L I G H T
Y E A R S

LIGHT YEARS

MAGGIE GEE

St. Martin's Press
New York

Library of Congress Cataloging in Publication Data

Gee, Maggie.
  Light years.

  I. Title.
PR6057.E247L5   1986   823'.914   85-25186
ISBN 0-312-48608-1

First published in Great Britain by Faber and Faber Limited.

10 9 8 7 6 5 4 3 2

This book is in memory of Peg Rankin, who climbed Mount Kilimanjaro, and taught me to look at the stars: and for her son, Nick

ACKNOWLEDGEMENTS

I should like to thank Lyman Sargent in America for an apposite
piece of information; and London Zoo.
My friends Musa, Nina and Rachel Farhi, Barbara Goodwin and
Grania Jones have given every sort of kindness and support.

The wise man only wonders once in his life, but that is always; the fool never. The education of the wise man begins with wonder, and ends with devout admiration . . . Coleridge, the most encyclopaedic of men, declares, 'In wonder all philosophy begins, in wonder it ends, and admiration fills the interspace . . .'

It is to excite . . . wonder . . . that this work is written . . . While relating, so far as our space will permit us, all that is most wonderful in . . . science . . . we shall intersperse our narrative with relations of Amorous Siege and Battle, Perils of Sea and Land, of the Dreams and Fancies, the Ambition, the Wisdom and the Folly of Man . . .

Let us consider shortly one of the commonest wonders about us – SPACE. Gaze up into the sky from off the page you are reading, and try to pierce as far as your eye can reach, and then as far as your mind can conceive . . . The mind, it has well been said, fails to comprehend so vast an area . . .

The World of Wonders, c.1884

L'amore, che muove il sole e l'altre stelle
Love, which moves the sun and the stars
Dante, *Paradiso*

LIGHT YEARS

PROLOGUE

In a year, light travels six million million miles.

'When will you be back?'
'I shan't.'
'When will you be back? You *will*.'
'If I come back, it will be to see Davey, not you.'
'You'll be back tomorrow. In a week at the latest.'
'A week? A fucking *year* more likely. Ten years . . .'

In a year, light travels six million million miles.

It flies from the sun to the earth in eight minutes. It crosses the whole solar system in eleven hours.

Light flies to the nearest star in our galaxy, Alpha Centauri, in four cold dazzling years. But there are several hundred thousand million stars in our galaxy.

After eighty thousand years of travel through interstellar gas and dust and stars, light has crossed the galaxy. But it is only one galaxy among unimaginably many. Light from at least one hundred thousand million galaxies is travelling towards us, through us, beyond us.

The whole observable universe would take thousands of millions of years for light to cross. But a single year is a very long time to us; see how far the light has gone already.

It is December 21. The Winter Solstice, the shortest day of a year in the mid-1980s. Around the five thousandth year since writing began, and the five hundred thousandth year since Upright Man began.

Only nobody thinks like that. They just think it's getting near Christmas.

A fan of light spreads suddenly into the cold and dark. A door swings open on to the city street and there are voices, screaming with laughter, or screaming. A couple of dark silhouetted figures, embracing or fighting.

13

'When will you be back?'

'I shan't.'

'When will you be back? You *will*.'

'. . . I could take a lifetime without seeing you!'

'Where are you going?'

'None of your business. Look, as far away as I can possibly get from you. Continents. *Light years*, Lottie. I'm through.'

Not embracing, fighting. He pushes her back against the light, slams the door and runs into the darkness.

Soon everything's quiet again.

☆

Darlington Road, Camden Town, North London, England, Great Britain, Europe, The World, The Solar System, The Galaxy, The Universe, Chaos.

The people who live here or lived here are Harold Segall (forty-five years old) Lottie Lucas (thirty-five years old) and her son Davey (sixteen years old). It was Davey who wrote that address on a letter to his mother from a drab school holiday two long years ago.

'Why *Chaos*?'

'Well, it *is* Chaos, isn't it?'

'Hmm. It arrived all right, anyway, darling.'

Actually things weren't really chaotic then. Harold and Lottie had just got married. The chaos was only wedding presents, and Harold's terrible dusty books, in tottering piles, unsorted.

Now chaos *has* arrived, with Harold gone.

Lottie stands on the wide white stairs lit up like a stage set and beats, beats her palm against the wall, the knuckles flashing heavy gold. Her green oriental eyes are dry bright slits and her cheeks are blazing. Davey is up in the roof, glad the shouting has stopped, flung clumsy as a cuttlefish on his bed. He turns on his back and tries to look far away, through the skylight, as Lottie tries to look through the wide white wall of the stairway, seeing nothing.

In a cold back room of the house in a foolish antique bird-cage with carefully gilded ivy leaves on top, a tiny Golden Lion Tamarin monkey, whose ancestors lived on earth twenty-five million years before man, has started to die, on its own, quite quickly.

The faint urban glare of the sky above the dark streets is a lid which conceals the stars. But the light from the thousands and thousands of stars still streams on regardless over and through and beyond these infinitesimally tiny points on a tiny blue and brown and silver ball which is lost among thousands of millions of miles of stars and stardust.

The single most material fact about Lottie is that she is extremely rich. Lottie both knows and forgets to notice. Sometimes she remembers, and uses it.

The poor are acutely aware of being poor; not so the rich.

Lottie's life is pleasant, in normal times, because she doesn't have to work. She is quite without guilt for not working. Her father had worked till he died to make money. He seemed abstracted, bowed down with work. Lottie knows that work doesn't make people nicer. (Men had to do it; women did not. It was one of the reasons feminists were crazy. Why would it be better if women were like men?)

Lottie uses her money to buy things. This time she has bought herself something alive. Something very small and very golden, a Brazilian monkey twelve inches long, a Golden Lion Tamarin, *Leontopithecus rosalia rosalia*.

The day the tamarin arrives, her husband goes. She is left with her son and immense amounts of money. Henceforth, her life will be rather less pleasant.

When Harold stopped running he was near a bus stop, so on impulse he jumped on a passing 24. The glaring lights and his anger dazed him. The row ran through his brain like heavy traffic.

'*Where are you going?*'

'Fucking bitch,' he muttered. Then he realized it was the conductor speaking.

He was fat, he was tall, his mouth was very mean. He stared at Harold, and his lip curled up.

'Look, Sunshine, I'm a busy man.'

'Er, sorry. I was dreaming. Sorry.' Harold groped for his money. 'Charing Cross, please,' he decided. He suddenly knew where he would go. He would go and spend Christmas in Bournemouth. Everything else was complicated, so he'd start by doing something easy. At least the statutory Christmas Day phone call to his mother would be cheap. She lived in Poole, and so had he for seventeen years of his life . . .

On second thoughts there would be no phone call. He wasn't ready to start answering questions. Moreover, his mother would gloat. Sylvia had never, really, liked Lottie. No one, of course, could gloat more than Harold about his lucky escape. But he wasn't ready for his mother to gloat. If there was to be gloating, he Harold would start it.

On the high-speed train he did not gloat. He felt small and weak, rocketed from side to side through the empty, windy night. Not many travelling. The noise was terrific, and the lurching made him feel he might die. He kept reliving the final scene, her voice like a drill, her mouth wide and ugly. That shivering, brilliant, bedraggled thing in the stupid cage she had bought. The tamarin was at once beautiful and repellent, because pitiful. Harold was swept with rage and grief. From somewhere outside himself had come the strength to tell her he'd had enough. Almost ever since they got married he'd imagined that moment whenever they rowed. All the same, it all happened too quickly.

He is shaking, belatedly, with fear and surprise, to a rhythm much faster than the shaking of the train. He is cold, though the train is stuffy and hot.

What on earth has happened? What have we done?

And Harold goes rocketing back into his past, into Dorset where he'd lived as a boy.

He was only thirteen when his father, Harold Senior, left home and went to America. There were nights of fierce prayer that Daddy would come back. In the end he threatened God on his knees. God did nothing. He gave God up. Davey was older, which was a blessing.

Rubbish, he thought, lurching to the left, the back of his hand on the icy windows. Davey will probably be relieved. At least there won't be any more rows.

His father and mother had rowed horribly. Pure suffering; Sylvia's high actress's voice, his father's less frequent, a low puzzled roar, and the house seemed to tremble as she slammed the doors. One after another, and then back again. The final breakup was still somehow worse.

Harold examined his forehead in the rainy darkness behind the window. He caught himself doing that so often; bald, balder, baldest. Harold was unresigned. He had dreams where his hair grew back. Lottie always said she didn't care about his hair.

'You're frightfully handsome and distinguished. All clever men are bald.'

'I'm not exactly bald, yet, am I? Couldn't you call it receding?'

Maybe she *had* cared, all along. He was sure that women must care. I mean I shouldn't like a bald woman. I shouldn't think it was distinguished. (*Am I too old? Will anyone else ever want me?*)

He thought about women's hair. From a distance, his wife and his mother, walking together, might have been related.

Lottie's hair. It was painful to think of her from a gathering distance. Keep gazing out of the window. But it didn't work; lights from the carriage burned on the dark like Lottie's hair.

Chin-length, cut so it swung and shook, the top layers sunbleached, the lower layers darker. Every shade of yellow.

Suddenly Harold was out of his seat and lurching along to the Buffet.

'Give me a whisky, please. I mean, a *large* whisky.'

Superior smile, glazed flushed cheeks.

'We only *do* doubles, sir.'

'Then I'll have a *double* double.'

With the whisky scalding his throat, he felt all right again.

Never go back, never go back. All hard decisions were right decisions. In the end, you had to live your ideals.

I was right to leave teaching, all those years ago. That was the hardest thing of all. If I hadn't done that, I'd never have had . . . my new life. My London life.

The tide of certainty faded. It wasn't his new life any more. He was leaving it behind, as the train began to slow.

The new life was becoming the old life.

The train pulled into a long, empty station. Bournemouth already? He wasn't prepared. Shuffling his suitcase. Not much in it. He wondered if he had any ideals left.

But I've never put up with things for too long, Harold thought, pushing out into the loud, wet night. At least I left teaching. At least I left Lottie.

His anger returned, and he blamed her for the pain of the wind that howled down the platform. He suddenly needed a lavatory badly and was just turning into what he thought was the Gents' when he was brought up short by a shout from the ticket collector (*damn, it was the Ladies'* . . .)

"Scuse me, sir. Where do you think you're going?'

'Oh – sorry, sorry. You can't read the sign.'

'Can't read, sir?'

The *sir* was ironical. Harold summoned some authority.

'I want a taxi. Can you direct me?'

'Taxi, sir? Yes, well, for that you'll have to leave the platform. And show your ticket at the barrier.'

The man beside the ticket collector snorted. Harold wanted to punch them.

'Are you always this helpful to strangers in Bournemouth?' He meant to sound cutting, but he sounded pathetic.

'This way, sir. *Merry* Christmas.' There was alcohol on the breath they laughed at him.

'Go fuck yourselves,' he yelled over his shoulder, a safe twenty yards away. He wasn't going to put up with things any more. There were going to be changes. Yes.

'And Happy New Year,' came back his tormentor.

The driver of the lone taxi hovering must have heard Harold swearing; he pulled noisily away, and Harold was alone.

Lottie walked up and down in the long front room of her large and splendid house. She had bought it, and no longer noticed it. There were two other houses she hardly noticed, one in Provence and one in Scotland, less than an hour from Perth.

Well after midnight. Every light was on. She walked in and out of many mirrors, and her anger was minutely softened each time she glimpsed her furious passage, thick hair blazing as it tossed against the dignified angle of her neck and chin.

'You'll regret this, Harold,' she muttered to the mirror. 'You'll be *so* ashamed.'

What was the good of trying to please him? You'd have thought she'd bought the tamarin for herself. She had so looked forward to showing him Goldilocks, she just couldn't bear to wait till Christmas. The whole thing had happened in a frightful rush. There were times when you had to make quick decisions.

Poor slow Harold could never see that. But despite the rush, she had thought of everything.

Even the cage. The antique shop was a flash of genius. Detail mattered to Lottie – she'd always had an eye for things. Those gilded leaves were so pretty, perfectly restored, of course. And *of course* little Goldie would appreciate it too. Not all hard straight clinical lines, like those enormous modern cages she'd turned down flat in the pet shop. The extra expense didn't matter a bit, since Goldie herself had cost thousands.

Still the subject of Goldilocks was not entirely comfortable. Tiny, smaller than Lottie had thought, shivering and scratching in her brief grasp. And Harold said it had been sick, but he probably made that up to upset her. It wasn't likely; on that first day she had given it tinned lychees and loganberries, just to be sure that the 'fruit' recommended by Dr Lambrequin was digestible. Nothing but the best for Goldilocks.

Harold even hated the name. 'This is *not* some stupid fairytale.'

She caught sight of herself in the wide gold frame, brow furrowed in a way that didn't flatter her, and a square tight set to her jaw. Instantly she drew herself up, shook her hair forward, gazed bright and imperious back at the glass: *Lottie Lucas*.

Subject dismissed.

But the subject of Harold was rather more complex. The subject of Harold could not be dismissed.

This evening Lottie had been drinking hard, and several glasses caught the light around the room, melted ice-cubes, abandoned lemon. She could never bear to spend time looking for things. If something was lost, she would simply get another.

She had married Harold as she did everything else; knowing what she wanted, going for it. She'd meant this marriage to be so different from her first disastrous marriage to Carl. Harold was brilliant like Carl, of course, but so much quieter, so much less wild.

Tonight his behaviour had been appalling, but on the whole he was – well, *sweet* . . . she had to admit they had mostly been happy. And they'd settled into a pattern, although they had only been married two years.

She felt a sudden pang of disquiet. It couldn't be over. Of course it couldn't.

19

He'd stopped being shy with Davey. He'd stopped wearing some of his more embarrassing clothes, and she'd thrown the others away. He'd almost stopped trying to take her to peculiar restaurants where he could pay. 'Authentic' little Indian places with ghoulish green strip lighting. Wine bars where you squashed up at tiny tables and ate red kidney beans and raw garlic while a pianist murdered Gershwin. In the end she had made her position plain.

'Darling, frankly I'd rather take a cab to Odin's where we can relax. The money is irrelevant.'

'To you. Not to me.'

'Look, it's so boring to go on about money. For the millionth time, I have vast amounts of money. Lagoons of it. Oceans. *We* have vast amounts of money. We don't have to talk about it all the time. I rather prefer to forget about it.'

'But I . . .'

She had kissed him to stop him talking.

'Sweetheart, I'm ravenous. Go call us a cab.'

In the end he came round to her point of view, more or less; and she sometimes let him take her to their local Greek, where the meat was perfectly acceptable.

'I can see I've been rather stupid, Lottie. I can't promise to stop trying to pay all the time – but I'll *try* not to try.'

'*Wonderful*, Harold! Admit it, darling – nice things just are rather nice, aren't they?'

'No no no. I mean, yes, they are. But my decision is on feminist grounds. I think my reaction's been basically sexist . . .'

' – Harold, you do sound pompous –'

'. . . I just couldn't take being paid for by a woman, which is too pathetic for words.'

'No, darling, it's marvellously gallant of you. It's adorable. But I'm not just a woman. A wife's different.'

'Lottie, you're not listening. It's easy for a woman to take money from a man, right? Well, if there's mutual respect it ought to be just as easy for a man to take money from a woman.'

'Well I assure you, Harold, I do *not* want every Tom, Dick and Harry proving their respect for me by taking my money.'

'You just don't see the point of feminism, do you?'

'I don't need to, darling. I have everything the feminists ever wanted, and more. I don't have to go round in hideous woolly hats hating men and secretly longing for them. I do whatever I like – always have done – so of course I don't whinge about being frustrated and dominated and castrated and whatever it is they all create about.'

'Not *castrated*, Lottie,' Harold mildly replied.

'Anyway, Harold, I'm sure the feminists don't mean men to go round lecturing their wives on how to be one.'

'Now there, Lottie,' said Harold, giving one of his yelps of laughter, 'You do have a point. Forgive me.'

He was best of all when he laughed. Best when they laughed together.

Harold sat on his case in front of the station. The desire to piss was urgent. The desire to cry was quite urgent, too. The wind blew straight from the stormy sea. Something scampered in the shadows. A dog? A rat? Not even a rat deserved cold like this.

Suddenly he thought of the tamarin. So little, so delicate, those round dim eyes and worried brows, the glory of its red-gold coat even now as it cowered at the back of the cage. The smell of excrement, sick and fear, sharp as a knife, so he moved back a pace. The black bars had looked like great sticks to beat it. Only Lottie would buy a cage as stupid as that.

'You've gone insane,' he had shouted at her, he who so rarely shouted.

'Harold, what do you mean? You're not going to be a spoilsport, are you?'

'How can you talk like that? What do you mean, *spoilsport*? This is a living thing.'

But it wouldn't be for very long, he reflected, shifting about on the case, trying not to put his weight on the mean sharp locks or the handle. His sorrow as he thought how the little thing might die was slightly lessened by another thought – how upset and ashamed stupid Lottie would be. Considering this lessening, he too was ashamed.

We're a horrible species.

The night wind howled.

Sprawled in an armchair of blondest leather, sucking up gin through the piece of lemon, Lottie drew up a balance sheet.

They agreed to differ on voting; America; The Bomb; feminism; religion (Lottie wasn't religious, but she was sure there was 'something there', some nameless God who favoured her); butter (Lottie spread it thickly, Harold feared for his arteries); bedtime (Lottie usually went early, Harold liked to read till two in the morning); and dope (on this point, Harold had given in – it was only nostalgia for the 1960s. It wouldn't do with a child around.)

So what did they agree on? She'd told him once, over a drunken lunch. A year ago, not so very long. Or maybe a year was a lifetime long.

Loving Davey (though Harold at first found it hard to show it), sex, beautiful things, fun, walking, 'really odd jokes', and each other.

'. . . oh, and history.'

'History, Lottie? You must be joking. You don't know the difference between Charles I and Charlemagne.'

'Don't be silly, Harold, of course I do.'

'You don't know your history, Lottie, honestly. Not that I married you to bone up on history.'

Her mouth was too full of crème brûlée to reply. But only for a moment. She swallowed energetically.

'You're the one who's being stupid, Harold. History – isn't History.'

'Aaaaah!' Mock enlightenment.

'History is your life, what's happened to you. It's . . . meanings, and memories, not dates. And we do share that. I love telling you things.'

Harold's beautiful brown eyes moistened; Harold apologized.

'Sorry, darling. I'm an arrogant shit. You're very wise. I adore you.'

The memory made her smile even now, but the glass in her hand was cold and empty. The taste was old gin and lemon pips, not sweet hot caramel and white Bordeaux. The memory was – rather lonely.

But Lottie was never lonely. Lottie refused to be lonely.

It was just that right now she needed someone to talk to. And Davey had been absolutely useless, going off and hiding in his bloody attic. She imagined his soft dark head on the pillow and was touched, as usual, with tenderness. Davey was still a love.

Or else he didn't give a fuck.

She hated both her menfolk. She gave so much, and what did she get back?

She tried to put down her glass. As it slid off the arm of her chair and crashed down, she realized she was the tiniest bit drunk. She made a great effort not to be maudlin. She made a great effort to be fair.

Of course, Harold hadn't meant any of the things he'd said tonight. He'd be back tomorrow morning at the latest. He was bound to ring before bedtime. Lottie looked longingly at the phone . . . but it was – God, it was two in the morning.

Still she sat on, and stared at the phone.

Things hadn't begun with the tamarin, no. Perhaps they began when she declined to go to Poole with Harold to visit his mother, a week ago. She quite often declined. It was fine in theory.

But this time Harold had been worried. 'I just think she didn't sound well. You know, whatever you think, Mother loves to see you.' (This wasn't strictly true. Harold meant, *I love to have moral support*.)

She didn't go, and he came back sullen and still worried about Sylvia's health, though he wouldn't be drawn after the initial statement – 'I think she's got angina – ' with the silent post-script, *not that you care*.

'Angina is the same as heartburn, isn't it, Harold? Sort of indigestion but worse?'

'No. It isn't, in point of fact.'

That evening they went to Claudia's Christmas party, and Harold drank far too much Chianti.

'Harold,' she'd hissed as he briefly turned away from a predatory-looking redhead, 'you'll get horribly drunk. You don't even like Chianti.'

'I see,' he whispered back grimly. 'Thank you for telling me what I like.'

And he hadn't said a word to Lottie for the rest of the evening.

Even drunk, he was graceful. That lean muscled back in tight jeans and cashmere. Cashmere she had bought him. Half-twined around him was the very tall woman. Her limbs seemed to go round him at least twice, and her magenta head was on a level with his. They were 'dancing', but none of the right parts were moving.

Lottie wanted him. She hated him. She would punish him. But first she'd go home.

Just as she was pulling the car away from the kerb, a maniac hammered at the window. *My God, that's all I need.* Then she realized it was Harold, too drunk to open the door.

'Get in.'

'Oh Lottie – Lottie. 'm sorry. Bes' wife in a world.'

He slumped in the seat beside her as she drove, trying to knead her thigh, which she shifted irritably about.

'You decided not to bring that giraffe home, then?'

'Sh'raffe? Oh yes. *Vampire,*' Harold burbled. 'Noragiraffe. Vampire. Eat me up . . . Y'see, I think Sylvia's dying,' he continued without a break, and his hand fell away from her thigh.

'Are you serious, Harold? Oh dear. Oh dear.' Then 'You don't mean it, damn you. You're just trying to get sympathy.'

She hoped he hadn't heard that. He probably didn't hear it. For Harold was snoring. Harold was asleep.

Next day he brought her breakfast in bed at some unearthly hour of the morning. His eyes were tomato-red, he was cravenly apologetic, and yet he was somehow withdrawn. She 'forgave' him without forgiving him, and went shopping very early to escape the atmosphere of guilt and crossness and headaches which hung in the house like old smoke.

Wandering around the glittering aisles of Fortnum and Mason, already crowded before 10 a.m., she felt out of sympathy for once with the mounds of pâtés and truffles, tinned frogs and tinned birds, marzipans and mayonnaises. It usually cheered her up, coming here. Marriage is spoiling my temper, she thought, and promptly bought a ribbon-waisted jar of snails, admiring their elegant coiled shells, the colour of gently burning sugar. It wasn't enough. What did she want? What could she do with her discontent?

Suddenly she remembered the man at Claudia's party with the very good suit and unreadable eyes. Either enigmatic or frightened. Today she deserved something really unusual. He was half-Belgian. She'd never met a Belgian before. And he had his own plane, which sounded fun. She had a hunch he would bring good luck.

Harold often teased her about her hunches. He said she had too many of them. It was just that Harold was rather low on intuition, as most men were. She deserved some luck.

She riffled through her snakeskin bag, and his number was there, on a pleasing card, a marbled grey.

> Dr R Lambrequin, FZS
> Specialist in the Zoology of Exotic Fauna
> Premises Centrally Located

It sounded frightfully respectable. Unusual but respectable. And he'd offered her a rare opportunity. Something very special he could show her; the would-be purchaser had changed his mind. Something he could offer at an advantageous price. Something for the very discerning buyer. Something for the woman with everything. She went to see him that morning.

'Unique, Madame,' he smiled. 'Not generally on the market. I obtained it as a very special favour from my good colleague in Belgium. You will never see another in private hands, I give you my word of honour.'

Lottie loved the Golden Lion Tamarin on sight. 'I'll take it,' she gasped, enchanted. She refused his other offers. Her house was a little too small for a bear, though they could have kept it in Scotland.

'No. I'll just have the . . . tamarin, did you say? And . . . yes, why not? I'll call her Goldilocks.'

'It's male, Madame,' Dr Lambrequin said, with the thin-lipped ghost of a smile.

'Nobody's going to know that,' said Lottie. She definitely preferred it female. Delivery on the twenty-first. And so she was undone.

As she drove home she passed a six-foot, model-like redhead piled with bright red-gold furs who reminded her briefly of the woman at the party. Love for Harold seized her heart painfully.

I want him, I love him. I should have gone to Poole. *I'll make it up to you, Harold.*

And so she'd decided to give him Goldilocks. Doubly, trebly undone.

☆

Time to put out the lights. She bent to one and found the mirror again and again she saw what she didn't want to. Tired and sad. Put out the lights. She never looked tired or sad in the morning.

Prologue

Everyone said she was beautiful, everyone said she was 'incredible' for thirty-five. She felt about fifty, fumbling for the light switch with the gin knocking at her skull and making her unsteady.

Once the room was dark, in the instant before she passed on to the lighted landing, she realized that she was suffering, that he had made her suffer.

Folding her strong arms around her as she padded upstairs, she renewed an old vow: *Never suffer for a man. Never, never suffer.*

Halfway upstairs, she stopped, swayed, and went reluctantly downstairs again. The cage was in the utility room, since Harold hadn't helped her take it anywhere more suitable (the sun-lounge might be nice). She noticed her breath catch a little as she opened the door, as if she were nervous, so she strode in boldly, making kissing noises.

'Goldilocks? Goldie?'

There was a scampering sound like mice as she switched the light on, but she saw nothing behind the black bars. A wave of panic – had it escaped? Then she saw something bright huddled in the cage's farthest corner. Its little face was fixed on her, eyes wide, nose and mouth aquiver. She told herself it was curiosity, but she knew in her heart it was utter terror. Closer to the cage the smell hit her. She went and flung open a window.

God, I can't cope with this now. I'll sort everything out in the morning. Harold will come back and sort it out.

She turned on her heels and as she closed the door she leaned against it, safe outside, unconsciously trying to close it tighter.

Sleep didn't come as readily as usual. The gin was dry and fretful in her brain, no help. A tiny worry like a tiny worm. *What if he doesn't come back for Christmas?*

Above Camden and Bournemouth the stars burned on as they always burn, without night or day. The earth rolls away from that endless brightness. Protected by the turn of the earth from too much brightness, all the little creatures slept, Lottie and Harold in their different cities, Davey twelve feet above his mother, thin arms spread on the peaceful dark.

The little monkey on its rack of rigid metal did not sleep, could not sleep. The tamarin came from a tropical forest. The world for him has become very cold. Time should have been for hunting insects, seeds, fruit. But he cannot hunt.

Prologue

He is living a dream. His dream is the forest, great trees, great richness, and he bruises himself as he flings himself towards it, scratching and tearing at the painted-over rust.

He is dying so much faster than any of the others. Tomorrow, more of the dream forest will die. The animals scamper towards the collectors.

The twenty-second, the twenty-third.

'Mum, it hasn't eaten any of that carrot.'

Davey had decreed there should be no more tins. Davey flattered himself that he knew about nutrition.

'Well, Dr Lambrequin *said* it would eat vegetables.'

'Perhaps we haven't hit the right vegetable yet.'

'I'm not going to worry about it every second. Most pets get fed *far too much*.'

Lottie sounded firm, but her heart was heavy. She could see Davey didn't want to upset her, and that upset her more.

'Has it – been sick again?'

'Not since I cleared up the last lot.'

'*You* like her, Davey, don't you?'

'Yes, yes I do . . . I mean, she's beautiful. But I wonder . . . do you think . . . just to be on the safe side . . . do you think we should call a vet?'

It rushed out, once he got started.

'*We are not going to fuss.* I've got enough to worry about with Harold disappearing. If only he'd come back, he *knows* about things like this.'

Her voice suddenly slipped off its note of forced irritation. She heard her fear come through, and could not prevent it.

'Anyway, Davey, I'm scared. It might be . . . against the law. They might say I shouldn't have taken it. It will be all right if only . . .'

If only, if only. Christmas Eve, and Harold had not come back.

One shopping day till Christmas.

Desperate, Lottie went out and shopped. If I get more food in, he'll have to come back. It will have to be eaten. He'll have to come home.

Crystallized oranges, round as suns. Rough boar pâté, dark in its dish. Mistletoe for magic healing. A twenty-pound tip to

27

deliver that day. Wrapping paper, though she'd done all her wrapping, the nervousness growing as her arms filled with emptiness.

She got home at two in the afternoon. No one but Claudia had telephoned. Davey wouldn't look at her. She couldn't ask about the tamarin (she would never again call it Goldilocks.) But she started to imagine she smelled it everywhere, the acrid smell of fear.

'It's been sick again,' he announced to the window, staring miserably out at the greyness. She rang Dr Lambrequin's number; there was no answer. Frantic, she drove to his address.

Lottie hammered on the recently painted front door, its shining letterbox a rigid mouth. Mocking her. The door didn't open. Then she kicked it, enraged, and her heel left a deep scratch on the new blue paint. I'm going insane, she reflected, shaking, feeling tears start to prickle.

Without warning the door opened. It was a tiny woman, mid-European-looking, very old. Lottie stepped back so as not to alarm her.

'I'm looking for Dr Lambrequin.'

'You know where is Dr Lambrequin?'

The little white face twisted upwards, horribly eager, and Lottie saw that her neck was shrivelled and pulled like the skin Amanda skimmed from warm milk.

'No. *I want* Dr Lambrequin. I want to talk to him.'

'Oh.' The little old woman shrank back into herself, life gone. 'No, cannot help you. Is gone. And he leave such horrible . . .' she tailed off, pale eyes wrinkling together, as if she regretted beginning. She half-turned away. In horror, Lottie saw the door was already closing.

'No, wait,' she said. 'You have to help me. I bought an animal. From him.'

The little body swung round, fierce energy was back in her mouth and fists, which clenched at shoulder-level, tiny and angry as a child's.

'*All – his – animals – dead*. Horrible, so horrible. No food for them, nothing. Your friend is wicked man. How do I help them? Too old. He tell me nothing. He ask for flat for one month, holiday let. Such gentleman. Suit – everything.' (Lottie nodded in agreement.) 'Such gentleman, I ask nothing in advance. Then noises – dreadful noises all the time – he tell me I have nightmare. Then I discover, he bring here *zoo*. Then he go, and pay me nothing. Except – dead monkey, dead bear, dead snake! Then police come here, and men from Customs.'

She stared at Lottie with something like hatred, but the white-ringed irises didn't focus on Lottie. They looked through her at a history of suffering.

Lottie was swept with hopelessness, something she never let herself feel. 'I'm sorry,' she said, but the blind pale face didn't yield at all, and the door was closing. Closed.

Oh God, thought Lottie on the icy step. Help me, please. Help.

She didn't tell Davey where she had been.

'Did Harold . . .?'

'I'd *tell* you, Mum.' Then he came and put his arms around her, and she thought how lovely his black hair was, blue and sheeny in the thin sun from the window. My lovely son.

'Good news. The monkey drank some milk and ate some lettuce and banana.'

'Did it? *Thank God.*' She hugged him until he gasped for breath. 'By the way, it's a *tamarin*, darling.'

That afternoon they decorated. She forced herself not to look at the clock. She decorated frantically, obsessively, with the energy that . . . she stopped herself.

The energy Harold said he loved. 'Lottie, you're a force of nature.'

Nature howled outside the glass, spiteful winds, acidic sunlight which slowly dimmed and reddened. The trees had shrunk to their own dark bones, the very last yellow leaves blown down.

But the Christmas tree was wonderfully healthy, a bright dark green, taller than Davey. (Harold had insisted on getting one with roots, and carried it home himself through the streets, ringing on the door without warning, a bristling green amazing apparition with his thick dark eyebrows just clearing the top. Harold, Harold. *Just a week ago.*)

She tied more balls, knotting forcefully, green, red, blue. Red, red, red. Blue, blue, blue.

'Watch it, Mum. You'll knock off all the needles.'

In the end she had piled on so much glitter you could hardly see the tree underneath. Outside the house, the sky turned violet then black, and street lights were hung on the darkness.

☆

But nobody came, and nobody phoned, or nobody that counted, and the night settled down.

At eleven that night, she was up on the step-ladder hanging her ninety-ninth paper chain. The room was a mad multi-coloured cats-cradle of colour and her neck and shoulders ached. The phone rang and she nearly broke her ankle jumping down and ploughing through the mess to reach it. Wrong number. Lottie wasn't polite. Davey went and made her cocoa.

'Mum, let's go to bed. Or tomorrow will be ruined.'

'Looks as if it's ruined in any case.'

Oddly she slept like her old self, easily, and woke up happy: it's Christmas. And then remembered: *this* Christmas.

But Harold would ring. It would be all right.

The day is unreal, like a frozen tooth, not as painful as expected, and removed at the end by the dizzy spin of champagne they drink at Claudia's. They drive off the dark with lights and laughter; the Boar of Winter has an orange in its mouth. The sun cannot quite be swallowed up. The days are already minutely longer.

'You see, Lottie, I know Harold's type. All talk and it doesn't mean a thing. You'll get home and find him sobbing on your answering machine, calling from a Sally Army hostel. Be nice to him. Let him come back.'

'Bastard,' Lottie giggled, sipping and burping. 'I wouldn't have him back if you paid me.'

She had eaten vast quantities of rich dark meats, pork and venison and fat dark duck, she had gorged the crystallized oranges she brought, and her body was soothed with the warmth and the sugar. Her mind was full of air bubbles, floating, pain-free. The table was forested with candles gleaming in lovely confusion from every bright surface. Davey was kneeling on the carpet, thick hair fallen forward over his face, reading *another* book in the firelight. Life, Lottie thought, is *very* beautiful.

Claudia watched Lottie smiling, head poised on her long strong neck like a fruit, perfectly in place, sure of her welcome. Her husband's left her and she's still unruffled, Claudia thought as her lips smiled back. She's always had whatever she wanted.

What if Harold *doesn't* come back? It can't be easy, living with Lottie. It isn't easy, being her friend.

'Claudia, you've been wonderful this evening,' Lottie shouted on the doorstep. (Lottie was always slightly too loud; at least it was less noticeable at Christmas.) 'Davey and I should have been so gloomy if we hadn't had somewhere to go.'

'She *is* wonderful, isn't she?' said Justin, Claudia's limp attachment, one arm draped over her thin shoulder as they stood together in the lit doorway. But his eyes only flicked very briefly to Claudia and then they were fixed on flushed, moist Lottie, narrow bright eyes, wet wide lips, deliciously wide, full lips. Her curls blew wildly in the wind as she stood for a second sturdily facing the light with her thin son propped against her. She blew a last kiss, and Justin blew two. Harold must be mad, he thought.

Claudia did not agree.

'Can you entirely blame Harold?' she murmured, as they slipped back inside.

'Well, I do think a marriage is worth preserving,' he demurred, trying to be diplomatic, achieving a consummate lack of tact since his failure to propose was a sore point with Claudia. Not that she would have accepted. Not that she believed in marriage.

'Don't be so fucking pompous, Justin. Will you help me load the dishwasher?'

It was five past midnight. Christmas was over.

Really, thought Justin. She's getting too sure of me.

Lottie and Davey were walking home. She was full of drunken energy. Davey would have much preferred a taxi. He was way past his normal bedtime, and a little bit tipsy, though less so than his mother.

'Mum, did you switch the answerphone on?'

'Of course I did.' She was putting all her concentration into not falling off the icy pavement. She slipped a little, and giggled. Harold was entirely irrelevant.

But Davey was brooding on Harold. He'd better have rung, or I'll hate him for ever. He rushed upstairs and pressed the button on the machine by the light that shone in from the landing.

Pressed the button. The dim light shone.

Pressed the button. The wrong button.

Pressed the *Erase* button in the half-light and went straight to bed, too locked in his misery to go and check the tamarin, went straight to bed and sniffled like a baby. Everything went wrong, everything. Next day he'd have to tell her the truth.

☆

Next day she was much too cross to be told. Booze and sugar no longer muffled the truth which dinned in her ears like traffic. Her husband had left her. She was mad with rage.

'Yesterday you seemed all right.'

'Bullshit. Yesterday I was vilely canned. And repulsively sentimental.'

She drank black coffee, sucking it in aggressively, hair scraped back in a rubber band, strong jaw thrust out at him like a fist. Her skin was patchily inflamed by drink, anger in red untidy patches.

'I mean. It's outrageous. He might be dead, for all we know. And Good Riddance. God, I didn't mean that. Oh fuck it all, I'm going to phone Sylvia.'

'Um – do you think you're in the right mood?'

'I think *I'm* the best judge of my moods. Honestly, Davey, sometimes you'd think that I was the child and you were the parent. If you want to look after somebody I suggest you go and see how – you know – is' (jerking her head dismissively in the direction of the thing downstairs).

'I did.' Flat.

'How is it?'

'Not good.'

'Oh, for God's sake don't look at me in that awful reproachful way. I swear I'll get the Queen's own vet to that thing but no one'll come on Boxing Day. Look, I've got a human being to worry about. Don't expect me to fret about an ape.'

'Monkey.'

'TAMARIN!' she screamed at him, smashed down her coffee-cup, and strode to the phone.

Davey didn't want to hear this. Davey didn't want to live here at all. A lot of his friends seemed to feel the same way, even more often than Davey. There's thousands of us, he considered, appalled by the behaviour of adults, all over the Western World. I wouldn't want to say about Russia.

He got out of the room in the nick of time as she dialled the final digit.

Prologue

'Hello-o-o-o-ah?' was what Lottie heard, an actress's voice of perennial hope for the perfect phone call with the perfect part, though Lottie was sure Sylvia recognized her voice.

'It's Lottie, Sylvia.'

'Oh *Lottie*.' Pause. 'Did you ring to wish me a Happy Christmas? You're a day late, you know.'

'Sylvia, I have *other things on my mind*. You may know your son has walked out on me.'

'Don't be *short*, dear. I was only asking because *Harold* didn't ring to say Happy Christmas. And he always does. Every year. Mind you, he did ring on Christmas Eve.'

'*Sylvia, did you know Harold had left me?*'

Pause.

'Oh *yes*, dear. I am his mother, you know.'

Lottie placed the receiver on the ground and shook both fists at the stupid air. When she picked it up again, Sylvia was complaining about Christmas.

'. . . of course you can't imagine what it's like being on your own if you've never had to do it. I do not blame . . . I merely observe.'

'Sylvia, will you listen to me? Do you know where Harold's gone?'

'Aaah . . .' Sylvia trailed into silence.

'You *do* know. Will you tell me at once?'

'Lottie dear, it's no good shouting at me. I'm quite an old lady now, you know. I don't think Harold likes shouting either. He was always a quietly spoken boy.'

Lottie knew there was no going back. Nor was there any way to go forward. Suddenly it was all too much.

'Now Lottie, don't be agitated. He's bound to get in touch with you sooner or later. I'm *almost* sure he said he was going to . . .'

The intonation made it deeply doubtful.

Lottie hung up. She had never done that to Sylvia before. She found she had sweated profusely.

That day was appallingly long, as long as Christmas Day had been short. *He's trying to drive me crazy.* Harold became a malignant presence, an absent presence, his malignant mother's son.

The tamarin rallied that evening, drank some water, did the ghost of a jump. Next day it lay dimly in the dark of the cage.

Diarrhoea had begun as well as sickness. Lottie forced herself to go and see it, but when she opened the door she was stopped in her tracks by the harsh, quick sound of its breathing. Davey was always closing the window. How would it manage without fresh air? She flung it open again.

For the first time she heard a little question, small and distinct, as if planted in her head from a long way away, somewhere even colder where she was not loved.

Lottie, what have you done?

But she wasn't going to listen to that. It was Harold's fault for abandoning her. He had never loved her. Right then. She hadn't ever loved him.

The next phone call to Sylvia was very different. Lottie was in control. She prepared her script before she started, and put the phone down smartly at the end.

'Sylvia? This is Lottie. I'm sorry I hung up on you yesterday. I was a little . . . tired. I'm ringing to give you some information. I'm getting all Harold's things packed up and Pickford's will bring them down to Poole. I'm sure that's best for everybody. Give your son my good wishes when you see him. *Goodbye.*'

As she placed the yellow phone precisely in its cradle, she felt power flooding back. Good, she was in control. Lottie was in control.

☆

This was not how Harold found her when he finally got through on December 31. She progressed from hissing to fury when she realized it was him.

'. . . dead . . . you don't give a damn . . .all your fault . . . *I hate you! I HATE YOU! I NEVER WANT TO SEE YOU AGAIN!*'

(It has been very hard for Harold to ring. His voice trembles, but she is too far beyond herself to notice, too far from reason and too far away across miles of cold dark senseless earth and leafless trees and howling winds, and she feels her anger as vaster than everything, millions of miles below the scalding stars, a billion times vaster than the planet they are on, two little living points jerking unconnected signals.)

'I did ring, Lottie. On Christmas Day. I left a message asking you to ring back – '

'LIAR! LIAR! Can you imagine what it's like? Davey looks at me as if I'm a murderess. I hardly dare go downstairs, just thinking of the awful thing – going rotten – down there.'

The injustice helped him get his voice back.

'For God's sake, Lottie, who went and bought it in the first place?'

'HAROLD! Come back at once and see to it!'

Suddenly he was shouting too. His voice wasn't really very good at shouting. It showed the strain, breathy and torn.

'Why should I come back when I hear you're sending all my stuff down to Sylvia's? Mother was in tears, by the way – did you have to upset her too?'

'Your mother is a spiteful cow and her tears are worth about as much as . . .' Lottie wanted to say, *don't be so unfair. She hurt me, not the other way round. '*. . . They're worth about as much as our marriage,' she finished. 'FUCK – ALL!'

'Look, Lottie, I'm in an extremely depressing hotel in the south of England, and I don't want to hear this.'

'You don't want to hear this! *You! YOU!!*' She was barking and spluttering with fury. '*You* did all this. *You* walked out on me . . .'

He held the receiver away from his ear, feeling cold and odd. She sounded like a fishwife. The hotel wasn't actually as depressing as he had said. Looking round the lobby it was faded but comfortable, rather as his own life had been before Lottie annexed it, two and a half years ago.

'. . . bought it for *you!*'

He clearly caught her conclusion.

'You're being completely irresponsible, Harold!'

She thought: *Please come back. Please come back and help me.*

'Oh shut up, Lottie. This is getting us nowhere.'

But Lottie had moved into a strange red country of screaming sound that he couldn't enter.

Harold wasn't really any good at all in the presence of extreme emotion. It made him want to slip out of the picture, leaving his shoes and his clothes propped up, dive through the window and at the end of his naked jackknife through miles of air, find himself floating out to sea . . .

'. . . so when are you coming back? Harold, *are you there?*'

He came back reluctantly. Docile suit, uxorious shoes.

'Harold, I'm TALKING TO YOU!'

Something gave. He kicked it off, with a sense of excitement, shoes, clothes, meek stupidity.

'Lottie. I mean, look here. I don't have to come back if I don't want to.'

Not the right note; a sulky small boy.

He tried again. 'Stop haranguing me. It's me who's supposed to be angry with you.'

Not much better. It was all unreal. Weary, he wondered if he cared any more. He wanted to get a drink from the bar and watch *Casablanca* on the TV.

'HAROLD! YOU'RE DRIVING ME INSANE!'

'Lottie – is there any point in this?'

'What shall I do with the bloody monkey?'

A sudden image; small, broken. Anger twisted in Harold's gut. In all the years that stretched ahead Lottie never forgot the cold speech that followed.

'Get the vet to take it away. Or burn it. Or give it to a lab for research. It's absolutely *nothing* to do with me. I'm just *sick* – with sorrow – about it. Disgust, if you like. I'd better ring off. Please give my love to Davey.'

Click.

Burr.

It could not be true. The electric burr of loneliness.

Eleven-thirty, December 31. The real parting had begun.

January

CHAPTER ONE

There are a lot of bodies in the Solar System. Everybody knows, working in towards the sun, Pluto, Neptune, Uranus, Saturn, Jupiter, Mars, Earth and its Moon, Venus, Mercury.

But there are many others who are virtual strangers. Strangers with fantastic names.

Orbiting Pluto, Charon; orbiting Uranus, Titania, Oberon, Umbriel, Ariel, Miranda; orbiting Saturn, Titan, Rhea, Iapetus, Dione, Tethys, Enceladus, Mimas, Hyperion; orbiting Jupiter, Ganymede, Callisto, Io, Europa, Amalthea, Himalia, Elara, Metis, Adrastea, Pasiphaë, Carme, Sinope, Lysithea, Ananke, Leda.

Such an enormous number of strangers you may never think about or meet again.

They have a lot of space to move about in. The solar system is around six billion miles across.

Earth itself is vastly more crowded. Around eight thousand miles across.

Harold is in a very small space with a lot of strange bodies in Bournemouth. A space about five yards across. Strangers with fantastic names he may rarely think about or meet again.

Harold is in the Bella Costa Guesthouse. His life has changed utterly, totally. The strangers crowd all round him. The television blares 'Auld Lang Syne'.

They are waiting for an invented date which is only important on some parts of Earth. The 'beginning' of the New Year, as if the planet were about to start turning.

Harold nearly spent it alone. After the apocalyptic phone call to

37

Lottie, he stayed in his room, trying not to listen for feet on the stairs, in case she phoned back. In the end Mrs Limone had called him, more genteel than usual, from the landing.

'Coo-ee, Mr Segall! Are you there?'

He had crammed his shoes on, flung the door open.

'I hope I'm not intrudin', but I was wonderin' whethah – you might like to join us all deown in the *leownge*?' (She was pulling out all the stops.) 'Mustn't be all on your own at the Witchin' Hour, you know!'

Harold heard himself saying, 'Yes, very kind,' as his disappointment faded.

Harold liked beer; Mrs L did not. Her 'Bar' stocked port or sherry. But it wasn't unpleasant, in the warm half-light, sitting listening to yells of television laughter, watching little men in kilts telling jokes (*but what am I doing here?*).

Every time he shifted in his seat, the white-and-gold wood of the arm creaked. There were two of these chairs, with scrolled bow legs, patently chairs for ladies. There wasn't any choice, tonight. Every other seat in the leownge was taken. Some of the faces were already known to him, but that didn't make them any less strange.

The Honeymooners had the sofa as of right. Groom, who was bouncing with health and muscle, took up at least three-quarters of it. Bride was slender and pale as a hair. Harold often caught himself looking at her.

Mrs Limone's fat boyfriend Francis sat at his mistress's feet, his bottom almost as large as the pouffe. Mrs L had a vast leather chariot. She looked pink, and fragile, but her hair was sharp yellow. So were the glances she cast about.

Two very old ladies whose names he didn't know sat in two carvers with their backs to the wall. Their bones showed through; their hair was very white, as Mrs Limone's should have been by rights.

Harold was glad that the chair which matched his was in a faraway corner. The woman who sat there troubled him, though she sat away from the light. She held herself in with bulging arms. Every other second she let herself go and drank some more, in untidy gulps.

Harold had seen her arrive. He was down in the lobby, just about to phone. She would 'take a single room, if you have one'. She was 'not with my husband, at the moment'.

She had suffered through this evening, without her husband. Every eye avoided her. The beginning of a year was very important. The beginning of a year was for booze and smiles, not for alcoholism and dreadful grief.

At the first stroke everyone looked slightly apprehensive, as if it was their turn to go on stage. Their glasses hung suspended. Then Mrs Limone's swansdown toe dug Francis sharply in the base of his spine. Nothing registered until the fourth stroke, when he suddenly sat bolt upright and bellowed 'And a Very Happy One! To all of you! A Very Happy New Year!'

Relief. They all drank to the TV set. The two old ladies chinked glasses with each other. Harold realized they were drinking whisky, not sherry. A bottle of – surely Glenfiddich? – peeped from an enormous Gladstone handbag.

Nothing of this was real. He might have died, and been reinvented. Lottie and Davey, he thought, sipping, Lottie and Davey, not all these strangers.

The beginning of a year was important. Why am I here? Must I be here?

He tried to decode the TV show. But he couldn't *understand* it, let alone decode it. A host of men in tights with the upper halves of fancy waiters leaped fantastic leaps waving (empty?) champagne bottles, landing at the feet of what might be shepherdesses, if you could go by their beribboned crooks, and the shapes of giant sheep lying dead in the distance. They all wore mauve crinolines and crimson nylon wigs, and all screamed in unison as the trouserless waiters landed.

This could not end well. At twelve forty-five Harold stood up, made a circular, summarizing 'Happy New Year,' and trudged up to bed.

Happy New Year, Harold.

He lay in his narrow bed, tipsyish, empty and very, very old. But tomorrow's a new beginning, he told himself, drifting away on a dinghy of sherry . . .

. . . someone joined him, swimming beside the dinghy, someone frightening in a crimson wig wearing two champagne bottles like waterwings, and he twitched violently, beat her away before he realized it was Lottie, Lottie . . .

☆

Drawing the curtains on the new beginning, he found it was

grey sea-mist. Downstairs in the lobby, the woman who had drunk and grieved last night in the fragile chair sat grey and trembling, counting her money by a row of shabby cases.

Breakfast: greyish porridge, startlingly orange kippers and greyish tea. Mrs Limone looked absent, though she served the kippers with a flourish. The beginning of a year was important. You didn't get kippers every day.

The two old ladies sat greyly at their usual table by the window, side by side, with their backs to him. They always spoke in very low voices. They seemed to talk a lot. He supposed they must be complaining, reminiscing, that kind of thing. What hell to be old.

Suddenly a peal of laughter as loud and clear as a bell rang round the room. He turned towards them, startled. The two narrow backs were shaking with mirth. He felt a little put out, and then a little cheered up. On cue, the sun outside the window seeped weakly through.

All right. He would drive himself out for one of his endless walks beside the sea. It was good for him, of course it was. The terrible straightness of the promenade was merely in his mind. So was the sameness of the shells, the uniform grade of pebble.

You go out there and enjoy it, he told himself.

Money. Hankies. Key. Scarf.

Lottie's scarf. Oh *damn* Lottie. The scarf she knitted when she could have bought him a gross of scarves. He remembered her sitting knitting after supper, quick impatient movements, the tip of her tongue very pink between her teeth, not seeming to think about what she was doing as she talked her usual nineteen to the dozen but her fingers flew like humming-birds' wings, and the tail of mauves and blues and pinks grew down before his eyes.

'Nice and bright,' Mrs Limone remarked, when he walked through the lobby. 'Cheerful, is that.'

There was something Harold didn't like about her tone of voice.

'Thank you,' he said, repressively.

'Don't get cold,' she trilled. 'The wind is somethin' shockin'.'

To Francis, who sat in Reception with her, she said, once Harold was out of hearing, 'Bit *fanciful*, that, for a man. Wonder what their – *marital life* is like? I'd say there was quite a *sensitive* side to Mr Segall.'

'Queer?' blurted Francis, sucking a sweet.

'I don't like that sort of talk.'

Francis looked down, his heavy mouth sagging.

'Oh, don't look so gloomy, Franky. Give mummy an incey wincey kiss.'

Harold popped into the newsagent on the corner to get some peppermints. Anything to take away that heavy, fishy taste.

'You always seem to be open,' he said to the angular proprietor. 'You were open on Christmas Day, weren't you?'

'Much good it did me. Rubbish, this time of year. Now summer – summer's different. I can make a nice bit in summer . . . You've been in a lot, last few days. 'Oliday, is it?'

'More or less.' Normally Harold hated talking in shops. Now he was alone, he welcomed it. He wished he could think of something to say.

'Well, there's not a lot of 'em open at the moment. *Sea Strole? South Chines? Bella Costa?*'

Harold nodded eagerly.

'Oh, so you're with *Mrs Limone.*' A dreadful sarcasm italicized *Limone.*

'Why, is it the dearest place for miles?'

'Nah, nah. Nothin' much in it. No, but I always have a little titter to myself about Mrs *Limone* . . . When I first knew her, she was married to a Mr Lemon. That'd be thirty years ago. Then after he ran off with someone, she changed her name to *Limone.* This is it,' he added, smirking to see Harold's face break into a grin of pure joy. 'Nice to see you smile. I'd started to think you'd given it up for Christmas.'

'I did. I left my wife,' said Harold, and went out of the door, still smiling. The bravado of that kept his smile in force all the chilly way to the front.

But part of him knew he was boasting and smiling because he didn't believe it. Today he would sort it out (would he?) Just as soon as it was cheap rate, he would phone her. Or was it cheap rate all day, on New Year's Day? Or *none of the day?* Living with Lottie, he'd almost forgotten the feel of that kind of worry.

As he came out on to the actual front, the wind off the sea hit him full in the face, making him weep and gasp and pull his scarf up over his stinging nostrils, over the lobes of his aching ears. In London there simply weren't winds like this.

Then the sun switched on from half to full, blazing out from behind the last skin of mist. There was nothing at all between Harold and the wide cold glitter of the sea and sky. Lines of surf which stretched for ever, flat bands of dazzle between the lines.

Above the horizon the massed winter sunlight hit him in the eyes in a frozen sheet.

He was used to tall houses. He was used to rows of city trees. He was used to tame little patches of sky, and winds which were blocked by walls and roofs. He stood there a second, taking the shock, eyes screwed up at the source of all the trouble. This was winter sun. It was supposed to be weak. Unshaded, though, he couldn't bear to look at it.

There was something in all this raw whiteness he would have to come to terms with. But not just now. His hangover nudged him behind the eyeballs.

☆

At six he rang from the callbox in the Bella Costa lobby, watching his timid movements in the vast, pompous mirror.

'Lottie?'

'No, Davey. It's Harold, isn't it?'

Davey's voice was very very tired.

'*Davey*, how are you?'

Harold just stopped himself wishing Davey a Happy New Year. After a pause he did it anyway.

'Happy New Year, kid.'

The matey tone sounded false as hell.

'Look, Harold, she's just told me to say she doesn't want to talk to you.'

'She doesn't mean it, does she? What have you done about the monkey? How *is* – your mother? Is she *all right?*'

'The tamarin's dead, *I* had to wrap it in loads and loads of dustbin bags and we took it to a skip. *Re*-volting. We probably poisoned everybody in London.' Another pause. 'Mum says I'm to tell you she's really happy. To be frank,' (he lowered his voice) 'it's a bit awkward talking to you right now because she's right next door in a fucking awful temper.'

Harold's heart thudded miserably in his chest but he tried to be bright, *mustn't depress Davey*.

'I'm glad you still feel OK enough to swear, Davey.'

Davey's voice grew more distant. 'Yes, well it's nothing to do with me, is it? It's you two, isnit. Or else it isn't. Look Harold, goodbye.'

And the line was cut.

Returned to the dim, hot lobby, Harold felt utterly bereft.

Six tenpenny bits on the box, unused. But the money would run out if he stayed too long.

The Bella Costa was fine for a bit. Full Board, Own Bathroom was fine for a bit. The crocodile of couples was fine for a bit – Mrs Limone and Francis, the honeymooners, even the two old ladies had each other.

The honeymooners were fine for a bit, and then they were less fine. There was an empty room between them and Harold but he still sometimes heard her cries, disjointed cries like cries of birds. After a while, the echoes began. The echoes were less pleasant.

All echoes were less pleasant.

New Year's Eve seemed a long time ago. His memory of it changed. The fragile chair which matched his own was no longer in a far corner. It was in the centre, shivering and groaning with the grief of the woman who had left next day. Only the honeymoon couple couldn't see her. Nobody else could look away. Her large red arms in their lacey frills held the pain in, held them all together.

CHAPTER TWO

In the first week of January, Amanda came back from her twice-yearly two weeks with her grownup daughter. She found the house in very much more than the mess she expected (and hoped) would result from her absence, to prove she was missed.

The second floor, where Harold and Lottie slept, was strewn with angry swathes and occasional neatly-folded stacks of clothes, stray sponge-bags hastily stuffed with razors and damp, unhealthy sponges, paper files spilling forth bits of paper which had clearly not been filed. Lottie herself strode about amongst the wreck in pink pyjamas, a pink headband sternly pulling her hair back off a brow which looked worried and shone with sweat.

'Ooooh, Mrs Segall. Whatever's the matter?'

'Matter? Nothing's the matter . . . Harold has left, that's all. I mean, he's left me, that's all. And I'm trying to send all his things to his mother.'

'Oooh. Mr Segall left. Oh dear, Mrs Segall, oh dear.'

'Yes. *Thank you*, Amanda.'

The tone was discouraging to say the least.

Amanda always felt 'partial' to the employers she stayed with, and she'd stayed here for six years, and to her it was just a continuation of staying with the nice Sinclairs who had lived next door. Them she had really stayed with, for over twenty years. She took on Lottie at their suggestion, and at first she wasn't quite what Amanda was used to, a little bit on the decorative side – and led you a bit of a dance. But the boy was always a lovely boy, and ever so good to his mother. And she'd felt a lot happier after the marriage. It always steadied a woman down. And Mr Segall was a charmer, on the vague side, maybe, but then, men *were*. Very polite and nice to her. Never – short, as Mrs Segall could be. As Mrs Segall was today.

But nothing could really shake Amanda, after forty years in service. An employer *is* an employer. They have their little ways, she told herself if anything got her down. But then –

that's what money does for you. I wouldn't change places, not for anything.

Her daughter thought she was mad. 'Mum, I'd rather die than be in service.' What did Noreen know about it? She took after her granny, who liked a bit of posh. Look at the name she saddled me with.

In any case, Noreen had a man to look after her. She was one of the lucky ones. Whereas Arthur only looked after himself, even before he took ill and died.

Amanda was proud of her record. I've always been in work. I've always paid my debts, in the end. I've always had a roof over my head.

So when Mrs Segall was – well, hoity-toity – Amanda was indulgent. It was money, also, that Amanda needed. If Mrs Segall didn't want to tell her what was going on, Amanda didn't care. Davey would tell her, later.

'Well, it looks as though I'd better start by helping you with all that to-do, Mrs Segall.'

'It is not a *to-do*, and no, thank you, Amanda. Just carry on as usual. The floors all need some attention. Oh – and the utility room needs a special clean. We had . . . a *pet* . . . in there over Christmas.'

Lottie rallied some of her old flirtatious charm, remembering the unpleasant smell that lingered in the utility room. Amanda had always been absurdly possessive about that room.

'Just give it some tender loving care, will you, Amanda, be a darling, and let in some nice fresh air. Oh – and can you possibly manage some fish, for lunch? With that marvellous lemony sauce you do? I can tell you we've been living off *baked beans*, with you away. Davey's been dying for you to come back.'

Amanda was quite appeased. She knew Lottie was really a perfectly adequate cook when she wanted to be. In a separate part of her brain, however, Amanda kept another mistress, frivolous, helpless, entirely dependent. It made her feel she did some good in the world, looking after these rich and helpless girls, brought up with much more money than sense. Someone had to do it.

Sally Sinclair had been the same. And before her, Jane Hart-Woodes; and before her, Whatsername, sweet little thing – Miranda Buchanan-Couttes-Hughes. What a mouthful. Tiny, with a lovely big smile, seemed much too young to be married. Seemed ever so much younger than *me*, though we must have been the same age. Mean, of course. Very mean. But then – that was the thing with money. If you had it, you never understood it. You had to need it, to understand it. It wasn't her fault, not really. Money was money, when all's said and done.

'. . . and if you could give the oven a special clean, I'm afraid I made rather a mess of it on New Year's Day. I put in a soufflé and forgot it . . .'

It was comforting, getting back into harness. After the first week staying with Noreen she always got itchy fingers. She liked to make herself useful, she liked the feeling of a job well done. This was what she understood: sorting out other people's messes, putting things right, making nice bright surfaces. You could feel pride when the job was done. A job's a job, that was the thing.

☆

When the quiet feet had padded downstairs, Lottie was swept with relief. She had felt like a vandal, discovered here in the middle of the wreck.

Of course what Amanda thought hardly mattered . . .

Of course what Amanda thought *always* mattered. More than Lottie liked to admit. In her greys and navies and sensible shoes, in her flat, lacquered perms and hygienic colognes, Amanda always came on her as a judge, an ambassador from her parents' world.

She was infinitely less beautiful than Lottie's mother, but the two women had shared their quietness. Kindness too; Amanda was kind. Lottie saw that, though she didn't much like it.

Amanda's bond with Davey almost made Lottie feel jealous. She supposed he just needed a grandma-substitute. He'd only seen Carl's parents two or three times since she and Carl divorced. And Sylvia was hardly good grandmother material, she kept on getting his name wrong, and then explaining at very great length who she was confusing him with. Amanda was not a bad choice for a grandma . . . dull, of course, but then, the rest of his life probably wasn't dull enough.

Lottie had forgotten where she'd got to again. Was she folding, or sorting? Was she throwing things away? They were very easy questions, but she didn't feel capable of solving them. Did dirty clothes have to be cleaned before you packed them off to somebody's mother?

Lottie didn't want to give Sylvia the satisfaction of calling her a slut. There seemed to be a *lot* of dirty things. He *would* have to leave when Amanda was away. Dirty things meant things which smelled of Harold.

He was a clean man, showering once or twice a day. The things which were dirty did not smell of sweat. They smelled of Harold, and lemony Eau Sauvage.

Before he met me, he didn't wear perfume.

Lottie stopped herself in mid-air, frozen with his t-shirt pressed against her face. Get on with it, she instructed herself. Get on with it. Get it over with.

What about things of his that she liked and wore herself? Could she keep those? His pants, for example.

Don't be ridiculous, Lottie. Of course you can't keep his underpants.

The enormous royal blue woollen dressing-gown she gave him for their first Christmas. She loved snuggling up to that. She slipped it on now over her pink pyjamas.

'You cold, Mum?'

Davey looked in through the door. She felt guilty and embarrassed, started pulling it off.

'Nope.'

'Are you sure? Do you want a cup of coffee? By the way, was that Amanda I heard on the stairs?'

'No, I drink too much coffee. It'll give me broken veins. Yes, it was Amanda. She's probably brought you something ghastly from Ireland . . . oh, why not go down and see her and make us *all* some coffee?'

She wanted them all away. She wanted to be alone with Harold – with Harold's *things*, that is. Yes. And be done with it.

Yet when Davey was gone she picked up the dressing-gown and cuddled its bulk in her arms.

The piles of paper were easier; she knew she wanted to be shot of that. Harold's scribblings, tiny ants of ink. She found his handwriting impossibly frustrating. Even in the first thrill of their affair when she longed for those ants on an envelope, she would tear it open and soon get exhausted, never managing to reach the end.

Harold had been outraged. 'It can't be that bad. Are you serious? You didn't read to the end?'

'Look, Harold, be reasonable. I mean, there were all of six sides of it! I have to get on, in the mornings. Life's too short to spend poring over writing as – well – idiosyncratic, as yours.'

Her own writing was nearly half an inch tall, bold and black and simple. Anyone could read her writing, anyone could understand what she had to say. It was one of the things she was proudest of, that she could make herself plain. Writing and speaking were communication. Spreading doubt and confusion seemed almost wicked.

She often wished she could make that point to modern poets and novelists. Harold liked them, of course. Harold's own novel might turn out obscure. That thought was insanely irritating. Everyone would think that Lottie approved.

Painting was vastly superior to writing. Painting said things in one. It asked you to look, and feel, not burrow and ferret and fabricate meanings. Harold, of course, enjoyed all that. Harold had been a critic himself. Worse, he had *taught other people to criticize*, writing those frightful textbooks for schools.

She wasn't being strictly fair. He had given up teaching, and reviewing. He had taken up Lottie, and writing fiction. Her sneer relaxed against her will.

I wonder if he was happy with me.

She nested two socks inside each other, having sniffed them to make sure they smelled of soap, not Harold. He seemed to have an awful lot of socks, and the pairs were spread remarkably widely. Maroon, blue, cream, grey. There was a pleasure when you finally matched them up, when you could tuck them in and forget them.

Pairs of things. Tucking them in.

Oh sod it, sod it. She'd had enough. She threw a pile of socks in the air.

'*Amanda!*' A shriek. She modulated it. 'Amanda, could you come up here?'

The stately, quiet feet began their predictable plod up the long stairs. When Amanda was only one floor away, Lottie kicked a pile of Harold's shoes about, just to show she could.

But when Amanda came in, she was looking demure.

'Oh, bless you, Amanda. Look here, I'm sorry, I've changed my mind, I've got to rush out. Could you see to all this? Just bundle everything together somehow.' (Amanda's thin lips took a disapproving twist. She never 'just bundled things together', *ever*.) 'I'll get someone round to get rid of it all. Pickford's or somebody. Could you manage it for tomorrow?'

'You can get a lot cheaper than Pickford's,' Amanda frowned. 'Yes, I can manage it. But what about lunch? I haven't started yet.'

'Oh, I'll bring back some takeaway Chinese for us all.'

'Beg pardon, Mrs Segall, I never eat Chinese.' She had told that to Lottie fifty times.

'Will fish and chips do you?'

'Thank you, Mrs Segall.'

She would put it in the bin. She hated frozen fish. Frozen was frozen: fresh was fresh. But if you were in service you couldn't go objecting to everything, could you?

She'd make herself a sandwich with the last of that turkey, it would do her nicely, with a slice of Christmas cake. Eat it as she worked. She'd soon sort out this pickle. As Lottie's feet ran downstairs, Amanda felt her good temper settle back. She started putting the shoes in rows, one and one, it was nice making pairs.

What a mess Mrs Segall always made. She was like a hurricane, couldn't keep still, made too much noise to listen to anybody. Always felt more than anyone else, and had more to say about it, too.

Mr Segall would be finding it quiet.

'Probably glad of the change, I'd say.'

She said it aloud, and as soon as she heard it she felt ashamed of herself. It wasn't up to her to have opinions. And it wasn't even true. She knew Mr Segall loved Mrs Segall. Doted on her was more to the point, always fussing around her in the middle of the morning when he should have been busy with his typewriter. Kissing her and doing. It was quite embarrassing the first year they were married. Like being with a couple of teenagers. She'd find them canoodling out on the landing, or he'd be chasing her round the garden.

But lately things hadn't been like that. There'd been a lot of shouting. She bossed him about, made him fetch and carry. No way to treat a man. Sometimes he looked at Mrs Segall in an awful way which reminded Amanda of Noreen's little dog. When it wanted some food off your plate, or a cuddle. Noreen's little poodle, with its sad brown eyes.

Folding shirts she always enjoyed, making a square of something so very un-square. He'd guess she'd done it. Well, there wasn't much else she could do for him. With that sort of woman, there was no changing them. When you'd worked here as long as she had, you knew a thing or two about Mrs Segall. Before Mr Segall's day, there had been plenty of gentlemen, and now she supposed they would be round here again.

It wasn't for her to judge; she'd never had the chances.

But even if I had had the chances. Even if I had had her kind of looks. I think *one* would have been enough for me, if he'd been kind-hearted, like Mr Segall.

And if he'd had a proper job, of course.

Which was the real snag with Mr Segall. A woman couldn't respect a man if he didn't have a proper job to go to. Looked at that way, she couldn't lay blame. All Mr Segall did was play about with books, and scribble this and that in the study. Probably made a bob or two; probably made enough for someone ordinary.

But Mrs Segall wasn't ordinary. Mrs Segall was rich.

It was only natural that a woman with money should expect more money to be given her. And of course she would expect it from her husband. And if he couldn't make it, that would be that. If you've got money, you see things different.

She went on packing all that day, packing Harold away in the cold of the bedroom, making pairs where she could make pairs, making things square that were not square.

CHAPTER THREE

Bride was really very beautiful, pale and bright as the January light which had dazzled him on the sea. Her lashes and eyebrows were nearly invisible until you got up close. Harold only once had the luck to get close, in Reception when she was collecting her key. They were soft and thick and baby-white.

She dressed very badly in shapeless pastels that seemed to have been laundered far too many times. Her limp pale hair was rather too long; her feet were also too long.

She looked so fragile. It couldn't suit her, being with that preposterous man. Yet at breakfast the flat quiet sound of her voice would suddenly break into cheerful giggles and in the same way in the afternoons and evenings and sleepless early mornings she would break into Harold's loneliness with those wild unforgettable bird-calls, crying easily through two thin walls.

Her speaking voice, however, was nasal, northern. Unlike her appearance, it said very ordinary things. 'No thanks, Eric.' 'No, I'm not cold.' 'Give over, Eric. I don't fancy any more.'

Harold longed to talk to her. It wouldn't be ordinary. However, she only had eyes for Eric.

He was like a walking, talking steak, red-faced, damp-eyed, bursting with go. He teased and chatted all through breakfast, and held her hand so she couldn't eat, though he ate on relentlessly, feeding in beans and eggs with his fork. He didn't ever say her name, so Harold didn't even know that. In his mind she was Bride. Or – Ingrid . . . he wondered about Claire.

One morning, Harold came down to breakfast early. Eric, for once, was late, so Harold was alone with silent Bride in the ticking dining room. Today it was he who could not look. The glass-fronted reproduction clock had a very loud and lonely tick.

Suddenly a miracle happened. She turned to Harold (to *him*, to *him*!) across two empty tables and said, 'I'm thinking about me canary. Eric gave me a lovely canary. Me flatmate that was is looking after it. I 'ope it's all right.'

Harold was deeply gratified. He started talking much too fast, of caged birds, caged animals, and finally Poole Zoo.

'There are three leopards and two black leopards. It's astonishing, they were just in cages of wood and wire when I last saw them, you'd think they'd be out in seconds and scrunch up the people.'

'Were you afraird?' Bride asked, leaning towards him, eyes brightening.

'Sorry? Oh, afraid. Well, yes. I suppose I was.'

She instantly burst out laughing and he dropped his eyes to his cornflakes, nettled.

'They'll 'ave to ayah you a goan.'

That was what it sounded like. He couldn't make any sense of it at all, and she was still laughing hard.

'I'm sorry?'

'I say, they'll 'ave to *ayah* you a *goan!*'

He still started without understanding, and she stopped laughing and started to blush.

'I'm going quite deaf, I'm afraid.' This was awful.

She spoke very slowly, using her lips, her pale full lips, very carefully.

'They'll 'AVE to AYAH you a GOAN.'

Two spots of angry red in her cheeks. It suddenly made a meaning in his brain and he laughed inanely, full of relief, applauding her with his whole body.

'Oh *hire me a gun*! Yes, they will! Yes, of course! Of yes! Very good! Sorry!'

She was white and removed and cold again. She waited till he'd finished convulsing and then addressed her own table-cloth.

'Well, it wasn't even foony in first place.'

At that moment Eric entered the room with a full-blooded 'MORNING!' and jogged across between the tables to kiss his new wife juicily. His slab-like back made a perfect screen. Harold was on his own again. When he passed her on the stairs later that day she didn't even nod.

I never even asked her about her canary, he realized. I never even asked her her name.

Time to go, time to go. Lonely people behaved this way, focusing their emptiness on others.

Lonely men. He was a lonely man.

Rubbish. I refuse to be lonely.

The blackest cold he had ever known had settled outside the windows. The blinding light of New Year's Day was a distant, confusing memory. There hardly seemed to be any day at all between breakfast, when all the lights were switched on, and around three o'clock when the shadows started thickening out in the road behind the pines.

He went out once or twice but it didn't help. Everyone had died, except the newsagent, who looked bleaker every day. The wind and rain found the tiniest gaps between cuff and glove or scarf and collar. Harold felt defenceless out there. He longed to get back in the warm. Besides, the phone might ring. His life had shrunk to the sound of that phone.

He made himself walk round the block, skirting the Central Gardens. Trees and bushes stood entirely bare, reduced to the merest scratching blackness, uncomfortable elbows, broken twigs, thin wretched bones beneath the rain. He was sure nothing lived upon those twigs. He could hardly bear to look at them. Inside *him* there were things like that.

Only the evergreens still had leaves, depressing, lightless, dreary leaves. Harold had always found pines depressing. Bournemouth seemed to be full of pines.

Nothing was alive, and nor was Harold. Harold was merely waiting to live.

Lottie would surely forgive him soon.

Or else she would not.

Then what, Harold?

Time to go, time to go.

Mrs Limone seemed abstracted, and flashes of pain crossed her criss-cross lines as she bent to pick up the breakfast things. She announced that Christmas hadn't suited her, she'd felt 'liverish' ever since. Francis was there as often as before but he didn't look very happy. His 'Mornings' and 'Evenings' formerly loud, were muffled, indistinct.

At six one evening Harold was buying a sherry from Mrs Limone when Francis came in and hardly looked at him, plodded straight through to the kitchen. His face, glimpsed in dull collapse, was fatter than ever, and sadder.

Mrs Limone rather artificially continued talking to Harold. No one could ever fail to notice someone Francis's size. She was clearly Making A Point. She rang up the till with an air of secret triumph, said 'Good 'Ealth', walked into the kitchen after Francis and firmly closed the door.

Harold turned to find both the old ladies staring after her, intensely interested.

'Is everything all right?' he asked on impulse, choosing a boyish, trusting tone. He had classified them in his mind: *old ladies*. It was quite all right to talk to old ladies.

'I don't believe we know your name,' said the smaller, older and yet markedly stronger-looking of the two.

'It's Harold – Harold Segall. And would you be so kind as to tell me yours?'

'Violet Isabel Ponsonby. And this is my companion, Pamela Troop.' She extended a tiny freckled hand, which had a grip of iron. Pamela Troop bent towards him and her hand felt light as eggshell.

'Now what' (*h*what) 'was your question?' Violet angled her head towards him. Her eyes were a remarkable speedwell blue. A little bloodshot at the edges.

'I was, er, just wondering, er, if there was anything – er – the matter with – er?'

Harold gestured helplessly kitchenwards. That glittering blue gaze made him feel silly.

'Ah yes, we *think* she turned him down,' Violet said very firmly. Then she leaned forward, clutching the arms of her favourite carver chair. 'But come and sit down here beside us and tell us what is the matter with you.'

Not knowing what else to do, Harold settled awkwardly on Francis's pouffe. It was a long way down.

'I've come down here to think,' he said.

Violet's eyes pronounced him a liar.

'We think you have a broken heart,' she said brightly. Pamela laughed a mild little laugh and nodded her well-kept white-fluffed head. 'We think your lady-love has left you,' Violet continued.

'I left *her*, actually.'

'It doesn't really matter, does it. Who leaves whom. Do you still love her?'

'No. Yes.'

'You see, he still loves her,' Violet trilled to Pamela, and they smiled, leaned back and closed their eyes.

'Do you want me to tell you about it? It's a hopeless case, I'm afraid.'

'Then what is there to tell?' Violet sounded cross, and the startlingly youthful eyes snapped open.

'We know all the sad stories. We expect them, dear.' Pamela's eyes were clouded, warm.

Harold didn't like the assumption that his story was one of many.

'A lot of it wasn't sad,' he muttered. 'It's not quite like you think. She asked me to come back. But that was some days ago.'

'She asked him to come back!' Violet gently, affectionately squeezed the lambs' wool of Pamela's thin arm. 'Is there a child?'

'Yes. Well, but he's not mine . . .'

'Oh *dear*. The trouble is, things are all so very different now.'

Violet sighed rather wearily. He felt their attention slipping away.

'No no, first marriage. I'm her second husband. We broke up because . . . she's very dominant, that's part of it . . .'

'You look as though you *need* a bit of organizing, dear. Not awfully practical, one would suppose.'

'Little Johnny Head-in-Air,' Pamela added and smiled innocently.

'She's . . . rich and selfish and loud,' Harold insisted, his calm disappearing, 'and she does incredibly stupid things. *Important* stupid things.'

'*Is* she stupid?' Violet asked from a thousand miles and years away.

'No, on the contrary, truly she's remarkable,' Harold rushed, and heard what he'd said, and stopped.

He saw they were back with him again, attending very carefully.

'Do you wish she was here in this room?'

'Do you wish she was sitting as close to you as Violet is to me?'

The questions were absurd, and yet his heart leaped to answer.

'Oh yes, yes, of course I do. But feelings aren't the point, are they. I mean – I feel all this for Lottie because she's my wife, we've shared . . . everything really, for two years. You can't stop feeling just like that.'

'But feelings are the only point,' said Violet fiercely, her jagged brown teeth showing, eyes blazing in their dark eaves. 'As long as you feel for her, there's hope.'

'You're very romantic.' He sighed, heavily. He wanted them to tell him something real.

'Don't patronize the old, young man.'

He started, and felt himself blushing.

'I didn't mean to – I didn't mean . . .'

'We've lived a very long life. I can tell you, only love in all the world can make living together bearable. Only *longing* for her to be here, as near to you as Pamela is to me, and we have to be near, always near, because we're a little deaf, you see – only longing for her to be here could make you bear her always being here when you're too old and too ill to move apart. So you have to look at her, every day, and see . . . in her . . . your own self growing older.'

The end of that speech took a tremendous effort. It came very slowly. Each word was said with such passion he almost believed it.

Pamela was nodding, lips sucked in, lids half-dropped, a wry accepting.

When Violet spoke again her voice was brisk.

'You'd better get on with it, Mr Segall, and get her back. No time like the present. When you get to our age you feel that keenly . . . Naturally one wishes one had known it sooner.'

Harold felt galvanized for a second. The sherry lifted him, fired his blood. He tipped the last drop back, pointing the stem at the ceiling like a boy.

'You're still very young, you know. Though of course no one ever feels young. But you haven't spoiled your life yet.'

Violet's voice was just a little hoarse; the effort of wishing him well was immensely tiring, but she had to make it. Pamela closed her pinker, smaller hand over Violet's yellow-white freckled one, and Violet leaned back for a moment and listened.

'How old are you, Mr Segall?'

'I'm forty-five.' It didn't sound much.

'Forty-five,' Pamela sang it lightly, making it brief as a grace-note.

Violet sat up and rejoined the game.

'Then if you are as fortunate as we have been, you have as long left to live as you have lived already.'

'That seems to give me some sort of obligation to make a better job of the rest,' said Harold, standing up and bowing to them both.

'There aren't any obligations,' called Violet as he walked away. 'There is better, or worse. There is choice.'

In Reception, Mrs Limone was reading a book behind the desk. Francis normally sat in there with her; now he had been banished. Now his great seat was spread across two of the upright chairs which faced the desk. His eyes were dog-like, six feet away from her, tracking her hands as she flicked the pages.

'We think she turned him down.'

Lottie will turn me down.

I tried to make friends with . . . Ingrid, Claire – but I just made a mess of things.

Harold creaked along the landing. The door of Number 6, the honeymooners' door, was pushed ajar with a slipper.

Just before Harold got there Eric hopped out backwards in a cherry-red dressing-gown, wearing one slipper and grinning at something inside the room.

'Sandra Smith, if you lock this door I'll tan your bum till you can't . . .'

He realized Harold was there a split second before they collided, and instantly planted both feet on the ground, bellowed 'Evening' at Harold, and darted back inside the room, kicking the slipper before him, so the door slammed hard on the girl's coarse squeals and Eric's baritone laughter.

We used to laugh like that.

Harold was glad to get off the dark landing and into his own lit room. He wanted to laugh like that again.

'There is better or worse. There is choice.'

OK. He'd ring Lottie directly after supper. He'd be terribly cheerful and funny in whispers about all the weirdos here. He always made her laugh. She loved him making her laugh.

Yet *Sandra Smith* had turned him down. (She was frightfully common. Those hideous sweaters!)

He sat there staring at the mirror, practising terribly cheerful expressions.

And then he just sat there, staring, waiting, combing dark strands over the emptiness.

CHAPTER FOUR

I'd have thought it would be more decent if there was a little bit of grief.

Amanda stood at the cold glass watching as Lottie rushed out two floors below, slamming the door as she always did. The street lamp made a brief flower-like thing of her hair against the blue velvet.

It must be somebody special; that coat was Yves St Laurent. One up on Dior, or so they said. This year's collections, as well. The money probably stopped them grieving. You'd think twice before you cried on ten grand's worth of velvet.

Amanda would stay inside, picking up the pieces as she always did.

And Amanda answered at nine o'clock when Harold made his nervous, hopeful phone call, ready to be terribly funny, ready to make Lottie laugh.

'I'm afraid she's gone out, Mr Segall.'

'Oh Amanda, it's you.' His voice was utterly disappointed. 'When will she be back?'

'She never says, Mr Segall.'

'Anyway, it's nice to hear you, Amanda. Happy New Year.' He'd never sounded less happy.

'Well, thank you, Mr Segall, and the same to you.'

There was an awkward pause. She ventured an opinion.

'I'm ever so sorry about what's happened.'

'I don't really know what *is* happening. I think you could say I'm in a bit of a fix.'

Hearing that familiar, bun-like voice, Harold's own voice had started to quaver. He wanted to blub, and tell her all.

He does sound in an awful state, Amanda thought. Ooh dear. All on his own in the middle of winter and probably hasn't any clothes to put on. A kind and fatal impulse moved her.

'You don't have to worry about your things. I've packed them all up, just this evening. They're going down to your mother's. And all your bits and pieces of paper. She was very particular I packed up those. I know you'd feel lost without them, Mr

Segall. You've always loved your little bits of paper.'

Harold's heart lurched sickeningly and he couldn't speak for a second.

'Has she done that already? Well, well. I suppose – I should have expected it.'

Amanda realized she'd said the wrong thing. Noreen said she did it all the time.

'I've put my foot in it, haven't I, sir?'

'Don't call me that, you know I don't like it.' He didn't like the rather sickly kindness in her voice, either. Even Amanda could patronize him now. He rallied his last resources of dignity.

'Look, Amanda, thank you for all you're doing. Please tell Mrs Segall – I rang up to ask about my possessions. Please tell her I'll be leaving this hotel. And please,' (his voice sounded real again suddenly) 'please give my love to Davey. Is he OK?'

'Well, he seems a bit quiet.'

'Oh.' It was all so hopeless, so stupid. 'Well, thank you, Amanda. Goodbye.'

And then he had to drag back upstairs, past the honeymoon couple's squeaking nest, back to his own bright silent cupboard. He'd never felt so lonely.

So she had got rid of him, just like that, cleared him out. He was last year's model. He should have expected it all along. She had no heart (*I hate her, I hate her*).

He caught himself grinding his teeth in the mirror.

Jesus, Lottie. You've turned me into a maniac.

For an hour or so he tried not to think. He'd left home without a thing to read. The Bella Costa's glass-fronted bookcase was mostly stocked with love stories. Who the hell still read love stories? – (Mrs Limone, of course.)

Who the hell still *wrote* love stories? He thought they'd gone right out of fashion, in the era of the New Brutality. And indeed they all seemed to be 1950s rubbish with ecstatically happy endings . . . not *quite* what he needed at the moment . . . at last he found a thriller. That should be good escapist reading.

But it didn't transport him anywhere. It didn't anaesthetize him, either. It just condemned him to an endless sequence of meetings with more strangers. Everything made him feel homesick, now.

How long till I get to the end of this . . .?

The book fell heavily on the carpet, jerking him awake. His

head ached, and he was very cold. He'd forgotten to switch the radiator back on. He sat there shivering, less than nothing.

Right. He would leave this dump in the morning.

Lottie would never mope like this. She seemed so far away already.

He remembered what she said about her parents.

'What's gone is gone. I don't believe in mourning.'

Now Harold was part of what was gone. He was swept aside like the tamarin.

His image of her began to shrink and harden, a cold white face far away in the night, sleeping dreamlessly, feeling nothing.

I can escape, if she can.

Lottie came in at ten o'clock. She had been for a drink with some neighbours. Ivor and Elspeth seemed more boring when Harold wasn't there to take the strain. They were more his friends than hers, really. She sometimes wondered if she'd ever liked them. She had worn the coat to boost morale. Elspeth had deliberately not noticed it.

'Mr Segall phoned, Mrs Segall.'

'Well?'

She jammed in another cigarette. All this trouble, all due to him.

'He said I was to tell you he phoned about his things. And he said he was leaving wherever he was.'

'Is that all?' Lottie felt the anger rising and burning in her stomach. 'Did he say where he was going?'

'No, Mrs Segall.'

'Didn't you *ask*?' Lottie whirled towards her. Her eyes were frighteningly bright with what Amanda thought was rage.

'I didn't presume to ask. I didn't know if he wanted to tell me.'

Amanda stared at the carpet, trying to escape the glare of those slitty green eyes. She wouldn't get cross if she knew what she looked like.

'You didn't *presume*,' Lottie snorted. 'In case no one told you, it's normal practice when taking a telephone message to ask for a number where the caller can be contacted.'

Amanda resolutely said nothing, stared down. The carpet

needed a vacuum. No one did a stroke while she was away. You'd have thought they could manage a vacuum.

'*Do you hear me?*' Lottie suddenly shouted.

Only once had she shouted at Amanda before. Years ago when Davey had German measles, and Amanda kept taking him nice mugs of soup. It was chicken broth she had made from bones. '*Just leave him alone, will you,*' Mrs Segall had suddenly screamed as Amanda went upstairs with another steaming mug. '*He's very ill. Just leave him to sleep!*' Later, she had apologized.

Amanda would *not* be shouted at. Up with that she would not put. She folded her arms to make herself feel more solid, and risked a short glance at Lottie's burning, furious face.

'Well, if he wants you to contact him, I expect he'll give us the number,' she said, and sidled to the cupboard where she kept her long broom. She started sweeping, emphatically. If she'd dared, she would have got out the vacuum cleaner, and turned the engine full on.

Just at that moment Davey wandered downstairs yawning with his Walkman headphones on. 'Hi everyone!' he called, from whatever distant place he was dancing in.

'WHY AM I SURROUNDED BY FOOLS?' yelled Lottie, and ran upstairs to their bedroom, her bedroom, with the boxes piled in the adjoining room, dived face first on to the bed and cried so hard her mascara made long smears of charcoal on the yellow satin of the coverlet. She wept till it all turned dark.

After a bit she realized it was getting out of hand; the sobs were stopping her from breathing. She was frightened, and the fear of not being able to breathe was suddenly strong enough to slow the sobs. Her face felt like a streaming mask of tears and phlegm.

She looked at herself in the mirror. Her eyes had narrowed to tiny pink slits, the rest was shapeless and swollen. I look like a horrible dummy, she thought. That can't be me, it's someone else.

Jesus, Harold, you've turned me into this.

'I hate you, I hate you, I hope you die.'

She watched the monster mouthing in the glass. She was shocked by herself but she liked what she heard. If she wanted him to die, then she could be free. More than anything in the world, that was what she wanted.

I don't need any of this. Sobbing and raging and waiting for phone calls. Being in somebody else's power. Being in bloody Harold's power. I want to be myself again.

But it wasn't so easy just to stop suffering.

☆

That night she lay awake, Lottie who never lay awake. She lay and thought about the past, refusing to think and thinking, thinking. After the thoughts, she dreamed. Lottie never remembered her dreams. She took a pride in not dreaming.

Her parents' house had always been dark, dark red Gothic in a dark green wood of pines which only grew brilliant in early summer. Then it was suddenly gorgeous, reds and purples and lovely soft pinks.

One day when Lottie was young her mother had pinned, with great difficulty, a purple head of rhododendron in her thick black hair. 'Mummy, you look like a lady in a film.' Lottie somehow knew that Daddy had picked it. She remembered their faces pressing together and smiling as she ate her tea. She had tea earlier than usual, and was sent to bed while it was still light. She knew she was shut out from a party. Her parents stayed downstairs all night, dancing up and down that long dark hall.

Later when she was a teenager the whole memory seemed unlikely. Her mother wore sensible fussy clothes and her thick black hair was divided and braided and nailed to her head with great tortoiseshell pins which didn't go well with her diamond earrings.

'Why do you always wear those earrings? They're much too dressy for day.'

'Your father gave them to me. He likes to see me wearing them.'

'Well, you shouldn't wear that brooch as well. Not on tweed. It looks sort of cheap.'

It was a brooch of a deer, with oversized green glass eyes and an unlikely red body.

'Ma fille, you know nothing. It is Fabergé, it is emeralds and rubies. For myself, I think it too – fantastic. But again, it was Daddy who gave it me.'

Now all those elaborate and tasteless jewels sat in the dark of Lottie's bank. Fossils of grief, shells of grief, useless things which should be disposed of. She had her own jewellery, lavish stones which spilled in the sun on her dressing-table. Her mother's little animals meant nothing to her. But her father's ghost laid his hand upon her, the weight of his arm in the heavy black coats he had worn all his life, summer and winter, as if he had always been waiting to mourn.

Norman had always treated his beloved Anne-Marie as if she was delicate, fussing over whether she was tiring herself, fussing over whether Lottie tired her. She was truly French in her love of the kitchen, cooking with passion and with flair. But Norman was afraid she would wear herself out, and constantly threatened to engage a cook, and there was a ritual argument.

And then she died early of a heart attack and Lottie realized, astonished, that his worry had been real. Then mourning became Norman's reality.

Nothing at all would be changed, he decreed. The house became thick with taboo and shrine. One Saturday when Norman was in London seeing to a new consignment of skins, Lottie crept into their forbidden bedroom.

Her mother's clothes, three years more out of date than they were in the year she died, stood across three-quarters of the wardrobe, headless ghosts at an airless party. Heavy brocades, expensive knitted jerseys, stiff Chanel suits with their buttons and braids. Norman's striped suits hung sadly alongside, squeezing themselves into what world was left. It was horrible, sickening, unnatural, and fifteen-year-old Lottie had run outside into the fresh green garden and made a vow.

'I'll never grow up and be like them. I'll never be miserable on purpose, like him. I'll never hide away like Mama and not have a proper life of my own. I'll never kill myself cooking. I'll never end up in a cupboard, like her. Just horrible clothes and mothballs and nothing!'

Now she renewed that vow. She was not going to mourn and brood over Harold.

It must be two in the morning.

I'm going to sleep sweetly, and dream of whiteness. Maybe tomorrow I'll paint everything white.

In fact, she dreamed of that lost, dark house, a confused nightmare of dancing with Harold, then seeing him lying dying in bed. She was weeping. Amanda was clearing the wardrobe. 'It's all for the best,' said her father. 'He's not what I wanted for my daughter.' She tried to walk away, but no one had noticed that she and Harold were woven together. On a crest of relief, Lottie called out, and woke herself. The dream had gone.

Outside the window, a few birds were singing, little scratches of light on the black. The first she'd heard that year.

She imagined his face, very tiny and white, miles away in the darkness. Already too far to see the detail . . . she willed his memory to shrink and harden.

I can escape if he can.

They have all been so far inside, this month. Outside, a lot is happening.

In the city, there are foxes now. A vixen screams in the dark like a peacock, calling for her mate.

In Bournemouth, where Harold sees dead black branches, there are actually thousands of millions of buds, the cells stirring and multiplying as the days get minutely longer. Cherry-tree buds push out from the ends of the twigs like the points of a child's star. By the black roots, the very first snowdrops.

Very very far away from all this at the edge of the solar system, so far away that the sun from its surface looks no brighter than a star from Earth, Pluto, the smallest, coldest planet spins through the freezing darkness. Its surface of methane ice glitters like glass, immensely brilliant. Though the sun is around three thousand million miles away, Pluto cannot escape.

February

CHAPTER FIVE

Harold complains about winter to the man in the paper-shop. The man in the paper-shop agrees. 'Shocking, these winters, lately.'

Actually, they are quite lucky.

Saturn has winds of nine hundred miles an hour in its yellow-orange cloud-tops. Such winds could blow down shops, houses, hotels, little humans in seconds.

Harold is looking for somewhere to live. Something a little more permanent.

☆

The thought was novel, and not unpleasant. After all, with Lottie there had been no looking. He had merely been added to her ménage. The weather was atrocious; snow and ice and screaming wind.

He'd put off starting the search for ages, anticipating a thaw. The little hotel was now boiling hot, and seemed to get hotter as the weather got colder, just to prove that it could; and there were odd hissing and clanking sounds, as if something might explode. The hotel began to close in on Harold. Violet and Pamela must be watching him, to see what effect their sermon had had.

(They weren't, of course. They had better things to do. Violet was absorbed in *Vanity Fair*, reading it for the twentieth time. Pamela was trying to decide, as usual, whether it was time to make peace with her brother. Her brother had taken against Violet, and she hadn't seen him for fifty-one years.)

Harold scanned the paper for flats, and gave notice to Mrs Limone. But the truth was, Harold had nowhere to go. He didn't know where to start. 'Flats to Let' was a miserable inch of newsprint in the *Echo*.

'It's not the time of year, see,' his friend in the newsagent told him. 'This place goes to sleep in winter. All the landlords are whatsit, *hibernating*. You'll just have to go out and dig something up, if you want to get out of Madarm Limone's. Good luck to you, in this weather.'

Out of the shop into the punching cold. Harold didn't mind the weather that much; it wasn't any worse than he felt inside.

As long as Lottie was suffering too. He imagined the breakfast room piled with snow, he packed solid ice into the double glazing so all she could see was ice and snow and she stood marooned in a cold grey prism. Then he was sorry and melted it all.

He'd always wanted to keep women warm. If that was sexist, then he was sexist. He hoped it wasn't, though. It was an instinct, wrapping your arms around what you loved. Women must want to keep men warm too.

At that moment his feet in crêpe-soled boots shot out from under him, *sod*, *black ice* and he landed awkwardly in shallow snow, jolting his spine and scraping his hand. Bastards. Bitches. Treacherous cows. He sent an avalanche down Lottie's neck. Hailstones buried her up to her waist. Her face became strange, whitish, greenish, all the bones showing in the weird snow-light.

The overcoat he had borrowed from Francis was very warm, a Forces' surplus. It wasn't, in itself, particularly scruffy; the tiny white spots were probably toothpaste. On Harold, however, it was gigantic, and he was uneasily aware that his face looked thin and shifty on top of that mountain of cloth. He loomed on doorsteps, much too large, very far from the image of a desirable tenant.

'What do you want?'

'I wondered if –'

'I'll get my husband. *Ronald!*'

All of them denied letting property; denied letting it in winter; denied letting it to *men*; or said it was let already. One said, 'We like to take a family. It works better that way, with a family.' One husband said, in a quite kindly way, 'Round here we don't do it like this, you see. We like to do it through *channels*. Formal channels, see what I mean. Not just going from house to house, asking for it, like you.'

None of them asked him in.

'We only do it in season.'

'No, we don't start till May.'

'You won't find anything at this time of year . . .'

He got to the end of a very long road of rejections wanting to shout at them all, 'All I want is a roof for a bit! I don't take drugs! I don't molest women!'

He suddenly bore right towards the sea. He'd go on the cliffs, and get blown off. Then they'd be sorry. *She'd* be sorry.

Hitting Overcliff Drive, he saw the sea, and just as he saw it the sun came out. Along the horizon, solid silver. The rest of the sea was the intense cold grey of the clouds overhead, but torn with breakers. Durlston Head and Old Harry Rocks to the right were buried in lighter grey mist, but Hengistbury Head rose into the sunlight, dazzlingly white against the sea. The wind blew straight into his nose and mouth so he had to turn away for a moment to breathe. The view behind was so dull by comparison that he wheeled and, suddenly feeling light-hearted, set off stoutly against the wind. He would take the clifftop path to Boscombe, make towards the sheer white cliffs of Hengistbury, make for the future, see what came.

The promenade below was a long blank ribbon. No one, it seemed, went out in winter. A few gulls bent and spun and clung to the crashing walls of air. The violence was exciting, blowing him about as if he were a bird himself. He made himself walk as fast as he could and soon felt hot inside his greatcoat, though his ears suffered immensely from the icy pummelling, slowly shifting from an ache to a pain.

The actual cliff slope was fenced off with 'natural' green wire fencing. Harold objected to all such fences. Harold was a nature-lover, now. He wanted to see nothing but trees and snow.

What kind of trees were they, he wondered, under their coats of white? Not that he would have known, even if there hadn't been any snow. The pines he could recognize, of course. He knew a pine tree, any old day, with snow or without. As the clouds shifted, the nearby bushes were – miraculous, there was no other word. White too bright to be silver.

All this was waiting if you went outside. He had never seen such a wide stretch of sea, now the sunlight spread from shore to horizon, such a massive, crawling weight of bright water.

No wonder these cliffs were slowly crumbling. Beyond white Hengistbury you could see faintly the Isle of Wight and the Needles, just holding on against the battering. Pillars of crumbling chalk like teeth. Harold's teeth felt the cold quite badly. 'Sensitive teeth,' his dentist said, and Lottie had sneered, and asked him if even his teeth had to be more sensitive than other people's. That spiteful streak. Perhaps his teeth *would* crumble.

Teeth made him think about his mother. Her pet obsession was teeth. One of the few things he knew about his father was that he had bad teeth.

'Your father never looked after his teeth. I daresay your father has paid the price.'

Her remembered voice made him shiver more sharply than the cold coming off the sea. With love, as well as fear. He hoped she was all right. On the day after Boxing Day she'd given him lunch and seemed on tremendous form, avid to hear about him and Lottie. The split had given her a new lease of life.

As long as somebody's happy.

Suddenly the raw light made him feel tired.

The path sloped down towards Boscombe and he followed it down quite gratefully. Here the pines half broke the wind. At the foot of the path, he came out at a little roundabout facing the pier. This was Boscombe Pier then; he'd seen it from Bournemouth often enough, a small black finger pointing out to sea. Close up it didn't look much larger. Shops at the entrance were shuttered. A hand-lettered poster, 'CRUISES FROM . . .', had run in the snow, mascara tears.

Lottie only cried to get her own way. She never felt a thing.

The wind on the front was terrific again and he wandered up a path beside a miniature golf course, flashes of brightly-painted reds and blues shining through their blankets of snow. I like this place, he thought. The pier was just the right size for one person. There was a little curving row of gabled nineteenth-century houses, built identically, painted variously, cheering in their determined difference (*was* he really a socialist? Of course he was, a *libertarian* socialist.)

They nearly all had signs outside: PRIVATE GUESTHOUSE,

PRIVATE HOTEL. Then there were some others, HOLIDAY FLATS. His heart rose, and fell again. It would only be in season. He stood in the lee of one of the porches, gazing hungrily up at a promising balcony.

Suddenly the front door opened, without Harold so much as ringing the bell. A rare and radiant flash of optimism. Of course, it was going to be easy.

And just for once, it was. The man who emerged from the blue front door stopped as he was just about to unlock his car, and said, 'You lookin' for something?' He was small and thin in a long thin coat with a long woollen scarf and a long kind face. He looked like an elderly student, but he talked like the country, slow and broad.

Harold, of course, would have thought most faces kind that showed any interest in him. This man had actually asked what he wanted. For Harold it was love at first sight.

Harold was looking for something, yes. Mr Sedley had it.

'It's not really meant for winter let. Just got the bar fires, see. Rent won't be much, this time o' year. Heating'll cost you a packet, I reckon.'

'It's perfect,' said Harold and meant what he said.

It was a top floor flat, with views of the sea, looking over the pines of Boscombe Chine, over treetops heavy with snow. From above, pines weren't depressing, he thought. It was all a matter of point of view.

The furniture was rickety: he loved it. It was much too big for him: he begged for it. He knew he'd be cold: he welcomed it. That morning he left a deposit, and arrived bag and baggage next day.

On his first night there he lay suspended in the new empty space so near the sky. He was trembling . . . Half with excitement at the new wild sound of the sea, liberating him from the Bella Costa's familiar stirrings and whisperings. Half with fear as the window-frame shook and he realized how little there was between him and the endless roar of the water, trying to break the shore. He hadn't thought it would sound so near. But the fear led back to excitement.

He got up, stared out of the window. There was a moon, unnaturally large. Everthing wide and white and raw. Something he had been looking for.

February

In London, Lottie lay in their bed. It was the only piece of furniture not covered in dust-sheets. The moon stared in at the unfamiliar snowy shapes in the sleeping room. It fell across Lottie's rippling face, whitish, greenish, the wide bones showing. She breathed as regularly as the sea, but she dreamed she was floundering across great snowfields, hiding from someone or looking for someone, lost in the February snow.

CHAPTER SIX

Amanda was peeling potatoes, a job she particularly liked. Light from darkness, she always thought, throwing the mucky black peelings away and tipping the smooth creamy egg-like potatoes into the pan. *Results*, she liked. But today she peeled almost absent-mindedly, solemn brown eyes looking elsewhere. She was worried about Mrs Segall.

Davey was eating fruit cake for elevenses at the kitchen table behind her back. He was usually such a caring boy. But today it seemed he just couldn't be bothered.

'I just don't see why she does it herself,' Amanda muttered, for the umpteenth time.

'She likes it,' he said, going on munching.

'But it's so much work for a woman on her own. A place this size. She'll wear herself out.'

'She enjoys it.' He was trying to read *Time Out*, and they'd had this conversation before.

'I mean, it's not as if she was short of money.'

"Course she's not,' he agreed.

Amanda turned round and gave him a Look. 'I'm surprised you're not more bothered. I mean, if she doesn't want to get people in, you could help her yourself, come to that.'

'Look, she doesn't *want* any help.'

'A lot of sons like to help their mothers. A mother's a mother. You only get one.'

That was the sort of Amanda-assertion that drove Davey insane. He was very fond of Amanda, but not of Amanda's assertions. It was the worst thing about grownups, the way they thought they knew general truths.

'Come off it, Amanda. I mean, I do help her. She's doing all this to take her mind off it. Harold leaving and everything. That's why she's going mad on painting.'

'*Going mad* is just about it.'

She grimly poured bleach into the sink. To her eyes, Mrs Segall looked sickly. Lost her nice colour, wasn't eating

71

properly, and hadn't done anything but paint for days.

'It's not as if it was just the undercoats, is it.'

Davey stopped reading, and stared at her amazed.

'What are you talking about, Amanda? Why is it all right for Mum to paint undercoats, but not top coats? Is it etiquette, or what?'

'It's not as if it was just the undercoats that's going to be *all white*, I mean,' Amanda pursued her thoughts regardless as the bleach attacked the stained enamel, working its weekly miracle. 'It was different when it was just the stairs. I never minded cleaning the stairs. I mean, it's enough to drive everyone mad, having everything white, *everywhere*. It's not really normal, doing that. Most people like a bit of colour.'

'Lots of houses are all painted white,' said Davey, but he didn't sound entirely certain. 'Are you *sure* about that, Amanda? She's usually mad on colour.'

'I said to her, yesterday, Mrs Segall, what colour's this room going to be? What do you mean, what colour, she said, can't you see that it's white? So then I said . . .'

But Davey shut up his *Time Out* with a slap. Amanda's voice was really very dreary when she got into one of her complaining moods, particularly with reported speech. (*'And then she said . . . and then I said . . .'*)

'Amanda, really, it's just white paint. She's not spraying everything with arsenic. It's just . . .' (he raised his voice to cover hers) 'it's just a phase, I expect.'

'I *see*,' said Lottie, behind him, coming downstairs in a white-streaked boiler-suit. Her face was white and tired and smaller than usual, and there were big spots of paint in her hair like peppermints stuck on a golden plate.

'Davey, you are an *insufferable* brat. I won't have you discussing my *phases*. I presume this house is mine to paint exactly what colours I like?'

Amanda pretended to scrub the sink. That was what came of having opinions. That was what came of getting familiar. She was over sixty, but she still hadn't learned.

'Don't call me a brat. It's a stupid word. Well, you can't paint *my* bit, anyhow.'

'I shall go up there and do it tomorrow.'

He was suddenly furious, red with rage and dangerously near tears. He dashed up to Lottie and blurted 'You won't! You think you can push *everyone* around! You always used to push Harold around! If you touch my room I'll hate you for ever!'

He suddenly sounded sixteen, the sixteen-year-old child he really was.

'Don't say stupid things,' Lottie snapped, thin-lipped, but her breath was coming in unhappy jerks. She sat down at the kitchen table, suddenly feeling too weak to argue. It always shocked her when Davey got angry.

Davey ran up to his room. Lottie sat and stared at her paint-stained fingers, then at Amanda's dour back and busy elbows. She pondered a crushing remark, but she didn't feel she had the weight to crush. Nor did she have the energy. She needed her energy to paint. So she took her usual course of action and carried on as if nothing had happened.

'Amanda, I'm ravenous and exhausted. Will you bring up some cocoa and some scrambled eggs? With cheese in? And some of your cake? And has that boy had something to eat?'

'Yes, Mrs Segall. In the upstairs sitting-room? Davey's had his.'

The sink was gleaming, white as the snow on the lawn outside. At last Amanda dared to stop scrubbing. Mrs Segall sounded quite normal. Only Davey was in the doghouse, then. Amanda ventured to be peacemaker.

'He doesn't mean any harm, Mrs Segall. He's only a child, you know.'

Lottie found scalding reserves of sarcasm under the wastes of tiredness.

'Amanda, I'd rather you cleaned the sink than told me what *my son* means. I know what *my son* means. And I know how old he is.'

As she fluffed the eggs and milk together, Amanda had to resist a temptation which hadn't visited her for decades, not since she was first in service. She wanted to spit into the saucepan. But she swallowed, and just added salt and pepper a little more fiercely than usual.

White, white, everything white. Poised on her ladder, Lottie tried not to think. Just think of the roller, smoothing on down, and the narrowing narrowing swathes of pink as the cool white covered it up with snow. Damn Amanda. Damn Davey. And Harold, Harold, curse him to hell!

Pressing too hard, nearly overbalancing, white before the eyes, she wished him ill.

CHAPTER SEVEN

Harold's last action before leaving the Bella Costa had been to ring his mother.

'Harold, *dear*. How are you? When are you coming to see me?'

'Soon, Mother. But not just now. I'm moving out of the hotel today.'

'Oh.' Pause. 'I thought you'd go back to her.'

The voice was audibly disappointed.

'*No*, Mother, I'm not going back.'

'Darling. You must come to me. It's the only sensible solution. After all, it seems that *your wife*' (the *wife* was mockingly intoned) 'is sending all your possessions here.'

He'd managed, just, to stay the flood, telling her the flat was signed and sealed, making lying promises to come to Poole just as soon as he'd settled in.

'Of course I'm just an old woman.'

'Of course you're not. Look, I'll have to go.'

'Harold, darling, *whatever* you do, remember I love you, in spite of all.'

'Yes, Mother. Thank you.'

'Darling, I'll come and visit you, and make sure you're all right.'

'Yes, Mother. But not just for a bit – '

' – so that's arranged. God bless you, Harold.'

He couldn't feel easy for several hours after that call was ended.

But once he was in possession of the flat, he forgot about his mother. Wonderfully free of memories, these high-ceilinged rooms overlooking the sea. Although geographically they were quite close, in his mind he severed Poole and Boscombe. He didn't want the past to seep in here. He wanted to be properly alone at last. He wanted to get a grip on his life.

'*There is better, or worse. There is choice.*'

'*. . . as long left to live as you have lived already . . .*'

He was forty-five years old, in the middle of his life, and there

74

were so many things he had never even thought about. There had always been too many people, and too much background noise.

He and Lottie had long lists of friends that neither of them liked (on reflection, *she* probably liked them. On reflection, they were *her* friends; it was Lottie inflicted those lists on him. Ivor and Elspeth, for example. He never had a thing to say to Elspeth, and Ivor blatantly flirted with Lottie. On reflection, she flirted back.)

There had always been someone expecting him to do something small *immediately*. So somehow he'd never had the chance to think what he *really* wanted to do – not today, or tomorrow, or to pay the rent, or to get him through till Christmas. What to do with his *life*. His life. The only life he had.

You made the little decisions, disposing of hours and days and weeks. You didn't see it all added up. There was never a point when you could stop and see the shape of it all. From your own point of view, not other people's.

He saw himself as somebody's son, somebody's husband, somebody's stepfather, too many people's ex-teacher. He saw himself as a non-writing writer. He saw himself as a disappointment, to other people and himself. But he didn't see what was in him; there must be quite a lot in him. Until he knew what was in him, how could he bring it out?

Somehow the years had passed like probation, always deferring the true beginning, the moment when he would play his part. Surely that moment must come soon. He wasn't . . . a stone. He was a thinking person. There should be a moment when he could say, 'This is why I'm here.' Or even, 'I think this is what I want.'

Perhaps there was hope at last. Here for the first time he could remember he didn't feel fogged by rubbish. Bric-à-brac, letters, telephone calls. He didn't even have his diary with him; left behind in London. He was suddenly glad of that. It seemed to Harold in retrospect that that diary had never been his. Full of dates that Lottie made. Lottie could keep the diary.

It seemed to have always been the same. His life was divided up by others. Cut up into such tiny strips that he couldn't use what was left. Parcelled out by Lottie. By school, and Carol, the woman before Lottie. By other women before her. Before them by his PhD, squeezing the hours into quotes and footnotes. And then, before that, by his mother. The greediest of them all.

This morning the sun was out in a childishly blue and brilliant sky. It made no headway against the cold but it made the sea a wide sheet of colour, a freeway stretching to the end of the world. No fences, no divisions. The pier made a tiny effort and failed. The sea swept grandly back and beyond.

Despite the cold of the glass on his forehead, Harold pushed open the french doors which led out on to the balcony. He blew like a steam engine in the cold and blinked at the light as he stepped out. Harold would overlook his world, the world he was going to make his own. The rail was rickety, rusty iron, but for a moment he leaned and looked down.

And there, on cue, for she never missed one, he saw the little mauve car. Panic nearly throttled him. It couldn't be. It was. The doorbell rang loud and long, resonant with pain and emergency, ringing every loose connection in his nerves.

Fuck. Oh fuck, I don't believe it. Mother, come to see me.

Frozen on the edge of the balcony, he decided, too late, not to answer; for she had stepped back and stared upwards, and their eyes met, Harold's wide with alarm, hers tiny in an upturned round of white. She looked small enough to tip backwards easily, flick her out of the way for ever. But she wasn't small, oh no she was not, she was here, she would stay for ever . . .

All his life he would never be free.

'*Har-old*! Aren't you going to welcome your mother?'

'Mother.' He tried, but it came out flat. 'Hang on, I'll be down in a minute.'

On the doorstep, she looked enormous, wrapped in an orange fur coat and surrounded by parcels, her hair puffed out in a large pale bun. Harold sometimes wondered where she got her money from. Of course, she had had her good years, but the theatre didn't look after its own. There had been a little money on her mother's side, but surely not enough for luxuries?

All the same, the fur looked distressingly new, little gold hairs which gleamed like life, and he smelled the familiar, expensive smell of her sweetish vanilla scent. Much too sweet for him.

The words poured out, a river of sentiment gushing upstairs

76

without pausing, swamping his silence, settling stickily on all his clear sunny spaces.

'Darling dearest boy, how *are* you, oh dear, your face feels frozen, I've brought you some blankets and an eiderdown and some underwear which I thought was yours but when I looked I wasn't too sure, they may have belonged to your father . . . *darling*, how lovely to see you. And I know how bleak these places can be, so I've brought you some cushions and rugs and things, most of it's in the boot except for some teensy bits and pieces I've got in here, oh and Pickford's, sweetest, brought *mountains* of things, I don't want to complain but my poor little house is snowed under with boxes, I hope *your wife*' (that elaborate mockery: did his departure make the marriage so funny?) 'doesn't expect me to unpack them, as you can imagine I'm far too busy . . . Of course it's different for her, she never does anything, does she, really.'

'*Mother*,' said Harold. '*Please*. I do not want to talk about Lottie. And let me have a look in those boxes before you unpack it all.'

She was always more than he bargained for; noisier, stronger, louder, less restrained. Yet, also – older, more passionate. That great fur embrace really did mean love. He knew he was all her family. He knew it all too well. He could imagine the joy and energy with which she had planned this visit. And he also knew he must send her away frustrated and resentful. He always disappointed her; both of them expected it.

(And yet she hoped, as well. Her entrances always shone with hope.)

'Cushions – no. Well, I'll take one for sitting out on the balcony. Blankets – yes. Eiderdown – marvellous. And woollies, thank God. What are these? Certainly not – must have been . . . Father's. Oh sit *down*, Mother. Please don't fuss. I like it that way. What? No, I don't want plants. I don't want to look after things.'

She was in the kitchen, concealed behind her coat, crashing things out on to the table. When he managed to peer round the shiny orange fur, he groaned.

'Mother, what *is* all this?'

He caught her by the shoulder. She turned. Her face was briefly youthful, a pinkish mixture of pride and guilt, the flush of blood still pretty under her freckles. Her mouth was already prepared to plead, flirt and cajole as it always had. She was a little out of breath from the stairs. Lately, she often seemed a little out of breath, though she hadn't mentioned the angina again.

'Just a few goodies, Harold darling. I thought we could have an early lunch . . .'

Gafelbiter. Lumpfish roe. Rich black pâté in greaseproof paper. Croissants, golden crumbly crescents leaving crumbs on his new clean table. Eclairs with great bulging entrails of cream.

Crash came a bottle of Nuits St Georges which she tried to hide behind her huge orange elbow. Harold could quite well see what it was. A bottle of noise and useless emotion and headaches through long sunny afternoons. He had seen those bottles before. He had suffered their contents before . . . (hadn't he enjoyed them too? He *would not* think of that).

'Mother, I've just had breakfast.'

'*Please*, darling. You're awfully thin.'

'Mother, you should have warned me.'

'Darling, there isn't a telephone . . . anyway that's what you *said*.'

'There *isn't* a telephone.'

'Exactly. What will you have to begin?'

The fur, or the sun which was trying to get past it, made him sneeze explosively. Curiously, it helped. In the second of silence that followed, he made up his mind, a faster and firmer decision than he had ever managed before.

'Mother, sit down this minute and listen to me, for once . . .'

Staring at the sea for strength, Harold pleaded to be left in peace. He also did a lot of lying, since strength wasn't quite enough.

'. . . just for a bit, completely alone . . . it's a kind of reaction from Lottie, I think . . . if I wanted to be with anyone, *of course* it would be you . . .'

She changed her role quite quickly, quaveringly gallant in defeat. Pouting, her pale eyelashes drooping to shield a mother's pain, she began to repack her packages. She was very thorough, immensely laborious. He wished she would leave at any rate the croissants and *one* of the eclairs. He knew that she probably guessed as much and he knew she would not leave them.

'Goodbye,' he called helplessly after her as the silly mauve car roared away down the road, a fluorescent wasp weaving much too fast. No pale, fur-ringed hand waved back.

Upstairs her perfume hung in the air. Vanilla for sorrow and regret. Lone orange hairs on the sofa, crumbs and grease on the 1950s' Formica. Her heart must be better, all the same. She would never have a pain and not mention it.

He sat in the sun on the eiderdown, and the silence was different from before. An absence, not a presence. The wind must have changed. It was colder.

I'm never fair to her. She was terribly brave when she had those gallstones. In any case, I didn't exactly give her a lot of time to mention things . . . Harold shifted on the eiderdown. Mother, Mother. What could he do with her?

(Another bottle of Nuits St Georges. The memory was clear, and entirely uncomfortable. On Mother's lawn, with green striped deckchairs, just after he left Carol, before he met Lottie. He'd come home thinking he would never smile again. Within minutes she had made it a party, flinging the windows of the front room open and aiming the record-player full blast over the roses – 'Mother, I'm *not* in the mood' – 'You *will* be, darling, you will be' – her red glass flashing and dipping in the sun. He'd blurted out the story of Carol, and she was almost listening. Then she wove back across the gravel and the grass with a second bright bottle, one free pale arm thrown out in abandon, laughing, declaiming to him or her garden

> I'll offer up
> As many kisses as the Sea hath sands . . .
> Oh here he comes, love, love, give Dido leave
> *Something something something, Harold*
> And I am made a wonder of the world . . .

'Marvellous, Mother. Who is it?'

'Don't remember, darling. Did it in rep. Marvell? – *Marlowe.*'

Of course things went wrong before that bottle was out; of course the sun went in and his pleasure faded, but even now he could hear that throaty voice, containing the roses, the bees and the gravel.

Why can I never applaud my mother until she's gone and I'm alone?)

And yet, after sitting for a bit and letting the echoes play themselves out, after making some coffee, black and strong, and wiping the table briskly, the guilt receded, and he almost felt proud. She was all very well, but not here, not now. Harold had repelled the intruder. He had been tested, and had not failed.

His life could now begin.

☆

What really began was a kind of boyhood.

Up in his flat, on the bridge of his ship, Harold led the life of a boy. He lived on cocoa and Kendal Mint Cake and tins of tomato soup. He kept two rooms just warm enough to live in, and relished being wrapped in sweaters and socks. Lottie's central heating had been unnatural; no wonder he'd spent his life half-asleep. Now he stayed up till 4 a.m. His face in the mirror as he finally brushed his teeth was the face of a different person. Excited, tired and very young, with a thick moustache of cocoa.

He had started to read like a boy, as well. He plundered the leftovers from January sales, sliding back through the snow freighted with wonders. They weren't his usual reading matter. He didn't want novels, he didn't want poems. He wanted to find out about the world.

At first he didn't know what he was looking for; then he found it, wherever he looked.

In Bournemouth bookshops there seemed to be shelves full of popular books about science. Tables groaned with them, dump-bins burst, window displays couldn't fit them all in. They were mostly reduced to ridiculous prices, the price of three or four tins of soup, not that he wanted to go without soup. At first he completely ignored them, as he would have done in London, passing them by with unnatural speed to prove he was not the sort of person who read them. They were rubbish books, for non-readers.

But in one bookshop he was forced to have a look, since all the other books were film-star biographies. Harold dipped, and then he plunged. With shock, he realized what he had found. All that he needed to know about.

Life on Earth . . . The History of Life . . . Stars and Nebulas . . . Sagan's Cosmos . . . Evolution – What Does it Mean? . . . Gem Guide to Nature: Life on Our Shores . . .

So much to know, so late in starting. He sprawled on the threadbare carpet roasting his cheek by the electric fire, the books spread round him in rays.

And I'm an intellectual, he thought. I'm over-educated, some would say.

Isn't this food for the intellect? Isn't this part of being educated?

Lottie seemed very far away, and smaller than she had ever been. Dwindling to a little point in the darkness, the furthest, tiniest point of bright pain . . .

Neither people nor their pain seemed real. Most of the world, after all, wasn't human.

What about bears and plankton? What about cacti, and stars?

Halfway through his life on earth, Harold Segall started to learn about it. Dizzy with print and excitement, he would look out of the window at the end of the day, staring at the long bright curve where the shape of the planet was clear against the sky.

CHAPTER EIGHT

Lottie had been painting for two solid weeks. When she closed her eyes at night, she saw whiteness, and the roller grinding down on her like fate. But she would not stop till the thing was finished. By an irony she could not control, as the house grew whiter the snow outside retreated and browns and greens wore through. She stifled a recurring mad desire to rush out with her brush and erase them again.

She had liked to feel the world simply wasn't there. It made things easier, just for a bit. Let the whole world be reduced to white. Whiteness worked as a bandage. And the physical work helped the physical ache she still felt when she stretched alone on the bed.

As the white tide advanced, two-thirds, three-quarters, she felt a dreary kind of pride. Another week, and it would all be done. Her neck was breaking, her nails were broken, but Harold was nearly bleached away.

The white flood had cut her off; she had hardly spoken to the others for days. Davey had ignored her since she threatened to paint his room, and Amanda seemed to be sulking. You couldn't be sure, of course, with Amanda, whose features were not of the most mobile kind. It was not the best time for sulking; but servants were selfish. Lottie didn't care. Lottie did not expect sympathy. Whiteness, that was what life was for.

She was halfway up the ladder, examining a wall where the white looked suspiciously thin, as if colour might suddenly burst through, when she heard a little sound and two bony boyish arms closed round her knees from behind.

'Mum. It's me. Don't drop your paint.'

'*Davey.*'

She was drenched with relief. Lottie was often astonished to discover she knew almost nothing about her real feelings. She always forgot this quite quickly, and so she would soon be astonished again.

'I'm sorry I got so mad at you. But I thought you meant it, about my room.'

She put the paint pot on the window-sill, jumped straight down and flung her arms around him.

'I've never done anything up there without asking you. You ought to know that.'

'You said you were going to.'

'Oh, never mind. I say lots of things. I say I love you, you'd better believe it. Let's go out. Shall I take you out to lunch?'

'No. It's too sunny. Let's go to the zoo.'

Normally Lottie would have demurred, but the joy of his presence was too strong.

'Right. I'll go and put my coat on.'

'Great. Oh . . . and Mum . . . no furs, please.'

'Bossy,' she said, but she grinned as she got ready. Peculiar boy. What did it matter what she wore? She supposed he was growing up faster than she realized. Men *did* care what women wore.

'I haven't been here for years and years,' she confessed, as they swung along, arm in arm, and an old tramp turned his grey face after them. *Rich people. Lucky people.*

'Harold used to go.'

'I *know* he did,' she snapped at him, and then she was sorry. 'I'm sorry, he still exists, I know. But don't expect me to talk about him.'

Davey was proud to go in through the gate with his golden mother, who everyone smiled at. Today she was looking tireder than usual and older than usual, but she was still beautiful. The sun lit her cheekbones and yellow springy hair, and the little lines just made her look kinder.

He had promised to take her to the Moonlight World. The name was thrilling; she was keen to go. She was sure it hadn't been there before. It sounded elegant, and cool, and romantic.

She couldn't know Davey had regretted it as soon as the name had passed his lips. The Moonlight World was in the basement of the Small Mammal House. There were many kinds of small mammals. Among them were Golden Lion Tamarins. Since the horror of Lottie's tamarin dying, Davey had often gone to see them. They were timid things, staying close to each other, but their fine coats shone and flashed like golden silk behind the silent glass.

Lottie was in a very delicate state. She hadn't mentioned the tamarin since it died. *Not mentioning* was a bad sign with Lottie. Still, you didn't have to go right past their cage. As long as he remembered exactly where it was. Luckily Mum was pretty unperceptive.

Together they went under the echoing tunnel which led towards the Small Mammal House.

'It's for animals who are only active at night. So they show them by artificial moonlight.'

'I guessed that, thank you,' said Lottie. 'Your mother is not a halfwit.'

Round the moonlit cages, though, there was rather more darkness than she had imagined. Lottie started to feel peculiar. It was a labyrinth; rows of silver-washed cells, connected by endless tunnels through which vague humans surged and lingered and stared. The tunnels were warm, and airless. She lost her bearings, and reached out blindly for Davey. The arm belonged to someone else.

Then she recognized her son in the glow from a cage where an animal hung upside down, inert as a bag of sugar.

'It's a sloth,' he whispered, his face intent.

She tried to look inspired. But everything seemed to be hibernating, only half-awake in the confusing light. Things hid, and lurched slowly out, half-formed. There were things like mice and rats and bats but somehow different, when you looked close. Things might be animals, and might be shadows. In the end she got cross and wanted to get out. Nothing was clear in this prehistoric moonlight.

'Davey, let's go and see the elephants.'

'I'd like to see the apes.'

'Marvellous.'

But it was chilly to linger by the outside cages, and Lottie was irritable when Davey stopped too long by the orang-utans, face pressed against the glass, ignoring her.

'Mum, look how he is with that baby. That's Bin-Tang, the big one. He's male, he's not even the father, but he's great with it. Oh, look at that!'

What was there to look at? She just saw a funny-looking, long-faced monkey wrestling with a smaller long-faced monkey.

The baby monkey's skin showed white through his scanty covering of dark hair.

His belly bulged out like the photos of children in the advertisements for famine. She said that to Davey, who did not comment. It wasn't easy to talk to the young.

Then she thought she'd make friends with the monkeys, and made loud kissing noises at the glass. They didn't show the slightest interest. They were obviously not very intelligent animals, but still it felt discouraging.

'I think I'd like to see something big. The elephants. Or a rhinoceros.' Lottie was eager to enjoy herself. She didn't want the treat to turn out to be boring.

'OK,' said Davey. He liked the apes best, but he wanted her to be happy.

They splashed past the other monkeys through the melting snow to the elephant house. Inside it was warm and smelled rank and rich. The roof was very high above them.

'It smells of hippo,' Davey half-whispered. It felt a bit like a church in there.

Lottie whispered back, because of the silence.

'I don't think I remember this. I think the elephants were outside.'

'There's an outside part to this as well. There used to be two elephants, but one of them died. They tried to move it to another zoo. Something went wrong. She had to be shot.'

'That one looks like a baby. That's *down* on his back, isn't it?'

There was a layer of long brown hairs which seemed to float down the curve of the elephant's spine.

'Actually it's quite tough and thick,' said Davey, but she didn't hear him.

'How weird to think of elephants having down.'

Elephants were weird altogether, she thought. Very weird to think of humans and elephants chancing to live on the same planet. Weird the way it looked at you as if you might be the same species. As if you ought to know how to talk to it. It seemed to look especially hard at Lottie. She probably had that special kind of sensitivity an elephant might pick up.

'Hallo,' she ventured, not very confidently. The elephant waved his trunk in the air. 'Hallo, sweetie,' she said with pride. She suddenly thought *it would look beautiful white.*

'Come on, Mum, come and see the hippo. It's showing its teeth. They're about a foot long.'

'D'you think he's lonely, the elephant?'

'It's a she. Of course. They're supposed to live in groups. But they found her abandoned, so I guess if she hadn't been brought to a zoo, she would have died.'

'He's got a chain on his leg.'

Her attention span was about an inch long. '*She*, Mother. I *told* you.'

'Poor thing. I think it liked me, though.'

She wandered off towards the rhinoceros. Behind her, the elephant stamped and pulled and suddenly let out a series of bellows which echoed round the high vault of the house. Up there in the roof, some tiny marmosets scampered, and Lottie jumped, which was not like her.

It was a curious day, unsettling, not the jaunt she had expected. He took her to see the tropical birds, thinking some colour would be good for her. She found them quite extraordinary. Bright as a Mondrian, bizarre as an Ernst, complete and extreme as Ibo sculpture. She thought that out and said it to Davey as they wandered on towards the ostrich and the emu.

Davey was notably unimpressed. 'It's just because you don't know about birds. So you have to see them as something else.'

'But *that* thing really isn't like a bird.'

She pointed at a cassowary.

'It just depends what birds are like,' said Davey, enigmatic.

She pondered the cassowary for a long time. The more you looked, the more surprising it was. Tall as a tall, awkward child, no wings to speak of, thick shiny feathers on its body like fur, bright orange neck, and a head of stunning iridescent turquoise. Perched on its forehead was a kind of fez of dull wrinkled bone.

Really, it was like – a cassowary. None of its parts seemed to fit together. She nearly said, 'It's surrealist,' but out of respect for her son, did not.

In the Snake House there was a wonderful dry heat, the heat of summer on a Greek island. She pulled off her gloves, and laughed with pleasure. Wrinkled silver-green dragons ('Mum, they're *iguanas*. Get it *right*') lay higgledy-piggledy over each other, soaking up the rays of their sun-lamp, a pile of bodies like a single being. I shouldn't like to live like that, she considered, stroking her own thick hair. Human beings are lucky to be separate. But not *too* separate. She hugged her son.

She had vaguely thought the snakes might be sexy, but they were extremely alien. Their bodies were made of cold wet gristle gleaming in the light. Mambas, slender as branches, hid so skilfully they startled her, suddenly darting across her vision, thin tongues flickering, swaying up towards her.

'I hope I don't dream about those. Horrible cold-looking things.'

'I thought you never had dreams. Anyway they're not. They're warm and dry.'

'Don't talk about them. I want to forget them.'

She didn't dream about the mambas. But she drew a deep breath much later when she opened her dressing-table drawer and a string of ebony heads coiled mamba-like on white tissue-paper.

The zoo had captured her imagination. Images floated on the blank wall that evening when she started work again. Images clung at bedtime as she drifted off to sleep.

The elephant balanced on two of its feet, the two which were joined by a hobble-chain, the free feet neatly lifted, practising that again and again. Possibly aiming it all at Lottie. He'd certainly waved his trunk at her. Definitely there was a bond between them.

Less comforting, those slow and grey and hidden things in the Moonlight World. Things which were only half-realized. Things which might suddenly wake up and be not at all what people expected.

Amazing heads in the Bird House, fierce jungle colours she didn't want to whiten, songs which jolted her inner ear.

How did they grow like that? Where can they all have come from?

Most of the world was human, of course, so you never got time to think about the rest. When you did think, it was both astonishing and not quite comfortable.

(Naturally, animals could let you down. The orang-utans, ignoring her . . . something worse she could not forget. The quivering horror which died in her house. She'd never try to help an animal again.)

Still, Lottie felt more alive that day than at any time since

Harold had left. The zoo was so wonderfully removed from all the boring important things in life. No one there worried about things like money, houses, husbands, the future.

She remembered, now, the last time she'd been. Guided by Harold, when they came back from honeymoon. Two and a half years ago.

He'd known a lot of the Latin names (or, as she suspected, read them off the labels) which grew annoying, after a bit. He hadn't known practical things, like Davey. *Real* things. Next time, she'd really listen.

She would certainly go again.

Falling asleep, drifting away.

The rhinoceros had a gigantic penis, hanging down like the elephant's trunk, suddenly stiffening and swinging out backwards, not what you expected at all, when the rhino wanted to piss. The urine shot backwards through his legs in a fountain.

And she thought, though the thought somehow needed correcting, *when Harold comes back he'll get a surprise. He'll find I know some amazing things.*

They are all moving further into the sunlight, though Lottie only notices the snow has gone. In cities there are little stirrings, little brightenings.

Cold as death to the human hand, dormice are still asleep in the country. Hedgehogs curl in the bottom of ditches.

But blackbirds and yellowhammers sing, less harsh than the birds in the Tropical Bird House. The raven lays its blue-green egg. Squirrels and rabbits are already mating.

On warm days, the first butterflies emerge, rarer than they were before. A Small White staggers up into the sunlight.

At London Zoo, men sit in suits in small offices worrying, as usual, about money. They ought to be building new animal houses . . . The government, as usual, gives more money to the Natural History Museum, to keep stuffed animals.

The snow is going, at least. It will not come back until it is needed.

Looked at from very far out in space, complex patterns of brown and green and blue gleam through the planet's whiteness.

March

CHAPTER NINE

Rocks and dust and craters and dust and rocks: the reddish surface of Mars.

If there was life, many years ago, if it was warmer, with running water, there seems to be no life now.

Humans made Mars their God of war.

Actually it seems that only humans spoil a fertile planet with war.

Davey had never been crazy about King Henry's, though he'd always found school easy. One thing which annoyed him about King Henry's was that you didn't get positions in class. That was because it was not progressive, giving people positions in class. Well, for some people that was probably true, but Davey was the cleverest kid in his class, and he thought coming first would have felt extremely progressive, once in a while.

Now he was in the lower sixth, it was already too late. In the sixth form everyone did different things, so there wasn't any way you could beat your enemies. Now Davey would never come first. He felt he had been cheated.

Most days he drifted through lessons, hardly noticing as the subjects changed. It was boring, that was the trouble. It stopped you reading whatever you were reading, though he sometimes read underneath the desk. This was a problem unique to him, since most of the others weren't keen on reading. 'You're a mutant,' Charles hissed at him in English. 'You're an extra-terrestrial.'

Davey normally read two novels a day, or one book about something real. That was the fault of King Herod's; at weekends he could read three novels or two non-fictions, on a good day. If he could have read like that all the time, he might have ended up *knowing* a few things. That was how he looked at school; it got in the way of your education.

The best thing about it was meeting your friends (and Mary, of course. Not meeting her, but thinking about her, watching her. Mary was never quite part of school.)

Breaks and lunchtimes, you remembered those. Which made school a stupid waste of time, since that was just a tiny bit of the day. It was like grownups in offices, living for evenings and holidays.

At the moment, though, home didn't feel right, so he was quite glad to get out of bed with Mum still asleep, grab his things and be off. Years ago Amanda had stopped trying to make him eat a cooked breakfast, but she still left coffee percolating, four slices of bread by the toaster, and on the table cornflakes, milk in a little blue jug, and two kinds of marmalade.

All Davey wanted was coffee, swigging down three mugs as he stood by the sink. Sometimes he'd have a few spoons of marmalade, eating the bread as an afterthought, munching a folded piece in his hand as he emerged into the winter grey.

'Your muvver don't look after you,' the milkman jeered, one morning.

'Dead right,' said Davey, untroubled.

Amanda would have been mortified. She never appeared, first thing in the morning. Her people didn't like to talk in the mornings. But she always saw they went off all right. A good breakfast was a good breakfast.

The bus was always crowded with schoolkids, most of them not at progressive schools, most of them in uniform. Davey, of course, didn't wear one. Sometimes he vaguely wished he did, since he wouldn't have had to decide what to wear. It was nearly always jeans and sweaters, but recently jackets and coats were a problem.

When he first got his leather jacket with the big padded shoulders he thought it was ace. But now he was worried about animal skins. People draped in dead animal skins.

His mac wasn't that much better. He was wild to have it, at the time. Lottie didn't go in for it too much, but he'd bullied her into buying two the same, one beige, one black, long military greatcoats, big collars, epaulettes, the lot.

Now he was worried about fascism. They definitely weren't anti-fascist coats.

Lottie said that he worried too much, and she'd be buggered if she'd buy him *another* coat. But she was too simple to understand that what you wore was a statement. Or rather, to be fair to her, she thought most statements were so much balls.

He said so, that morning, to Charles, at break. Charles was the son of an architect, pale and plump with carroty hair. He looked like an absolute creep. But actually, he was what they called 'disruptive'. He knew how to drive teachers quite insane, without doing anything crass. He had a really good sense of humour, and he had peculiar friends. Davey was actually quite straight, he sometimes thought, by comparison.

'Would you call me straight?' he asked Charles.

'Straight as a pencil,' Charles replied. 'It's your mother's fault, I suppose.'

'Do you think *she's* straight?' Davey asked, with real interest. 'I wouldn't have called her straight, myself. I mean, she does whatever she wants to. She doesn't worry about anybody else. She doesn't *work*, or anything. And she doesn't believe in anything. Politics, or morals, or all that stuff.'

'You're straighter than her,' judged Charles.

'I think my mum is an anarchist.'

Once Davey had said it, he knew it was true.

'What, like Smeggy? You must be joking.'

Charles hooted, showing rabbit teeth.

'She did meet Smeggy once, remember. She thought he was rather good.'

Charles had a certain delicacy, otherwise he might have told Davey what Smeggy said about Lottie. ('She still looks quite a good lay. I think she fancied me a bit.')

Tuesday was not too bad a day. Double History, Break, Free Period, Arts Biology, Lunch, Double English, Free Period. The tricky one was Arts Biology. They were supposed to do Reproduction again. You did it in the first year, when you didn't understand, then they had another go when you did. All term it had been rumoured they were going to do humans. It was even rumoured that a film went with it. Mary Granger sat well away from him, on a bench at the back where Todd Argyll often sat.

Davey would have died with embarrassment if she'd sat any nearer; all the same, he didn't like her sitting quite so far away.

He glared round once as they waited for the teacher. She didn't look up, and Todd Argyll was beside her. At any rate, only half a bench away.

In the event, it was Frogs and Toads, no film, and Davey was massively relieved.

In English they were reading *Under Milk Wood*, which he definitely enjoyed. He watched Mary's face as Stebbings read. Her head was dipped, her cheeks were pinker than usual, her hair hung heavy and dark over her forehead. She was sucking her thumb. He wanted to touch her, and at the same time he wanted to hide her, so no one else in class could see her so enthralled.

Stebbings was a creep but he read superbly. They were supposed to call him Julian. Mary did. It was a stupid name. Davey said so, but she didn't agree.

Most of the teachers liked you to call them by their Christian names. They got annoyed if you called them *Mister*. Davey only called Stebbings *Mister*, but Charles *Mistered* everyone. It made the class giggle, but new teachers often missed the point completely.

Davey thought Charles was being too subtle. After all, most teachers came from ordinary schools with rules and prefects and uniforms. So they just thought Charles was a nice polite boy, until they found out different.

On the way home, Davey stared at the damp-smelling, navy-blue bodies packed on the afternoon bus. Kids from St Sebastian's. They looked so meek, even when they were playing with flick-knives. Davey tried to imagine Smeggy in uniform. He couldn't even imagine Smeggy sitting on a bus.

He'd only ever seen him use the tube. There he seemed almost *natural*, at night, in that lurid light, against bright graffiti, with his blue-red-mauve-striped crest of hair and the mauve ink webs he painted round his eyes and the long queer nose like an ant-eater . . .

He was like the spirit who lived there. Patrolling the tunnels, night after night. So people would find what they feared to find.

He'd been a bit worried his mother would faint when Charles brought Smeggy round to the house, one Sunday afternoon last summer. Harold and Lottie and he were finishing lunch, rather late. Amanda had let the two boys in, then clearly got worried, and was hovering behind them as Smeggy strolled into the dining-room, legs like a stick-insect's next to plump Charles, his crimson halo a foot above Charles' relatively tame-looking orange curls.

Harold's eyebrows shot up towards his hairline, which left them a lot of head to shoot up, but Davey was proud that Mum didn't blink and didn't seem at all embarrassed. She'd been just the same as usual, in fact more so, and talked a lot and poured lots more wine.

After they left, Harold pulled at his hair in the mirror, as he often did, but looking slightly more frantic.

'I'm surprised that's still the fashion,' he grunted. 'I thought punk went out years ago.'

'It's punk *revival*,' Davey told him.

'It wouldn't be *you*, Harold,' Mum remarked, with the wicked look that Davey liked, her eyes very narrow, her dimples very sharp.

'I shall go and write my book.' Harold made a dignified exit.

'Do you think Smeggy's ugly, Mum?' Davey asked.

'Ugly? No. *Extraordinary*. Is he a fan of Mick Jagger?'

'You must be joking. No one is. Jagger's gone senile and lost his memory. Why should he be?'

'Well, his mouth is . . . rather Jaggerish.'

'Well, Smeggy couldn't have changed his mouth, could he? Even if he *was* a fan.'

Davey was a little put out. There was something he hadn't quite liked about the way she was reacting.

'What does he do?' she asked, as if he might be something in the City.

'Well, he doesn't, does he. He's just a kid. He dropped out of school, he's the same age as us. Not our dump, though.'

'Oh. I thought he must be at school with you.'

'They couldn't afford King Herod's. He lives in a council flat. His family does, I mean. Somewhere near Euston. He's on the dole.' Feeling he'd squashed Smeggy rather too flat, Davey added, 'He's a really good vocalist. One day he's going to have a group.'

'How *interesting*,' said Lottie. She looked as though she meant it, though in fact she'd stopped listening after 'council flat', which was quite exciting to her.

Now she was thinking about something else.

'You know it's a most peculiar name.'

'Smeggy?'

'No, King Herod's. When you come to think about it. I'm sure he was the man who slaughtered the innocents. It's rather comic, as a name for a school.'

'It's a *joke*, for Christ's sake. It's what we *call* it. You ought to *know* the name of my school. Sometimes I think you're not on the planet . . .'

'So's Smeggy, anyway. It's simply disgusting.'

'What do you mean? He's always called that. His real name's Simon McGuire.'

But Mum had given him a very strange look, which he still didn't quite understand. Then she came over and kissed him, fondly.

'I'm glad you don't know *everything* yet. If he wasn't at school, how did you get to know him?'

'He's Charles' friend, actually. I dunno – they just met somewhere.'

(Davey *did* know. Smeggy supplied Charles with dope, which Charles sometimes resold to Davey.)

'Well, I think it's very interesting to meet people from *different backgrounds*.'

Davey grinned to himself, remembering. She was wonderfully innocent, his mum. At that moment she'd sounded like a social worker, not an anarchist at all. Half of what she said was just talk. She neither believed it nor listened to it.

He got off the bus into the icy rain. It was getting dark already. He usually looked forward to coming home from school, but things weren't so simple with Harold gone.

He hoped she wouldn't go crazy. She had always been very *un*-crazy. But he knew that she had loved Harold a lot. He hoped she'd stop painting soon.

It wasn't much fun, being his age. You were always dependent on other people. You could only do things *if*. *If* it wasn't a school day. *If* Mum hadn't got some mad idea that she wanted to drag him into. Before Harold, the various boyfriends. *If* they didn't complicate things. He'd hated most of the boyfriends. He hoped all that wouldn't start again. *If* Amanda wasn't away. *If* there wasn't trouble at home.

And there often had been trouble at home. Not that that was unusual; homes were troublesome places. All of his friends felt that. All the same, at the moment it was *real* trouble.

That was why he loved it up in the roof. In his room right under the sky. Smoking, with his windows open. The stars were his own, and never troubled him. Well – they *weren't* his own, but they weren't other people's.

That glittering point looked faintly red. Star or planet? He didn't know (there were only a few dozen light years of difference).

At first you thought all the stars were white; then you saw tiny variations of colour. To understand, you must watch for *ages*. You couldn't live long enough to know the stars.

Compared to them he was an atom of dust, a speck of frog spawn, not interesting. That was why they left him alone. Stars didn't care about people. Sometimes it was better not to be cared about. Sometimes it was better to be left in peace.

Other people's lives still leaked upstairs, other people's worries could seep through the floorboards. He wanted peace, and a life of his own. His real life hadn't begun.

CHAPTER TEN

Harold stood out on his balcony just after the sun dipped behind the pines. His notion of time had changed, attaching itself to light and darkness, except when his stomach urged him to note the opening and closing times of shops. It was half-past five in the afternoon in the second week of March, but he couldn't have told you that.

The windows and the balcony were his favourite part of this new world. His personal god's-eye view of things.

The sea was never the same. Cloud shadows swept across it like giant birds lifting and landing. Light blazed, unpredictable. You could never grow bored with it.

('You'll soon be *insane* with boredom, darling,' was the last thing Sylvia had said. 'Then you'll go running back to London.' That was all *she* knew about it.)

This afternoon there was as little wind as there could ever be beside the sea, and almost no cloud, so the sky seemed vast. In the centre it was still bright, like the blue-pink heart of a giant shell, where sun slanted up from below the horizon. But the sea was already night, a uniform dark blue-green, and the pines silhouetted in front of it were black with a black pigeon settling down and soon it would all settle down to night and the pines would fall black into the black of the sea. He had watched it many times, though never as slow and still as this.

Lights flickered on in Sea Road, which led down fifty yards to the pier. Then the pier lights came on, throwing a track of shimmering fluorescent green on the water. Tomorrow I'll take a look at that pier.

Close up, the pier was a slight disappointment. Just an amusement arcade, really, with fruit machines and video games. It wasn't worth spoiling the view for. A pier should not be a compromise. Harold liked a pier to have character, photographers, a fortune-teller, candy-floss.

'Like Brighton Pier,' he told Mr Sedley. He was now supposed to call him *Ted*.

'Waste o' time,' said Ted. He was a man of few words, or rather, a man who seemed to *hoard* his words. Harold suspected Ted had a lot and didn't want to waste them.

'Piers?'

'Machines. Bloody silly things. Today's teenagers. That's what they like. Won't find one reading a book these days.'

'I know a teenager who still reads books.'

(*Davey*. Sprawled on the yellow sofa, awkward elbow crooked round a book.)

'Doan' believe you.' Ted sucked his pipe, long jaw working, not unfriendly. He'd come for the rent, and stayed for a minute to show Harold how to make the hot water work.

'See you're a reading man, though.'

Nobody could miss it. Books were piled on the coffee table, stacked along the fireplace, scattered on the carpet, even two on the draining-board.

'Yes, I love books.' Harold feared to sound ingratiating. Ted's preferred style of conversation was clearly more abrasive.

'Mostly rubbish those though, arn' they?'

Ted pushed a pile on the table with his pipe so they fell and he could see the covers.

'Animal books. TV spin-offs. 'At's your typical modern book.'

Harold straightened them, nettled.

'No offence – ' The pipe pushed Harold in the arm.

'Oh, no, no, no. As a matter of fact I find them very interesting.' He covered his flank before he thought about it. 'Mind you, they're not my usual kind of book.' (And immediately felt disloyal. Why did he have to say that? Were his Lit Crit textbooks 'my usual kind of book?' Who the hell wanted those except the poor sods taking exams?) 'They, uh, reflect my interests at the moment.'

Whenever Harold opened his mouth he felt pompous, a windbag compared to this dry, slight man.

'I'll show you *books*, if you like.' The old voice suddenly shook with passion. The skin round his eyes were crinkled like leather. Dirty brown leather.

Porn, thought Harold. *Oh no*. The bond between lonely single men. I'm *not* a man, he insisted, hopeless.

Luckily he said nothing.

'Real books, these are. *Victorian* books. The Victorians, now, they knew about books.'

'Er, thank you very much,' said Harold.

He was glad when Sedley had gone. The less you saw people, the odder they seemed.

He wished he could seal his door completely so the only way out was the balcony. Into the sea, the sky; a bigger world, a planet. Never again would he go back to the tiny pocket of world he came from.

The same thing was true of time. He didn't want a time that restricted him, time to be at this place, time to be at that place, time which nibbled your time away. He wanted to grasp the stream of time through which the stars and planets moved. The sort of time in which the Earth cooled and life began in the sea.

He wanted to find if he had a place in all that space and time. He wanted to make that place his home.

And the scale of the sea encouraged him, the way it signed the curve of the Earth, the way it pounded and crashed on the cliffs and eroded careful human building. It encouraged him to be grandiose who had always been wry and careful.

Of course he had been wry and careful. He lived in wry and careful times. Intellectuals, he thought, are wry and careful, and human society is mindless, careless. Intellectuals think at desks, in little rooms, in little buildings . . . no wonder they get the scale of things wrong . . .

Whenever he passed a cliff-fall or a bit of sea-wall collapsing, he felt an exhilaration. The promise and threat of freedom.

Ted came back at teatime. Harold hid his annoyance.

'Here's *books*, if it's *books* you want,' Ted said, jovially aggressive.

He shoved a pile into Harold's arms (smell of dust, feel of cold embossed binding); grinned like a skull; in a flash, was gone.

But the books, examined in the sunny kitchen, turned out to be miraculous. *The World of Wonders* and *The Universe*, 1884. *La Géographie Universelle* . . . *The Birthday of the Earth* . . . Harold read the preface of *The World of Wonders*.

March

The wise man only wonders once in his life, but that is always; the fool never . . . Coleridge, the most encyclopaedic of men, declares 'In wonder all philosophy begins, in wonder it ends . . .'

Let us consider shortly one of the commonest wonders about us – SPACE. Gaze up into the sky from off the page you are reading, and try to pierce as far as your eye can reach, and then as far as your mind can conceive . . . The mind, it has well been said, fails to perceive so vast an area . . .

Harold placed it reverently beside his bed. He climbed out on to his balcony, and stood there shivering a little. His favourite time of day. The pier looked fragile and temporary.

The pearl-light had started to fade from the sky and two minute pink feathers of cloud were suddenly blue, and then black. Beyond the black feathers, on the deepening sky, brightening, steadying, a single star. Please not a plane. No, one star.

He stared at it, and it shone on him. Light streamed across millions of miles of space. He felt he was the only man in the world. And just one star. Maybe a universe beginning.

Or else it was a planet, not quite so far, a world still brilliant in the light of the sun, hanging in our sky as earth must in theirs. Mars? Venus? He would look it up.

Was anyone out there watching him?

His desire swam out across the sea towards it. He stood there watching till it was quite dark and the first star fell into a sea of stars.

The immensely great, the immensely far.

Did I eat lunch?
What time is it?

CHAPTER ELEVEN

'Do you know what day it is?'

Lottie burst into Davey's bedroom, and light burst under his lids. The sun was dismayingly bright on her hair, pushed up into a ponytail. Mauveish dress and some kind of painfully shocking-pink object in her hair.

Davey closed his eyes again. He wished you knew where you were with her. For the last few days since she finished the painting she'd been really low. Today she looked manic.

'Yes. Christ, Mum. What time is it?'

'Eight o'clock.'

She sat down on the bed, and tried to ruffle his hair on the pillow.

'Oh *look*, Mum. I'm supposed to be ill.'

'Of course you're not ill. You said it was Drama Day.'

Once a term normal lessons ceased at King Henry's and a day of plays was put on. The progressive parents were supposed to come in and meet the teachers in between plays. A lot of TV actors and newsreaders and people had kids at the school. They came and sat in the vast modern hall looking very famous, and apologetic, and less famous parents turned round and pretended not to recognize the famous ones or stare, since staring at fame wasn't too progressive. All the same, the room was a thicket of stares.

There was one big problem with Drama Day, which dated from Stebbings' arrival at school. He had decided it was unprogressive to have compulsory rehearsals. So once a term, from ten till six, there was a day of total shambles.

Lottie hadn't gone for the past two years. In one way Davey approved of that, in another way he was cross and hurt. But *he* certainly wasn't going to turn up if *she* couldn't be bothered to.

'It *is* Drama Day. So I can have a lie-in, can't I. Anyway . . .' he turned over on his back, squeezing out from underneath her hand, and rubbed his eyes crossly. 'What are you doing up at this time? Did the clocks go back or something?'

'It's the Vernal Equinox. It says so in my diary.'

'What the fuck is that?'

'Don't swear. In the morning. It's the first day of spring, I think.'

'Oh, great. Terrific,' he said, in a voice which meant the opposite.

She tried to tickle him, her face like a cat, slanted eyes very green in the sunlight, little teeth showing, sharp tongue showing, and her fingers were steely, and she was on top of him –

Davey felt almost frightened. Sometimes his mother seemed very large. Sometimes his mother seemed very strong. He wondered what Harold felt like having her in bed with him, but the thought was extremely uncomfortable and he pulled up his knees convulsively to try and push her off him.

'*Mum*. Look, I'm not in the mood.'

'Right. Spoilsport. Come down and have breakfast. Amanda's cooking me mushrooms. I suddenly felt like mushrooms.'

'I never feel like mushrooms in the morning.'

She suddenly lost her temper and her whole face changed, lips closing like a trap, heavy brows settling. She flung herself off the bed and stood with her arms folded.

'God! You make me sick. Whining and moaning. You remind me of your father. And your fucking stepfather. You are not going to spoil my day.'

And when he finally came downstairs, she had adopted a resolutely cheerful expression, and was being unnaturally sweet and talkative to Amanda on the landing. (That wouldn't please Amanda. She was never chatty till lunchtime.)

The smell of mushrooms was admittedly delicious. By now he rather fancied some. But he wouldn't take the risk. He went and sat in the window. Beyond the roofs, blue bright sky. Little clouds like children's drawings of clouds. And the gardens opposite had tiny yellow splashes which from close up must be crocuses.

'It's not a bad day,' he said, very cautiously, not *to* anyone, just trying it out.

'It – is – a – perfectly – beautiful – day,' said Lottie, with such coldly stilted diction that she stopped at the end, heard herself, and laughed, rather sourly. It broke the tension.

'You're a *pig*, Davey.'

He smiled at her. Down here, she was no longer scary.

'You're a cow, Mum.' It was a bit of a risk, but he smiled very beautifully. 'I'm sorry I was mad. I had a bad dream.'

She came over and sat beside him. The hand she put round his shoulder looked quite lined in the full sunlight.

'Well, I'm sorry I . . . never mind. As a matter of fact, I'm just feeling about eight trillion times better than I have for weeks. I think I am *finally* over Harold. And it calls for a celebration.'

His mother's celebrations. She celebrated everything. It was great, in a way, of course. It could also be really tiring. Now Harold was out of it, Davey knew the supporting cast was him.

He kissed her on the cheek. He knew she liked being kissed. Harold was always kissing her. Davey suddenly wondered, did Harold feel like I do sometimes when I do it? Sort of, *oh well, here goes; I know she likes to be kissed* . . .

She smiled and her cheeks sucked into deep dimples. Yes, Lottie liked to be kissed.

'Thing is, I said I'd go and meet Charles. He's "ill", as well, today. We'll probably go to a film.'

'Well, bring him back here for tea.'

'OK, Mum.'

She was waiting for more. Her will to be loved was a physical force, as real as the sunlight, as dazzling to walk into.

'That'd be great. Of course we'll come.'

She smiled, appeased, turned and looked out of the window.

'It really is spring-like, isn't it? I'll have to think of something.'

They didn't go to the pictures; Charles had agreed to see Smeggy. Smeggy's mother was at work so Davey and Charles went round to his place. Davey had never been there before. He was quite glad he was with Charles.

It was like going back into the nineteenth century. Like Dickens, but not so jolly. Not jolly at all. Blackened brick. It was right at the top of the block. There wasn't a lift, just stairs. They were covered with violent drawings.

The flat had very small windows and smelled of ashtrays and steam. Washing was stretched over most of the furniture. Some of the curtains were drawn. The heat was on full, though the day wasn't cold.

Smeggy hadn't got his makeup on. He looked milder, and less

beautiful. Nor had he got any dope. 'Too broke at the moment,' he explained. They couldn't go into his bedroom because his brother was asleep. 'Got pissed last night.'

'Why can't he sleep in his own bedroom?' Davey asked. It was a let-down, not seeing Smeggy's bedroom. Charles had told him about it.

'Shares wiv me, doesn' 'e.'

They listened to Motorhead, and Charles and Smeggy watched an old movie on the TV. Smeggy was bored, and kept making rude comments, and started painting his face as he watched.

Davey couldn't settle to anything. He gazed through a crack in the curtains down on sunlit, spoiled London. There were flats like this for miles and miles. Hardly any trees, compared to where *they* lived. The ones he could see looked small as weeds. Cars crawled through the endless blocks of darkness like glittering, greedy insects. It wasn't clear what they were after. There wasn't anything here. Davey wanted to go back home. He hadn't read a book all day.

'My mum asked us to tea.' He interrupted the movie.

'Your *mama*?' said Smeggy, with a smirk. 'Did she really? Right, fans.'

He shook out his crest of hair, gorgeous in the electric light, and with deliberation wriggled a red glass stud into his earlobe. Smeggy was ready to go.

Davey couldn't really explain that only he and Charles were expected.

Nor did it matter, as it turned out. Lottie might have been expecting a wedding. Lottie had thought of something. Lottie had celebrated spring.

Lottie had rung up Harrods and asked them to send five hundred pounds' worth of spring flowers.

The unnatural whiteness had suddenly broken into rainbow bowls and banks of blossom.

'Amanda's used every bowl and vase in the house,' she laughed, seeing their faces. 'In the end she got down to tea-cups. You can imagine, Davey, she wasn't pleased. You'll have to drink your tea from saucers.'

Camellias, irises, tulips, daffodils, columns of white narcissus. Hot-house roses, very cool and clean, tight little whorls of pink and blue and yellow against the blue of the china. Open red roses, florid as velvet. Orchids, elaborate, strange and single, like tropical butterflies pinned on the sunlight. Almond blossom, some already falling, heavenly pink and white.

Every piece of furniture was covered. The window-seats had all sprouted flowers, every polished surface reflected flowers, the mirrors glowed and swam with flowers, and even the peerless white of the walls had developed blushes and washes of colour, reflected light from the sea of flowers.

The tea-things were balanced on tiny islands of space on the shining mahogany table. She had bought a lemon cake: the yellow icing had caught two white petals. Davey cast a glance at Smeggy. He was looking rather pale. Smeggy was gazing at Lottie. 'Blimey,' he said.

Smeggy hardly ate a mouthful. He kept looking round at the flowers. Lottie was in her element, golden, excited, playful. She stroked Davey's arm as he ate, and made Charles laugh a lot. In the window a red sun hung, and the colours became even richer, denser; coppery daffodils, deep mauve freesias, heavy ivory narcissus.

'Well, Smeggy, what do you think?'

Lottie looked at Smeggy, one dark brow lifted.

'Blimey,' said Smeggy. 'I mean, *blimey*, Mrs Segall.'

CHAPTER TWELVE

The sun did not stay in the city. Once celebrated, the sun retreated. Harrods flew flowers from overseas, but London's buds stayed tight and cautious. A wintry cold returned. Reluctantly, Lottie dragged out her jumpers and told Amanda to dead-head the flowers.

After a week, very few remained; five or six vases, say. But the colours faded from being indoors, or absorbed the lead in the sky outside, and before they were truly over Lottie lost patience and threw them all out.

(Flowers had to have *splendour*. Flowers should have no half measures.)

Shivering as she stared through the window at her black, sullen garden, Lottie was struck by a happy thought. If she was this cold in London, Poole must be like the South Pole. Harold must be with Sylvia; where else would he have gone? Harold and Sylvia on the horrid little lawn of that horrid little house, two snowmen.

Lottie didn't know the comparative annual figures for sunshine in the United Kingdom. She didn't know how often Bournemouth had claimed the highest figure. In London there were hard black buds; in Bournemouth they swung open. In London there were smudges of green, but Bournemouth leaves were out.

The sea was warmer than the land, curling into the wide blue bay. Clifftop gorse was already alight. From Seabourne down to Branksome Chine there were dunes of blowing green and gold.

The formal gardens were ready for guests. Ornamental cherries and crabs and peaches foamed pink and white across windy skies. Underneath them rows of polished tulips and daffodils stood to attention in the sun. Well-wrapped trippers took walks again. Harold, of course, was not a tripper. Harold needed a little urging.

Two weeks of reading obsessively had made him strange and pale. Ted Sedley, who came in to look at the cooker, peered at his tenant instead.

'You look like a new potato,' he said. 'They keep 'em out o' the light.'

You couldn't say much to that. Harold retired to the bathroom, injured. The fluorescent strip above the cabinet mirror showed him yellowish, with bloodless lips. He bared his teeth to make sure they were still there. Ted Sedley stared in through the open door.

'Tulips is out,' he said. 'Boscombe Gardens is famous for tulips.'

Harold went out, and looked at the tulips, and looked at the cliffs, and found them good. Tulips, daffodils, gorse – cherry trees? Things he could name with simple pride. There were far more things that he *couldn't* name. Once he'd got the stars more under control, he would buy some guides to trees and flowers.

At first, the sunlight hurt his eyes; he would have to get used to it again. His calves felt weak and stiff; he would walk them in again. It was part of the same grand plan, after all. Indoor research and outdoor field study. Naturally, there would be more field study now they were into the last week of March.

But Harold was sure of one thing – everything tended towards one end. Nothing at all could distract him from the grand purpose of understanding.

Nevertheless, it was rather cheering to find he was looking better. The bathroom light was never kind, but very soon he saw an improvement. Faintly yellowish-*brown*. A definite hint of weather.

Walking down Boscombe's exceptionally long straight high street one morning, he watched his plate-glass reflection walking meekly along beside him. The basics weren't too bad. He wasn't stout. He wasn't short. What was there to be meek about? He tried pulling his shoulders back, lifting his eyebrows, raising his chin.

A plain girl walking slowly towards him glanced at him appraisingly. When he returned the glance, however, she assumed a haughty, artificial expression which made him want to guffaw with embarrassment. Safer to practise on the plate-glass windows.

He might be bald, but he wasn't fat.

He was deaf in one ear, but he didn't need glasses.

He hadn't thought much about his appearance since he had settled with Lottie. That was one of the things it did to you, having a settled relationship. You saw yourself as part of that, not an object for other people. And sometimes it was quite nice, to be an object for other people (but he felt a little pang; nice to be intimate too. Nice to be so close to someone that they didn't really look at you.)

He'd begun to notice girls looking at him, even when he wasn't trying. He was sure they didn't do that in London. In London, *women* looked at him occasionally, usually drunken women at parties. Women who wanted affairs, and didn't mind that he was married. Until he made it clear that that wasn't what he meant by married (but at Claudia's party, last December, he hadn't been clear, and *he* was the drunk. Why should he feel ashamed? He was hardly married, any more. That bitch had swept him out of her life. He'd never trust a woman again . . .).

He caught himself grimacing in the window of a bank and crossed the road hastily, determined not to think about it. Lottie wasn't going to spoil his morning. This morning was an outing. An outing for research, but still, an outing. He had read till two last night; now he researched the sunshine.

A bus swept past him, daffodil yellow. Just what he needed. It slowed, Harold ran. *If I catch this bus, my whole life will come right.* Just as it started, he hauled himself aboard.

Upstairs or downstairs? Upstairs, of course. The spiral stairs nearly finished him. Why couldn't they just have the straight variety? His breath rasped like an actor hamming as he sank into a seat. He began to feel rather faint. It didn't go back to normal again.

A girl with very straight brown hair turned to look at him curiously, showing a grave and clean-cut profile. As she turned back, she seemed to smile. *Laughing at me,* thought Harold, stung. He stared with envy at her sheer smooth cheek and her hair the colour of clear dark honey. He'd never be truly young again.

Still his breath came back, and with it, good temper. Never mind being an object for others, he was a subject too. A cat can look at a king, and Harold could look at women. If Lottie didn't want him, he could want other women. He also wanted some breakfast. His appetite was good.

He strolled through Bournemouth's Central Gardens, the long slope down to the sea. The seats along the narrow stream were already packed with people. Their arms and legs were still covered but their faces turned hopefully up to the sun, as open and helpless as flowers, quiet, orderly rows of flowers. Most of the faces were older, but some of them were quite young. Swooning into the sun, lids closed, they were curiously similar. Harold scanned them eagerly, looking for some little sign, someone a little bit different, someone waiting, maybe, for him.

How very trusting they seemed to be, yielding in public, all together, sitting as closely on their bench as lovers in a narrow bed. Yet most of them couldn't know each other.

Lottie and me in bed.

He was hurrying into the dazzling sun, suddenly sick and hungry. Should have had breakfast before I set out. Get to the pier, must eat something . . .

Lottie, Lottie. When we first began. He crouched on the grass for a moment. The bliss of being close to her. Looking back, he could see them, very small, curled tightly round each other. He stood up swiftly, started to run, then closed his eyes, hopelessly dizzy. Big stars burst behind his lids and he groped for the nearest seat, for the nearest . . .

'Is he *drunk*?'

A great angry voice. A man's? A woman's. A Yorkshire-woman's. He was sitting on her lap. Oh God, he would die. He made a great effort like a terrified chicken and flapped to his feet through her red flailing limbs.

'I'm sorry. I'm very . . .'

A cool young voice was arguing with the other.

'He's ill, can't you see. He was ill just now, on the bus.'

A hand pressed his head down towards his knees.

'I'm frightfully sorry. I'm all right now. I think I just need some breakfast,' he gabbled. Then he knelt down. It was easier there. He held his head down till the blood came back.

A curtain of flashing brown light beside him. And then a face he half-recognized, but slewed by gravity, kneeling beside him.

'That's better. You've got some colour back now. You fainted, that's all.'

It was the girl from the bus.

He straightened up, and smiled a smile of pure love.

'How *terribly* kind of you to bother.'

'Come on, let's go and get some coffee. They do some not-bad salads on the pier.'

Harold relaxed into this benign dream. It couldn't last; he might as well enjoy it. Her profile was absolutely perfect, and she wasn't laughing at him. She looked French, with that profile, or maybe just rich. And she couldn't be more than twenty.

Over lunch, he revised these opinions. Full-face, she was still very pretty, but marred by a definite squint, her irises yearning towards each other. It was rather endearing, he decided. It made her short-sighted, like a brown-eyed puppy. She laughed at him quite a lot, but in a way that made him feel warm. She was an art student from Bournemouth. She was poor, and twenty-three.

He could see, though he didn't dare believe it, she found him attractive. Or *very* attractive. He spun out lunch till it got ridiculous, frightened she'd go away.

In the end she got up swiftly and gracefully, shaking her long hair over one eye.

'Do you want me to show you the Russell-Cotes?'

'What's that?'

(Never mind. His heart hammered *Yes*.)

'It's a museum.'

'Oh.'

A museum. It didn't seem spring-like enough.

'You'll like it. It's a house, really. Wonderful views of the sea. And this super stained glass with suns and shooting-stars and things . . .'

Harold's heart leaped. More gifts, more grace.

'Oh yes, yes please, I'd love to.'

She smiled. A minutely chipped front tooth. Her skin was so smooth, so young.

'I don't even know your name,' he mumbled. She'd told him when he was dizzy. He couldn't help wanting to touch that skin.

'It's a silly name. It's April.'

In London, the sun refused to break through. Lottie was bored, and restless. Amanda kept hyacinths in the kitchen. She loved the smell, and Lottie said nothing though she always thought they were vulgar things. Now the hyacinths drooped and browned.

'Are you going to throw those out, Amanda?'

'I was going to ask you, Mrs Segall. If I could put them in the garden. They might recover, and flower next year.'

'I'd rather they *didn't* flower in the garden.'

'Yes, Mrs Segall. I'll throw them out.'

The exchange left Lottie feeling vaguely guilty though of course she was perfectly right. Servants asked such impossible things. There would be painted gnomes in the garden next.

Lottie hadn't been in the garden this year. Last year she was out there nearly every day.

With Harold. We watched those bulbs as if . . . I suppose as if they were our kids. Something I shared with that bloody man. I'm not going to share it with bloody Amanda.

I'm getting bad-tempered, she thought. She looked in the mirror at the two little lines which seemed to have deepened between her eyebrows. She smiled, artificially, laughing at the glass. But the smile was pale, and the lines remained.

Lottie thought, life is dull. I need some colour. I need some . . . *fun.*

☆

The colour of the daytime sky on Mars is a warm pink, a flesh colour. The surface of the planet by day is iron-red and apparently barren. Long ago, there was running water. At sunrise or sunset, the sky is deep blue. Night on Mars, when the dust has settled, is clearer than earth's, with trillions of stars.

It seems there is nothing alive to see them.

A late March day on Earth; the surface of the planet swarms with colour. On a little island in the northern hemisphere, primrose, violet, daffodil.

In Boscombe Gardens more tulips have opened. They are crimson, particular, sharp as knives; to a sleepy ant, enormous, from a nearby planet, infinitely small. They open more slowly than the eye can measure, immeasurably faster than history can record.

In London, a large queen wasp which has slept in a fold of a velvet curtain wakes up and feels the cold.

A great deal still to be done.

Lottie walks to the phone.

April

CHAPTER THIRTEEN

Venus is the closest planet to Earth. When it is close, it is very close: twenty five million miles away. A hair's breadth away, in cosmic terms. Nearer the sun than Earth is.

Its surface is shrouded with uniformly shining lemon-yellow cloud. Venus is close but mysterious.

Astronomers map it with names of lovers: Guinevere, Sappho, Helen, Diana.

Humans dreamed in the nineteenth century: was it a world of seething swamps and swarming tropical forests?

Some things are clear at last.

For example, Venus shines most brightly on Earth when it is still a crescent.

For example, on Venus the sun rises in the west and sets in the east.

On Earth, the streets near Lottie's house are bright with the blossom of Norway Maple, lemon-yellow, preceding the leaves.

Lottie phones Hugo Gatling.

'I can't believe it's April.'

Hugo sounds rather low. Hugo is an 'ex' of Lottie's. He has a lugubrious voice but a cheering, persistent passion for Lottie. He asks her to openings at his gallery. He asks her advice about pictures, though he rarely listens to what she says.

More to the point, he once gave her a heavenly small Bonnard. She suspects he's always regretted it, too. He stares at it fixedly, sometimes, between courses, if asked to dinner. If Lottie isn't nice to him, more fixedly than ever.

'Come to lunch tomorrow, Hugo, and I'll cheer you up. Though really, how *I* can cheer anyone up . . .'

'*Wonderful*, darling. You know perfectly well just the sight of you cheers me up.'

I wish I could say the same, she muses. But the thought of male company is very agreeable . . .

Next morning it was cold but bright.

She sprayed on a lot of Givenchy 3 and rolled up the sleeves of her dress (though it wasn't really warm enough) to show off her well-shaped wrists. Its pale turquoise green picked up her eyes. She added some bracelets of turquoise jade.

Thank God I'm pretty, thought Lottie suddenly, peering out of the bedroom window. Down in the garden, just visible, Amanda's brown perm with its thick white parting bent drearily over the cabbages. I don't know why she bothers to dye it.

All Lottie wanted to grow was flowers, but Amanda insisted on having fresh vegetables. First – 'It'll help young Davey to grow. He's just at the age for growing pains.' Later – 'With menfolk, they need their greens. Greens is greens, Mrs Segall.'

They were squashed in a corner, screened by rose bushes. Lottie insisted that they should be screened. Amanda sighed, and washed her scratches. Hugo was going to get his greens.

He arrived looking as he always did, terribly handsome from a distance. Women always felt that. Across the room at a party, they longed for him to come closer. He had aquiline features, kind sad eyes, thick black hair which was not retouched, and a stoop which only added to his agreeable air of gentleness. He had been married three times.

In closeup, he disappointed.

First, he was wildly unfaithful, feeling it rude to refuse a lady, and rude not to ask a lady, in case she wanted to be asked. Secondly, infidelity always made him terribly sad. Thirdly, whenever he drank too much he developed allergic catarrh. His snores, normally hearty, bloomed into horrible, gas-bubbled roars. Lottie knew all these things. She had slept with him on and off for years and turned down three marriage proposals.

The first time she was touched, but only moderately flattered, since he was married to his second wife, a friend of hers. The second time she was irritated; he was newly married to his third

wife. 'Oh Hugo, don't be so *wet*. I'm not the marrying kind.'
Within months she was married to Harold, and Hugo became a
little more lugubrious, gazed at her with a little more sentiment
when they met at dinner parties.

Now he didn't try to conceal his glee that Harold had left
home.

'I say, Lottie, how *frightful*.' He tucked into his duck
energetically. 'Must say you're looking well on it, though. God,
you're a beautiful woman.'

He ate with relish, precision, control, carving the rich brown
meat into parcels, sucking them down with the darker skin. He
liked his duck; he liked his cabbage; he liked to drink, despite
the catarrh.

Hugo likes sex, as well, thought Lottie, watching him. As he
eats, so he fucks.

She crossed her legs, a little excited, looking at his well-
manicured fingers flexing and relaxing round his fork. He looks
nice undressed, she remembered. Suddenly no longer apologetic, he sprawled half-smiling on the bed. How long ago?
Three years ago . . . we're both ageing well. She flashed him an
appreciative grin.

Maybe I should put my diaphragm in. The thought was
shocking, but not impossible. First she'd drink some more
wine.

Over apple charlotte and a second bottle of Muscadet he
became expansive, pouring cream with a generous hand.

'You know – it must've been awfully difficult, Harold not
having what you'd call a job. I mean Emma complained about
me being late at the gallery and that sort of thing . . . and other
sorts of thing . . .' (Lottie knew what sort of thing) '. . . I mean
to say, but *surely*. No woman wants a chap under her feet all the
time. I mean.'

'Most of them don't,' said Lottie rather coolly, not meeting his
warm, sympathetic gaze. He didn't notice; Hugo never did. His
perceptiveness was just for sex and paintings.

'I mean a woman must want a chap to have a bit of an *income*,'
he ejaculated messily, swallowing crumble, licking cream fatly
off his lips. He didn't know he was taking a risk. He was only
stating the obvious.

Hugo had income from property, income from his gallery,
income from inheritance. *If income is what she wants*, a dim

113

aroused voice in his belly urged him, *I've plenty of income to give her. I'll give her income till she howls for more.*

'Hugo, dear.' Her voice was acid. 'I know you have a simply enormous income. And Harold didn't. But I do. And I don't need another one.'

'Of course you do,' he said, abashed, laid down his spoon and unconsciously, swiftly, folded his hands to protect his crotch. 'Of course you *don't*, I mean. I mean, you do have an income of your own. I know that, Lottie. Now don't be touchy.'

'Men always imagine –' she began, throwing out her hands with such grace that Hugo caught one and kissed it, gallantly; and interrupted, rudely.

'Oh, don't say you're going feminist, Lottie, just because Harold's left you. You're much too clever for that.'

'Too clever, am I.' Lottie twisted her hand so sharply he had to drop it. 'Thank you, Hugo. For God's sake, feminism bores me to tears. *Harold* was the feminist, not me. But I don't want you telling me why my marriage broke up. I don't tell you about yours. Though I could, you know, Hugo. I could tell you a few things.'

The clock ticked loudly, unhappily. Wine made the dangerous moment extend, Lottie's heart beating not unpleasantly. Her cheeks burned with sugar and temper.

'Lottie – don't be cross with me. You're such a lovely woman.'

Hugo toppled was not a lovely sight. Hugo deflated was . . . rather repellent. Thus they must have left him, those three wives, finally tiring of his glamour – at which precise moment, it disappeared. And what was left was not very nice.

As he walked through the drawing-room, putting on his coat, he stared very hard indeed at the Bonnard.

After he had gone, Lottie went to her bedroom, and lay on the bed, and considered. Lunch left a sour taste, a low-grade headache and a surfeit of grease. The truth was, being with a man on her own was not as nice as she half expected. Hugo had thought her available again. He was right; she was – *ready to be* available.

It's all so different from being with Harold. Sex was so easy, then. Nothing to win, or lose. Well, I'll have to get used to it again, won't I? I'm sure I enjoyed the whole business once.

Downstairs she could hear the dishwasher grinding into

action. It was a relief to think of all that foaming hot water. Greasy lipmarks being washed away. The stain from her weeping three weeks ago had disappeared from the golden satin. How did people manage if they didn't have staff? She supposed it was different if you'd never been used to it. Since she was a child, there had always been staff. Some habits you could never change.

But it's only two years since I married Harold. I must be able to change that habit. I'm sure there were lots of things I liked about being a free agent. (Were there? There must have been . . .)

Wondering whether you'd do it, when you began a date. Feeling powerful and weak at the same time. Then the growing certainty you *would* do it. Watching them take their clothes off, wondering what it would be like . . .

Lottie rubbed her nipples, irritably. She'd forgotten about sexual hunger. It wasn't only sexual. It was wanting a body to rub and touch and cuddle up to and stretch against. On impulse, she got out her silver fox whose very feel was sexual, consoling, and rubbed it against her cheek and neck. She knew what she would do.

She took three aspirins, applied bright lipstick and went to the zoo, wrapped in her coat. The mauve-nosed man on the gate stared hard. She could still dazzle, then. Gratified, she gave him a beautiful smile.

There were monkeys called Diana Monkeys which they must have rushed past before. White and black, very elegant, with long slim tails and tiny faces. She watched a bit before she spotted the baby, neatly clasped to its mother's breast, the fit so close that the mother ran and leaped with little loss of economy.

At least I have my son. Someone to cuddle; someone to touch.

The male pulled and jumped at the mother, wanting sex or perhaps just jealous, pulling her tail, batting at the baby. Then his mood changed – or her mood changed – and he started licking and grooming them both, treating mother and baby as if they were one.

Maybe I should have had Harold's child. But I was too old to start again. And kids aren't glue. They grow up and leave you.

What did keep people together? Did you have to change

partners all the time? Weary, weary, weariness. She watched her reflection passing the cages, the same silver animal in every cage.

The two young gorillas couldn't get away from each other, sitting indifferent on concrete shelves. 'Kumba and Salome' said the notice. Davey had told her something sad. Lottie peered in, and concentrated. She found them disturbingly sexual, with their powerful muscles and gleaming black chests.

What was it Davey had said? That they didn't want to breed. Or Salome, the female, did, but Kumba wasn't interested. They'd been brought up together, so the male saw Salome as a sister. And they'd never seen older gorillas doing it (was that how humans learned? But Lottie had always felt sexual.)

The more you looked, the more interesting they were. But the glass kept cutting Kumba off from her sight. Instead she saw her own silver-puffball reflection, annoyingly vast, less interesting than usual. The coat just got in her way, stopping her pressing close enough to the glass. She couldn't see beyond the reflections.

Then she hit the right angle, and saw something curious. The gorillas weren't looking at each other, or moving, but they were holding hands. Or rather holding hand-and-foot. Kumba was holding Salome's foot. Wrinkled black noses, bored mild eyes.

We were friends, weren't we? she asked herself, as she went out past the gatekeeper. We did get on, Harold and I. That should have kept us together.

She didn't smile at the gatekeeper. His stare seemed less friendly this time around. Indeed, it was almost a glare.

She told herself that was paranoia, pulling her coat of dead animals round her.

CHAPTER FOURTEEN

Harold was not himself at all. Harold was hopelessly over-excited. Harold bit his nails to the quick, then panicked and filed the ragged edges. Harold had bought some new scent. Aramis, not Eau Sauvage. He was shocked by how much the damn stuff cost; Lottie had always bought his scent.

Harold began doing sit-ups. At home he did them twice a year. In the bathroom, he looked at his body. He was really in pretty good shape. But he knew young bodies were – frighteningly different. He had watched Davey flash along the landing, everything smooth and unmarked. No bones, tendons, lines, folds. The older body had nothing *but* . . . Still, it was tall, and – *sculpted*. She's an art student. She ought to like that.

Up, down. Up, down. He schooled his body for what lay ahead. Yet the very idea of making love to April was still unlikely and faintly indecent. In the week or so he'd known her, his behaviour had been chaste. Once on a cliff-path, they held hands. One chilly night he put his arm around her, walking her back to her small bedsitter. After a few minutes he took it away. They said goodnight awkwardly at her door.

She had made him lunch there last weekend, toast and tinned pâté, very bland pâté, then scrambled egg with tomatoes. The tomatoes were sweet and shapeless, the kind that came from a tin.

'This is *marvellous*,' he told her, and meant it. It was marvellous that she cooked for *him*.

And the room was marvellous too. She had made hangings, rugs and cushions, all in shades of orange and red. Sunny, summery colours. The designs were abstract, but not hard. He was anxious to say the right thing.

'I don't like a lot of abstract things . . .'

'Most people don't.' Her voice was disappointed. '. . . I mean, because they're more like geometry than life, somehow. But your shapes are beautiful. Flowing, and . . . living.' He looked at the glowing rug, unsure of her reactions. 'When I look at your designs, the word that comes to mind is *organic*.'

She was pink and pleased, stroking her hair. 'That's exactly right. It's a lovely word. That's just what I want, for the shapes to look living.'

She made instant coffee; Lottie never touched it. But somehow it was charming, now. Drunk black, in orange mugs. April was transformed by his admiration, talking much more than she usually did, confiding and bright-eyed. She shone with pleasure in *his* pleasure.

He used to make Lottie light up like that, though it hadn't happened in ages. It was wonderful to make someone light up. You forgot that you could do it.

Now April wanted him to be perfect. 'Do you like Georgia O'Keeffe? She's my hero, my heroine I mean. You know, she does great big shapes, very simple . . .'

Harold panicked, though the name rang a bell. Great big shapes.

'I *ought* to know . . .'

'She's ever so famous. Hang on, I've got a book about her.'

She scrabbled on the bottom row of brick-and-plank shelving. The book looked familiar . . . oh, no wonder. Lottie had it. A present from Davey. Christ, it would be her birthday soon.

Whatever happens, I mustn't forget it.

The thought confused him, and he lost the thread.

April talked on regardless. The words didn't register, but *April* did, standing closer to him now, her slender shoulders, *oh*, the smell of her hair. She was smaller than Lottie so she had to look up at him, trusting eyes which touched him with their shine, their slight blindness.

Almost exactly half my age.

She was suddenly looking very nervous. Her eyes strayed off to the side.

'It's funny, me being young to you. I'm quite old, really, for what I'm doing. I'd better tell you the whole truth. Painting . . . is what I love best. I *am* an art student . . . *part-time*. I go to evening classes. And I get day release from Bingles.'

'Bingles?'

'*Bingles*. You know, *Bingles*. Everybody knows Bingles. It's the biggest department store in town. I . . . well, I work there. In Furnishings and Fittings. But really I'm in charge of the Art section. Prints and things. And Objay.'

'Ob Jay?'

'*Objay d'art*. Sculptures and models and vases. We've got some quite nice things.'

'Oh,' he said, a little disappointed. It wasn't so romantic as a student.

'First of all I didn't think I'd bother with college at all, so I didn't copy anyone. Then I realized that you more or less have to copy everyone. Till in the end you find something of your own.' She saw his face fall. 'I'm boring you, aren't I? . . .'

'Please, please, you're not at all boring. It was just what you said about "finding something of your own" . . . It reminded me of lots of things I've got on my mind at the moment.'

She still looked anxious. Harold had an inspiration.

'As if you were reading my mind, April. As if you were a little bit psychic.'

And she smiled so beautifully, so easily delighted, so pleased to be psychic, that he almost forgot the guilt which touched him, briefly. *Things on his mind.* He had the *world* on his mind, the *universe*, up till the last few weeks. Since he'd met April, his mind had slipped off it.

Harold had forgotten the oceans of smiles which stretch between new lovers. The island where things begin, endlessly lapped by meeting smiles. He knew – it was beginning. He knew, and he'd never been very quick, that April was – keen on him. He knew, but was frightened to face the words, that April was falling in love.

They sat and talked in cafés, promenade snack bars, ice-cream parlours, seafront shelters, museums, and twice, at lunchtime, April's room. But when she offered him coffee after he'd walked her home in the evening, he always refused, clumsily, stupidly. Walking away, he cursed himself. And he'd never asked her to Boscombe. He knew that would be that. But *that* is precisely what you want, he exhorted himself in the bathroom mirror.

Combing, shaving, spraying. Changing his underpants twice a day. Sitting with her in buses, trains, pubs . . . where would it end?

This evening it was a pub. It was April 19. The date rang a tiny bell in his mind. Maybe he was psychic, too. Harold had made up his mind. He'd put two bottles of wine in the fridge, though she wasn't much of a drinker. He had a suspicion, for things to go right, *he'd* have to be a bit of a drinker.

There were two dozen candles from Woolworth's, though two would probably have done. Candlelight wasn't economy size, but the pack insisted; Economy Size. Nor were the candles cheap. Economy Size just meant *more than you wanted*. He had bought some Durex Elite Superlite. He hadn't used Durex in ages. He didn't feel part of the Elite as he fumbled among the counter display. The chemist seemed to leer at him. But he knew all chemists would be ill from leering if they leered every time they sold a packet. There were hastily purchased and scantily planned ready-cooked treats from Marks and Spencer: Haddock and Courgette Bake, Barbecued Chicken, Lasagne and a last-minute thought, a packet of smoked salmon. He didn't know what she liked.

Nor was he sure he would ask her. They'd been drinking beer in the Buccaneer for one and a half hours. Whenever he opened his mouth to ask her, she'd talk about something else.

'I never knew anyone, not personally, who had a PhD, before.'

He laughed, pleased at her innocence. 'Lots of people have PhDs.'

'Don't laugh at me. I know that. But it's nice going out with one. Dr Harold Segall. Doesn't that sound posh?'

Dr and Mrs Harold Segall. On so many formal invitations. How could he scratch out all those miles of gleaming gilt-embossed cardboard? How could he say to April, *I'm free. Do you want me?*

'Segall's a good name for you.'

'Why?'

'Your eyebrows.'

Sometimes she made him feel slow. Her mind darted like a dragonfly's.

'What's special about my eyebrows?'

'Well . . .' Embarrassed, she blurted it out. 'I think they look like a bird. *Seagull*, see. I mean, the wings, flying.'

She let her hair fall forward. Under bright light it could look blonde; by day it was caramel, soft, kind.

(Even at the very beginning, Lottie never *admired* me like this.)

'You can't have a black seagull.'

'You *can*, as well!' She shrieked so loudly that the barman looked round and Harold saw his face, admiration followed by envy. He'd seen that look before, from other older men.

They'd all like to be with April. The realization was a little frightening. He wasn't sure he was up to this. It was almost too late, in any case . . . Could you eat supper at nearly ten? A relaxed little four-course supper?

Right. He would blurt it out.

'April . . .'

'You're not *listening*. Come on, we're going to Boscombe.'

'What?' he said, jaw dropping.

'I'll show you a pub with a black seagull.'

Maybe she was just a little bit psychic. The Seagull was on Sea Road, fifty yards up from Harold's turning. When they got to the pub she reached up gently and turned his head towards the sign.

On a light background, a large black seagull was silhouetted, flying seaward. The artist had made it a bit like a bat, but there it was; a black seagull.

It must mean something. There must be a pattern.

The bright waves lapped round their shared island, the smiles which promised *tonight, tonight*.

Is it a promise?

Will she?

CHAPTER FIFTEEN

The evening before her birthday, Lottie felt – full of potential. Life had been hard since Christmas; but she had coped, frankly, *splendidly*.

'*Amanda, could you be an angel and bring me a cup of coffee? And one of those cakes? I'm upstairs on the phone.*'

This sudden shrill command to Amanda deafened Claudia, nearly two miles away, though she held the receiver inches from her ear.

Lottie was retailing her state of mind. In sum, it was triumphant.

All her other friends had breakdowns or face-lifts when their husbands left them, or went into analysis. But she was too restless for analysis, and she didn't need a face-lift. '. . . Yet, darling, anyway.' Lottie could not break down; how on earth could people break down? She had always felt too all-of-a-piece to *bend*, let alone break down.

'Lottie, you're doing marvellously. Only – don't be, you know, too sure of yourself. It's not always the first few months that are the worst, with a breakup.'

There was a little silence, full of fear, her fear of Lottie's anger. Claudia always found it hard to speak her mind to Lottie. If you annoyed her the slightest bit, Lottie let you know. Claudia couldn't deal with it. Lottie always . . . *bore her down*. Claudia always ended up saying sorry.

On the other hand, Lottie annoyed Claudia frequently, sometimes to the edge of insanity, but Claudia never showed it. Never dared show it, to be precise. It made her feel hopeless, and very tired. It was mostly men who affected her like that, but Lottie could flatten her just as well. Every now and again, like tonight, Claudia would make the effort to be honest. You can't be friends if you can't be honest.

Lottie considered her cake: a large cream slice, intricately layered, delicately fluted, flushed with pink, billows of cream frilling out of the edges. The cake was satisfactory, Claudia was not.

'Thanks very much. Very cheerful,' said Lottie. 'It'll all get worse then, will it? Is that what you think or what you hope? You're just like everyone else . . .'

'*Lottie* – '

'Everyone's livid that I'm not prostrate with grief over Harold leaving. I'm sure half the women I know were delighted Harold walked out on me. They thought it would bring me to my knees. Well, it hasn't. So there.'

'Lottie, you know me better than that. I'm just warning you, that's all.'

'Well you've chosen an excellent time to warn me. It's my birthday tomorrow. I'm looking forward to it. Well, I *was* . . .'

The unfairness stung.

'LOTTIE! I know it's your birthday, I've sent you a present. Now stop it, *please*. I'm very sorry if I upset you. What I'm really saying is – don't be surprised if you feel grief later. It wouldn't be letting the side down.'

'So you want me to have a breakdown. You think it would make me more human.'

Lottie was very audibly eating, which added to Claudia's irritation. She suspected Lottie enjoyed all this. A sort of mental isometrics.

'But breaking down occasionally isn't *having* a breakdown.'

Claudia could hear in her voice a tone of agitated, reasonable pleading which all too often crept into her dealings with Lottie.

And Lottie must be eating a large bowl of stew at the very least. A voluptuous *shloop*.

'So which would you like me to do? *Break down*, or *have a breakdown?*'

The cake was really delicious. Lottie licked the cream and enjoyed herself.

'Let's drop this, Lottie, please. Look, I only want what's best for you. It's just like all the magazines say – it doesn't hurt to express your feelings.'

'So *have* you expressed your feelings, Claudia?'

Claudia felt very tired, and yielded. 'Yes. I'm sorry.'

Shit.

No wonder Harold left her.

Feminism left some things out. There are women just as obsessed with power.

But now that Lottie had won the point, she returned to being so wickedly funny about Hugo Gatling coming to lunch that Claudia was soon laughing again.

Just before they said goodbye, Lottie said what she'd wanted to say all along.

'I bet I get flowers from him tomorrow. I bet I get three dozen roses. He'll ring and beg to come creeping home.'

The contempt was strangely forced. Claudia suddenly knew that Lottie couldn't bear to say Harold's name. Her much-tried heart went out to her friend.

'Of course you will. I bet he will.' She sounded a bit more convincing than Lottie.

'Of course I'll refuse, if he does.'

Of course she wouldn't. But he won't remember.

One thing Claudia knew about Harold was his appalling memory for dates. But Lottie knew that too.

She ought to; she's had to remind him enough. She told me he actually made a date to play squash with someone on his wedding day. So why is she kidding herself? Perhaps she's having a breakdown.

☆

But Lottie felt happy when she rang off. It helped to have Claudia agree that Harold would get in touch tomorrow. Sometimes you needed a second opinion. Someone impartial, who told you the truth.

Lottie licked the last cream off her plate. She would take a long bath, and condition her hair. There'd been too much effort and worry, of late. Time for fate to be good to her.

She fell asleep thinking of roses, mounds of sugary, creamy roses, detailed, old-fashioned, intricate roses served to her on a silver plate. But the dream went wrong. Lottie woke in the early morning, frightened, very alone. It was almost 3 a.m. She couldn't deny that she had been dreaming.

Something about a loss, or a burglary, something stolen she wouldn't get back. She touched her face to make sure it was there and was surprised to find her cheek was wet. She realized, I'm thirty-six, tomorrow. Over halfway to three score and ten. The fear took a long time to drain away.

If no one remembers me.

What then?

CHAPTER SIXTEEN

The pint at the Seagull made three. Three was really Harold's limit. He was intensely happy, and full of hope. They leaned so closely over the table in the red alcove that he could feel the velvet warmth of April's breath. Her shining eyes never left his face.

(*After all this, she can't say no.*)

There weren't many people in the upstairs bar, and for him there was only her. His face ached from smiling so much, his stomach felt bloated but empty. Ever since they'd reached the Seagull, Harold had been erect. The faint gold down on her skin, her red lips parting, a musky smell . . . was it really true that sex smelled of musk?

In the rosy light she was astonishingly pretty, her wide mouth showing those regular, gleaming, ever so slightly imperfect teeth. (Lottie's looked wonderful, but two of them were capped.) So very – *new*. A *new* woman. Somebody new to push inside. Somebody who would let him in.

Harold veered between tingling, voracious lust and shame; she was surely too young to kiss. *Don't be stupid,* his erection told him. *The kids all do it from the age of thirteen.*

Harold was sweating. He took a deep breath, and full of fire, he spoke.

'I don't suppose you like haddock?'

'*Yes.* Well anyway, *quite.*'

'Right. Let's go,' said Harold. Time to be masterful.

The night outside was surprisingly cool, without stars (he had somehow imagined stars. It didn't matter; April's face was resting on his shoulder.)

Self-consciously up the stairs, through two floors of emptiness. He had never brought anyone here. Ahead of him, her slim belted back, her *specialness*. How trustful she was, coming here with him! He almost felt he should warn her.

He saw the flat quite differently as April looked at everything, timid at first then flying from room to room and calling to him in the tiny kitchen where he sweated and dropped things.

'It's ever so big. It's enormous. You could fit a family in here.'

A very faint bell of warning.

'Well, it's big compared to yours, I suppose. It's jolly cold, as well.'

'What?' She was in the bedroom (*April was in his bedroom!*) He hoped it looked all right. He'd dug up a surprisingly flashy yellow paisley bedspread from Mr Sedley's store. It turned out to be full of tiny holes, but they wouldn't show by candlelight.

'I'm not cold,' she said, reappearing, though the ghastly fluorescent of the kitchen made her suddenly white and chill, a different person he couldn't touch. 'I love it here. It's wonderful.'

'Sit down by the fire, I'll open some wine.' Harold was desperate for her not to watch as he dug all the frozen food out of the fridge and tried to make the bits add up. 'You'll soon have something hot.'

But before she went, very biddably (Lottie had never been biddable) she put her arms round him and his freezing, slippery parcels, pressed up against him and before he was ready for it passionately kissed him, and all he could think was *don't drop the haddock, help.*

He wished he was completely sober.

Wine, that's right, that's what they needed.

He dumped everything on the table, and bent down for the wine. *Plop.* He slopped two beakers of wine.

She was perched on an armchair in the sitting-room, with her knees together, like a girl at a tea-party. Somehow, the jeans were a party dress, and she took the glass like a cucumber sandwich.

'Thanks!' She drank the wine like water.

'To us,' he said on impulse, and chinked their glasses so a tiny stain fell on her jeans, on those tight-pressed thighs.

'How lovely,' she said, 'I'm enjoying this.'

Back to the kitchen.

'Harold.'

'Yes?' He wished she'd let him get on with it.

'Do *you* like haddock?'

'Yes. Love it.' He sounded short.

'Oh.' Pause. 'That's good.'

He switched the oven dial to MAX. The picture on the packet looked delicious, but a long way off.

'Harold . . .' She was back in the door again. 'Is that smoked salmon in that other packet?'

'Yes. It is. It's *smoked salmon*. Why?'

(How on earth did Amanda manage to cook and talk to Davey at the same time? He supposed because she didn't want to sleep with Davey.)

'Well. I mean. It is quite late.'

'I *know*. I'm *trying* . . .'

'We could just have the salmon.'

Relief swamped him. A *marvellous* girl.

'I say. Could we really?'

'I *love* smoked salmon. I ate it at my brother's wedding. It's really nice with wine . . .'

Whatever she said seemed so fresh. Could anyone really have only eaten smoked salmon once, at a wedding? Could anyone think it was *nice with wine*? April could, and did.

(Could I ever get bored with anyone whose world is still so unshaded? The thought wouldn't come till tomorrow. Tomorrow it could, and did.)

But this was tonight, and not to be spoiled, for nothing in life had quite the promise of the first time, any first time, even though he had had many first times, and the last one had been with – *No, don't spoil it.*

(– *Lottie. See, I can manage without you.*)

She balances candles on the coffee table; he goes and puts out the central light. The bottle of wine is half-empty. Pink curling tongues of salmon are eaten ravenously with their fingers. Salty, silky, raw. They sit on the sofa, side by side, his denim thigh at last touching hers, every nerve-end tingling as they press together.

Pink curling fingers, interlacing.

Now the salmon is gone and someone is shrieking with helpless laughter.

Now they are both on the floor, one candle is lit, and the glow of the two-bar fire shows their arms and legs have got confused and his hands are combing her red-glowing hair and now the colours have changed and the red light gleams on long inlets of naked skin.

Now someone blows out the second candle. Two thin bare

figures, breathing very audibly, cross the firelight and pad next door, too urgently to switch off the fire.

It is way past time; it is 3 a.m.

This tableau waits for the morning.

Two bottles, one empty, one quarter-full; two plates, with the cutlery splayed like legs; a lemon, which no one remembered to cut, the colour of an orange in the firelight; clothes like a spill from a laundry basket, a married couple's, all intertwined, tumbling together, twisted together, yet in their stillness become domestic.

Lottie, thought Harold, half-waking at five, nuzzled against someone warmly asleep. Bliss flooded through him. *Back with Lottie . . .* and slept again, and forgot it utterly.

When he got up next day at ten the first thing he did was to pick up his clothes, separating them from hers.

CHAPTER SEVENTEEN

Lottie woke at eight, five hours after the bad dream woke her. *Harold*, she thought. *He'll ring today.*

The sun was creamy through the curtains. Creamily dozing, it's my birthday. Something is bound to happen. I'll snooze a bit longer and wait for it.

Yet some little worry, an emptiness, some confusion or foolish dream, stopped her falling asleep again.

The door-bell rang, loud and peremptory.

She shot out of bed, quick with joy, pulled on the sky-blue dressing-gown and started downstairs in her warm bare feet. Amanda called up towards her.

'Some lovely flowers, Mrs Segall. And Happy Birthday, Mrs Segall. Many Happy Returns.'

The bouquet was as large as the chair it lay on, glistening with cellophane and golden ribbon. She looked for the card; there wasn't a card – of course he knew she would know it was him – so instead she ripped off the cellophane ('Oooh Mrs Segall! I'll bring some scissors!') and plunged her face into the warm smell. Beautiful, tight-budded, hopeful roses, at least three dozen, the petals shaded from cream at the edges to butter yellow. The hearts were tawny pink.

'Amanda, aren't they wonderful?' Lottie held them up in the sunshine.

'There's a card, Mrs Segall. Here.'

Lottie shoved the flowers into Amanda'a arms and snatched the tiny card in its envelope. Trying to open it too fast she accidentally tore the card in two.

'Oh, bugger, why do they make them so *small*?'

Impatiently, she pieced it together.

> STILL UN   FORGETTABLE
> HAPPY BIR   THDAY, DARLING
> LOVE ALWAY   S XXX CARL

'It's from *Carl*,' she gasped, and slumped against the table. 'They're not from Harold, they're from Carl.'

Nothing could change things, then. The calendar hadn't any magic. Just because it was her birthday, it didn't mean that her present would come.

(There were lots of presents, of course, but not the ones that counted. 'You have been lucky this year, Mrs Segall,' said Amanda, arranging the cards in a line, salvaging the prettier wrapping-paper. 'Bollocks,' said Lottie, half under her breath, but Amanda heard, as she half-intended.)

Mid-morning, there were more roses. This time Lottie wasn't hopeful.

YOUNGER THAN SPINGTIME. EVER YOURS, HUGO.

The message made her feel very old. When she read it again, she noticed the florist had left the 'r' out of 'springtime'. *Spingtime* was even sillier and emptier. It sounded obscene, and vaguely Chinese.

People just didn't care any more. Literacy was disappearing.

But Davey, bless him, cut a Double English and rushed home early from school. They went for a walk along Camden Canal, past the edge of the Zoo. The birds shrieked down from the aviary. It looked somehow sinister, like black net stockings. Under the bridge a body was lying, smelling of alcohol and sour milk. As they passed it, one foot suddenly kicked. Neither of them mentioned it.

Lottie was talking about George Grosz, whose paintings the aviary brought to mind. She was hectically cheerful, but her face was strained, and she'd put too much rouge in the centre of each cheek.

Davey bought her an optical kaleidoscope from the man who sold them at Camden Lock. It was a wonderful instrument which split whatever you looked at into tiny repeating segments, centred like stars or flowers. The most casual thing became jewelled and deliberate. Normally Lottie would have loved it.

She kissed him, rather desperately, exclaimed a lot, and waved the thing about, but she didn't concentrate, she didn't look properly. You couldn't see the pattern if you didn't look properly. Davey was cross, especially since he'd have liked to keep it himself.

But he knew quite well what the matter was. Sodding Harold. Sod him.

In the café where he took her for tea, she ate two pieces of chocolate cake as if they were meat, hungrily, goring them with her teeth.

'Ex – *quisite*. I was so *empty*.'

Then she smoked two fags, emphatically.

This evening Mum would drink too much.

On the way home through the evening chill the sun was a stagy, ominous red. The canal footpath was already closed; the birds would be smothered in their thickening stocking, the tramp would not be kicking any more . . .

There were shouts as they came into Camden High. The traffic was solid all down, horns blaring. Then they saw bodies, quiet and still, spread flat, three-deep, across the road. A sort of bandage of bodies. Lottie stopped in horror. They were women, mowed down, and nobody was helping them. She broke into a run.

Then she saw the banners on the pavement.

CAMDEN WOMEN AGAINST CRUISE. CAMDEN WOMEN'S DIE-IN.

And she saw the faces, plain unpainted faces, shining with virtue, like nuns.

She turned to Davey, her jaw thrust forward, two spots of rouge, eyes hate-filled, brilliant. Her voice shocked him with its viciousness.

'Stupid – *cunts*. God, how I hate them. If you ever do anything like that, I'll kill you, I swear I will.'

For once he didn't contradict. Sometimes her strength was terrifying. And her ignorance, that was the trouble. A lot of his mother was frightening. How much she wanted things, as well.

And Harold is just a stupid prick. He doesn't care about Mum at all. I'll always hate him, I swear I will.

It was comforting to get back inside out of the raw red sunset. The house was very light, and smelled of flowers, and the cake Amanda had baked. Lottie's mouth unclamped a little. The world was no longer entirely hostile.

That evening she didn't get drunk. Carl's roses were ranged round the walls. The phone rang at nine, when they'd just finished eating a cheese soufflé and watching TV.

Davey had forgotten it was *Dallas* that day, Mum's favourite soap opera. It always perked Lottie up. Maybe the oil barons who starred in it were *ineptly* wicked, but at least they were wicked. There wasn't a single socialist or social worker in *Dallas*. The plot was absurd, of course, and she always said so when she switched it off. Yet she sniffed, audibly, in glorious relief when the star-crossed lovers stared across the room at each other, at the Oil Barons' Ball. 'Go get him, stupid,' she whispered. She always joined in, in Dallas.

The phone rang just as they were ready for it. Davey hurried to answer it. *Please be Harold, please.*

'Oh, hallo, Dad.' He always sounded indifferent when Carl rang, but today disappointment made him border on rude. Lottie came and took the phone, giving Davey a disapproving dig. He moved away, rubbing his ribs. Mum's playful digs left bruises.

He listened half-heartedly to the conversation. Mum always used a different voice for men. He supposed it was sexy, but it grated on him.

Christ, she's been *married* to this one – so why should she try and sound sexy? The interesting thing was, what she was saying contradicted the voice she was saying it in. Dad must be asking her out. He tried it, every so often. It was odd that everyone who'd ever been out with Mum still seemed to want to again. They wouldn't if they knew what she said about them. He slid their two plates together.

'He never gives up,' she crowed, as soon as the phone was back in its cradle. 'He asked me to go to Venice with him. Failing that, for a drink this evening. Of course I turned him down flat.'

He normally hated it when she went on like that, sort of *look at me, I'm Queen Bee*, but this evening it was a relief. He knew it was getting her own back on Harold. Davey played up to it.

'Dad's never really loved anyone but you, has he?'

'Silly of him,' purred Lottie, content. 'There've been dozens of girls, but I suppose you're right.'

She corked up the wine and put it in the tray.

They watched the ten o'clock news, which he hoped would mention the Die-In. It didn't, of course. It showed lots of shots of pregnant Princess Diana, smiling and waving at some cordoned-off children, who waved back vaguely from miles away.

'Do you think she's pretty?' Lottie asked him.

'I suppose she is. But . . . sort of awful.'

'Yes. You're right. She's much too skinny,' Lottie said, with considerable satisfaction.

It wasn't what he meant. So what, if she was happy. As he left the room, she was still speaking her mind to the TV screen.

'I don't see why people are obsessed with her. Everything's Diana, wherever you look. Even those nice little monkeys . . .'

'Eh? *What?*'

Never mind. She was watching the weatherman.

'Goodnight, Mum. I love you.'

The only person awake in the house, Lottie went out into her garden. It was hers, after all, not Harold's. I think I'll get back to gardening again.

The bulk of the building cut off the street lights, and though the whole sky was faintly orange, against the orange she could see a few stars, and after her eyes got used to searching, more and more stars, till she felt quite dizzy. Sometimes she felt very small. She never enjoyed that feeling.

She thought about Carl, instead. It was gratifying, thinking of Carl. Carl as he was at the moment, sentimental about her, wanting her back . . .

When they were married was a different matter. I was so horribly, painfully young, and so stupidly in love. Impossible, now, to believe how much . . .

Carl was the hero from *True Love Stories* and *Imogen* and *Boyfriend*, the one she had dreamed of night after night as a teenager, reading her comics till midnight. Carl appeared at her birthday party. Standing in a leafy summer window. At last the descriptions fitted. He was, just as she had promised, *devilishly good-looking . . . muscular, blonde, grey eyes that raked you.* When he asked me to marry him, I didn't hesitate. So many birthdays ago. I was twenty, and already pregnant. And then we were married, and the pregnancy got bigger. And then his eyes started raking other women. I couldn't bear it, or cope. He enjoyed it when I raged and pleaded. I felt so clumsy, and sick all the time. I put up with it for four years. I must have been mad. One day I woke up.

The stars above had no comment to make, steady behind a frieze of leaves (leaves already; it would soon be summer . . .)

Fifteen – *sixteen* years ago. Sixteen years to the day, of course . . . there were other stars, which seemed to say *yes* to Carl and her as they kissed in the garden.

And now it was another husband. Now she needed another

bit of help. She looked up, hoping for a sign. But the stars had moved so much further away.

I never think about them, but they're always there. Lottie was suddenly curious. Is it windy up there, and immensely cold?

She imagined great winds blowing down from the stars, blowing them off into emptiness. Sometimes the world was frightening . . . Lottie, of course, refused to be frightened. But sometimes, recently, she'd felt there was less of herself than there used to be. And more of other people. People she couldn't control.

Those horrible, stupid women, showing off out in the road. And the drunks you saw sometimes out in the park, slobbering, trying to paw you. There seemed to be more and more people talking out loud to themselves in the streets. They looked lost and angry and stared at Lottie as if they hated her. Bus queues straggled everywhere. Lottie never travelled on buses, of course, but recently the queues had begun to bother her. Poor people, old people, mad people, spilling from buses or trailing towards them. The queues got longer and longer. They didn't seem to know what they were queueing for.

Maybe it was jobs, or money. But with all the taxes that Lottie paid, they should have had enough money. Why did they just wait around like that with hopeless faces and querulous voices? Why did the government allow it? Why were their clothes and expressions so ugly?

Why won't Harold come back to me?

Something is wrong with the world. Maybe we *ought* to be blown away. Maybe we shouldn't be such a loss.

But Lottie herself is still full of life. She likes the right things: order, beauty. She tried to say so to the orange sky.

It's my birthday. Listen to me.

All she can feel is emptiness. The empty spaces between the stars. She shakes her head, determinedly, and tries to engage with those distant lights.

What she sees is clear.

The stars are there. And the emptiness.

In the country, though, not a twig is empty.

White willows bear erect male catkins, yellow, pointing at the clouds. April is in flower; cowslips, wild strawberries.

April

Ladybirds whirr out to eat the greenfly. Rhododendron heads push up, purple, lush as *True Love Stories.*

Thousands of years ago, humans made Venus their goddess of love.

Some things are clearer now, on Venus.

The heights are higher, the depressions are deeper than mountains and valleys are on Earth. *Freyja Montes, Diana Chasma.*

Up into the lemon-yellow clouds, and down.

Some things remain mysterious, under the uniformly shining cloud.

On Earth, in Bournemouth, old trees look much older under their new green leaves.

May

CHAPTER EIGHTEEN

Harold and April walk by the sea. Lottie absently approves her garden. Earth surrounds them with brightness, substance. The cosmos, though, is mostly empty.

Lottie sits by her window, absent-mindedly sketching on an envelope. Clematis hangs in a heavy white rope across her sunny garden. What she draws is a rope of stars.

Emptiness cannot be seen or drawn. Astronomers map stars and planets, not the gaps between them.

On a clear night in May, the observer seems to see more stars than darkness. The single viewpoint foreshortens space; each star is swollen by a ring of starlight.

The truth is, stars and planets are almost infinitely rare compared to space. Set down at random in the cosmos, the observer's chances of arriving near a planet are one in a billion trillion trillion.

1 in 1,000,000,000,000,000,000,000,000,000,000.

That tiny '1' at the beginning is us.

So very small, so very light, surrounded by such emptiness.

What do we do with such great luck?

We take it lightly.

We play it light.

'But what on earth does – *Lottie* – do?'

In their first idyllic weeks, April didn't ask about Lottie. She seemed to want him to be newborn in a world with just the two of them.

That suited Harold fine. It helped him to forget. Perhaps he could turn into someone else who would be entirely in love with her.

When he'd first entered April, she gasped, 'I love you,' and to his surprise he heard himself say, 'I love you too.'

Would she remember? He half-hoped not.

And yet, she was so lovable.

Running on the cliff like a ten-year-old. Laughing helplessly at his jokes. Sometimes their ages seemed reversed; she would stroke him, and tell him not to worry.

She often thought he looked worried.

'We all look worried, at my age, April.'

Love was worrying, too.

There was more to April than he thought he wanted (he wanted them to stay in bed all day). She had a history (he hadn't asked her), she would have a future (older, heavier?).

Guiltily, Harold made an effort. He wasn't a shit. He would do her justice.

One evening he programmed himself to ask questions. He asked her about her paintings, her parents, and (quaking inwardly) her politics. He felt much better for asking.

I'm not that bad a chap, he told himself, lifting his eyebrows to HOLD. He sat as the words washed over him.

I care about her as a person, don't I? You could say I'm the New Man.

But he worried about his short memory. He was sure what she said wasn't . . . *boring*. It was just that he'd put a whole evening into it. No wonder he felt tired.

Later her questions began. Very often, the same question.

'Does she do *anything*?' The tone was petulant.

He knew who she meant. He fobbed her off.

'Lottie? She keeps very busy, yes.'

Every few days, she asked again.

'Well what *does* she do?'

When she frowned, the slight squint was less attractive.

'Thing is, you see – she's rather rich.'

April was frankly disbelieving.

'Are you rich then? You don't seem very rich. You don't act very rich – ' (he'd only taken her to pubs).

'No, I'm not rich – '

' – you don't *look* very rich – '

' – *my wife* is rich. On her own account. Family money. They were in the fur trade. Very rich, actually.'

There was no way of saying these things, in England.

'*Shush*,' said April, crossly. He thought it was because he was talking about money. Actually it was because he said 'wife'. Other people in the pub might hear him. She went on talking, elaborately quietly.

'That's all she does, be rich?'

'Well . . .'

It did seem feeble, put like that. Harold hadn't really asked himself the question since he first met Lottie at a Private View, all those years ago. Admittedly then it had seemed very odd that someone so forceful didn't have a job. But once you knew her, it wasn't odd. She was always rushing somewhere: to galleries, films, theatres, shops, lunches, drinks, dinners. Reading or walking or travelling . . .

The catalogue seemed a bit empty. He cast about, feeling absurdly defensive.

'It's different, when people . . . are rich. She's got a lot of interests . . .'

'It must wear her out, having interests.'

The sarcasm was childishly vehement, and her lip curled back from the uneven tooth. But she saw him withdraw, and stroked his arm, and suddenly looked her old self. Her *new* self, her *young* self, the self that he was in this for.

And most of the time she was wonderful company. Certainly a better listener than Lottie. *Certainly* better company than Lottie.

But every so often, quite unpredictably, she plunged into depression. Then the questions began.

'Does she know you're here?'

'I don't suppose she knows about me?'

'Is she . . . fatter than me – *is she fat*?'

'Have you ever been unfaithful before?'

And, oh, he didn't want to talk about the past. It seemed so seedy, in such bad repair. So full of failures and absences.

Bedroom chat was different. It pleased his vanity to drop little titbits about past lovers. April's past was only three loves long. Harold pretended his lovers were countless. She would never see any of the odd scraps of paper on which he made lists of women's names, always appearing in a different order, lists that he made while writing his novel. A basic query he had never resolved: was it nineteen or twenty? On a good day it would come out twenty. Thank you, April, he thought. Now it was twenty, or twenty-one.

'Is it – *nice* – with me?'

'Wonderful.'

He was watching her bathing, late at night.

'Are women . . .do we . . . all feel different? I can't believe we do.'

'*You're* different,' Harold muttered fondly.

'No, but *really*.'

'Really. Of course women are all different.'

She seemed to be waiting for something else. Harold cast about among his memories.

'I knew a woman once who only let me make love to her while she was having her period.'

'Catholic?'

'No . . . she just didn't think contraceptives worked.'

April shrieked with laughter. 'Wasn't it messy?'

'No,' he lied. 'After all, it's quite natural. It's just that men have always bullied women into being ashamed of their bodies.'

Her brown eyes looked impressed.

'I've never done it with my period. But *you* can Harold, if you want to.'

'Hmmm,' he said, not committing himself. She was rather too literal-minded.

There was silence for a few moments. Harold felt perfectly at ease with April when they were silent and he could watch her. Looking down on her now, he vowed, 'I've never seen anyone as beautiful as you.'

She curled in his poky blue bath, very pale in the soapy water, her nipples cloudy red, her hair floating out like fine dark weed in the milky sea all round her.

'My baby . . .'

He sponged her tummy, and his fingers ran through the curls beneath it. 'Little Mermaid . . .' He loved her drowsy, like this.

He had just made love to her twice, which still seemed something of a feat to him. With her he managed the double quite often; with Lottie he never even tried. (With Lottie the first time was good enough. Don't think about her, don't think about that.)

'I used to know that story, *The Little Mermaid*,' she mumbled, curling her toes round the tap. 'Hans Christian Andersen, isn't it? Beautiful story, I seem to remember.'

'*You're* beautiful.' Harold felt humble.

'Did it have a happy ending, that story?'

He didn't answer.

He thought not.

'Sometimes I think you don't listen to me.'

April had insisted on a coffee after her bath, when Harold longed to sleep. As he warned her, it woke her up. Well after midnight, she was still talking.

'Of *course* I listen.'

'Well, I really want to know.'

'I tried to answer you the other day. Lottie *doesn't* work. She's just – lucky.'

'I thought they did charity work, rich women.'

'I can't see her doing charity work.'

He couldn't keep the mockery out of his voice. The target was Lottie, but April was wounded.

'I don't see what's *funny* about charity. If she's got so much money, she could help other people. With famines, and things.'

It was twelve-fifteen. Harold was suddenly impatient.

'April, a famine isn't something you hold on Saturday, like a jumble sale.'

'That's stupid, what you said.' She was very angry. 'I'm not naïve – '

' – *No.* Look, I think we're both just tired.'

(God. She's *exhaustingly* naïve.)

'Well, maybe I am. I ought to go home.'

She said it to be contradicted, but Harold quickly agreed.

Their first real quarrel was already almost over. Things were simpler when you weren't married.

'I'll call you a taxi from the callbox.'

She was very quiet till the taxi came.

'Goodnight, darling. Sleep well. Will you meet me in the Buccaneer tomorrow?'

'Do you want me to?'

'Of *course*.'

As she got into the taxi, he kissed her, glad she was going, glad she would be back.

In bed, he read from *The World of Wonders*, savouring the silence.

Astronomical Wonders

A railway train at the average speed of thirty miles an hour, continuously maintained, would arrive at the moon in eleven months, but would not reach the sun in less than 352 years; so that, if such a train had been started in the year 1512, the third year of the reign of King Henry VIII, it would reach the sun in 1864. When arrived, it would be rather more than a year and a half in reaching the sun's centre; three years and a quarter in passing through the sun, supposing it was tunnelled through, and ten years and one-eighth in going round it. How great these dimensions are may be conceived from the statement that the same train would attain the centre of the earth in five days and a half, pass through it in eleven days, and go round it in thirty-seven days.

The figures amused him, but went terribly slowly.

Everything now goes unimaginably faster. I'd have been courting April for *years*. They didn't even have planes, in those days. They had to imagine space-flight with *trains* . . . we understand so much more than they did . . . Harold felt pleasantly superior.

An odd sub-title attracted his eye.

Curious Fishes

A few years ago, there was exhibited in Piccadilly a 'talking fish', as it was called, but . . . in reality, a seal. It could stand on its tail, and overtopped its keeper. It was amphibious, and a female seal . . . It had a fine dog-like head, and beautiful eyes, sparkling with intelligence, showing that what you said to it was understood . . . It was very docile, and would dance when bidden, rolling itself with great vehemence in its bath. It could say 'Mamma' and 'Pappa' and could call its keeper by his name – 'John'. It could use its fins as hands and arms, and clasp them together in the attitude of supplication . . . Its brain cavity was large, and the brain highly convoluted, being ranked by Professor Owen as the highest of the animal brain types . . . At night it reposed on damp boards, and the species can exist for days out of water; yet this specimen did not live long.

He laid the book aside, with a sigh. Our ancestors were savages. *Not* what he felt like reading at the moment.

He fell asleep thinking about April on their second date, silent, smiling into the sunlight.

In her bedsitter, April lay awake.

She doesn't do anything. Nor does he. And nor have I, since I met him. I'm on at nine, and I'll never get to sleep.

But oh – I love him, I do.

CHAPTER NINETEEN

Long after Bournemouth trees unfolded, the row of horse-chestnuts in Regent's Park is a mass of white and pink cones of blossom. There are animal rides at the Zoo: ponies, camels, a gaily-decorated llama-cart, always something new for Lottie to see.

Today she has stroked the baby elephant.

Dilberta was going walkabout, trotting obediently between her two keepers. People assembled in a ring. A keeper addressed them briskly.

'You'll notice the elephant wears a chain loosely attached from its neck to one of its forefeet.' Lottie hadn't noticed. What a shame, she thought. 'This doesn't restrict her movements at all. It just ensures she is easy to handle as she goes around the zoo. You'll see we also have a hooked stick with which we might tap her lightly on occasion. It's essential that animals be trained if they are to live happily at the zoo . . .'

That's all right then, thought Lottie, though she didn't believe that the chain did not restrict the elephant's movements. It would restrict anyone's movements, having their head chained to their foot. That must be the point of it, restricting the elephant's movements. And very sensible too, she thought, surveying its massive bulk.

'May I stroke her?' she asked the keeper, who nodded, smiling at her breasts. She reached out for its broad, deeply lined forehead, but the elephant jerked away to its right.

'Never mind,' she said, but the man was irritated. He uttered a sharp command in a language she didn't know, then pulled Dilberta hard by her left ear, pulling her back.

Lottie stroked her. It felt wonderfully – *real*: when she touched what had looked like soft dark down it turned out to feel like the bristles of a brush.

The training seemed so clever; the way she heaved down into a kneeling position, back legs canted like falling trees, while the trunk curled upwards in a cheerful loop, an 'OK' sign which seemed aimed at Lottie. Some bits were almost like ballet.

'Can you believe such a heavy animal can balance on two legs with the others in the air?' she asked Davey, when they met at the gate to go home. He had been to the Reptile House on his own.

'Yes,' said Davey grimly. 'Men'll train animals to do anything.'

'Don't be a spoilsport. Surely you can sometimes give credit for something?'

'Why do they get credit for making animals look stupid? Kneeling isn't natural for an elephant. Or standing on half the legs it was born with.'

'I didn't say *natural*, I said clever.'

'Why is it clever to turn an elephant into a fucking ballerina?'

Lottie sat down on a seat, resentful, not unlike the elephant sinking.

'Don't swear so much,' she said. She had somehow got it wrong, as usual. That was where enthusiasm got you, in England. *Fuck* the young. So fucking superior. She remembered something else she had gleaned.

'They talk to it in Singhalese. At least they make an effort.'

'Elephants don't speak Singhalese. Elephants don't *speak*.'

'You think you own this zoo.'

'Wouldn't want to.'

'Liar.'

'You don't understand. It's *interesting*, but – it's not paradise. If the world was different, we wouldn't need zoos.'

'Are you saying that zoos are bad for animals?'

'They're not for animals. They're for people.'

They started to walk home in silence.

Davey was grateful for the silence.

He'd really only suggested this trip to get away from the breakfast table. For a Sunday, she'd been oppressively talkative. But walking turned out to encourage the talking.

Lottie was thinking about what he had said.

'Look, I hate bullying too, you know.' He didn't say anything. 'Admit it, pig.'

'All right.'

It wasn't satisfactory.

The park was satisfactory. Lottie assumed a happy smile, staring with interest at the horse-chestnuts. She couldn't keep quiet for long.

'Why are the red trees always smaller?'

'They're *hybrids*. Not natural. They're not so healthy as the white ones.'

'Why do boys paint their faces these days?'

'It's not just these days. They've been doing it for ages.'

'Well, why? Why does your friend Smeggy, for example?'

'He's Charles' friend.'

'I don't *object*. But he'd look perfectly nice without it.'

She meant he'd be rather gorgeous without it, but kept the thought even from herself.

'Look, dunno. It's a fashion, isn't it?'

'Why don't *you* then?'

Davey said nothing. He watched a pigeon being stalked by a puffed-up, demanding male. Every time the smaller one flapped away, the tyrant goose-stepped in pursuit. It wasn't much fun being the only person around to distract his mother.

He answered, in the end, but didn't look at her.

'People do what they want to, don't they? I might not want to. Don't think I do. Anyway, you'd go spare if I painted myself with spiders' webs like Smeggy.'

'No I wouldn't, darling,' she lied. 'I don't think I'm an old-fashioned mother.' She shook her yellow, youthful hair, and walked a little faster.

She always walked too fast anyway. Davey sighed, and trotted after her.

'Anyway, Mum, what's the big deal? You wear makeup nearly every day.'

Every day, Lottie reflected. Since I've been in my thirties.

'Yes, but . . .'

'Well, why do you?'

'I suppose to look more . . . *exotic* . . . or . . . yes, well, forget it, all right. No reason why he shouldn't.'

Lottie didn't want to go into why she wore makeup. Partly to repair the tiny changes since she was nineteen. Little marks that were no longer temporary, a skin – not *sagging* – but losing its spring. If we could be renewed like trees . . . if it could all just be natural . . .

Sensing her retreat, Davey pressed in.

'Do you agree there's no reason why a *man* shouldn't wear makeup if a *woman* can?'

Lottie stopped, and wrinkled her eyes up at the sun. This sort of trap came more often these days.

'You know I hate all those boring generalizations. I got it from Harold all the time.'

'It wasn't a generalization. It was specific. It was about makeup.'

Lottie couldn't find the words to back her distrust of his proposition. She started walking again, uneasy.

'All right, so what? So men can wear makeup.'

For the rest of the walk she wore a little frown. And when they got home, ten minutes later, she started talking again as if there hadn't been a break.

'It's probably because men have to do jobs. I mean, you'd look mad with makeup in a board room. Smeggy would never in a million years go to an interview in that spider's web business.' She was using her hands in the square, dogmatic way he hated, beating the air as she made her points.

'That's rubbish. Most women do jobs too. You're out of touch, that's your trouble. With what this country's like, I mean. Nearly *everyone* does jobs except you and Harold. And people who can't get one . . .'

'Like Smeggy. There you are! That proves it.'

'Look, Smeggy isn't really looking for a job. He's going to be a vocalist. I told you. He's already made some demos.'

'What? How ghastly. Does he go on demos? I shouldn't have guessed it. He seems quite nice.'

'Demo *discs*. So people can hear his music. Where have you been all these years?'

It was Amanda's day off; Davey always got lunch. He banged knives and forks on to the table. Then he stopped and picked his pair up again.

'Look, I think I'll have my lunch upstairs. I've got a lot of homework to do.'

Her face and stance suddenly changed completely, melted into an attempt at charm. The attempt sagged badly. Her smile wobbled.

'Davey.' The tone was pleading. 'Don't leave me all on my own. You know I hate eating alone . . .' (she knew he knew that wasn't true, and improvised) 'on Sundays, I mean.'

He sighed and stayed. There would be more trouble. She was bored and low and for once he felt he couldn't help her. He didn't want to. He was only sixteen. It just wasn't fair.

She never thinks about *my* problems. I mean, I might be missing Harold too. Of course, I'm *not* (of course I am . . .).

They ate home-made mackerel pâté which Amanda had left. The toast was thin and dry and the pieces kept snapping uncomfortably as Lottie ate.

Davey knew she was brooding. She kept looking up at him, but saying nothing. Then over salad she began her speech.

Everyone she knew had heard this speech. Davey had heard it in all its variants; it never failed to make him cringe. She had some oily lettuce stuck between her teeth and he comforted himself by watching that.

Harold, come back, he prayed. Christ, it's not even summer yet. I'll go mad if you don't come back . . .

CHAPTER TWENTY

Harold didn't really understand what had happened. Things had gone wrong much too soon. He felt as if he'd bought a beautiful new book and the spine had cracked within days.

I only met her in March. Christ, it's not even summer yet.

It really went wrong at Tucktonia. Tucktonia was *his* idea. He'd seen it advertised in the local library. 'Europe's largest model landscape'.

It was a sort of Great Britain in miniature, boasting a Post Office Tower twenty-six feet high. That was pretty high, for a model. (Harold once knew the real Post Office Tower very well, a red-tipped finger pointing up at the sky when Harold walked – home – from Regent's Park. How many hundred feet high? How many miles away?) He thought it would be very amusing.

But April didn't seem to see it that way. She wanted to go to the movies.

'Oh, go on, April, it'll be fun. And we'll get a ploughman's afterwards.'

He doesn't understand, she thought. She'd told Emmy, her friend in Furnishings and Fittings, that Harold was really glamorous. An older man, a writer, a man of taste and culture. What will she think if I tell her he took me to Tucktonia? It's where all the tourists go. Great fat mothers with great fat kids.

'At Tucktonia we aim to ensure that you Have a Nice Day.' The bus dropped them ten minutes' walk from Tucktonia.

'Pity you don't have a car,' said April, hanging a little behind him. 'I suppose you've got one in London.'

'Yes,' he said, but doubtfully.

'Well have you got one or not?'

' – *We* have.'

(Normally he never said *we*; his history had been forcibly cut in two, '*I* went to Morocco,' '*I* have a big garden.') 'Well, actually, there are two. But they're Lottie's – Lottie drives them. It probably sounds odd, but I never learned to drive.'

148

'I learned to drive when I was *seventeen*. Me mum said I'd be useless if I couldn't drive.'

Harold was stung, but there was nothing he could do about it. Useless, he kept on walking. It wasn't an auspicious day; dreary grey clouds which made even April's skin look grey and drained. Her nostrils were inflamed, pinkish. They were silent, except for her sniffing.

A lot of other people had the same idea for getting through Sunday. The coach park they passed looked full. Next to that was a giant amusement park. Harold stared, bemused.

Cars with shrieking youths inside roared round a giant go-kart track. There was a quivering, inflatable rubber castle where children were falling on top of each other, and two boys wearing plastic helmets were blazing away with plastic guns. Definitely not a miniature castle, definitely an *oversized* rubber castle. Next to it there was a sort of spaceship, an obviously non-flying spaceship, emblazoned with stars and stripes and the legend 'ASTRO-LINER' on the side. It looked like a Super Giant Economy-sized tube of toothpaste.

The whole thing looked very wrong; nothing like the place he'd imagined. More American, surely, than British. Though these days you couldn't tell.

April's expression was not encouraging.

'I – er – thought it was meant to be *miniature?'* he asked.

There was definitely scorn in her eyes.

'The Model Great Britain's just a little part of it. It must be round the side. This is the other rubbish.'

There weren't a lot of people queueing to get in to Model Great Britain. April fumbled in her bag.

'I'll pay,' said gallant Harold.

'I hope so. I was only looking for my hankie. They don't pay much, in Bingles.' As soon as she had said it, she regretted it. 'Don't take any notice of me – I've got a headache, that's all.'

But she didn't want an aspirin, thank you: she didn't want a cup of coffee; she didn't want to sit down. She wasn't getting her period – thank you *very* much for asking. And she didn't want to go home – but she sounded less certain of that.

Once they were through the turnstile, Model Great Britain was open and windy. The first thing they passed was two fat women in little felt hats, holding on to them. One of the women had twins, two fat red faces in the same pram. A snatch of words came on the wind.

'It's not much, is it, not really?'

'Norafter what we've seen.'

April didn't try to keep up with him as he strode about, being interested. She hovered in the partial shelter of the grey plastic St Paul's, a miserable grey giant with tangled hair. It was odd looking back and seeing her, huge, lost in a shuffled dream of London.

It must be too early in the season, or else too long since the model was built. Harold looked it up in his booklet. Nineteen seventy-six. The text promised to depict 'Britain's . . . architecture, her natural beauty, her transport and industry, her technological achievements'. The pictures made it look bright and glossy.

But the Model Great Britain of the mid-1980s had suffered some great depression. And pitiless winds, or the blast from some bomb. Lorries lay heavily on their sides which should have been delivering to the miniature Kelloggs' factory. There was a model oil-rig on a real lake, surrounded by tugs, a 'working model'. If you put in tenpence the tugs would put out a fire on the oil-rig, or so the label said, but there wasn't a fire, and the rig looked wretched, pointlessly sprayed with cold water.

Cars in the car park of the Auto-Chef had been tumbled together, some on their roofs. Blue electric trains which ran smoothly, emptily round the perimeter of this strange country only made the desolation sharper. Concorde kept its white nose low as it taxied round the airport, round and round, never able to lift. It looked obsessed, and faintly spiteful.

April spotted something brighter and newer-looking down one end of the landscape. She went towards it hopefully. Its towering chimneys shone among the greyness, on a slightly larger scale than everything else. It dominated the view, from there.

'That looks quite smart,' she said. 'What is it?'

'Some kind of factory.' He wasn't very interested.

'Well, *look it up.*' Her eyes were determined. *He ought to make an effort, if he cares about me.*

He shuffled through the booklet.

'Good God, it's a nuclear power station.' Harold was grimly amused.

'Well, I don't know why you're so pleased about that, I thought you were an Anti.'

'Yes. Oh, never mind, April.'

But she did mind. There was lots to mind.

The trains moved and the planes moved but the people were all dead. The model people of Model Great Britain had been frozen where they stood, many of them in the last convulsions of mystery diseases.

'They all look *drunk*,' said April. She said it as if she had never been drunk. But she giggled a lot at the cricket match, where some of the cricketers were out for the count, flat on their backs on the plastic turf, and others were wildly dancing about, faces lifted to an absent sun. There was a batsman, but the ball had vanished.

Harold's favourite was the wedding. The bride was a tiny trollop with a crimson mouth and coal-black eyes. Her parents appeared to be having a fight and the priest leaned absurdly to the left, trying to touch up the bridegroom. The guests had wandered off, indifferent, and were falling down dead on their own. Meanwhile the church bells tried to toll but the tape had stretched to the point of exhaustion and what emerged was an eerie caterwaul, tired and ominous, never giving up.

'I *hate* all this,' said April suddenly. Her face was thin and set.

'Oh, come on, April.' He tried to put his arm round her. 'You have to see it's funny. I think the whole place is magical. It's a metaphor, don't you see? I mean, Britain *is* like this. Nothing working, and everything going to seed, and all the old rituals going wrong. I think it's simply *classic*.'

She shook him off. 'You're so . . . *superior*.' Her colour was coming back, with temper. 'Why is it funny, things going to seed? Why is it funny, things going wrong? It's all right for people like *you*.'

He was winded, completely taken aback.

'What's the matter? Why are you so angry?'

(So it *was* too good to be true. She had somehow already seen through him.)

But she was too angry to explain. She could only repeat herself. The lack of words brought a rush of tears, clogging her lashes and glazing her cheeks. 'It's all right for *you*! It's all right for *you*!'

'There's a pub next door. Let's go and sit down. Oh, *don't* cry, please don't cry. It was a stupid idea to come.'

The Tucktonia Pub, the Golfers' Arms, was a nightmare of dogs and bags and electronic rock and Space Invaders and shouting people, trying to get drunk enough to drive into a wall before Sunday early closing . . . after he'd fought his way to the bar, leaving her squeezed into a space by the door, he looked round to see if she was all right and caught a look of such blank distress that he plunged straight back towards her, past a gigantic white nylon belly balancing a brown-scummed pint of beer and a riot of teenage girls with mask-like, floury faces and cold black eyes and matted hair which smelled sickly sweet, of banana, seized her pink and human hand and said, 'Come on, we're going home.'

The bus journey seemed to take for ever.

They went to bed and didn't make love. As the sun came weakly through for a troubled sunset, she made him hold her tight.

'You're . . . different from me. I mean, you're from London, and you've got a PhD. And you went to Oxford, and you talk like it. You're used to living in a beautiful house' (he'd never told her it was beautiful) 'and you go to places like – well, I bet you go to that Langan's Brasserie' (she'd read about it in the *Mirror* 'Diary') 'and cocktail bars, and – *Paris*. Wherever you want to go. So for you it's fun to go slumming with me. But your real life's still back there. Well, why shouldn't *I* be part of that? I'm not . . . *common* . . . whatever you think.'

It hurt her to get the word out.

He was horrified, touched, and embarrassed.

'Of course you're not common. I don't know what that means – '

'You're a liar. Everyone knows what it means – '

'Look, I'm hardly of *royal blood*, you know. My mother was a second-rate actress – '

'Actress is posh. My mum does school dinners – '

' – and Lottie may like the high life, but I've always eaten fish and chips, when I could – '

'Well, I eat fish and chips all the time, to save cooking! I'd like never to eat it ever again! I'd like to have a life like *her*, your . . . *wife*! Except that I'd do something, not like her. That's another thing that I hate – ' (she was sitting up now, the bedspread pulled tight across her knees, staring fiercely out of the window; the sunset made a mess of her tear-striped face) – 'you don't have to live in Great Britain, not really. If there's a depression, you just . . . *look* at it, and it's *interesting*, and quite *funny*. You don't have to work, you don't have to live here. You – and her, can just *take off* somewhere. Well I want a life in Britain! And a career! And a future! I don't want all the stores like Bingles to go bust! I like things . . . bright . . . and comfortable . . . and hopeful . . . but they're *not*, are they? That awful place. It was a nightmare. You *made* me go there, you *made* me.'

Stroking, apologizing, plying her with wine, nothing seemed to make it better. The wine made it worse: she drank fast, rather wildly, and became less logical and more angry.

This time he didn't have to ask questions. He learned, in detail, a lot about April. There was more to April than met the eye. He grew increasingly weary of this.

At nine he got up and started putting his clothes on.

'I'd better walk you to the bus stop.'

He couldn't get taxis every night.

That made her start sobbing in earnest, clutching her listing glass to one small hanging breast as she searched for her tights in a fury.

'You're chucking me out! That's typical! You don't give a sod about me as a person! You've just been taking advantage of me!'

'You don't know what you're saying. I really think you'd better go home.'

He was impressed by how cold he sounded. In fact he just felt old and tired.

At the bus stop, puffy and strange under the street lamp, she told him not to bother to wait. He didn't argue, kissed her on the forehead, and walked back, pulling a long hair from his mouth. It lodged unpleasantly under his tongue.

It's all a bit much, he thought. The young are so self-righteous.

CHAPTER TWENTY-ONE

'I must say it's a bit much when my own son starts telling me I don't do anything. *You* don't know what *you* want to do – '

Lottie's hand jabbed with awful regularity. The lettuce trembled on her white front teeth.

'I never said that. I'll change to science, and be an astronomer. Or maybe a tree conser – '

' – *Harold* never knew what *he* wanted to do. I must say it seems just a tiny bit feeble. *I've* never had that problem.'

' – conservationist.'

'Listen to your mother, will you! You *ought* to listen to your mother. That's the trouble with men, they never listen – '

'That's a generalization, if ever I – '

'I was saying, it's never been a problem for me. I could have been anything I wanted. I might have been an actress. Sir Terence Delaney – well he wasn't Sir then, but anyway – *begged* me to test for a role in that play which ran for *six years* in the West End. What was it called? *Maybe* something. When I was *eighteen*. Not much older than you . . . I could have been a journalist, *easily*. Whenever Claudia writes anything, I can see masses of ways it could have been better. I sometimes tell her, not that she enjoys it. Naturally I'm the soul of tact . . . Lots of people say I ought to write books, when they read my letters. They are rather good. I *should* have been an author, I've got the right temperament, I shouldn't waste all my time agonizing, like Harold . . . I could have been in television, too. When I see that ghastly Delia whatsit talking rubbish about paintings, in orange lipstick and spotty dresses, I really itch to put her straight. I mean, she isn't even pretty. Don't look like that, I assure you it's true, I did a diploma in Fine Art, you know – '

'*Everyone* knows, you *tell* everyone – '

' – And it should have been a degree, it was quite *hard* enough to be a degree, but at that time they just called it a diploma, which sounds like a cookery course . . . Where was I?'

'All the things you could have done, much better than anyone else, et cetera.'

Davey said the last half of the sentence so quietly that only he could hear it.

'Hmm. I could have been an art dealer. Years ago Hugo begged me to go into partnership, when he moved into Cork Street . . . I could have done absolutely loads of things. I could have done whatever I wanted.'

Why didn't you then? thought Davey, but all he said was 'Yeah.' The 'Yeah' came out like 'Who says?' How on earth did Harold put up with this? He stared disapprovingly at a tomato, plump and greedy, alone in the bowl.

But Lottie's speech had run down. When she spoke again, her voice was different.

'I know the truth about jobs, you see. They seem very glamorous and splendid from the outside, and everyone oohs and aahs and admires those TV women a lot. Princess Diana, too. A Princess is only a *job*, you know. When it comes down to it, you lose your freedom. You go where they say and do what they say. Look at Claudia – '

'That's not *television* – '

'It's the *media*, it's all the same thing – she's always exhausted, and she says they never print what she actually wrote. It's probably the same with Princess Diana.'

'Then she should give it up. Claudia, I mean.'

'Oh don't be a prig, she *has* to work, Claudia's poor as a rat. Anyway, I think she enjoys it – she wouldn't meet men if she didn't work – '

'Mum! You can't say things like that – '

'Don't interrupt. She's poor, I'm rich. Exceedingly rich – thanks to your grandpa. That's the difference. And I've always had men.'

Usually Mum never mentioned Grandpa. Davey was interested despite himself.

She continued, a little too vehement: 'I've never, ever been bored. It's never been a problem, filling my days.' (Till now, she realized, with Harold gone.)

'How can you be so sure about jobs if you've never actually done one?'

'That's complicated,' said Lottie. But she didn't bite his head off. 'Let's have some coffee, darling.'

Standing in the kitchen, watching the percolator, Lottie talked to Davey as he stood beside her. Not meeting his eyes, it was easier to talk.

She said things she'd never said before about her father, his grandfather. The terrible zeal with which he worked, long after he was a millionaire.

'He'd been so poor, you see. His family was dreadfully poor. And none of the other children made good. Well, think of Great Aunt Evie. And his dreadful old brother, Leonard. He waited till he was already rich before he dared start a family. There was only time to have me. I think he was terrified if he eased up for a second we'd be back in squalor. He didn't see that he'd made us safe. I don't think he ever *could* feel safe . . .'

'So money was all he cared about?' Davey sniffed the coffee.

'Oh no, he didn't *like* money. It terrified him, so he had to control it. The only thing that mattered to him was my mother, your grandma. He really *adored* her. I mean, he was still – quite *besotted* with her, I suppose, when she was in her fifties. And then she died. And the ghastly thing was, he'd gone on slaving with those bloody furs and hardly seen her, day after day . . . Never doing the things he wanted to do. He wasted his whole life. I vowed that wouldn't happen to me . . .'

As she talked of the past, her voice grew depressed. Davey headed her off.

' – You were saying, about jobs. You're clever, Mum, in your way –'

'It sounds as if it isn't a very *big* way –'

'I didn't mean that, I mean, like you said, when you see that Delia woman, or read Claudia's drivel – don't you ever wish you had their job, so you could do it better?'

'No.'

'Just a little bit?'

'Um – *yes*,' said Lottie, pouring coffee, watching the black boil up in the white French bowls. 'To be truthful, yes, a bit. But you see, when I finished the diploma, I fell in love with your father. And then I had you. You were quite a handful. The nannies kept leaving, like servants do. And Carl didn't want me to work. We just had fun – well *he* did, especially – and travelled. And by the time we were through, I was already twenty-four. Believe it or not, it seemed quite old. And I didn't *have* to work. There was *pots* of money. And maybe I didn't want to fail.'

Stirring in cream, licking the spoon, enjoying the thickness of the stuff on the silver. Darling boy. She put her arm round him, and squeezed, and Davey smiled at her.

I underestimate her.

Yet, he wanted to get away.

She thought his smile had a tinge of pity, and when she spoke again she was brisker. She looked through the window into her garden. The sun was out, the roses were out, the birds were singing, sharp and sweet.

'I've lived my life as I chose to. Nobody's pushed me around. How many of the feminists can really say that? They'd like to make me feel guilty, though. It's just another kind of *duty*, the things they're talking about. It's all invention; you *ought* to have a job, you *oughtn't* to get married, you *oughtn't* to like men. You shouldn't ever listen to oughts. You should listen to the voice inside your own head.'

It was rousing, but Davey wasn't convinced. She's always telling me what *I* ought to do. *You really ought to listen to your mother.* How often have I heard that?

Her voice had gone quiet again. 'I enjoy – *every day.*' He didn't like the sound of that moved little quaver. She thought, it *used* to be true. 'The world's so *interesting.* And when I met Harold, I think I convinced him' (*thought* I'd convinced him) 'we could live that way. Oh, he could write his books. But live for pleasure . . .' (almost inaudible) '. . . and each other. Well. It sounds stupid now.'

Davey was absolutely cringing. Was that the lot? Please let me go.

She drank a great gulp of coffee, gasped, and added more cream.

'But don't misunderstand me. I'm the luckiest person I know.'

(She *would not* let Harold defeat her. She could still make it true.)

Davey jumped and spilled his own coffee as she suddenly slammed her coffee bowl down on the table.

'Maybe *PARIS!* That's it!'

'Wha . . .?'

'That Terry Delaney play. The one he begged me to star in. The title, the one I forgot. Look, I think that's the answer. Darling Davey,' (she was radiant, hugging him, so more hot splashes jumped up his arm) 'will you be all right with Amanda for a bit if your mother goes to Paris? I think I deserve a break. Paris in spring. How corny. How lovely.'

And so it was settled, as simply as that.

Next afternoon, she was on the plane, in a private atmosphere of Je Reviens. She had sprayed it everywhere, arms, knees, ears. Her makeup was immaculate. White frosted eyeshadow, clear pink lipstick. She'd dressed for Paris and happiness, in draped white jersey with a huge white hat, Schiaparelli-inspired, shaped like a swan. It was rather a nuisance, even in First Class, but one made an effort; one shone. She rose on the bubbles of a huge white gin. The steward was clearly in love with her, and the clouds were as white as her hat's long feathers.

I'm the luckiest person on Earth.

And summer is well on its way, in the little island that Lottie leaves. Trees are thick with rank white may. Clouds of it shadow the creamy cow parsley. Hedges and ditches are dense with leaf. The cuckoo sings all day.

At twilight, the long-eared bat is flying, carrying her solitary infant with her wherever she goes, clinging tightly to her fur, and as she chases moths, he suckles.

Hard to remember the emptiness, above the bats, the birds, the clouds, above the plane where Lottie flies, immensely lucky, on a foam of bubbles.

Very small, and very light.

One in a billion trillion trillion.

1 in 1,000,000,000,000,000,000,000,000,000,000,000.

June

CHAPTER TWENTY-TWO

The middle month of our year. The sun is 'at its highest', viewed by sun-lovers in tiny Europe, spinning helpless round the sun.

Ninety-three million miles away, over a million times as large as Earth, it moves the Earth, the lovers, love.

Ninety-three million miles away, life on Earth faints in the heat. Horse-chestnut flowers spread and fade, becoming yellow ghosts.

Other things ripen. Tiny cherries start to be flushed with pink. Grass grows tall; the mower needs to be oiled again.

This is the month of scent. Wall-flowers smelling of oranges, tobacco-flowers smelling of cool vanilla. Everywhere in the air, cut grass.

Daisies follow the sun, dotted like milk across the lawns and fields. On all the grass in England, no one can count how many.

In the Milky Way, our galaxy, astronomers guess at the numbers of stars.

Compared to space, the stars are rare.

Around four hundred thousand million stars in the Milky Way – 400,000,000,000 stars.

In the solar system there is only one.

For Harold, there is darkness.

He is walking back from the bus stop on one of the blackest nights of his life. Not a ray of hope, not a gleam.

Every second, billions of solar neutrinos, tiny particles sent from the sun, shoot towards him, go straight through the planet, straight through Harold, effortlessly on.

Two months ago, Harold knew about that. Now he is wretched, and forgets.

The bed is disgusting, wrinkled, grey. Bottles, glasses. No energy. He has another glass, eats a tin of sardines, and crawls into bed. He sleeps instantly, heavily, but wakes too early to a taste of metal.

All day he skulks inside. The first of June, with a hangover. It isn't a beginning, but another messy ending.

I'm a messy person, he thinks. Now I've messed up another chance.

But it's only Lottie I care about. I'll do anything if she'll take me back (but if she won't, will April? How can I make it up to her?)

☆

His books, so shining with life and detail only – a month, *two months* ago – over two months since he'd *really* read them – now seemed almost irrelevant. He picked up *Cosmos*, but the numbers of stars and the numbers of miles between the stars blew like so many grains of sand. He tried Kaufmann's *Stars and Nebulas*, instead.

> An eclipsing binary is a double star oriented so that the two stars alternately pass in front of each other. Usually astronomers discover eclipsing binaries by noting that the brightness of a single-appearing star exhibits periodic, temporary depressions . . .

Harold dozed, a tiny man running down a very long promenade, looking for someone lost in the distance, but the sand blew across and concealed the end.

Waking, he saw it was six o'clock.

He ran up the steps of the pub, picked up the phone and before fear could stop him, dialled her number, *his* number, *their* number.

'Yes?' It was Davey, sounding suspicious.

Harold felt a rush of love.

'It's *Harold*, Davey.'

'Oh. Yes.'

Definitely hostile. Harold pressed on.

'Can I speak to Lottie, please?'

160

'You took your time.'

'Davey – *please*.'

'Well, she's not here.'

'*Davey, please*.'

'I said, she's gone. She's gone away. I haven't a clue when she'll be back.'

'Oh.' Stunned.

'You forgot her birthday.'

'Oh NO . . .'

'Yes. Well done, Harold.'

'What do you mean she's gone away? She can't go away without telling you when she'll be back. I don't believe you.'

'It's the same as what you did, isn't it?'

The question was quiet but extremely – *blaming*. There'd been enough guilt, today. Harold wanted to cry.

I forgot her birthday.

The pips went for another 10p.

'Hang on, I'll put in another 10p – '

The coin jammed, then went straight through, then the phone started howling, unobtainable. He tried again, but it was either engaged or off the hook.

Two people were queueing, too close for comfort. One looked a bit like Francis from the Bella Costa, but he had a huge growth on his cheek. He was chewing something, and the growth shifted. He stared at Harold, meaningfully.

Harold picked up his coins and went away.

For the rest of the evening he sat alone, hugging the pain of his love for Lottie. I never realized how much I loved her. You never do, until someone's gone.

And he listened, stupidly, for the doorbell, listened, although it was hopeless, for April, come by bus to forgive him. No one rang, no one came.

He lay in bed, still listening.

An idea came with the wakefulness. How much money did he actually have? Around three thou in his deposit account. In the building society, maybe seven. I could do it, if I want. In the lonely night, he definitely did.

Smelling of Aramis and a dozen roses, and wearing his tightest jeans, Harold went up the escalator at Bingles during the lunch-time rush.

Fancy Goods . . . Leisurewear . . . *Furnishings and Fittings* . . .

Somewhere in that lot, Art would be. He walked through shelves of glittering dishes and vases, walking gingerly lest his great prow of roses poke the whole lot to the floor.

Past a painted menagerie of porcelain animals, oversized pussy-cats and puppy-dogs, tiny winsome lions and tigers, egg-shaped owls without feet or wings. A powder-blue elephant pirouetted happily on its stand. These were the *Ob Jay*, then.

And – there she was, and there was the Art.

IS YOUR CHILD A PICASSO IN THE MAKING?

She was straightening paintboxes in the display, with the question posed above her. A second later, she looked up and saw him. She was Crimson Lake, with Rose Madder highlights.

'Oh . . .' she said, then her mouth stayed open.

'There's a note in this envelope, asking you something. Read it and tell me what you think.'

He kissed her cheek. She looked strange and lovely in a high-necked white blouse and navy skirt (April hardly ever wore a skirt) and her hair was wound up in a complicated coil. For once she looked all of twenty-three.

'Will you meet me in the Buccaneer after work?' he asked, made timid by her novel air of propriety.

'Where do you think I'm going to put these?' she asked, waving the roses doubtfully. But really she was gratified. Emma watched them, boggle-eyed. The Van Gogh 'Sunflowers' she was trying to sell wavered and sank on the counter.

In the Buccaneer she was radiant, the April of their first evenings.

'When are we going?' she asked. '*Paris*. Oooh Harold, how *lovely*.'

'How long could you take?'

'I get five weeks. But I usually save two for Christmas . . .'

'Three weeks would be all right,' said Harold hastily.

Three weeks would cost a packet, in a decent hotel.

'No, don't be silly, I'll take it all. We can really get to know each other. Oh, I don't *believe* this!' She kissed him full on the lips, so sweetly that tenderness rose in him.

'You're very lovable,' he said. (Too good for me, much too good.)

'Do you love me then?' she asked, the focus of her dim brown eyes just short of him.

He hesitated for a fraction of a second; baulked; yielded – and was lost.

'Yes,' he said, unhappily, but the jukebox covered the unhappiness.

As lovers do, as lovers will, they travelled hopefully to Paris.

Harold had wavered between one-star and two-star and settled on a two-star hotel. The stars, however, did not blaze. The lobby smelled very faintly of cabbage, though the restaurant only offered breakfast. But they had their own bathroom and WC and a sunny, blowing window, curtains of delicate spotted white voile through which they could see it shining; Paris, silvery, still surprising, three long floors below.

'Oooh Harold. It's just lovely.'

And for all the weeks that stretched ahead, lovely, he thought, it will have to be.

April's endless energy. Paris affected her like neat spirits. The hangover never came.

'French men seem to like me. Maybe I have a Parisian look,' she told him, smiling as she smiled all day. Whenever they were parted, even just for an hour, it seemed that at least three Frenchmen approached her.

Harold didn't think she looked at all Parisian. But he did feel proud, and so he should, bald but distinguished in café windows, swinging in the evening down Boul' Mich' with her on his arm, hair flying loose.

She was fascinated by the tall blacks who sold mechanical birds which really flew. Those graceful men made a beeline for April. Their instinct was right; her strange brown eyes swung after the blue-and-white or green-and-white or white-and-gold wings which were whirling, whirling – against the grey attics – against the pink sky – then clattered earthwards.

These demonstrations never hurt the birds. To her it was miraculous. Each time one landed near her (as intended by the gleaming salesmen) she glanced at Harold briefly, though she never explicitly asked him to buy one.

'They're tourist things,' he said. He found them threatening, the coal-black men so impeccably sheathed in pale skins.

Where did they come from, where did they go? They couldn't be young in Paris for ever.

And nor can we. But she was so happy.

Where would they go in winter?

'They're beautiful,' said April. 'Harold, I'm so happy.'

She would see *everything*, all *today*. She walked for miles on her slim pale feet, which soon became very brown.

'In Bournemouth you weren't all that keen on walking,' he remarked one day at breakfast.

'Oh, *Bournemouth*,' April said, dismissively. 'Bournemouth isn't Paris. I want to go to one of those cemeteries. The special ones with tombs like houses. That American lady told me on the landing.'

'It's a good idea. But not today. Today you said you were going to go to the Jeu de Paume and the Orangerie.'

'Oooh yes, let's go.'

Her amazing smile. At other tables, there were solitary men, men like Harold had been in Bournemouth. He knew how they must envy him. It was all so different when you were alone. In January at Mrs Limone's he had been obsessed with the other couples. Maybe he had imagined them; Bride and Groom, Violet and Pamela.

'What are you thinking about?'

Not his favourite question. 'People you don't know. Nothing important. What did you say?'

'Let's go to the Jeu de Paume this morning.'

'Thing is, April – I've been there rather often. I thought – well, I humped along all those books. I thought I might do a bit of reading.'

She pouted, but made a bargain.

They had sometimes eaten bread and charcuterie and cakes in their room for supper. This was not her idea of Parisian romance, though he said it was *très typique*.

'Will you take me out for dinner?'

'Yes.'

'But properly, I mean. A proper *meal*, not steaks and *frites*. A *treat.*'

Was it greedy or was it touching? Ugly or innocent? Sour or sweet?

In any case, to refuse was ugly.

'Yes, darling. It can be a treat.'

She kissed him, thoughtless as a bird landing, once, twice, and then flew off in her thin blue t-shirt and tight white jeans.

June was all around her.

CHAPTER TWENTY-THREE

I'm not really sure I should ever have married, thought Lottie, sitting up slowly and yawning as the maid in her delicious black and white uniform bent to draw the curtains. Little white bow, biggish black bottom. No wonder men fantasize about maids.

The coffee she had brought smelled particularly good. Lottie grinned companionably at the woman, who was in her mid-thirties, basically a peasant, large-breasted, with knowing dark eyes, and dimples.

She's the sort of woman men like, like me, Lottie thought. I'm basically a peasant, too.

The peasant who heaved herself upright on the enormous frilled and monogrammed pillows looked benignly on the other peasant.

'*Merci mille fois,*' said Lottie.

Three hot gold crescents of bread, reeking of butter, flaking in her fingers.

All for me if I want them. Really, I *love* being on my own.

The crumbs fell on and off the tray. Lottie thought with wonder, as she often did, how impossibly messy other lives must be. If the mess just lay where people left it. Hers never did, that was the blessing . . .

Marriage was my mistake. Even Davey, much as I love him.

Having to look after him, day after day, *thinking* about him, *worrying* about him – (Lottie frowned slightly; hard to think of the *precise* duties she performed for Davey) – was a frightful bore. You didn't think of all that when you gaily went ahead and had children.

Thank God she had thought of Paris. She'd been feeling *crushed* by the weight of it: that great house, floors and floors of things and people all looking to her for animation, Amanda dreary in her basement, Davey dreamy in his attic . . . Lottie had to carry the lot. And a teenager wasn't easy. And as Amanda got older, she seemed to get more moody.

Lottie sighed, and dug into her second croissant, lavishly,

luxuriously. How many times had she asked Amanda to find a shop which sold truly French croissants? How many times had Amanda palmed her off with inferior imitations? You would think Amanda had never been to France . . .!!

I suppose it's just possible she hasn't. Nevertheless, she is *very* trying.

Here, in the third most expensive hotel in Paris, Lottie would not be tried. She could think of *herself*, for once. She started her third croissant.

Paris in June was the perfect place (except for the English tourists).

The sky was blue, cloudless, or the most frivolous pastry-cook's curl of cloud. The long beds in the Luxembourg Gardens blazed with clear-edged, paintbox colours. The first June roses were Crimson Lake. The horse-chestnut trees were a mass of green as the white flowers yellowed, crumbled away and the petals lay on the ground like confetti, blowing a little in the summer wind.

The humans also appealed to Lottie. Parisian youth was freshly stripped, excited by the first really hot sunlight, skins in the early prime of what were going to be deep brown tans. And they did undress so well, in amusing layers of cotton and linen cut away from the body to be free and cool. They were all too skinny, of course . . .

(But then, Smeggy was skinny. And Smeggy was very attrac . . .)

Lottie shifted, briefly, in the silly but stylish cane chair in Le Départ. She shivered, although it was hot. She was having a coffee and *fine*, and she swigged one after another to make it burn her, to teach her a lesson.

Don't be stupid. How old are you? You can't go fancying a kid like that.

But the brandy expanded in her bloodstream till she let the little mouse-thought out again, patted it with a slow cat's paw.

Yes, I really do fancy that boy.

She wandered slowly up Boul' Mich', a little merry, a little dizzy, admiring *everything*, the red of the awnings, the chinks of light on lifted glasses, the bright green wings of the plane-tree leaves which the five o'clock sun poured through. Long sticks of golden bread wove home from work, stuck under the arm of an overalled workman with five o'clock shadow, broken and nibbled by a yellow-pony-tailed girl.

Early evening in June, with so much still to come.

I love life, Lottie thought. *I'm lucky. Give me a long, long life.*

Who did she tell? Who did she ask?

Lottie did have her idea of God, or rather her sense of 'something there'. God was something you saw and felt, not something you could think out. Lottie's God was the sum of things, the *rightness* of the world. In the fan of pale veins on the plane-leaves, in the fan of pale yellow from the pony-tail, in the bright brass rims of the circular tables, the gilded lips of the glasses. Everything connected, everything sang, everything told her that she was happy, and full of desire, and young . . . and that somewhere, God applauded.

Men tried to catch her eyes as she wandered, leisurely, half-smiling, up the street. She combed her curls with her fingers, pouting at herself in a *pâtisserie* window.

'Mignonne,' whispered a tall, ridiculously sharp-suited pimp of a man. His shoulders were padded to an acute angle and his shirt was striped like a barber's pole. She caught a brief smell of marzipan which seemed just right for his yellow sugary skin and oiled dark eyebrows. In fact, it came from an open stall of Tunisian sweetmeats, and she stopped to look. She nearly applauded the colours: coral pinks, sand yellows, pistachio greens.

Was she hungry or was she randy?

June, she suddenly realized, January, February, March, April, May – it's June already. *I haven't had sex for over five months.* Christ, I should hope I'm randy!

And she smiled very beautifully, tickled to think that she knew what she wanted and needed next, at a tall, Germanic-looking, fleshy man who was guiding his girl into a restaurant. Surprised, he stared at Lottie, speculating, and his arm fell away from the thin girl's shoulders – *they really don't like them that skinny, do they?* – but just at that moment the thin girl turned and her unremarkable, unpainted eyes had a look of such hurt and worry that Lottie walked on, ashamed.

Round the corner she flashed her smile again and was satisfied with three successes.

The sun was dipping behind the high elaborate attic storeys. She stared up towards some carved dormer windows and a dim pink curtain moved as she watched, blinked, whispering *private lives*. Paris was the city of private lives. London was shops and offices. (The curtain closed; she was left outside.)

I'm ready for a little private life. To be naked, in a high room with someone, the last red sunlight, the last glass of wine . . .

Suddenly Lottie wasn't quite so happy. Suddenly Lottie was just a little envious. Oh well, I'm hungry, she thought. I'm hungry, after all.

At the hotel, the receptionist called out to her as she passed. It always vaguely affronted her pride when someone addressed her in English, but these girls liked to show off their English. Probably fresh from college. *I went to college too. And I am almost bilingual.*

'Mrs Segall, there is a telephone for you.'

'*Now*? Oh – you mean a message.'

Something exciting. She unfolded it.

Monsieur Hugo Gatling telephone. He will retelephone this evening.

'We don't say that, you know. It isn't English, "retelephone".'

'Sorry? Oh, Madam, I didn't write.'

Lottie showered, playing the warm water over her nipples, her back, up between her legs. England, she thought. Hugo. He's the last person I want to see.

And when he re-telephoned, she was short.

'Well, how did you . . .? Oh, I see. Well, just this once you've struck lucky, Hugo. I hate to be thought predictable.'

Hugo had remembered her choosing this place when *he* brought Lottie to Paris. For a long weekend, four years ago.

'Different rooms though, thank God,' she told him.

'That's not very complimentary, darling. I remember you with great . . . fascination.'

The way he said that was very unpleasant. He is gloating over having slept with me.

'You're a dirty old man, Hugo. I can hardly remember you at all!'

Hugo gamely tried to recover. But when he had offered her a choice of lunch and dinner for the twenty-one days he would be in Paris on business, and she had committed herself to none, he rang off rather briskly.

He sat and thought of the Bonnard.

She sat and thought of quite different things, in her suite with its view of the sunset. She pulled off her blouse, which was clingy and hot, and smoked a cigarette. Then she pulled up her skirt and pulled down her pants over strong white muscular thighs, kicked her feet free, and her fingers stroked and teased and worked till she came, with a long, convulsive peasant's groan.

Lottie's God was also in the force of that.

CHAPTER TWENTY-FOUR

It must be nearly midsummer.

By evening, Harold and April's third-floor room was extremely hot, even with the windows pushed wide. Harold had been reading in there since breakfast. Harold spent much of his time like that. Normally the heat made him sleepy, but today he was gripped by god-like excitement.

What had fired his imagination was time, or rather, Time. He had just discovered he was living more or less at the centre of the lifespan of the solar system. Five billion years down, five billion years to go.

And man evolves now, so something is alive which can watch the pattern of life on earth. What's gone and what's to come (or bring the whole process to an end, of course . . .).

But the first idea was so thrilling: Man the Observer of the Universe. It's enough to make Man believe he is God.

And Woman too, he hastily added as he heard April's running feet on the stairs. His heart sank just a little. He wouldn't finish his chapter, now.

'Darling! I had a wonderful time. You should have come.' She jumped on top of him, sat on his lap in the fragile chair, took the book from his hands, kissed him.

'God! It's awfully hot in here. Have you been in all day? It's practically *unbearable.*'

Her voice implied he was unhealthy, and lazy. Harold felt defensive.

'I've been working. Look – there's some wine by the window. Pour yourself a glass. Do you mind if I finish my chapter?'

Her face changed. She didn't say anything. He retrieved his book and stared at the page. Peripherally, he was watching April, banging the wine and the glass about.

'The wine's *warm.*' Her voice was petulant.

'Sorry.' Why should I be sorry?

'Don't be stupid. It's not your fault.'

Silence. He tried the page again.

'Still, I think . . . never mind.' She stopped.

'Oh don't be so maddening. Finish your sentence.'

'I think – you might have poured me some.'

(Her accent had shifted subtly; she had become a lady.)

He put down his book with elaborate patience.

'*April*. Please don't let's have a row. Look, I'll have a drink as well. I mean, I'll come and pour it myself – ' (but she was already pouring it) ' – oh, thank you, darling. You're looking marvellous. Tell me about your day.'

She couldn't decide whether to sulk or not.

'Well, it looks as though you'd rather read your book. I suppose what I've done is boring to you. You've heard it all before. Like you said, you've seen the – ' she flushed as she tried to pronounce it right, and pronounced it worse than usual ' – JerdePaume lots of times. Well, it was marvellous to me.'

Guilt caught at him, and age.

'April, I do want to hear about it.' He stroked her hair, tangled from walking. 'Tell me about it, please. And I'll brush your hair, if you want me to.'

That was an inspiration. She'd adored it when he did it before, told him he was a 'smashing fellow'. None of her 'other blokes' had ever done that.

He started brushing, she started talking. But today it didn't work. The brushing stopped him listening properly; he kept on catching the brush on knots and in the end she said sharply, '*Stop*. Look it's not your fault but it really hurts.'

She often said things were not his fault; it usually seemed to mean that they were. He drank his warm wine, rather wearily.

But the wine (a generous tooth-beaker each, and another half for April) restored her good temper, or lifted a layer of resentment, released the romantic hope. Slightly *frantic* romantic hope.

He sneaked a glance at his watch. Half-past seven. She'd been talking for an hour! Gently, he tried, 'I'm hungry, darling.'

'Yes, so'm I. Where are you taking me?'

Christ. He had forgotten to book.

She bit his cheek, lightly, playfully, and pressed her hand against his penis. Both things were actually rather painful.

He made a gigantic effort. '*Surprise*. Somewhere quite different. You'll love it.'

Her hand was squeezing mercilessly. She obviously meant to

be erotic, but the penis is not an indiscriminate organ.

'I think we'd better get ready, April. These places do fill up.'

'I have to get changed though, Harold.'

'You look absolutely lovely as you are.'

'But this is supposed to be a treat! *You're* going to change, aren't you?'

Yes, he evidently was going to change.

It was difficult, pulling clean jeans on. They stuck to his sweaty skin in the heat. He had a feeling it wasn't enough. So he put on his fashionable baggy blue shirt, so comfortable he'd never believed it was fashionable, though Lottie had always insisted it was, and stared at himself in the mirror.

It looked a little – *bare*. She was flitting about, entirely absorbed, adding earrings and bangles and perfumes and shawls. Accessories, that's what I need, thought Harold. He tried a navy-blue spotted scarf knotted casually at the neck. But he looked like a phony portrait-painter, a refugee from the Place du Tertre. April would probably like it, having no grasp of kitsch. He pulled it off. He had his pride.

Then he had an idea: *dark glasses*. Everyone else wore them. He'd bought a rather nice pair in Bournemouth to impress April in the early days. He always forgot to wear them – besides, he rarely went into the sunlight. But for evening – *yes*. Sexy, mysterious, distinguished.

She was still far from ready. She seemed to be painting her toenails. He picked up *The World of Wonders*.

> *Spectres of the Air.*
> No organ is so liable to deception as the eye . . .

'Oh, Harold – you look like a film-star.'

This was going to be fun after all. She looked very pretty, if a little – 'April, you look very pretty. Are you ready now, or what?'

'I shan't be a minute, Harold.'

> Eastern travellers often tell scarcely credible tales of the mirage of the desert. Suddenly in the distance, where all is known to be arid sand, appears a sheet of water . . .

'I'm ready now.'

'Miraculous.'

His stomach yearned for Eastern food. Couscous, he thought. A mountain of food. He'd take her to a good couscous place and they would stuff themselves silly.

Following her downstairs, as he had often followed Lottie. White cheesecloth dress; gold sandals; gold Italian bangles; musky scent; white shawl; a synthetic, lacy affair. He added it up. Not at all like Lottie. April looked – less expensive. April looked a little *cheap*.

He chose the dearest couscous place he knew. No one should say he stinted. It was suitably dim, if a little too warm. She settled herself at a corner table. Her whites looked prettily pale in this light. Other men looked at her.

'Comfortable?'

'Yes . . . it's nearly all Arabs, here.'

'Well, that's a good sign. It's like Chinese restaurants. You know they're good if they're full of Chinese customers.'

'Yes, I suppose so. It's just . . .'

'What's the matter?'

'I suppose I was thinking of something more *Paris*. Oh never mind, Harold, this is fine, really.'

It soon became clear it wasn't fine.

They had ordered two Couscous Impériales. They arrived looking lavish, whole landscapes of food, mountains of golden couscous supporting hamlets of steaks and chops and long felled trees of *merguez* sausage.

The first mouthful was as dim and warm as the dim warm room of the restaurant. She ate for a bit in silence, then she laid her fork on the plate.

'Harold, this is *cold*.'

Meanly, Harold denied it. He was actually hungry enough not to care till the first hunger was sated.

'Mine's all right, darling.'

But the more he ate, the less certain he was. There was a layer of congealed white fat on the chop and the grains of couscous were like cooling sand. There were yards of it left. He drank deeply, and tried.

'I hope you're enjoying that.' The tone was derisive.

'Yes I am . . .' (I'm a liar) '. . . why?'

'Because you've hardly spoken a word to me, Harold, since we sat down in this restaurant.'

God, it was true. But so *unreasonable*. He'd had the bloody awful food to think about.

'Well, what would you like to talk about?'

'That's a stupid question. I can't tell you that. You ought to *want* to talk. Of your own accord. Normal people don't sit in silence.'

Harold thought of all the normal married couples he knew who sat in silence, much of the time. With Lottie there had sometimes been silence. Mostly – a *companionable* silence. Silent, he ate to an abrupt full stop.

'Look, darling, I'll order some coffee.'

'You haven't offered me a dessert.' Her face was crumpling over her wine glass. 'You *said* this would be a treat!'

The fatty aftertaste combined with despair. Harold spoke to stop her voice rising. 'April, you're being childish.'

'How dare you call me childish!' Her voice rose quite unstoppably up towards the dangerous shadows of the ceiling.

Oh no, she's going to cry. The silent couple (normal, married?) eating bravely at the next table were surely listening, heads tilted.

I suppose we're both drunk, thought Harold. But how do I ever get out of this? What have I got myself into?

He ordered foolishly lavish ice-creams, designs of banana and sticky custard with horrible labia of frilled cream which turned out to taste of dust. They lay and melted, uneasy. April was telling him what she felt. She felt enormously, desperately. The sentences were confused.

He tried to think about stars. The stars were clear, and brilliant. But they couldn't help; too far away. Dim warm food piled over them.

Then the door opened, and the night came in. It was a dark, gipsyish woman clutching a sheaf of dark-looking rosebuds. She was selling them for thousands of francs, he bet. Just let her try that on me, thought Harold. They ought to protect you, in restaurants.

She was hovering at his elbow. An incongruous smell of cough sweets. Her face was ravaged and wrinkled, its lines all etched in black.

Suddenly he felt a sharp pain on his shin. He looked up at April, unbelieving. Her mouth was a line of fury, her eyes grown small and hard as stones.

But her voice was torn, with a sob in it.

'Why don't you buy me one, bastard?'

Ashamed and frightened, the bastard did.

So when Lottie, who was eating at the Closerie des Lilas, sitting outside in the leaf-bright light, pleasantly gorged with the taste of *foie gras*, veal and a crisp little *tarte aux poires*, looked up from her plate of *petits fours* and saw them stroll past her, arm in arm, the pain which clutched and squeezed at her heart came mainly from the red rose April carried, held to her cheek, with her other young cheek (she's a *teenager!*) buried in Harold's shoulder.

It can't be. Of course it isn't. No.

They were already level – his beautiful mouth, fine nose, but why is he wearing dark glasses? – then past her – his long slim legs, his bottom. He seemed to turn and stare straight at Lottie. But the strange girl laughed and pulled him back.

The final image was that long straight hair, such – carefree hair. So *painfully* young.

CHAPTER TWENTY-FIVE

The body sprawled on top of him. He lay there thinking, trying not to think. He would never eat couscous again. He would never drink wine again.

The scene in the restaurant was bad enough but it all got worse after the sickening, breathtaking moment when he thought he saw Lottie (as if it could have been Lottie . . . if only. If only.) Sitting alone and confident in the Closerie des Lilas. So utterly *unlike* April. Who at that moment, grimacing with grief, had tugged his arm.

'What are you staring at? She's probably a prostitute, sat all on her own like that.'

Harold spoke dully, gasping. 'I think it's . . . I thought it was . . .'

But he kept on walking, into the night.

'What's the matter? *Tell* me.'

'I thought it was . . . *my wife* . . . if you really want to know.'

He hadn't been able to look at her.

After that, she utterly lost control. When they got back, she'd demanded, with pathetic *hauteur*, that he make love to her.

He couldn't make love to her. The penis is a discriminating organ. He felt he would never make love again. And then she'd started to weep. She seemed to weep most of the night.

He held her, helplessly, listening to the sounds of a fight somewhere in the distant streets, the wind groaning, occasional sobs and hiccups from the water pipes.

What are we doing here? She lay upon him like a corpse.

That night he did not sleep. Even an hour of sleep would have helped him, an hour of escape from April. An hour, just an hour on his own.

In Poole, on a cold and windy night, Sylvia worried about her son. She had indigestion again: lately it had disturbed her sleep. She pulled the covers up over her chest and hoped that Harold was all right. That flat had looked so windy, so empty, so horribly alone. And he hadn't rung her for two or three weeks.

He always rings on Sundays. He's a good son, really, is Harold. So what can be wrong? Maybe he's gone back to Lottie . . . it wouldn't be such a bad thing. Impossible girl, but I suppose she loved him. And I don't want Harold to be lonely. I've spent too much time myself being lonely.

She imagined him lying awake, alone, and decided she'd write to him, tomorrow, and planned the letter as she lay in the dark, with some kind of heartburn, awake, alone.

Every morning April woke too early. The spotted voile curtains didn't keep out the light and he'd offered to screen the window with a blanket so she could sleep a little longer. The offer didn't go down well.

'Look, I don't want to live in a tent. This is luxury, to me. I like things to be nice. Don't spoil it. I know you're trying to help . . .'

'I just don't want you to get too tired.' (I just don't want to be so tired myself.)

'Look, Harold, it's not your fault. Anyway, I wake up with my tummy.'

Harold knew that particularly well. The en suite bathroom had cardboard walls. Every sound came through, with certain amplifications (at least, he hoped they were amplifications). She had clearly been having diarrheoa for days . . . She wouldn't discuss the problem.

'Upset tummy again?'

'Yes, but it's all right, thanks.'

Harold wasn't used to people being prudish. Lottie and he had happily discussed the little triumphs and defeats of their bowels. The curious thing was the *power* of prudishness. If she couldn't mention it, nor could he.

What strangers they really were, trying to live so closely. Although the room should have been full of light – it gave on to long bright prospects of street, tempting balconies, trees like fountains – it began to feel small and close and dark. Except, he realized, when she wasn't there.

Could they have been here for only three weeks?

Could they possibly survive for five?

He tried his best to be what she wanted. He shaved off his sideburns, which she said were dated. He splashed on Aramis every day. But he knew that the central thing was missing.

He didn't adore April. He didn't love April. And as the weeks went by he thought he didn't much like April.

More immediate problems consumed him. The money was going too fast. April was surprisingly amenable when he said they must move to a smaller hotel. Perhaps she had been afraid he would say they must go home.

It turned out to be easier, in some respects, with the WC at the end of the landing. They looked out over the roof of the kitchen, and two wires came from the wall like worms, red and white worms which had eaten the light that should have been over the bed – but, 'it's nearer the Louvre,' he pointed out. 'And I think this bed is bigger.'

'I didn't mind a small bed. I like to be close to you.'

But the protest was quite subdued, and she'd taken to going out more on her own, with less preliminary complaint.

He tried to encourage picnics. The evenings were light and long.

'You know we quarrel in restaurants.' *You know it costs too much.*

'We don't *have* to quarrel.'

'But picnics are nice. Look, I promise – I'll see to everything. I promise I'll get some delicious food. I promise it'll be fun.'

The final picnic, however, was different; April was actually keen to go. It was lunch-time, which seemed more suitable for picnics. They were going to the wonderful cemetery she'd wanted to see for ages, Cimetière de l'Est. She was taking her (almost empty) sketchbook. Harold arranged the food. A carton of celery *remoulade*, a tender little Neufchâtel cheese from the market, tasty tomatoes, fresh *baguettes*. She poked about approvingly.

'Don't squash the tomatoes, April.'

'*Don't squash the tomatoes, April*,' she mocked, but cheerfully, picking up her skirts in a parody curtsey. 'I'm not a little girl, Harold.'

It wasn't entirely a joke. She was getting a tiny bit bored with Harold, organizing everything, making all the rules. *If only I had some money of my own . . . then he wouldn't treat me like a little girl.*

The Cimetière was a marvel, a climbing city of the dead, all competing for the highest pinnacles, the largest inscriptions, the richest marbles, whorled fantastically, greens and reds. The soil was rich, as well. The trees were fat and brilliant, surely the greenest trees in Paris. The tombs strained and jostled, as if they were bursting with pride and money. Some of them were literally bursting, though. Through the cracks the green grass grew.

It was a day of sun and wind. Cloud shadows were chasing each other over the sloping miles of graves, grey following silver, Harold following April.

Girls, boys, women, men . . . she worked out the ages from the dates on the stones. April felt sad for the children, lying with so many old people. She peered into the tiny chapels which the larger tombs contained. Some of the windows were broken, some of the altars held flowers which were not much more than a handful of rust-brown dust. Unvisited since they were built, perhaps.

Most chapels bore something more discreet, concealing duty or lack of duty, circular wreaths of wax anemones the colour of pigeons, cold pink, cold grey.

Perhaps they attracted the cats. Something attracted the cats. They slipped between the mausolea, sleek and black and fat.

It appealed to April's sense of romance. Pleased she was pleased, he unpacked the picnic.

'Ooh Harold, I'm ever so glad we came. It's really creepy though. Thinking about all those dead people. Sort of rich, but not at all rich. Underneath it's just – well, empty.'

'Yes, I agree. That's what appeals to me. Human beings want their palaces – even when they're dead. But you feel all the time things are falling apart. There's a marvellous *irony*.'

Briefly, long enough to eat the celery *remoulade*, they were truly friendly. Briefly, they were at one. His frame of mind was pleasantly melancholy.

Boys and girls and men and women, all of them lay together here. Briefly, looking at her long bright hair against the miles of inhabited marble, he wondered at this living girl. Almost – *loved* her.

Then he saw Lottie again.

She was sitting two or three sections below them on the long slope of tombs, some fifty yards away. She was doing, as she so often did, what April would not do. She had spread little pots and packets of food all over the top of a flattish gravestone. One of the few he remembered like that was Proust's relatively modest affair. Even Lottie would not eat lunch on Proust . . . *would* she? *was* she?

There was also a bottle of greenish wine. She was drinking from the bottle. As he looked at her, the sun came out and blazed through the glass of the tipped-back bottle and on her blowing yellow hair.

It can't be, *can't be*.

This time he managed to say nothing, but he couldn't sit there and go on eating. He stood up abruptly, wiping his lips.

'I think that's Proust down there. I'm going to have a look at him.'

She started to speak, but he had gone.

She saw the woman with the yellow hair.

'Darling . . .' April shrieked.

When he came back, she questioned him till he admitted the truth. April wept in the funeral wind, reduced to a little girl again. Not even Harold's little girl. A little girl who was all on her own.

Back in their room, he refused to talk, retreated into the *World of Wonders*.

Lottie's picnic was an impulse thing. She had neither glass nor cutlery. She had suddenly felt stifled by the smooth delicacy of the hotel dining room, shrimp-pale sauces, cream-pale soups. In truth, she had felt – not quite *herself* – since the evening when she imagined seeing Harold.

It's not like me, imagining things.

Life seemed a little insipid. Lottie would not put up with that. This cemetery was never insipid. She chose the most peppery, savoury food. She sat there sucking a *chorizo* sausage, pushing on the little lumps of meat with her tongue and wincing with pleasure at the tide of paprika. No, there was nothing quite like meat.

A cat shot out of the grass behind her. She turned to look, and saw Harold again.

Surely Harold.

It must be Harold.

But she was looking into sun. She shielded her eyes. She wasn't so sure. His distinctive sideburns were missing. Twenty yards away, he looked too thin.

Oh Christ, let it not be Harold, she thought, the food she'd bought randomly, abundantly, stretched reproachfully far over the gravestone. He'll think I've turned into a solitary drunk. A compulsive eater, too.

But she couldn't look away. Were their eyes meeting, or was he looking at something just beyond her?

Then a woman's voice (English? Yes, rather cross, a *common* voice) called petulantly, '*Darling*. What are you doing down there?'

Embarrassed, Lottie looked down at her lap. Of course it wasn't Harold at all. A perfectly normal married couple, a lower-middle-class English couple.

That woman must have thought I fancied her husband.

She took a swig more wine.

I think I've been too long on my own. I think I'd better ring Hugo. I think I need to talk to someone. I think I might be going insane.

Spectres of the Air
No organ of sense is so liable to deception as the eye . . . Eastern travellers often tell scarcely credible tales of the mirage of the desert. Suddenly in the distance, where all is known to be arid sand, appears a sheet of water. Here and there upon its bosom lie enchanted islands, above the top of whose woody groves rise the turrets of castles, or minarets of mosques. So real is the sight, that men and camels push forward, longing to bathe in the refreshing waters of this fairy lake; but as they advance, the mirage retreats, and all fades as the sun sinks beneath the lurid horizon.

July

CHAPTER TWENTY-SIX

By July, the horse-chestnuts change again. The skeletons of the flowers have yellow-green sexual bulges which will soon be fruit.

The first migrant birds fly south. The woods are quieter, with fewer flowers as the dense leaves block the light. Under the beeches there are Birdsnest Orchids, honey-coloured, leafless parasites.

Lottie flies effortlessly north-west.

In Regent's Park, pink bodies dream on yellow grass. The band plays jazz, in hot blue uniforms frogged with mustard. A black dog dances between the bodies. The saxophone blares. Small ducks drift black and sharp as notes on the bright blue lake.

Nights are a murmur of voices. Nightjars, and a few human lovers, down in the damp grass, stargazing. They think they have found Venus. From a distance, it still has infinite promise.

Astronomers find something else, as the camera presses closer.

Venus is very dry.

Venus is very hot.

The lemon-yellow clouds let sunlight in, but they let nothing out.

Leaving all her luggage in blazing Paris, Lottie flies home on the first of July. She tells herself she is doing it for Davey – darling Davey, the only one who loves her. In fact, the heat and glare of Paris have left her feeling a little washed out.

Lottie refuses to feel washed out.

She hopes it will rain in London. She will look very brown *indeed* in London. And it will be good for Davey to see her (good for her to see Davey).

Lottie wants to surprise him. In retrospect, a mistake. A *great* mistake, Lottie reflects, two days older and wiser.

London wasn't rainy: London was sweltering hot. Without her keys, she had to ring. After a pause, the letter-box clicked up, and Davey's eyes looked through. *Peculiar boy.* Then he opened the door and smiled, but with neither surprise nor enthusiasm. Rather a *vague* smile, in fact.

'It's you,' he said, and allowed her to kiss him. 'The fridge is bust, by the way.'

She had forgotten it was Amanda's summer fortnight. Amanda was in Ireland. There were dead flowers in vases. Davey had smoked in *all* the ashtrays. She'd thought he hardly smoked at all. And he'd been burning incense. It was quite a *nice* smell, but after a bit it was irritating to find it everywhere.

'Can't you just have that stuff upstairs?'

'What stuff?' he asked, looking worried.

'That bloody Indian stuff. Incense. It's everywhere. Don't you get sick of it?'

'Oh,' he said. 'All right.'

'How's school?'

'We just broke up . . . for all you care.'

'Of *course* I care!' She gave him one of her special smiles, which said *Davey, darling, Mum adores you.* But Davey didn't smile back.

That child is getting too sensitive.

It was not till next day that he suddenly said 'By the way, Harold rang.'

'Why didn't you tell me? Where is he?'

'He didn't say.'

'Oh, *not again.*' She dug her nails into her scalp. 'Well, *was it abroad*? You must know that.'

'Nah,' said Davey. 'Why should it be? At least, I don't think so. He sounded just like he usually does.' That was a relief, or half a relief. 'I've just remembered, it couldn't have been. He said he was looking for another 10p.'

'Bless you, Davey,' said Lottie, and hugged him. Thank God, so it hadn't been Harold in Paris. 'Did you tell him where I was?'

'No, I don't think he asked.'

'He must have asked *something*.'

'I don't remember.' Leave me alone.

'You must remember. Oh – *forget it*.'

She swooped on the ashtrays and started emptying them, crashing them together as she did so.

Leave me alone, all of you, thought Davey. I don't give a sod. They all bugger off and leave me, then they swan back and give me the Third Degree.

The milk went off in an hour or so: the butter turned to oil: cheese sweated vilely. Worst of all, there was no ice.

How am I supposed to survive without ice, thought Lottie, swatting crossly at a fly. Although she had told him she would stay for a week 'just to see that you're all right', by Sunday afternoon she was secretly planning on returning to Paris that evening.

They had to eat out, of course. You'd think the child would appreciate it. On Friday it was San Lorenzo, on Saturday it was Odin's. But Davey was hardly company. She tried her best to be amusing, but he just looked down at the tablecloth, or up in the air as if there were birds.

He was thinner, too, and looked – older? sadder? She thought he ought to confide in her.

'Is something the matter?'

'Matter?'

'Yes, *matter*. You seem to be somewhere else.'

'I was thinking about somebody.'

'Well, may we know who?'

'A friend. You don't know her . . .'

'By the way, did Cassandra Jennings ring? She had a picture for me.'

'She might have done. You've been away a long time. I can't remember everything. I've got things of my own to think about.'

'You're cross with me!'

She was rather flattered. It was better than being ignored. Besides, men always got cross with her, and she always charmed them out of it.

However, for the next thirty-six hours she could not charm him out of it.

After weeks of Paris, Lottie fancied a traditional English Sunday lunch. She dragged Davey off to the nearest place which did a three-course set Sunday lunch. 'Surprise!' was all she told him.

At first he was relieved she had chosen somewhere a bit less over the top. Then he saw the menu.

Oxtail Soup, Roast Beef, Yorkshire Pudding, Roast Potatoes, Peas, Spotted Dog and Custard.

'Mum, I'm a *vegetarian*. I'm your *son*. You *ought to remember*.'

In furious silence he ate potatoes and peas and both portions of Spotted Dog.

'I'm only eating it because I'm starving. I think the name is a fucking disgrace.'

In the middle of saying that, mouth full of suet, he caught her eye and started to laugh. His cross voice suddenly struck him as funny, and keeping up a fury was very hard work. Besides, it was fairly nice to see her, appalling as she definitely was.

But as soon as she saw he was melting, Lottie let her own anger rip. He had made her suffer for thirty-six hours. He would not get away with it.

'I'd forgotten how pompous you are. Brat!'

She said it so loudly that a woman turned round.

'Brat is a stupid word. Look, I *know* people round here. Do you have to shout all the time?'

'There you are, you're pompous.' Her voice hadn't got any quieter.

He stared at her, slowly reddening with rage.

'Well, I'd forgotten how selfish you are. Mothers aren't *supposed* to be totally selfish.'

Flushed with rage, with very bright eyes, he looked like a child again.

She softened, reached across the table firmly and trapped his hand before he could remove it.

'Children aren't *supposed* to criticize their parents.' She was grinning. 'I've never denied I was selfish.'

'Look, other mothers don't disappear all the time.'

'I don't want to be like other mothers. You're not like other sons. My beautiful, intelligent, *interesting* son.' And her smile became such a wide blaze of love that it drew him, despite his better judgement.

'Davey, let's have a brandy. You *occasionally* like a brandy.'

The Spotted Dog had made him feel sick, but an atavistic desire to please made him accept the brandy. Two large Courvoisiers lifted them. They left the restaurant laughing together.

On the way home he put his arm around her. Pleased, she wriggled her own heavy arm out of the niche between them and flung it gaily round his thin shoulders.

I haven't had anyone's arm around me for . . . weeks, months. Perhaps I'll stay longer.

'Darling, let's walk home through the Park.'

Lonely people, spread pink and naked with their Sunday papers around the bandstand, stared at the two of them, enviously. *Beautiful people, happy people.* The trumpet called them, the saxophone yearned. Lottie and Davey walked on through the music, yellow hair shining against blue-black hair.

Behind the shine, two headaches were beginning. The drum hammered, the horn complained. A long march home in the dizzy heat. Two large Courvoisiers sat heavily upon them.

'We shouldn't have had that brandy,' said Lottie, with an edge of accusation.

'I didn't want it,' said Davey.

'I suppose I forced you. You're so self-righteous.'

Nearly back to their empty house.

☆

In the afternoon something happened which left Lottie feeling uneasy. Around half-past three there was some shouting in the street. Some teenage fracas, she thought.

Then she heard Davey pound downstairs from the attic. Someone came back upstairs with him. She went out on to the landing, pulling at her hair.

It was Smeggy, looking astonishing in leather trousers which adhered to his legs, *must be hell in this weather*, and a t-shirt torn till there was hardly any of it left. His left ear-lobe was attached to his nostril by two glass studs and a thin gold chain. He had hard, protuberant nipples. He was white, and thin, but his muscles showed. He caught her momentary stare.

''Allo, Mrs Segall, do you like my diamonds?'

He meant, do you like my chest? Do you like my muscles, and my nipples, Mrs Segall?

'Hmmm. Well, they're . . . dashing.' She didn't feel quite so in control as usual. She had an unsettling feeling that this thin gangling boy knew something she didn't.

'Would you like some biscuits or something? The fridge isn't working . . .'

187

'I *know*,' interrupted Smeggy.

'. . . you could have coffee and biscuits.' The offer didn't carry conviction. 'Davey, get him some biscuits.'

'Mum, he doesn't *want* any biscuits.'

What he did want did not become entirely plain, unless he just wanted to arrange himself round the room in impertinent postures. Lottie struggled for a bit to make polite conversation, but the atmosphere was heavy and somehow constrained. Perhaps the boys were waiting for her to go. But that was ridiculous. She'd only just got back. The talk was entirely between Smeggy and her. Davey stood restlessly by the door, as if he wanted to leave for Australia.

Her and Smeggy. Smeggy and her. Her body told her what it was about.

'It suits you, having a tan, Mrs Segall.'

Smeggy's eyes were just avoiding staring at her breasts, or avoiding her catching his staring at her breasts, but Lottie still knew he was doing it.

'It quite suits *you*, being white.'

'Do you do a lot of, you know, lying in the sun, in Paris?' The question was more than the actual words.

'I *enjoy* myself. I do exactly as I like.'

He was sprawled on the arm of the leather sofa nearest her low armchair. His liquorice thighs were spread apart, his white hands held them as though they were not his own but someone else's.

As if they were my body.

Davey had fallen completely silent. He looked as if he was going to be sick. The room was electric, full of dry heat.

But Lottie wasn't sure she had invented this game. Her son's white face became painful to her. She made a great effort and broke the contact.

'You boys must want to go for a walk. Or play records upstairs, or something. I'm going to put my feet up in here.'

'Are you?' asked Smeggy, smugly. 'Are you feeling like a little *lie down*?'

Could he mean what she thought he meant? Suddenly Lottie was genuinely cross.

'Piss off, kids. I've got things to do. I've decided to get a plane back tonight.'

They only went upstairs for about five minutes, but her

temper had cooled when he came to say goodbye.

I'm just frustrated, and imagining things. He's a nice boy, really. And it's good for Davey to know boys of all kinds.

She made a special effort to be brisk but pleasant.

'Nice to see you, Smeggy. I'm sure Davey will invite you round for a proper meal another day. We haven't got help at the moment.'

At the last moment she decoded the slogan on his ripped T-shirt, HEROIN KILLS.

'By the way – what a very sensible T-shirt.'

That boy had a way of looking at her as if nothing she said was what she really meant, as if he would do her the favour of discounting it. He smiled. In his pale thin face, his black-lined eyes were a piercing blue. It was a real, friendly smile this time. Almost a smile of fellow feeling.

'By the way,' he said. 'Somefing I wanted to say. I thought those flowers – were *ace*. They were really good, those flowers. I mean, you *remember* those flowers.'

What bothered Lottie afterwards was the extent to which that buoyed her up. The dangerous extent to which she wanted to smile that fellow feeling back.

As the lift bore her back up into the skies of Paris, she stroked her hair consolingly.

Lottie, you need a fuck. And she started to dial Hugo's number.

'Darling. Did you get my message?' he asked.

'No – no, I just got back. The receptionist was busy.'

'Come to Maxim's tonight. There's someone you have to meet.'

Some things in this life are simple, thank God, thought Lottie, waking up next day. The head beside her on the frilled pillow was handsome even from the back. Thick black hair, strong neck. The naked curve of his shoulder. He was breathing peacefully; he hadn't snored.

Well, Hugo, you missed out, she thought. If you'd come on your own you'd have had me, love.

André Legros was his cousin by marriage. Lottie hoped Hugo wouldn't be cross. But I think he'd enjoy it, old pander. He'll frig himself silly, imagining us. There was a ghostly likeness, but everything was different. André was young, firm, decisive . . .

Young and *firm*, she thought. Should she go to her bathroom and take out the diaphragm? He stirred slightly, and so did a specific throb of feeling between her legs. I think I'll just leave it in.

She said to herself, *That's better. I really am feeling better.*

CHAPTER TWENTY-SEVEN

Sylvia waited five days after writing her letter to Harold before really starting to worry. Worry made her heartburn worse. He only has to pick up the phone, she thought. I mean, I can't ring *him*.

She drove down to Sandbanks Point one morning and left the mauve car in the usual gale. Natives of Poole are comfortable; Sandbanks natives are tough.

Two old ladies were sitting in deckchairs, side by side on the shining beach. Their faces, turned up into the sunlight, were almost identically white. The sand blew round the legs of their deckchairs, fine and bright as their caps of hair. My God, thought Sylvia, I hope *I'm* that tough, when I get old.

She stared down the bay to Boscombe, down the green cliffs, into the sun. It looked just a blink away, except for the tiny microbes surfing and swimming. Boscombe Pier was a slightly smaller finger than Bournemouth Pier just in front of it.

I am a mother, she thought. My son is just over there.

She tried the words on the wind, using all her training in voice projection. That settled it; the sound fired her blood. She hurried back to her car.

Darling, she informed it, we are needed, we are on our way.

Violet had persuaded Pamela that this was just the day for a picnic. They watched that poor woman talking to herself, amateur dramatics on their lovely beach. Forty minutes later Violet watched through her spy-glass the little people swimming around Boscombe Pier. A mauve car shot out like a crazy insect and came to a halt not far from the swimmers.

Pamela said, 'Don't tire your eyes.'

Violet said, 'I love you, dearest.'

She still sometimes uses her telescope at night, wearing both their dressing-gowns, sitting on the balcony. Violet ignores all the 'facts' about Venus. For her it is the Morning and the Evening Star.

☆

Sylvia felt marvellous on the road. Adrenalin flooded through her. I'm going to see my child, she thought. She had a rôle; she was wanted.

That was the trouble with growing – well, *older*. You thought, 'What shall I do with my time?' instead of, 'Who needs me most today?' Life grew slower, as you grew older. Life was less sparkling. Darker. Looking back, though looking back didn't do, she saw everything immensely bright, immensely fast, dizzily fast. Driving through a stretch of pines, her mood dimmed for a moment. Could they be over, her years of light?

– But the pines were gone, the sun came out, the sea to her right was dazzling silver.

Harold would be glad to see her. She had been – a little over-sensitive, after her previous visit to Harold. A little distant when he phoned her. Four months was too long to be proud.

She'd been proud with his father for thirty-two years . . .

Looking back doesn't do.

A bank of red roses flashed past like a kiss, and she pressed her foot on the accelerator.

Harold's hurt had been too fresh. She understood that better now. It was ever thus at the end of a marriage (and I should know, thought Sylvia. I suffered enough at the end of mine. I am the person to understand suffering. I am the person to comfort Harold.)

She was also the person suffering the presence of a dozen packing-cases of his things. Luckily, the garage was on the large side. Luckily the little car just fitted in (her fingers grazed the bonnet fondly as she turned to walk up from the pier).

The slope was steeper than she remembered. She was just the faintest bit apprehensive – would Harold be *totally* pleased to see her? And under that was a deeper worry. What if he was – *not all right*? What if he was ill, or depressed? She hoped she was strong enough to cope. Of course, she had always *had* to be strong. When you were the mother of a gifted child, there was always a tiny worry.

In fact, he was always a very good boy. Top of everything, all the prizes. Then later, that rather strange streak. Going into teaching in that dreadful Comprehensive when he could have had a brilliant future at Oxford.

That charming Professor had told her so herself, refilling her glass of sherry. (Perhaps he was only a Tutor. But a very *important* Tutor.) 'We think he has a brilliant future, Mrs Segall. And we're hoping he'll stay with us.' He was gallant, he bent very close.

I was beautiful then, thought Sylvia, sharply. On the whole, things didn't get better. You were stuck with the same memories. Life was no longer memorable. Sometimes even she herself felt dull, Sylvia Segall who could never be dull.

But Harold's life had been a little too exciting since he suddenly gave up that teaching job. It wasn't what she wanted for him, but it was still a job. She'd hoped he'd try and get back into Oxford – they must *sometimes* advertise professorships; or by now, perhaps, something more senior. When she hinted, he was very short with her.

'That's the last thing I want, Mother. And honestly, you haven't a clue. They don't want rusty old has-beens like me.'

'But, darling, you've written your marvellous books.'

'They're A-level textbooks, Mother.'

'Well, the one I looked at seemed frightfully hard.'

'They *wouldn't want* me. It's *too late* for that.'

That was typical of today's young people. They didn't understand about positive thinking. It was never too late, if you lived for the future.

It seemed a step backwards, this writing full time. All right as a sideline to teaching. But she suspected it might be novels, next. It was what he had wanted as a very young boy, but she'd always been sensible and practical (someone had to be practical) and explained that boys really had to have jobs. So many people, as she should know, wanted to be creative. So very few of us *could* (Sylvia *was*, of course. You would hardly get two in the same family. He'd want to be an actor, next.)

'Mother, they're only *textbooks*. And journalism. Bread-and-butter stuff. I'm not trying to be Samuel Beckett. I should be so lucky.'

But she thought of him as a dreamer. *Dreamer*, for her, meant *failure*, though she'd never admit that to anyone.

I think he married Lottie because that woman's more a man than he is. But she overplayed her hand. My son may not be a mogul (a word she was never quite certain of) – my son may not be a mogul, but he wouldn't let himself be trampled on. No son of mine would do that.

She rang the door with decision. Behind the stained glass, the hall looked very dark. She rang again and again. In the end, feet shuffled and lurched from some nether region along the hall towards her. Harold? Something was terribly wrong. Her hand went to her painful chest.

But the door swung open on a wizened little man with a long brown face and inquisitive eyes.

'Got pins and needles in me legs,' he said. 'Kneelin' down paintin', see.'

'Good Morning,' said Sylvia with extra dignity, since she had to say it for the two of them. 'My name is Sylvia Segall. My stage name is Sylvia Delaire. I am Harold Segall's mother. Will you lead me to him, please?'

'Warn me to go to Paris with yer?' The old man chuckled.

She looked at him disdainfully. Many, many performances had given her practice at expressing disdain.

'I wish to see my son.'

''Ave a look at this then, Missis.'

He took a sheet of paper from the hall table and handed it to her (beside it she suddenly saw her letter, boldly addressed in violet ink).

CALLERS/INQUIRERS AFTER HAROLD SEGALL: HAROLD SEGALL IS IN PARIS TILL FURTHER NOTICE.

It took her a few moments to understand. Her spirits slumped. Her disdain vanished. You need energy for disdain.

'And who are you?' she asked, flatly.

'Landlord. Name o' Sedley.' His voice was more sympathetic. 'Hope you ain't come a long way, Missis.'

She felt so very tired. 'Could I possibly sit down on your chair for a moment?' The chair by the hatstand looked ancient and rickety but suddenly tremendously attractive.

'You all right? You need a cup coffee?'

And now his voice was definitely – *charming*. Sylvia could not say kind; she certainly did not need kindness. She drew herself up to a smile, and relaxed into it, ecstatically. I don't think I've smiled for weeks.

'Oh, I say, how simply delightful. A *small* cup of coffee would be wonderful.'

He asked her into the downstairs flat which had almost finished being repainted.

'Last lot of tenants set fire to it. Bloody nuisance, in the season. You're losin' three hundred pound a week.' He lit up an ancient pipe. 'Your son now. Bookish, reliable type.'

He sat her down on the scorched pink nylon-velvet sofa and made her coffee. A mug of coffee. She drank it slowly.

He asked her about that 'stage name'. His syntax became quite *galant*.

"Ave I the pleasure of talking to an *actress?*'

She repeated the Delaire three times. In the end he remembered, rubbing his long bony hands together with excitement, that he'd seen her twice, in *Private Lives* and *Hay Fever*, many years ago. He didn't remind her how many years. The conversation warmed up.

After he'd made her three mugs of coffee and listened to her opinions on the dressing-rooms at the Winter Gardens, Ted nipped out for a packet of biscuits which they solemnly munched till twelve. By now he was describing, in quite fluent prose, his collection of Victorian theatre programmes. Perhaps he was a little hard to understand, and perhaps his teeth, detached, some brown, some white, standing up from his gums like dominoes, were a little distracting as he laughed and smiled, but she found him simply delightful.

When he suggested they go 'up the Seagull' for a beer, she declined, but gratefully. Sylvia Delaire did not drink beer. But at least she was Sylvia Delaire again.

Emerging into the sun on the step and the noise of the swarming crowds from the front, she silently blessed Ted Sedley.

People still remember me, then; people still want me, need me; I have to turn quite a few of them down. She had almost forgotten Harold.

Glancing back at the gabled house for a second, she remembered something else. That was Boscombe Chine, surely. She had come to Boscombe Chine.

Boscombe Chine was the long steep ravine of pinewoods leading up to the town. Boscombe Gardens were at the top of the Chine. And ten, twenty-odd years ago she had walked up the Chine with . . . *Harold's father*.

She tried not to think of her ex-husband as Harold, though that *was* his name, and it was she who insisted on giving it to their son. 'Oh, let's call him Harold, darling, I want a little boy just like you.'

Even a lifetime later, it hurt.

Nor could she think of him as 'H. Stanley Segall', which those frightful Americans apparently called him. Stanley was a coarse, comedian's name. And so he was always '*Harold's father*'.

But today some pebble in her mind rolled sideways and the pain was replaced by an odd little pleasure.

I walked up there with my husband, Harold, she thought, in spring, and on sudden impulse she walked up again, enjoying the air, which hummed with resin and distant children.

She walked briskly but she looked at things, enjoying the shocks of recognition. Pigeons fluttered through the pine branches, making a sound like clapping. The sun looked very far above the arched trees, making stars between the dark leaves of holly.

There was a duck, she remembered. On that little pond. She saw the duck still, though it wasn't there. And a dozen ducklings, swimming like sprinters. We went back two weeks later and there were only seven left. And he said it was OK, it was a lucky number.

Many things Sylvia was vague about; they were holm oak trees, less shiny than holly, and far more years had drifted away while she waited for parts and dreamed of stardom than she imagined; thirty-six, in fact. Thirty-six years of being a dreamer.

But the head of the duck and its fine etched patterns of light brown and dark brown herringbone silk, and then – Harold's – face as he smiled at it, were as sharp as anything had ever been, and the memory was a lifetime's happiness.

Then the pain, which caught her as she reached the top and turned to go back to the sea again, was as sharp and dreadful as a lifetime's pain.

She was stunned, frozen until the pain lessened. The day came back with its sun and wind.

It's the biscuits, she thought, as life returned. I shouldn't eat biscuits . . . Besides. I have to think about my figure. You never know what offers will come.

CHAPTER TWENTY-EIGHT

April imagined he was doing it to spite her. Just when things might have gone right again. Most annoying of all was the fact that she hadn't got a proper look at those women. She'd have liked some idea of what Lottie looked like, then she could have hated her better.

The more she knew, the more it inflamed her. For Lottie wasn't just rich. She wasn't just beautiful (she pressed him to that. In fact Harold said, '*Some people* think she's beautiful.' April knew *she* wouldn't think her beautiful. Anyway, Lottie was thirty-five. She must be a wrinkled, ugly old bat. April hoped she died.)

The beauty, however, was not the worst part. The worst part was Lottie being wild about painting. It all came out when April told Harold what she'd seen at the Petit Palais.

'They're called *intimistes*,' she said, with a flourish. Her French was beginning to feel more confident. 'Because they paint intimate things, I suppose. There were two painters I adored – one's called Vuillard, but the best is Bonnard.' Then April tried to describe the paintings. 'We ought to sell prints of them in Bingles. They're gorgeous colours – and they paint happy things, which is just what the public likes . . .'

Harold had been terse all day, and he suddenly broke in and stopped her.

'Look, April, I know about Bonnard. There's a vast exhibition on at the moment, at the Pompidou Centre.' (She hadn't gone there; it looked too cold, a bit like the factory where her father worked. She didn't know there was a Bonnard exhibition, but she knew when Harold was putting her down.) 'We've got a small Bonnard at home, as it happens.'

'What's it like?' She was mortified.

'Oh I believe it's rather good.'

'I mean, *what's it of*?'

'Oh. Quite unusual – two figures, not just the solitary nude. Bedroom, sunlight, you know the kind of thing. Very close, but looking in different directions. Beautiful woman, frightful man.'

And so it came out about Lottie and painting. So even *that* wasn't special to April. Lottie had got her hands on that too. So what was there left for April?

The sex was nice, but not what she wanted. She wanted to understand him. He was creative, like her. He was a thinker, like her. They could have been kindred spirits. But he didn't want to share things with her.

'I'm trying to understand you.'

'Well, people *can't* understand each other.'

Typical Harold; he liked despair. In some ways he was very *unlike* her.

'Did Lottie understand you?'

'I'd rather not talk about Lottie now.'

He kept on imagining he saw her, though. April *knew* Harold still kept imagining he saw her.

Whereas I'm here, and I'm real. And he doesn't see me at all.

In the early mornings April lay and looked at him, handsome, yes, but so superior. She knew he was pretending to be asleep. She noted each line, each bag, each vein.

He thinks he knows me. He thinks I'm weak.

He's weak himself. I'm stronger than him.

After the first two 'sightings', Harold saw Lottie wherever he went. A woman wearing Lottie's white suit, a woman in a café with Lottie's broad shoulders. Stupid, painful hallucinations which left him unsettled and wretched.

The room he and April shared became more and more of a nightmare. The chambermaid had got slatternly, now they'd been there ten days. She no longer changed their towels. She had never changed their sheets.

One morning Harold used April's towel by mistake and as he opened his eyes after rubbing them dry he saw a smear of lipstick on the white, and was shocked to feel a shiver of repulsion.

Lottie wore makeup too. Lottie got makeup on the towels. We never even had separate towels. But I didn't feel repelled, not once.

He found her hairs on his jackets: he found her hair on his

sweaters. They seemed to get longer and longer, and more determined to cling.

It wasn't that he had a low opinion of April. She had enormous – *potential*. But he, Harold Segall, was what thwarted her, stopped her being what she longed to be.

Yet she also longs to be thwarted, he thought.

Harold was the mean, unappreciative, maddening, unreasonable, bullying figure she hated – *exactly* the man she wanted. The script was written, the parts were fixed.

His wisdom pleased him. He understood.

Was it sexist to think she was a masochist?

- It was sexist to think *all* women were masochists.

Secretly, though, he did.

Then he thought of Lottie. Lottie was not.

- Never mind Lottie. April *is*.

No, he thought, I'll have to get out, I'll have to get back to England.

But the heat had its awful inertia. They woke up tired and cross and late. Each night he fantasized that in the morning he would tell her the truth, pack his bag, check out.

Each morning, he woke with a headache, and she would be lying there, straining to see him, those eyes which he once found touching (but now found creepy) turned in on him, blind and weak. Her hand would uncertainly stroke his neck, her slightly damp arm would stick to his.

That's what I can't bear: the intimacy. With someone I don't love. So the intimacy becomes sickening.

It was always far too late to check out.

The only escape he has is reading. Sitting in a café with *Life on Earth* spread out on the table in front of him, he can still be enthralled by jellyfish or flying squirrels or nautilus shells. Their brilliance blanks out her suffering face.

Or he reads from the *World of Wonders*. Some of the entries make him laugh.

Mermaids and Men of the Sea
Mermaidens and men have from early ages been reckoned among the wonders of the sea. Poets have sung of their wondrous beauty and power, historians of the most

irreproachable veracity have chronicled their appearance;
writers of natural history have asserted most decidedly a
belief in their existence . . . The latest mermaid known
was that exhibited by the American showman Barnum, a
few years ago, and was a singularly ugly object. It proved,
on examination, to be an ingenious combination of the
head of a monkey with the tail of a fish.

On second thoughts, it is not so funny.

At six, reluctantly, slightly late, he pays his bill, closes his
book.

Slouching back through the shining streets. Smells of strong
coffee, oil, oranges. The sun is brilliant, the air is alive.

By comparison, doorways are impossibly dark. Butchers are
cutting up meat for tomorrow.

Dragging his feet, he goes into the dark.

She was there before him.

'You're late.'

'Sorry.'

'Harold, I've got something to say to you.'

'Oh.' *Oh no.*

'It's gone wrong between us, hasn't it?'

'Yes. Well. But we talked about that. Only last night. I'm
doing my best.'

'That's not the point. Look, it's not your fault. It really isn't.
I've been thinking about it. I was dead keen to come. But . . . it
hasn't worked out. I think I want to go home . . . I don't want to
upset you, though.'

Harold's mind worked strenuously to catch up.

Oddly enough, he could hear that the voice which emerged
from his mouth sounded faintly piqued.

'Oh, well. Yes, you're right. Yes . . . I'm not upset. Don't
worry about that.'

'I thought you wouldn't be, some'ow.' Her voice held a little
bitterness. 'Any rate, I've seen Paris. I'll tell all my friends, I've
seen Paris.'

'Yes.' There was astonishingly little to say. She had started to
pack already.

But I must say something. I must do something. It's my last chance to do the right thing.

The initiative had left him, however. He sat and watched her folding, stacking. Had he given her *anything* that she wanted?

'Would you like a goodbye dinner tonight?' (If she's going, I can afford to take her somewhere nice. Somewhere that she will remember.)

'There's not much point to it is there, really?'

'Well, I mean, you know, a bit of a treat.'

The echo sickened him. *I must be getting stupid*. It was April's phrase. It sounded like mockery.

'Look, if you want to spend money on me. I mean, there is something. What I'd really like – *Harold, please, give me the fare to go home.*' – And her calm broke a little but she went on packing as the tears betrayed her in the last of the sunlight. Her face underneath them was set, determined.

Harold rushed to get his wallet. Action was a solace. He riffled through the pack of notes, thank God I went to the bank today. He'd taken out rather a lot of money on the theory that April might cost more as the situation between them worsened. Agitated, he dropped the lot, picked the notes up and dropped them again. There didn't seem to be as much as he'd thought. Maybe I already paid the hotel.

'What'll it cost? Are you taking the ferry? Single . . . hmm . . . forty quid . . . five hundred francs ought to do it.'

And he pressed ten fifties upon her. Of course the fare was really thirty-odd quid, so five hundred francs was generous.

She took the notes without looking at them, put them in her handbag, didn't meet his glance. She had thought of going hovercraft. But channel ferry was cheaper.

'I can keep the change then, can I?'

'Of course. Buy a coffee, or something.'

He caught a peculiar look in her eyes, eyes he had recently thought of as dog-like.

'There's no need to be sarcastic, April.'

She sat down, snapping her handbag shut. It was a cheap handbag, with a large cheap clasp. She told the handbag something, and her voice was not the slightest bit sarcastic.

'I miss Bournemouth,' she said. 'I miss Emmie. I miss the sea. I even miss getting letters from Mum.'

He'd remember that, and the sarcasm. The last two things that April said. Neither of them made him feel comfortable. But his brain had started to work again and he found that she hadn't a booking. Crazy for her to go tonight. But she was emphatic that she couldn't stay.

'I can't stay with you. It's not your fault.'

Then Harold would leave and find somewhere else. He *could* be decent. He could do the right thing. She should stay here, get a good night's sleep, and set off home in the morning.

He kissed her on the cheek. Her irises yearned briefly towards him, failed to find him, and her eyelids fell. She clutched his hand like a banister. But she didn't accuse; she didn't complain.

'Thank you, April. You were good to me.'

The words came out without his planning them. *Good to let me go, as well.* But she shook her head, and waved him away.

'Good luck – good luck with your painting.'

This time she didn't even bother to look up, and he left embarrassed by his clumsiness.

Out on the street he watched the street lights flicker into brightness. The possibility of being cool. Paris looked almost promising again.

In the end he took the least adventurous course and went back to the hotel they first started with.

'*Une chambre simple,*' he asked.

The concierge recognized him. Her bloodhound eyes hardly flickered.

A single room, this time.

No bathroom, just a shower. He stared at himself in the mirror. *You're a free man again.* He rubbed his naked cheek tenderly. *Time to grow back your sideburns.*

April, alone in the tidied room, had found something which cheered her up. Harold had given her too much money. *Ten times too much, in fact.* Four hundred pounds, not forty pounds. Five-hundred-franc notes, not fifty-franc notes. And she hadn't a clue where he'd gone. She smoothed the notes between her fingers.

I've never held this much money in my hands . . .

He told me to keep the change.

And a plan began to formulate itself.

July

I've still got one week's holiday left. I'm a *little bit* homesick, but not that homesick. I think it was Harold who made me feel homesick. It would be a bit daft to go home.

She had a hundred pounds of her own money left, though she'd been determined not to spend it. That meant that she had five hundred pounds.

If I stay somewhere else he'll never find me. I could – treat myself a bit, on five hundred pounds. I could go back and look at those Bonnards. And the other Bonnards, in the Pompidou Centre. Those intimate, *intimistes* Bonnards. I'd really enjoy doing that.

CHAPTER TWENTY-NINE

Walking down the Rue St Denis with André, laughing at the luridly mis-spelled signs –

GRILS! GLIR! NON-STOPH ARD SHOW!!!

– Lottie realized with unspeakable relief that for almost a week she hadn't thought about Harold. She probably never would again.

She'd wasted so much *time* on Harold. She had started to feel she would never escape, that in some frightful way they were tracking each other.

She watched herself in the plate-glass window.

You're a free woman again.

André's impressive reflection flanked her.

Wonderful being with a man again, too. Not just the sex, but the comforting sense of someone tall and solid beside you. Solid as her, and extremely handsome.

Almost absurdly handsome. He was thirty-eight, but looked twenty-seven, except for a certain air of power. His hair was as thick as her own, but softer, dark, with a wet-ink sheen; his cheeks were ever so slightly plump, which only made him look more sensual; his nose was a short Napoleonic curve, with elegantly clipped and tapered nostrils; and his eyes were caramel-brown, heavy-lidded, *lingering* eyes which lingered on *her*.

One tiny fault made perfection bearable; the merest hint of a double chin. But I'm through with skinny men, thought Lottie. It's time for someone more substantial.

Substantial in more ways than one. He seemed to be nearly as rich as she was. This was disconcerting. She was used to being the one with money. Once she got more or less used to the idea, it made a pleasant change. Just for once, it was lovely to sit back and watch while André looked briefly at the bill and then flipped his Gold American Express card on to the saucer.

He part-owned a jewellery firm in Geneva; that was just *one* of his occupations. He had been a commodity broker, but now he traded in Gold Futures. Lottie was vague about commodity broking, which sounded rather dull, but she liked the sound of Gold Futures. It had an optimistic ring.

In Paris he was nominally on holiday, but he spent a great part of his day on the phone. His secretary was staying at the same hotel. She was a tall, anorexic-looking girl who could often be found sitting down in the foyer, chain-smoking extraordinarily long cigarettes, as long and thin as her fingers. Lottie kept on forgetting her name. She wore clinging dresses in acid-drop colours, which made her knees look bony. She was exquisitely polite to Lottie, who felt rather sorry for her. But the floating secretary added to Lottie's pleasing sense of – *what?* – something that gave her vague unease even as she enjoyed it . . .

Her sense of André's importance.

She had never been attracted to that in men. Pompous things, most men were, and that was *before* they got important: and she was important enough for two.

All the same in the end it got boring, being married to men who were brilliant and creative (or brilliant and blocked, like Harold) but didn't have two pennies to rub together and thought Dress Formal meant a pair of clean jeans.

André wore cream or pale grey linen suits which were always perfectly creaseless, perfectly stainless, perfectly cut. His shirts were of natural silk. The light colours possibly made him look a little sturdier than he was . . .

. . . But I like a well turned-out man. And I like a sturdy man. And – apart from anything else, I bloody well like a bit of a change.

Money, thought Lottie idly, enjoying the light on the cedarwood of André's cigar box and the bright raised threads on his silk cuff as he tipped his glass. They'd taken a stroll after dinner, and popped in here for a coffee and *fine*, though most of the couples were eating. He was reading the financial reports in *Le Monde*. Sitting down, his shoulders were wonderfully broad.

Money. And sex. And looks. I suppose we're the couple with everything. If time could be stopped right now, as we sit here. If we were frozen in a photograph. The people who saw it would be sick with envy.

Lottie Lucas, who has everything. Sitting with the handsomest man in Paris. Lucky Lottie, Lottie Luck.

She felt *herself* in Paris. She always forgot that she was half French. The French knew how to enjoy themselves. Things were better arranged, in Paris. Those straggling queues which bothered her in Camden – madmen, drunks, cripples, tramps – could be forgotten here. Of course there *were* drunks in Paris. Of course there might be a tramp or two. But you weren't forced to notice them all the time. Lottie looked round the room, and glowed.

At every table, handsome couples reflected each other's sense of well-being. Well-dressed couples ate with the graceful greed the French perfected. Husbands and wives resembled each other, or else it was their expressions, which said they *would* be loved, they *would* be fed. How very *right* such couples looked.

I'm glad that I'm not here alone. Lottie had been too long alone. Across the table André sat, an alibi, a splendid anchor. She gave a little shiver of pleasure.

His eyes flicked up from the paper.

'Are you cold, my darling?' he asked.

'No, I'm fine.'

The sexiest eyes she had ever seen.

'So. I am hoping you will be cold. Then I have an excuse to take you home and see you are quite warm.'

The way André kept her warm was still so novel that Lottie spent most of her waking hours thinking about it. The hours, that is, when he wasn't doing it. Remembering him as she strode alone through the Grande Galerie of the Louvre, the heat would prickle through her body, hanging with specific weight low under her belly and between her legs.

She glanced at the people inspecting the classical landscapes with surprise and pity. Vast low landscapes with flattened people. Nothing happened to them at night. They all looked grey, insubstantial. Mere forms, they had no life in them; they were not being fucked by André.

Sensual, beautiful André. His silk cuff trapped the light again. The money somehow leaked into the sex. His penis seemed to wag the message *André Legros is loaded.*

But that's absurd, she thought. Harold's erections were just as strong, and Harold had no money.

Something less pleasant occurred to her. Did her own money signal to men? Did they see her body through a shimmer of money? That thought did not appeal at all. She finished her brandy in one gulp.

The man at the next-door table had summoned the waiter to send his entrée back. He was explaining, at excessive length, exactly what the chef had done wrong. His wife directed her eyes with concentrated longing at the ceiling fan. Lottie observed that the silent waiter didn't look very much older than Davey; his cheeks had reddened, as Davey's did.

Harold and Davey. *Damn.*

It never really mattered to me that Harold didn't have money.

It wasn't a problem for *Lottie*. Money was her natural element; she took her money for granted like the colour of her hair. You naturally shared it with those you loved. You didn't have to *decide* to share it; by being near you, they just absorbed it.

Except – Harold didn't always absorb it. Harold sometimes felt awkward. Harold wriggled – Harold refused. He tried to pretend she'd be happier if he could 'pay his way'.

It was all to do with ego, of course. It wasn't that he wanted to spend his money. If anything he was, well, careful . . .

He felt my money gave me too much power.

Maybe I should have made more allowances. I mean, one must, with men. Their egos are so much more painful than ours. They can't help *that*, poor darlings.

I thought we were working through it. He finally seemed to be accepting things . . .

Suddenly she was in pain. The café receded, André receded. *Harold's disloyalty.* That drunken party, just before Christmas, before it all went wrong. And after that I went crazy. I bought that dreadful, unspeakable, cheapskate, dying monkey to cheer myself up – and woo my husband back, of course. *Darling husband, see how I love you.*

Enraged, she bit clean through the nail she was proudest of, long and cyclamen pink. She clutched the torn pink shaving for a moment, pressing one finger on the spiteful edge. *Never again, never again.*

I've worried too much about everyone else. Harold and Davey and even Amanda. Nobody thanks you for being unselfish.

I think I need to be cosseted. I think I'll let André worry about *me*.

☆

Later that night, to her surprise, when she was already drugged with sleep after one and three quarter hours of love, André suggested she move in to his hotel. He would take a larger suite.

'Lovely idea,' mumbled Lottie, whose mouth and jaw were a teeny bit painful, and slept and dreamed of enormous sweets stuck in her throat and choking her. But when she woke up, he asked again.

'I'll have to ask my son. He's terribly worried about my morals.'

What awful rot I talk, she thought, as she waited for Davey to answer the phone. It's the worst thing about strangers. You can feed them any old garbage . . .

She longed with a sudden acute longing for people she really knew.

But Davey sounded vague and cool as before, and exasperation soon killed the crooning maternal register she started in.

(No one in England appreciates me. They'll be sorry. *Others* do. This'll shake the little sod up.)

'I've made this amazing new friend. Terribly nice, a cousin of Hugo's . . .'

'Well, *Hugo* isn't terribly nice . . .'

'Listen to me. We . . . hit it off. He's asked me to stay on in Paris.'

'You mean, with him.'

'Well, in a way. Yes.'

We *are* in the 1980s. I'm a woman approaching forty. All the same, his tone of voice made her feel a little anxious.

'*Mum*. You said you'd come home in August. Early August. You *said*. Don't you think you ought to?'

No one said *ought* to Lottie. Nobody spoiled her freedom. If anyone tried to stop her doing things, Lottie would always do them.

'Oh, nonsense, Davey, I'm sure you're having a wonderful time there all on your own, Amanda spoiling you and so on, and millions of noisy friends coming round and no miserable old Mum to cramp your style . . .'

'Mum, I'm serious. I wish you'd come home.'

'Davey, you're not lonely . . .?' But before he could answer with the kind of *Yes* that might stop her doing what she wanted to do, she carried on, '. . . because, darling, really, there's no need to be. I give you *carte blanche*, though don't break the Ming. Just invite whoever you want. That nice peculiar Smeggy. And Charles . . . and, well, girls, if you like. But for God's sake don't get anybody pregnant . . . *Look*, darling, Mum loves you. I'll have to go. Thank you for making up my mind. I *swear* I'll be back in September.'

She is blowing loud kisses; she is gone.

Davey is sixteen, and he has *carte blanche*, and millions of noisy friends coming round, and girls if he likes, though they mustn't get pregnant, and no miserable old Mum to cramp his style . . .

So why does he sit and hold the mouthpiece and not put it down for nearly five minutes, and why if it is all such fun do a few tears come?

In Paris the red sign glares all night.

GRILS! GLIR! NON-STOPH ARD SHOW!!!

Thunderclouds tinged with sulphur gather over Paris, London, Frankfurt. The days are past their longest, but under Earth's clouds it is getting hotter.

Beech trees shadowing the last of the Birdsnest Orchids have shed a few leaves; some are yellowing early.

In German forests, there are many millions of early-yellowing, falling leaves. In fir forests, the resin is leaking. Woodboring insects multiply.

Venus sets very bright an hour after the sun at the end of July. Davey sits and watches it. He knows which one it is, at last. It looks very white, though he knows it is yellow. He knows that the clouds on Venus aren't water.

August

CHAPTER THIRTY

Dog-days. Still getting hotter.

Every night of the year, the sky over Paris, London, Frankfurt is faintly orange. Thousands of tons of fossilized sunlight are being burned. The air thickens with carbon dioxide, sulphur dioxide, nitrogen.

In August, great flashes of lightning split the orange from top to bottom. The little humans pray for rain. When it comes, it is acid rain.

A third of the German forest is dying. The insects have lots of dead wood to bore.

In England, not very much is noticed. Dog-roses wilt in their proper season, horse-chestnut fruit grow tiny horns, thistles turn into plugs of pale fur.

Venus, the closest planet to Earth, was once much more like us. It did have water, once.

A little too close for comfort, now.

The yellow clouds are sulphur. Under that, carbon dioxide. The surface is hot as fire.

It has never been Harold's favourite month. The French didn't even have a decent name for it – what kind of month is *août*?

But he started this August with quite high hopes. He felt lighter, younger, now April was gone . . . *but at first she made me feel so young*.

It was safer to stay on your own. Less messy to stay on your own.

And you got so much more done. He woke early, got up straightaway, finding no long hairs on the shower curtains.

Breakfast wasn't spoiled by quarrels or sulks or simple incon-venience. (April had the unfortunate habit of thinking she couldn't eat a whole croissant but would just like a bite of his. And it wasn't worth her opening another little pot of jam when she could just share with him. Now he ate monolithic croissants, now he sucked dry whole lagoons of jam.)

And after breakfast, there was no long faintly irritable, faintly hopeless discussions about their plans for the day. So much more *efficient* to be on your own.

The truth was, you didn't even see a foreign place if you were with somebody. You walked through the streets looking at *them*, talking about things which interested *them*, which probably had nothing to do with Paris. April's hair blew like a sliding screen across so much of Paris. In the end he'd almost given up going out.

(He remembered something else, briefly. Coming here with Lottie soon after they were married, the whole city was focused through her laughing, tilted face. Her – *electrifying* face. When she was happy, it held so much life. Those pale green eyes, endlessly curious. She showed him the queer fountain with dogs and turtles in the Luxembourg Gardens, she showed him the chimpanzees in their sad, stately cages in the Jardin des Plantes . . . she agreed the cages were sad but said they were 'history, Harold'. Her version of history followed. 'This place was in the middle of the Revolution – the mob wanted to set all the animals free, then the lions and tigers, who had a lot of sense, started eating the revolutionaries. They locked them up again pretty quickly . . . looks like the original cages, to me. They must be riddled with *ghosts* and *bloodstains*. Don't you think it's marvellous?'

I was so in love with her then. I never troubled to contradict her. I should have pointed out how irrelevant human history is to an ape. And how relevant good cages are.)

The train of thought was unhappy.

Oh best, best to be on your own, to have no frightful burden of guilt that the other partner has thrust upon you. Better by far to be free.

And for the first few days in August, Harold did feel happily free.

211

April sat on the endless steps of the Grand Palais in the milky
sunlight. Her legs were delightfully brown. Emmie would be
wild with envy. She was looking forward to telling her all.

Now she had a chance to think it all out, she knew that Harold
had really loved her most of the time.

Some of the time.

Well, he said so once or twice.

Bastard. Creep . . .

And then she forgot him, shifting her seat on the warm stone
steps, and read her catalogue.

The first day after she checked into her new three-star hotel,
she thought about Harold all the time. Then certain facts came
home to her.

She was in a really nice hotel (she realized now that neither
hotel she'd stayed in with Harold had been *really* nice) with no
one but herself to worry about. She was in the most romantic
city in Europe – *everyone* knew that – and by some miracle, she
knew her way around it. There were five whole days of holiday
left.

Of course, those days were clouded by Harold. The weather
was heavy, not quite ideal. But Paris shone out in the gaps in the
cloud, pools of bright colour in a silver-grey paintbox.

She had scarcely used her sketchbook so far. Going through
hell, you could not be creative. Now she took her sketchbook
out in the streets and dashed in fountains, squares, arches. The
squares and arches might be frames for Harold, but she
managed to keep his ghost out of the fountains.

Good, she thought, but not *very* good. The truth is, I'll never
be *very* good. Maybe I'm – limited. I see some things very clear
and sharp, but other things escape me completely. I understand,
and I don't understand. And I'm not quite brave enough to
make it all up. I suppose I *am* limited. But – it's something to
know I'm limited.

I'm very good at my job, though. I could rise to the top of the
tree in Bingles. Or go to London. Liberty's, Heal's. I don't want
to be just average. I want to be rich and powerful enough for no
one ever to treat me like a child again. I want to be able to pay
for my own hotels, my own holidays. So I'm never palmed off
with second-best again.

I shall buy myself a Bonnard. I'll lend it to exhibitions, and
they'll have my name on the label by it, *Collection Miss April*

Green. They'll all know me at the Pompidou Centre. And I'll know *everything* about what's on.

I want Harold Segall to glimpse me, once, in about five years, or it might take longer, swanning in to the Ritz, or somewhere. And I'll wave to him, just casually, but I shan't have time to stop. Because I'll have a *really important* appointment. By then, of course, he'll be pretty ancient. Grey as a mouse, I expect, and most of what's left will have fallen out. Maybe his teeth as well. And he'll most certainly be impotent. Last fortnight he could hardly do it with me.

Good! Good! April triumphant.

Perhaps her sketch was not so bad. She'd added some made-up figures in the foreground. The lines were bolder, livelier.

She remembered Harold, felt slightly sorry, restored his teeth, and as she got to the door of the Ritz looked round and offered to take him out to lunch. *After* her appointment.

Harold had managed to read himself to the point where thinking was an easier option. Harold was thinking about likenesses. It was stunning to think that chimpanzees were 98 per cent genetically similar to humans. So we're not as unique as we think.

Then there was the question of likenesses *within* a species. We must look as alike to chimpanzees as chimpanzees do to us.

Lottie and I weren't alike at all. Utterly different people. But somehow, at least for a bit, the pieces fitted together. We were a real couple. I felt – *at home.* That phrase was still painful.

Differences, and likenesses. As Paris emptied for *la grande fermeture,* Harold was no longer tormented by cruel likenesses of Lottie. She had gone away and left him. Some final link had been broken. When he tried to imagine her face, nothing recognizably human came.

Once the spectres ceased, he missed them. But did any of them really look at all like Lottie? Was it all just wishful thinking?

An ironic footnote was that once, just for a moment, as his bus disregarded a pedestrian crossing, he'd seen a phantom April, days after she had gone. Now that wasn't wishful thinking. That was pure delusion.

He sat at his solitary table in a café which was soon to close until September, sweating in the electric heat.

Time to get back to reading.

And April, on her last evening abroad, sat faintly drunk in a *lovely* restaurant with red-and-white check tablecloths, candles in bottles, *pure* Paris, the kind Harold never once took her to. It was satisfyingly expensive.

The menu came complete with English translations, and the English was wonderfully, authentically French.

Daily Soup, Greens Bean, Steak 'Pepper-style' or *Dumplings of Veal, Fresh Prunes* or *'Beautiful Helen' Peers.*

There were also things which were more obscure, classified *'Chef's Commandments'. Scorpion Fish, Snout of Swine.* One day she'd be more adventurous. One day she'd show them all. One day she'd eat them all for breakfast.

Most of the other voices seemed to be English, which was slightly disappointing, but that must be because of things closing for August, so everyone had to come here.

The music was the finishing touch, making everything perfect. An old accordion-player, wearing a beret, with a very French moustache, was playing wonderful old-fashioned tunes: 'The Shadow of Your Smile', 'April in Paris', 'Catch a Falling Star', 'As Time Goes By'.

Thinking of Harold as the music played, her perceptions were kinder and wiser.

At least he loved me completely at first. I've learned so much. I'm a different person.

Then she drank another glass and stared at the couples, married couples surely, at the nearby tables. They were getting no more conversation than she was. They'd sat down, ordered, dug into their food. She'd soon put paid to Harold doing that.

Good job I'm strong, she thought. I wouldn't fancy being married.

And yet, with the little tables hardly keeping them apart, spread knees silently, grimly touching, they looked as tenaciously linked as slipper limpets slowly dying on the shingle at home. The dullest shells of all. As if nothing could ever separate them.

And the new, wise April, who could bear her wisdom, who

was lifted by it as she drank her wine, had this perception: he'll go back to his wife. He's probably back with her already. Running back where he came from. *Swine.*

Married men are all alike.

CHAPTER THIRTY-ONE

August 6. A difficult day. Lottie's wedding anniversary. She had no regrets about that marriage, absolutely none.

But perhaps she regretted the idea, still intact on that burning, distant day, that you only had to love once. That you found someone, and were safe, and could spend your whole life getting used to them.

She thought of herself as a loyal person. Yet two of her loyalties had snapped like matches. And once you found that certainties ended, how could you ever be certain again?

Of course, what happened with Harold was worse. With Harold, the choice wasn't hers. So everything was a lot more dangerous.

You thought you lived in a house. You thought you would live in it always. One day you looked up and the ceiling was gone and the person you loved wasn't there.

These thoughts made her rather quiet at breakfast. The day was thundery, hot, and bright. Too much bright linen in the breakfast room. André was solicitous.

Last night he had stayed with her, rather than the other way round. Odd how he made her suite feel small. The usual kind of night.

The strange thing was, all through the night your bodies could be writhing and melting together – but in the morning, life went back to normal. This morning she felt detached.

'Darling, don't you find it – not commodious – that we live in two different places? It means we must always take this decision, where shall we meet. It's bore,' he said.

'It's *a* bore,' she said, with her mouth full of croissant. 'Or you could say, it's boring.'

'So! You agree?'

'I can't think about it this morning. I may be getting a headache. It's August 6 today – '

'Darling, I know. I see three of my managers at ten. It is annoying, there are some little things, you know what kind, I

216

like to do with you, this morning . . . ' She knew what kind of things. She was a little sore again. 'But I think we can celebrate later, especially if you take this decision . . . '

'André, I'm telling you something, darling. Today is the date of my first marriage.'

(Sometimes she longed for fried eggs and bacon and sausage, which Amanda would cook on request. And coffee which wasn't quite so strong.)

'You know, my first wedding anniversary.'

'Oh, so you marry Harold since one year only? I am surprised.'

(Sometimes she longed for a conversation with a native English speaker.)

'No, André. I'm talking about Carl. My first husband. My first marriage.'

'So you are sad.'

'No, no, of course I'm not sad. I'm just thinking about it a little.'

'If you are sad, André makes you happy. You marry André today also.'

'Oh, André, *really*. Don't be silly.'

She smiled, rather touched by his boyish gallantry. She had been staring absently at a tiny trail of coffee-grounds on the white linen, delicately twisted like a curl of smoke. When she looked up to pass on the smile, she was surprised by a look of burning will.

'Oh no, Lottie, you must not call me silly.'

'I call *everyone* silly sometimes.'

The moment passed, but she had a sense that something had happened she didn't understand.

And this morning he wanted to talk. This morning he wanted her to understand him. It was eight-fifteen in the morning, not the best time for understanding. Oh well, at least with André there was rather less to understand. A little simplicity suited her fine.

He was a conservative, 'but progressive'. He liked strong women, *equal* women, though he didn't see why they should work.

'Look at poor Trudi, how tired I make her. It isn't proper life for the beautiful woman. But she is poor, she *must* do it. She must obey all my boring small wish. Lucky for me, of course!'

And he smiled his engagingly honest smile. 'Frankly, I like very much that she will do it!' And he laughed his honest, hearty laugh. 'But a woman like you, Lottie. This is another matter. You are rich lady. You like to stroll, you like to see pictures, you are cultivated, you like music, film, you have your milieu. Yes?'

'Well . . .' she beamed at him indulgently. His face was so pleasantly masculine; those full lips, that determined jaw. So what if he sometimes talked rubbish. All men sometimes talk rubbish.

'So, for you, you are strong *without* work. But you must have the strong man, also, my darling. The strong man like André is, *big* and strong.'

She felt herself flushing, prickling. He really *was* a very sexual man. Carnivorous teeth when his full lips smiled. She was licking her own lips suddenly.

'And a strong man ask you something also. He ask you – certain special work. Your big, strong man. He likes to ask the strong, beautiful woman to work hard for him. You know, I think, where he ask you to work.'

Congested, urgent, their eyes meeting. His fingers flexed on the tablecloth. And they were already standing up, hands brushing, and making their way from the breakfast room, and then they were in the lift, and she said, 'But you have an appointment,' and laughed, though her voice was huskier, more strained than usual, and he said, 'But first, I have an appointment with you,' and as the lift doors opened his fingers probed with precision the cleft of her buttocks.

After he had gone, she slept, exhausted. She woke with a start around three. The day had mysteriously slipped away; the light had a different quality. Could it be getting dark already? Everything had shifted a few degrees. She was astonished to think that other people were opening shops for the afternoon, choosing lettuces, sitting on trains, staring ahead with their knees together.

Other people's sexual selves were nearly impossible to imagine. Your own sexual self was scarcely less strange, because it was not consecutive. Sex moved you in irresistible bursts. It made you blind to everything else, until you had your orgasm. Then reality reappeared, unchanged, except for a brief feeling of distance. And you couldn't reconstruct that overwhelming urgency. Until you caught fire again.

And the same thing happened on a larger scale when you had a new sexual partner. For a while, sex was slotted through all your consciousness, bright thick blazes of erotic desire. Even then, there were gaps of ordinariness. And slowly the gaps extended.

But then, of course, just once in a while, there was love.

And then there was Harold.

Love changed the image entirely. Sex became fused with tenderness. And instead of desire fading away, or being cut off, it was part of life. You could weave it around the two of you, wrap it around you and sleep in peace.

I know that Harold loved me.

The words were as clear as if she'd spoken aloud.

Lottie realized that she was standing naked and dripping wet after her shower. She'd forgotten to dry herself. It was August, but she felt cold. And irritable, which wasn't like her, who always felt marvellous after sex. She dried herself and washed her diaphragm, dried it and put it away. She always hated doing that. She wished someone else would do that.

When she'd said as much to André he chuckled. 'My darling, we do everything to please you. I think I ask Trudi to do it.'

The memory cheered Lottie up. She had a vivid picture of six-foot Trudi, her anxious, fine-boned, aristocratic face, making exquisitely polite small-talk with Lottie while she solemnly washed her diaphragm (her fingers were quite *unnaturally* long, and her nails rather long for typing . . .)

And then she would say, rather as she did to André, 'Is there anything else, Mrs Segall? Are you sure I can't do anything else?'

Lottie suddenly stopped smiling. The joke left a rather unpleasant taste. Perhaps André himself was not always so pleasant.

Perhaps *my life* doesn't taste so pleasant.

Her first wedding anniversary. What should she do with the rest of the day?

In Camden, there would be flowers. For the past eight years, since Carl had forgiven her, flowers had arrived every year. She imagined Amanda receiving them with that small sardonic twist of the lips.

It's a good thing she's fond of Davey. We'd never keep her if it was just me. Amanda would arrange the flowers badly, perfunctorily. Davey would put them straight.

She hoped everything was all right. Of course, by plane it was hours away, it wasn't as if she had deserted him. But still – she hoped *Davey* was all right.

This world – the world of adult sex – must still be a total mystery to him. Despite my stupid joke on the phone. Why am I always so bad on the phone? I hope he's not screwed up about sex.

Lottie tried to remember what being a virgin was like, and failed.

I do hope it hasn't upset him, knowing I'm – well – having it off. He used to be such a strange little boy, hating any man who put his head in the door . . . those wild years after I broke up with Carl. But he must understand me by now. And he's probably inherited a taste for it; his father and I both shared it . . .

Yet it suddenly seemed rather abstract. The taste wasn't there, for the present.

Why am I here in Paris, hundreds of miles from my son? Why am I here on August 6, hundreds of years from the man I first married? Why doesn't anything last? Why does it all come crashing down?

The window was half-open. Outside, the sky had turned heavy and thunderous. People were shouting, down in the street. Harsh, unpleasant voices chanting something she couldn't make out. She went and closed the window, and stood for a moment, hugging herself.

What have I done with my life?

Why does it all feel wrong?

CHAPTER THIRTY-TWO

Why am I still in Paris? thought Harold, staring round yet another empty café. Hundreds of miles from anything I care about. Spending money I can ill afford.

And Paris was in a coma. Everything was in a coma. The plane-tree leaves looked grimy and shrivelled but not quite ready to drop. The roses needed dead-heading. Dressed salads had that faint sheen. Cooked meats were darkening in the heat because no one was here to eat them. People had left for the country, where things might still be green.

Harold mixed Perrier with his wine and thought the words, *my life.*

He tried to concentrate on those two words, on the size of a human lifespan. There were four or five billion of us on earth. Four billion lives being lived. But somehow the whole four billion lives were a tiny layer between past and future. A layer thin as human skin. The tracts of time each side seemed enormous.

On his own, he felt four billion times less.

I suppose my life is *this.* Me in Paris at forty-five.

That was a shaking thought. I can't just be . . . this hopeless mess.

Thank God, at least we live our lives according to our own minute timescale. Years seem a vast amount of time to us . . .

What if we lived by cosmic time? Everything gone in the blink of an eye. No time for regrets, or putting things right (though he wasn't sure he could put things right . . .)

He'd read somewhere that the sense of time is related to the speed of the heartbeat. A bird, a mouse and an elephant all live roughly the same number of heartbeats, so they feel as if they live for the same length of time. Harold approved of that. There was a lot of fairness in that.

Then he began to worry.

He had always had a fast heart, even at school when he played so much tennis. He took after Sylvia, who claimed it was a sign of a passionate nature. But if they had fast heartbeats, and their lives were counted in heartbeats, that meant they were ticking their lives away, that meant –

It meant Sylvia might die. She complained that her heart beat faster and faster, though her life was no longer exciting.

He didn't want to think about his mother. She hadn't answered his postcard. He wrote that months ago . . . he knew he should have phoned. He supposed he was still a provincial; foreign phone calls seemed so extravagant.

Tomorrow I'll phone home.

Poole hadn't been home for twenty-eight years, yet he still used that expression. Was Poole his real home?

He shook his head, and the waiter stared, then fell asleep again.

It was Sylvia's home with Sylvia's rules. She drove Dad away and she kept me down . . . to be fair, she loved me. I think she adored me. But she never quite *saw* me. Never will. She doesn't *want* to see what I am, because I'm not what she'd like me to be . . . (was he being fair? Well, *fairly* fair.)

Part of him hadn't forgiven her for depriving him of a father. She'd admitted it when he was twenty-one. His father had written to Harold three times a year for the first five years or so. She had never shown him the letters; she had never let him know. 'I didn't want to upset you . . . I didn't want to confuse you.' He understood perfectly well what she meant. She didn't want her son to have *confused loyalties.* 'Thank you, Mother.' He felt a deep anger.

By the time he was in his twenties, it was much too late to start writing to his father. Yet over the years his mind circled back to it endlessly, uselessly. If he could have had one wish . . . nobody offers you wishes. But Harold had planned a hundred letters, had met his father in a thousand airports, a thousand shuttered rooms.

Maybe your parents *were* home. You could never quite get free of them. Friends and lovers seemed more important, but they lacked that terrible staying power.

My life might have been so different if I'd had a different mother.

He knew the excuse was feeble. But then, maybe *he* was

feeble. Maybe he wouldn't be feeble, if he'd had a different mother . . .

Sylvia's dutiful son. More like a dutiful husband, once Father had gone.

He remembered the times when she was touring and they stayed in unfamiliar rooms. She would come in and wake him in the early hours, switching on the light so he woke, afraid. Her fine freckled skin would be shining with excitement, and she would smell exotic, of grease-paint and sweat. Sitting on the bed, often crushing his foot, she would launch into her story, tides of unfamiliar names, waves of wild laughter, both hands flying like freckled birds. 'Harold, are you listening?' 'Yes, Mother, of course I am.' Watching her hands, hypnotized. If they would sleep, he could sleep.

And yet, she had so much life, still does. On good days, she could light up a room. The same talent that Lottie had . . .

Around him, the café was still and dark. The waiter flicked his cloth, to keep cool. Harold drummed his fingers on the table-top, and when they stopped, he could still hear thunder.

Of course I'll phone her. I hope she's all right . . .

Of course she's all right. She's always the same. I'll phone her tomorrow, and she'll be reproachful and vague as ever, of course. And I'll feel bored and guilty as ever. Nothing changes. No hope of that.

Yet Harold himself could change. Harold did not feel hopeless. Tolstoy started writing in his forties, didn't he? Maybe I'll still write a novel. I've changed before, I can change again . . .

But *monuments*, like Sylvia. Amanda. Even Lottie.

They could never ever change.

He wandered back through the Tuileries, slowly under the stupid heat. The parallel lines went on for ever, and dust, and yellow grass, and dust.

Where the lines converged, great thunder-clouds.

In London, the clouds burst open just as the march crawled into Hyde Park.

Infinitely slow, the last two hours, to every marcher but Davey and Mary. They were still uncertain they were quite together, and looked at each other an awful lot. Davey didn't care how slow the march went.

Slow as the march, the clouds grew darker, and then the light started flashing and flickering over the thousands of waiting faces, and then they felt the first fat drops.

As the drops turned into a heavy bombardment, somebody, *Mary*, seized his hand. 'We don't have to stay. Are you coming?'

They run up Oxford Street, soaking wet, Mary still clutching a placard on which the 'CRUISE' had dripped black tears. Her lids and cheeks are shining white.

In Camden, Amanda is struggling back from the shops with a brand new pressure-cooker.

'I give you *cart blonsh*', Mrs Segall said, when she gave her the money for household expenses. Whatever that meant, it was a lot of money.

But money doesn't solve everything.

Davey is growing up fast. He makes her feel uneasy.

He complains that she overcooks the veg. She has always cooked it the same. But she wants to please, and who else is there to please, now Mrs Segall seems to have emigrated?

Amanda will give this a go. It will probably kill her, but she'll give it a go. All the same – she doesn't like changes.

The clouds open as she passes a house two hundred yards from home. A woman who was going to put out her rubbish but stopped in her doorway, watching the rain, sees Amanda trying to shelter with her enormous parcel under a tree.

'Coo-ee!' She calls. Amanda looks. They have sometimes chatted in the vegetable market.

'You'll catch your death. Come and have a cup of tea.'

The idea is a novelty. Well, why not?

By the time Amanda leaves for home, she is calling the woman Doris, and has taken advice on the pressure cooker.

'Take it back. They're horrible things. Good as having a bomb in the kitchen.'

☆

Why doesn't that child ring me? thinks Sylvia, beached in Poole. Sometimes she feels like an ancient shell abandoned by what had once lived there. Harold makes her feel like that. He makes her feel she is already dead.

He no longer *sees* me, really. He just *refers* to me, like a code. Well, I'll surprise him yet.

Not so much time to do it.

Sylvia knew by now she was ill. It was more than indigestion. The doctor still said it was angina, which he had been saying *months* ago. He gave her some pills, and waffled on. But angina was just a kind of heartburn, wasn't it? *She'd* thought it was angina once. Not any more. The doctor was old. *It's more than heartburn, dear,* she thought.

She fed the pills to her plants. Most pills agreed with plants.

The pains had been sharper, more regular since her climb up Boscombe Chine. She should have felt depressed. Instead she felt strangely light-hearted, like a nervous actress who suddenly starts to act well near the end of the play.

Whatever happens, happens. I think I'll enjoy myself, just for a bit. I don't intend to die just yet.

Sylvia had a sherry and reflected. All time was a special occasion, now. Confident as on her birthday, she rang – *my family* – in Camden.

'Yeah?'

'Davey, *darling.*'

'Oh *hallo,* Sylvia.'

Davey was genuinely pleased. He had always been short of grandmas. When your mother behaved like a bossy younger sister, you really needed a grandma. Amanda was great . . . *but.* Once things were perfectly simple. Lately he'd realized that paying someone money complicated things between you. As he got older, she became less free. She couldn't say what she thought. She wasn't that keen on Mary coming round, but she didn't dare say so. It made him feel guilty. He really didn't want to have power over people. It just made you both . . . *unnatural.*

Sylvia's crassness was quite a relief. Catch *her* not saying what she thought about things. And she had actually remembered his name, *in one.*

'It's great to hear you, Sylvia. You know Harold walked out on us. Well, Mum's gone too. I'm on my own.'

Sylvia was on good form. She asked if he was growing. She asked if he was eating all right. She asked if he was getting good marks, coming top of things and so on. He explained that his school didn't work like that.

There was a pause while she digested this peculiar remark. She asked if he had a girlfriend yet. She could never resist, though she knew he hated it. To her surprise he said, 'Yes, I think so. I'll bring her to see you if you like.'

(He didn't mean it; but he merely meant he was proud that he could answer 'Yes.')

But Sylvia rushed to embrace the idea.

'Darling, that would be wonderful. Soon as you like. I'm a teeny bit under the weather. Heart playing up, though I feel *marvellous*. But it would be nice to see you. Especially nice, in fact. You could go and look at the sea. Don't leave it too long though, darling . . . Oh, if Harold happens to ring – could you tell him I'm not quite myself? And Davey – regards to your terrifying mother.'

I'll go, he thought, as he put the phone down, but somehow he didn't, for another month.

The phone call invigorated Sylvia. It proved it was easy to call people back. She still had the pulling power; now she would use it.

And swiftly, gaily, as if he had just gone away for a week on a conference, she started writing to – *Harold's father*. She started writing to her husband, Harold, the only husband she had ever had. It was certainly time; it was just the moment. She'd always known she would write in the end. It was certainly time to forgive him. These years had just been a game between them, a kind of game that they both understood.

It was a long, breathless, gossipy letter on beautiful Indian watered paper. It might have gone on for weeks. At the end she might have got to the point.

But weeks weren't as long as she thought. The timescale got suddenly shorter. The pains grew worse, and more frequent. Her heart was beating much faster.

Sylvia was resourceful, though, and determined to have a good send-off. She cabled the university where Harold was Professor. She didn't hope for too much, since it was the long vacation. She didn't much hope, so she didn't much care (she cared entirely; hoped absolutely) and she hazarded all, as she'd hazarded certain amazing and beautiful improvisations, years ago when she was still Sylvia Delaire and the world was still her stage:

August

DARLING HAROLD AM THINKING OF BOWING OUT STOP
TICKER TICKING EXCESSIVELY FAST WHY NOT
FLY OVER AND SEE THE WRECK ABSURD
BUT I ALWAYS LOVED YOU STOP
SYLVIA DELAIRE SEGALL

CHAPTER THIRTY-THREE

It was much too hot, too heavy, too weary for Lottie to cope with a crisis. Yet a crisis seemed to have arisen.

August is *not the right month* for a crisis.

André's parents were coming to Paris. When he first told her, she felt relief.

'That's wonderful, darling. You'll enjoy yourselves. Don't give it a thought, I've got lots to keep me occupied.'

Fly to Provence, for a couple of days. Catch up on sleep. Some time to think.

'But of course, it is my chance to present you.'

'You want to present me to your parents? How charming of you. Of course. We'll have lunch one day, or something.' What a bore, she thought, that he still had parents. She'd rather have someone whose parents were dead.

'But Lottie, of course, I think they must be very surprised if you do not meet them. They know already many things about you. Not everything of course. They know you are of a certain age. Doesn't matter . . . ' he smiled expansively, generously, lifting his hands in the air.

'Thank you, darling,' she said, drily. His hands were so beautifully manicured, the whites of the nails so immaculately white, the rest such a matt and healthy pink. He had joked that Trudie did them.

And yet, his palms are the tiniest bit plump . . .

'But attention, my love. Something they do not know, and I ask that you don't tell it, please.'

He wagged his finger with mock severity and again her eyes were riveted by the nail. The cuticles didn't show the slightest unevenness; her own were rough, by comparison. Maybe Trudi *does* manicure them. Maybe secretaries *do*, in Switzerland.

'Of course, if they know that you still marry this Harold, they do not like it. So, we tell them that you marry him a very long time ago – maybe since fifteen years – with a beautiful son, naturally – and that he dies – you are widow.'

Lottie started to giggle. *Preposterous.*

'Are you serious, André? *Honestly.* What did my husband die of? Is my son dead, too?'

He drew himself up in his chair, which made him look imposingly large. He smiled, but it wasn't a wholehearted smile. His brows were raised, his nostrils pointed.

'Ah Lottie, you find it very amusing. I laugh also! Ha, Ha!' It was the most mirthless laugh she had ever heard. 'I also like the jokes, you see. But I think we do not joke so much with my parents.'

'André, I would never laugh at your parents . . .'

'And I think you agree, you are widow. We agree perhaps he die of the heart?'

'All right, André. Here I am, a beautiful, submissive, respectable widow. And my husband died of the heart . . .'

Died of the heart. At first comic, the phrase echoed a little unpleasantly.

Mort d'une crise cardiaque. Douleur de coeur, crise de coeur.

Why must he always speak English? . . . he says it makes him feel closer to me. He really believes his English is perfect ('like this, we understand *completely*'.)

The conversation left an aftertaste. The affair was starting to make demands.

☆

It soon became clear that André expected them to escort his parents round Paris together. She was rather touched, in a way.

He's a nice boy, at heart. His parents are probably sweeties . . .

Thank God they're only staying three days.

Luckily, André seemed impervious to Lottie's lack of enthusiasm. He had enough and to spare. But every so often he would check himself and look to her briefly for corroboration.

'We all have families, no? We all need the family, also. I am a very progressive man. But family is the most important tradition. Friends – yes. A man has many. But family never leave you.'

They turned out to be small and round and very faded beside their son. They both ate a very great deal of food very seriously, and went round the Louvre more seriously still. Quite often André excused himself, leaving Lottie as chaperone. Trudi was away for a few days, which left him a lot of work to do.

'And Lottie, they both love you so much. Like their son does also, of course.'

The Louvre seemed to grow and grow; the Legros were never tired. Her slightest remark made them chuckle approvingly, whether it was funny or not. And sometimes in the middle of a sentence of hers, one or other of them would suddenly remark, *'Mais elle est belle, n'est-ce pas?'* and make sketchy attempts at pinching her cheek.

When they left they both hugged her sturdily. Monsieur Legros remarked that his son was a very lucky man; Madame Legros hoped they would see her *very soon* in Geneva, and informed her that their house was her house – Lottie must think of her as a second mother. Her pale, fat-bedded eyes were moist.

But you aren't my mother, Lottie thought coldly. My mother was beautiful. My mother is dead. These people *aren't* my family.

Who are my family though? Davey. And a few old aunts and uncles I never see. People I send money to . . .

Sylvia. Oddly enough, I thought of her as family. Even though she doesn't like me. I love the old bat, in a way.

Then one of those voices she couldn't shut out.

Harold is my family.

☆

As they drove back from the airport, André was delighted with Lottie.

'Lottie, you were *formidable.* They really adored you. A great success.'

She was glad to see Trudi back in the lobby; it might check André's flow of words. That girl was looking as pale and tired as ever after her three-day break.

Her legs are really *abnormally* long and thin, Lottie decided, observing them as Trudi redraped herself in the chair. They crossed in too many places, twining together like swans' necks.

I wonder if Trudi's married. I suppose André pays her awfully well, but it doesn't seem much of a life to me.

'My parents now also love Lottie,' André was telling Trudi, praising Lottie as if she was a particularly well-behaved child. 'She is almost adopted of our family. Ha! Ha!' and one of his hearty laughs seemed to break over Trudi like a blow.

She flinched, and Lottie thought, Oh dear, he must be exhausting to work for. On the other hand, Trudi's colour was back. Indeed, it was rather high. It must have been just a trick of the light that made her look pale before.

Next day, André flew to Milan with Trudi to see some new designs. Lottie was on her own. She had a long day walking. Last night there had been a thunderstorm so massive that the air was breathable.

She wandered up through the Champ de Mars, crossed the Seine with the rest of the ribbon of glass and steel and fumes winding over the river, and stared up at the fountains of the Trocadero.

The water-cannons shot wide arcs of water over towards the Eiffel Tower. It came at her like a giant waterfall: white noise, sheer power. Walking up the steps beside the fountains, the fine mist blew across her. Not many people, just her and the water. Lovely to be outside, after all those days in the airless Louvre with André's fucking family.

Close up, you could see the muscle in the water. Thousands and thousands of gallons of water. Enormous concentrations of power. Exciting, but also frightening.

Hydrogen bomb. Atom bomb.

The horrible words shot into her mind.

What was she supposed to do with them? They didn't usually trouble her.

She remembered the mob on her wedding anniversary. Even in Paris you got this kind of thing. Some of them had seemed to be jeering at her, when she emerged from the hotel and walked to her taxi, though what did it have to do with *her*?

A boy who was really quite sweet-looking had pressed a leaflet into her hand. In the end she took it, in case they got violent – peace protestors were often violent – and carefully dropped it on the floor of her taxi, as soon as she got inside.

She walked a little distance from the fountains, out of the blowing cloud of water, and stared across the river. The long steep curves of the Eiffel Tower shimmered in the midday heat. As if it were slowly melting.

Unimaginable heat. Of course, it would never happen. Governments stopped these things happening. But sometimes things went wrong. We ought to build millions of shelters.

André was telling me about the wonderful shelters the Legros family have in Geneva, with everything from video libraries to wine cellars. It's something to take into account, I suppose . . . if Davey could come too . . .

No – she would rather do something herself. There wasn't room for anything *comfortable* in London, but she could do something quite nice in Provence. Scotland wasn't really worth bothering about; being stuck in Scotland would be worse than death . . . But Provence would be quite all right. She *liked* the idea of Provence.

The wind changed suddenly and blew a spiteful volley of ice at Lottie. It felt like an admonition. She told whoever might be watching her, *I didn't mean everyone else to die.* I didn't mean *that*, honestly. Governments ought to build shelters for *them*. Governments ought to look after things.

But she still didn't feel quite easy.

She started walking back down the sloping terraces, towards the Seine. Away from the fountains, it was very hot. The clouds were building up again, hazy, yellowish, across the water.

Harold always said I shouldn't think this way. He said it was a delusion. He said there'd be nothing left to live for, the world would turn dark and cold.

Stupid, impractical Harold. Gloomy, perverse Harold.

He said we could stop it happening. But if it happened, shelters wouldn't help. He said . . . things she would not remember.

I told him it was morbid nonsense. We'd get into the car and drive to Ireland. We'd have flown to Sydney *weeks* before . . .

She turned and stared back for a second. Little people shrieked as the white mist blew. There was hardly anyone left.

Maybe I do need a family.

CHAPTER THIRTY-FOUR

By the last week in August the relief Harold felt when April left had long since gone.

The thundery heat was an endless penance. His body began to complain. Aches and pains he had never experienced settled in his joints, his back, his shoulders. Strange pangs pulled at his soft innards, places he never knew existed, reminding him there were a lot of worries he hadn't worried yet.

And then, there was the itching. He showered daily, as he always did. But one day he'd started to itch. On his calf, then the back of his neck. And so he started to scratch, discreetly, since he was in a café.

Back in his room he scratched again, furiously, ruthlessly.

In the end it seemed his whole body was an endless riot of voices. A headache droned like an aeroplane, followed by commanding, frightening pains in his groin, from which he was summoned by the tiny twitch which began to pulse in his left eye . . . as he searched for a mirror to monitor that, the itch began to whisper again.

Far too much was happening.

On the other hand, nothing, nothing at all, nothing on earth was happening. Nor did he have any plans. There were only itches, and impulses. Once when he'd drunk too much wine he tried ringing Lottie's number. He gave it ten rings, then, just in case, another ten. After twenty rings he hung up and redialled in case he'd dialled wrong. The senseless ringing maddened him. She and Davey were sitting there, knowing it was him, deliberately not answering.

Not that he didn't communicate with them. Oh no, they couldn't stop him communicating. In his head there were endless dialogues, endless imaginary scenes. Lottie behaved disgracefully, shouting absurd insults. In time, she tended to weep. He felt better once she was weeping. Davey sulked, was indifferent. But Harold was splendidly forceful, delivering ace after ace, volleying, sprinting, shaking them up, smashing the enemy into the ground . . .

Actually, lying awake in bed, twitching, scratching, aching. Listening to the blaring of foreign horns, listening to people driving away. If only they would come back. But Paris belonged to pigeons and dust. So why did he stay on?

– To avoid deciding where else to live. To avoid his mother; to avoid his novel; to avoid the absence of his novel. To avoid deciding what the hell to do when his money ran out.

The royalties from his textbooks were quite nice as spending money, when your living expenses were paid by your wife. But they didn't increase, they diminished; like everything else, he thought. And he'd never write a textbook again.

'It is generally thought that . . .' 'It is believed . . .'

Harold no longer pompously thought it. Harold no longer believed. Harold no longer craved to examine, and feared to be examined.

Five A-level textbooks, a broken marriage, some yellowing notes and a handful of dust.

When Harold examined himself, it seemed there was nothing there.

Lighter and lighter.

Less and less.

On his own, he was hardly real.

In the end, a kind of panic got him as far as the Gare du Nord. Crazed with economy, Harold booked a crossing on the night boat home.

The hours on the Channel weren't pleasant, but they were extremely real.

Harold was old; the old tried to sleep. The lights shone pitilessly through his clenched lids. The young had fun as the tin box of bodies chugged over the water under clouds and stars.

It was very hot. The ceiling pressed down. The light in the boat was yellow and dirty. Harold read *Cosmos* for a bit, but you couldn't think in a football crowd.

The young drank duty-free whisky, belched, farted, yelled 'Excusy-moi!', dropped ash and nuts and crisps on *Cosmos*.

Frantic, he fought his way upstairs.

Outside, the night was relatively cool, but over the engines he could still hear thunder.

He stared up into the darkness. Erratic gaps in the muddy cloud. Maps of the stars never looked like this.

Much too close to Venus. The lemon-yellow, uniformly shining clouds are a haze of drops of sulphuric acid. Underneath them the carbon dioxide traps the heat; nothing escapes.

Lightning plays ceaselessly over Venus. Near the scorched surface the air is clear and the temperatures are higher than on any other planet. The pressures are intense.

A lethal yellow hot-house.

Too much cloud. Harold went below.

Once the boat docked, there was the waiting. Outside the window, the light increased. The rucksacks queued for the exit. It didn't hurt being butted by a sleeping-bag as long as you didn't hit the zip . . .

But something more urgent was bothering him. Something more painful made him feel real.

Suddenly, Harold was worried about Sylvia. Suddenly he knew there was something wrong. Messages must be waiting for him at home in England, terrifying letters he could not open. He felt sick, and guilty, and frighteningly real, as he stared at the backs of the travellers in front of him, strangers who stood between him and his mother.

And Harold feels very small. He is a tall man, he isn't used to being small. He and Lottie were once a commanding couple. He is standing now, with a lot of luggage, and yet he is dwarfed by the great clanking boat, the meaningless noise and the press of bodies, people in groups, people in pairs, people in families shouting, 'Stick together!'

On his own, he is nothing at all.

September

CHAPTER THIRTY-FIVE

Mercury flies past the vast bright disc of the sun like a tiny ant. It is very small – only Pluto is smaller. Humans call it the messenger. The fastest planet in the solar system, flying the closest to the sun.

A planet of extremes. Its coldest nights dip to –180 degrees Celsius. Its hottest days climb to 430 degrees Celsius. Its highest speed as it circles the sun is 127,000 miles per hour.

But it spins on its axis very slowly. Immensely long days, immensely long nights.

A long brightness, a long blackness.

It is 'small': 3,300 miles across.

On a ten-foot wall of dark honeysuckle leaves in a seaside town on the planet Earth, there is still one flower, parchment pale, about an inch and a half across.

LAST DAYS of the summer sales. Fogged pastel sunsuits, unsuitable hats, a row of sand-shoes in miniature sizes. Open-topped buses skim faster and faster along the front, with fewer passengers. Fifty miles per hour on a downhill stretch.

A police car passes, doing sixty.

Dover, September 1. Coming out on the gang-plank was like being born, dazzling, frightening. Above, the sky was a flat mass of cloud, compressed and very bright. Below, the pavements, ramps, walkways were black from thousands of weary feet, trying to get back home.

Harold creaked along in a line of bodies.

It's usually one of my favourite months. Behind the white there must be sunlight. Things will be clear. My life will begin (though it *wasn't* clear how his life would begin).

He passed through Customs like a dream, suddenly thinking of April, realizing with a kind of wonder that they'd left these shores together. And now he'd almost forgotten her . . . the railway platform opened up.

Not easy to think on the London train, with the hangovers, and the overtired schoolkids, and an old man snoring, looking desperately ill, scalp frail and freckled when his head fell forwards. Outside the window, salmon-pink houses were eating the fields, which had yellowed in his absence. Stubble was burning, some already black. Everything was suddenly going too fast.

But Harold knew one thing clearly. He wasn't going to do what a son should do. He wasn't going to slip across London like a ghost and take the next train down to Poole. He was going where his heart told him to go.

He was going to try one more time to see Lottie. He was going to the last place which had been home. Properly home. And it didn't matter if all his belongings had been packed off to Poole, it didn't matter if every small mark he had made on the walls or the sheets had been washed away –

It was still our bed. She can't change that.

He knew how Lottie felt towards Carl; she had simply erased him from her life. But you only repaint the present, you can't erase the past.

And however much time goes by. However many husbands Lottie may have. *Under that roof we slept. Under that roof we are lovers.*

He dozed for a little, comforted.

At Victoria all the large luggage-lockers were full, so he kept his big suitcase with him. That day he would grow to hate it.

He ate a disgustingly large English breakfast to give him strength for what lay ahead. The grease made him feel slightly sick, and he spilled some egg-yolk on his jacket.

She might be bad-tempered if he rang her early. So he went to a café and read the English papers. He read some pages several times. Then he trundled his case along to get some more money, and plenty of tenpenny pieces. He spent the money on a pint of

Dutch courage, then another two pints, then another half. That made him feel less courageous, and drunk. So he had to eat a large lunch, to get sober. In the mirror-lined café, Harold observed that he badly needed a haircut. But no one could fit him in till three. Then they kept him waiting, and cut it too short. Smoothing his ears back against his head, he wished he was brave enough not to leave a tip, and in the stress of discovering he *wasn't* brave enough, left all the tenpenny pieces.

Suddenly, it was nearly five o'clock. He couldn't put it off any more. Harold made for the bus stop, heart beating rather fast. The weight of the suitcase made him sweat profusely. It was comforting, though, to see the 24 bus. He stood his large case on the seat beside him and nervously combed his ears backwards again. They had certainly got more springy than before.

Had he got balder?

Well – not *less* bald. But the face in the window was certainly browner than most of those around him. A tiny glimmer of hope.

' 'Scuse me, mate,' said a robust voice. 'Is that thing a fare-paying passenger?' A vaguely familiar conductor's face, big, unhumorous, mean.

'Uh, no, sorry,' Harold panted, as he wrestled the thing towards the floor. One end hacked cruelly at his shin and the handle grazed his knee in passing. But it still wouldn't fit on the floor between the seats, so he ended up holding it jammed upright on his knees with a lock staring into his face. He felt like an untrained cello-player. The audience stared and waited.

A large fat perfumed West Indian woman strained into the seat beside the two of them. The scent was oily, sugary, powerful; in better times he would have appreciated it. But Harold was terribly hot, and unable to see where he was going. Harold was suffocating. Every part of his body except his scalp, which felt, as usual, uncomfortably bare, was squeezed against some surface, mostly surfaces of the woman.

As usual, everything felt out of control. He tried to get out at the Camden Boots, but he was completely stuck. The perfumed woman didn't get up. She just stayed put and tried to encourage him by shoving crossly at his pinioned arm and saying, 'Oh Lord, oh Lord.'

In the end he got off only one stop late by dint of ceasing to try. Suddenly, something gave. He was on the pavement and the bus had gone.

Three streets away was home. Nothing had changed but the season. The sky was smoky, city pink, an uglier city than Paris. The evening was cool on his damp skin. Of course, he thought, it's autumn.

He parked the case on the pavement, walked up two steps – brought his feet together. Walked up three steps – brought his feet together; stood in the wind for a second; swayed; *this will change my life* – pressed the bell.

No one answered.

Pressed the bell.

No one.

The lights were on in the drawing-room, but that meant nothing, since they had a system which switched on the lights when no one was there. Bloody silly system. Fucking silly system.

Pressed the bell, frantic, again and again.

One more try, staring hungrily upwards.

How could he ever have just slipped inside?

And heavily, wearily he backed down the steps, nearly falling backwards as he took a last look, and picked up the case, and stood undecided.

God knows what I'll do now.

(If so, God knew the most wearisome things. Harold would take a tube to Victoria, a dirt-cheap hotel where the sheets were nylon and the pay-phone had been half-wrenched from the wall. He would sleep till noon, despairingly. So he stayed for an extra day. In the end he stayed for almost a week in that blank little room with its black-and-white TV. The same worry nagged him about his mother, repeating ineffectually. The black-and-white picture rotated endlessly, slipping, slipping, driving him mad. He made endless journeys to Camden where the house stared blindly back at him. After six days he would leave for the sea.)

'What'll we do if he knows we're here?' Mary whispered to Davey, two floors up.

'Don't be daft. And you don't have to whisper. Course he can't tell, he's not psychic, is he? Anyway, not answering is your idea.'

'Well, Smeggy frightens me.'

'Well, he doesn't frighten me.' Davey isn't telling the truth completely. 'Anyway, how do you know it's him? It might be Amanda forgotten her key.'

'It's a feeling I've got. It's definitely Smeggy. A woman wouldn't keep ringing like that.'

'Anyway, he'll only come back.'

'Doesn't matter, does it, if it's after tomorrow? You'll be in Norfolk, with Charles.'

'I wish you could come with me.'

'His parents would have a fit.'

'What were you talking about before?'

'Oh . . . makeup. They test eye makeup on rabbits. Sometimes they go blind.'

Downstairs a door clicked, and the teenagers jumped and swung their feet down off the sofa.

But it was only Amanda.

She cleared her throat on the landing outside and came in after a second or two.

'Did someone just come to the house?'

Mary lied quickly to save explaining. 'No, only you.'

'I was just coming down by the Irish shop, and I saw a man on our doorstep. With a suitcase. Thought it might be that man sharpens knives. Doris said he was down this way this morning. I told her, we've got plenty of work for him to do. She said – '

'We didn't hear anything.' Mary shook her black hair impatiently.

She's as pale as lard, thought Amanda. And skinny as a matchstick. Funny-looking child, with that little snub nose and a great big mouth with no colour to speak of.

Nice enough girl, but not much to look at. She's done very well for herself, getting Davey.

Amanda had plenty of time to discuss her with Doris during the days that followed. Davey had gone for a week in the country with his carroty-haired friend, Charles. Amanda approved; it would do him good. Why should only Madam have holidays?

– Amanda herself took a holiday. Yes. *Other people might need holidays too.* It was a great departure; the first in years. Amanda only went away to her daughter's.

But now Mrs Segall had upped and left them, there wasn't a lot for Amanda to do. Davey fretted if she dusted too much. That veg of his took hardly any cooking. At first she had just felt at a loose end. But now she began to – *enjoy the freedom.* She said as much to Doris. Then she knew she meant it. You could have opinions, if you had a friend.

Timorous as if she was going to Africa, Amanda made a voyage of two hundred yards. Amanda went to stay with Doris. A friend's a friend, she thought with delight.

Someone who actually saw you as a person. A person, not a – *dogsbody.*

She couldn't say *that*, not even to Doris. But lying in bed in the lovely little room that Doris had made up just for her, *dogsbody* rang in her brain. *None of them guesses that I might have feelings.* But Doris guesses. Doris understands.

Doris and she had a lot in common. Doris had Dug for Victory, too. They talked about the war, and nearly died laughing about those awful recipes. *Mock Haggis, Hasty Pudding.* 'Take Half a Leek and One Bacon Rind . . . ' The young didn't realize how lucky they were. Doris and Amanda both realized.

Doris really had had her bit of luck. 'I'm sitting on sixty thousand quid,' she said. That startled Amanda, but Doris meant the house, which Ronald had picked up for a song after the war. And he'd left Doris with a nice little pension.

They walked Doris's terrier in the park. Amanda hadn't been in the park for years. She picked up conkers, which were not quite ripe. How long was it since she'd noticed conkers? She felt like a girl of thirteen.

They went to the last of the summer sales, not to buy but just to jeer at the prices. But Amanda, on a wave of euphoria, suddenly bought herself a hat with cherries, a beautiful straw, yellowy cream, with a bunch of cherries exactly like life. 'It'll come in lovely, next summer,' she said. They had a drink and a laugh together.

Amanda had never realized she was lonely.

Doris, who had only been widowed a year, was in no doubt that *she* was. 'What's the good of having this blooming great house if I tremble whenever the door creaks at night?' she demanded, pouring Amanda a little more apricot wine. 'I've slept better these past few nights than I have since Ronald died. Good riddance to him, all the same.'

In Amanda's mind, where nobody had looked or enquired for twenty years or more, things were growing, changing, incredibly fast.

Doris enquired, with interest.

Harold hung around till the following Friday. None of their friends seemed to be in town; Claudia was in New York again, the Jenningses were in the Dordogne, Rick and Liz had gone to Tuscany, Ivor and Elspeth weren't back from Ceylon, as their answering machine termed it. Harold was alone in his frightful room where the black-and-white screen flickered mockingly as the TV picture slipped and fell.

On Friday evening, Amanda was with Doris, sniffing at a film in the very front row. Davey and Charles were smoking dope on a haystack, staring at the stars, so much brighter in the country.

And Harold was staring at the stupid doorstep, blinding white under the stupid light. Above him the sky was entirely black. The bright porch light had put them all out, the millions of stars which might have helped him a little.

Barely catching the very last train, a defeated Harold, dragging his baggage, repeated the journey he made last December, from Camden Town to Bournemouth.

Lottie, Lottie. Where have you gone? Who are you with? What are you doing?

Lottie was almost totally happy. She was off to Provence for a fortnight, tomorrow. André was quieter than usual, tonight. They strolled by the side of the river, and there was a hopeful crescent moon. September was one of her favourite months. A dazzling pleasure-steamer passed them.

Across the water, the sound of a waltz. Tiny couples were circling each other. She smiled to herself as she watched the dance.

CHAPTER THIRTY-SIX

In the hall of Ted Sedley's house in Boscombe, Harold found utter darkness.

Groping for the light, he knocked a pile of things, must be letters, off the hall table. Curses. It took a little time for his hand to remember where the light-switch was. He found it. The bare bulb blazed.

There was a ragged clutch of messages. He knew they must be, they *were*, for him.

The first thing to hand was a re-used, resealed envelope. He flicked it open. A faded theatre programme (*Private Lives*, 1953) which he folded irritably away. Two handwritten invoices from Ted Sedley. There was a long and puzzling PS.

'Your delightful Mother the Actress called. We had a "good old Chat". Please show her the enclosed "Memento". Appreciate it back some day. Ted.'

Which cheered him up quite drastically. Sylvia and Ted having a 'good old Chat'. *She must be all right*. The relief spread through him.

A postcard from Davey.

H. SEGALL. PLEASE FORWARD.
Where are you Harold, please get in touch. Thought you were in Poole with Sylvia? She just rang up and said she was ill and doesn't have a clue where you are. Mum's in Paris with an AWFUL CREEP. Love Davey.

'with an awful creep' was the first pain, then
'said she was ill'   'said she was ill'
And then there were two police messages.
No.

The first asked him to contact Poole General Hospital as soon as possible, where his mother Mrs S. Segall was seriously ill. Dated two days ago.

The second one asked him to call at Boscombe Police Station as soon as possible. Dated yesterday.

It was as if he had always known. He felt very cold, and he sat on his case, with his old tired head in his old tired hands.

I knew in Paris, when I felt so uneasy. I knew last week when the Victoria Royal Boarding House phone was so horriby – dead. She's dead. I just had a feeling. When I went to phone, and the phone was dead.

It was nearly midnight. He'd go to the callbox and phone the police and the hospital. But first he dragged his cases upstairs, step by step by heavy step. The flat smelled damp and the bulb had gone. He couldn't believe he had ever lived there.

The affair with April, the months in Paris – it all seemed utterly unreal. As if he had woken from a long light dream at 2 a.m. in terrible pain. Nothing at all but the pain was real.

Harold spoke to many strangers that night. All of them were nice to him, and spoke to him gently. Next day, more phone calls. Trying to be practical. He needed an appointment to see his own mother. It seemed outrageous, but Harold yielded (perhaps they were making her look nice for him). Harold began to feel numb and distant. The undertaker's, at 3 p.m.

It felt like a dentist's waiting-room. The thin receptionist was also nice to him, seemed to be pleased to see him. She was telling him something, thought he couldn't listen, and gently taking his arm. They went down a corridor together. This last gentleness made him weep.

And he entered weeping, exactly as Sylvia Delaire Segall would have wanted him to. She lay looking slightly bemused to be there, very dry, very pale, very freckled. She was smaller and more contained than before (he must have feared spreading, wetness). Someone had combed out her sandy-white curls. From quite close up they looked yellow and young.

The first thing he felt was pride; how beautifully she was playing it. As a boy he had seen her act several swoons and a wonderful Desdemona. The first time he had been terrified. Any minute now, she would get up and smile and prepare for the Final Curtain.

I'm thinking what she would have wanted me to think, Harold realized, acknowledging her power. But it isn't a play. And she died alone. They found her lying at the top of the stairs. Never even regained consciousness, and died in hospital two days later.

I hate to think of her being alone. I should have been there. I *could* have done. Maybe I could have stopped it happening. I should have come, but I chased after Lottie.

Maybe she was waiting for me to come.

But her face, turned up, slightly smiling, remote, denied she had ever suffered. He wished she could move, just for a second, just somehow acknowledge he was there. But she had a look she sometimes wore in life, of being somewhere else, above or beyond.

I came in the end, Mother, he thought but his lips were as stiff and silent as hers.

I did love you, Mother, you know. You weren't like anyone else's mother. You were just a little too much for me. Ted Sedley fell for you. Davey was fond of you. Even Lottie in her own weird way admired you.

He tried to tell her, as he sat beside the coffin, all the things she might have wanted to hear. His tears fell softly, without a sound. In the end he sat dry-eyed.

The feeling that was left was for himself.

Did she *ever* know I was there? Did she ever listen to me? Did she really love me at all?

Why did she have to die?

He found he had clenched his fists. He relaxed them quickly, ashamed. He suddenly wanted to get away from this scented, silent, sunlit room and his leaf-dry, silent mother who was here and nowhere on earth at all.

It wasn't Sylvia: too little, too light. He suddenly bent and kissed her lips and half-stumbled towards the door.

Of the kiss he would only remember the cold, too cold to believe she had ever lived there.

CHAPTER THIRTY-SEVEN

Hanging baskets of brown-leaved geraniums swung at eye-level on Sylvia's porch. They all looked homesick for the ground below.

Round the side, under a tile, as if nothing had happened, the key he'd so often told her not to hide there. The door opened as if nothing had happened. The house smelled of everything familiar.

Everything's changed, everything. Harold stood in the hall in tears.

When he went upstairs there was something lying on the very top step. A telegram, ripped open. She must have opened it. She must have dropped it. A telegram from Boston.

WAIT FOR ME ARRIVING MONDAY HEATHROW AIRPORT
1200 HOURS MY TICKER NOW TICKING OVERTIME
THANK YOU FOR ASKING I LOVE YOU TOO
HAROLD

Harold sat down on the thick mauve carpet, stared at the thing and read it again.

Christ, he thought. Boston. My father. I don't understand. 'Thank you for asking . . . I love you too.'

Sylvia loved him? She asked him to come?

It didn't seem possible.

He read the telegram again and again. So he'd never understood anything.

And then he remembered it would never happen. She hadn't been able to wait for him. They would never meet, it could not be mended.

And he knew, with sickening finality, that he and Lottie would never be mended. They had left it too long. It was all too late.

Harold put his elbows on his knees. Harold put his head in

246

his hands, very slowly. He began to sob, enormous, wracking sobs that he hadn't sobbed since childhood. He sobbed till the terrible pressure was gone, and then it was very quiet. It had never been quiet with Sylvia there.

He washed his face in the bathroom. No hot water, of course. Dried himself. That must be her towel. And the rough soft feel of it comforted him, to think his mother was rubbing him dry, the last living traces of her. Before she was laundered and burned away.

He started to think more clearly. That man is arriving on Monday. I must telephone him. How can I? I don't know his number. I can't stop him coming. I'll have to meet him. He'll want to see her, I suppose. We'll have to stay in this house together. He'll want to talk about the two of them.

Why the hell should I feel sorry for him?

No one was sorry for Harold.

He wanted to go home. He wanted to be back with Lottie. Lottie would care. She listened to me. She never listened to anyone else, but she always *(usually)* listened to me. At least, when it was important.

And then he remembered the postcard, 'Mother's in Paris with an AWFUL CREEP', and another, unfairly extra pain made the grief swell up again.

That hadn't occurred to him, when he was sleeping with April. He'd hated Lottie and longed for Lottie but he always pictured her alone, maddeningly content in their big bed. Now he imagined her in Paris, laughing, her arm flung round – the AWFUL CREEP . . .

All her ex-boyfriends were awful creeps. If it was Hugo, he'd have to be killed. Perfectly simple. He addressed his wife: 'Look, we're still married, you know. Marriage is a serious business.'

Harold couldn't bear to stay here tonight. He'd have to go back to Boscombe. As he walked through the porch the geraniums loomed. Damn, damn. He went back inside. He filled the watering-can three times before the hanging baskets seemed slaked. They dripped, lugubrious but satisfied. Good. Sylvia loved her plants.

I'm doing what she would want me to . . . but what the hell can I do for myself?

The garden looked mournful, deserted. Not a flower remained

on the honeysuckle. The rowan tree, which had been her favourite, was shockingly heavy with bloody berries, occasional leaves flipped back by the strain so the silvery undersides showed. Outside, a great tree root was cracking the pavement.

Harold skirted it and started to hurry, a living man in a businesslike hurry – hurrying back to nothing. An early evening, a Saturday: but Saturday meant nothing to him.

And Saturday stretched round the world, to Lottie, in Provence, dressing up for a party, combing her hair, feeling nothing for Harold, and his father, in Boston, five hours behind them, packing and hoping, with nothing to hope for.

CHAPTER THIRTY-EIGHT

I'll run a bath. I'll make some tea.

He dimly remembered leaving some tea-bags in Sedley's flat, long ago in early June. If Ted hadn't pinched them, they must be there. Purposefully Harold started running the bath – a grinding pause, then a rush of water – and put the kettle on.

When the tea was brewed, he remembered. Without any hope, he flicked open the fridge. He emptied the pot in a sudden rage, spreading black leaves all over the sink. He padded along to take his bath, pulling off his clothes in something like frenzy; plunged his leg in up to the knee.

Plunged his leg into ice-cold water.

Gibbered and cursed in helpless fury.

That was the end. He abandoned the day. He crawled into bed – of course, no sheets – with his half-washed body and his unflossed teeth.

In the windy darkness, he could not sleep.

If only I could have *talked* to Mother.

The sun woke him with a feeling of well-being that didn't go away when he remembered. He pushed out on to the balcony. A brilliant silver-foil sea astonished him. Blinking, then opening his eyes very wide. He'd forgotten all this, and the pine-scented air. Breathing it in. He was still alive.

He'd have to go back to Poole that day to get the house ready for his father. Why shouldn't he take the scenic route? An open-topped bus along the cliffs?

So Harold soared down the dazzling cliffs to Poole in a yellow, open-topped bus. The wind was fresh, the gulls were blowing. Everything here was completely unchanged.

But Harold himself would never be the same. He stared at the glittering lines of surf.

Mother wasn't *there*, in that chapel of rest. Her body was

there, but she had gone. I didn't realize death was like that.

I hope she's here. In all this light. Darting about wherever she wants to. Part of it all. She can't just vanish.

Grief came again. *She had so much life.*

But the silver water refused to mourn.

☆

Slipping the key into his mother's door he felt a bit like a burglar. The feeling increased as he went into the dark. Worst of all in the kitchen. The kitchen was never a place for sons. She had only let him make cups of tea, and that was occasionally, on sufferance.

There were many kinds of fancy biscuits, unopened, two boxes of rather good chocolates, a Dundee cake in a tin (did she have a lot of visitors, then? What do I know about my mother?) Three bottles of the famous Nuits St. Georges (but does she drink that when she's not with me? I always thought that was something between us.)

Did she drink it. Everything past.

He didn't feel right in the kitchen. Maybe he'd see to the beds. Would his father want to sleep in Sylvia's bed?

In Sylvia's bedroom, as he pulled off the sheets (which smelled of her, vanilla) he was touched to see an old photo of himself, one he didn't recognize, standing on her mantelpiece. New since his visit last December, when he'd brought her tea in bed.

So maybe she thought about me, near the end. Maybe she wasn't angry with me.

But he wept for her nightdress, flung on the chair, entirely Sylvia, but empty.

☆

Next morning Harold was actually walking into the vast, noisy cathedral of Heathrow when he realized, looking at the swarming people, that he didn't really know what his father looked like.

He had a vivid image of a tall man with a thick dark 1950s quiff. Eating Shredded Wheat in orange pyjamas. Harold remembered the orange pyjamas. Today he would not be wearing them, and the faces came in a solid wave.

He stood anxious and afraid outside Customs, staring till the strip light made his eyes ache. What if this was the wrong terminal? What if he takes a different flight? It was a crazy idea to meet him.

(But he had to meet him; in so many dreams, through adolescence, in his twenties, thirties, he had crossed the world to meet this man. Now he felt mostly fear and anger, fear of missing him, fear of finding him, fear, above all, of breaking the news. Anger that he might have to give comfort; *he* was the one who needed comfort.)

Time and again he jerked into motion and then fell back – no, *can't* be him.

Once he approached a plump elderly man with thick black hair and a safari suit. Their eyes met, and held. Harold said, less confident with every word, 'Excuse me for troubling you, but I think you might be my father.'

The man looked distinctly disappointed, and gave him a ribald smile.

'Not my line, really, dear.'

Mortified, Harold turned away.

In the end it was his father who recognized him. An arm was suddenly flung round his shoulders. He turned and looked at an older, thinner, firmer version of his own face. An American voice said, 'You have to be Harold. I've been circling you. It's great to see you.'

And then they were embracing; curiously easy, as if this had all been done before, and indeed it had been imagined before, thousands of times, by both of them.

Yet nothing else would be easy.

CHAPTER THIRTY-NINE

The dialogue started badly.

'What do you want me to call you?' asked Harold.

'What do you want to call me? People mostly call me Stanley now. In the States, I'm H. Stanley Segall. Of course, you could call me Dad.'

'I don't think I'll call you anything, for a bit, if that's all right.'

Harold did not sound warm.

The train journey back to Poole was a lumpy mixture of confused emotions.

Resentment: how dare this dapper stranger tricked out in ghastly new American clothes try to pass himself off as my father? Besides, the last thing I need is a father.

Embarrassment: for it *was* his father. How are you supposed to behave towards your father?

Relief: for Stanley knew she was dead. Stanley did the talking.

'I wanted to see her. Just one more time. I shan't stick around for the cremation, though. Virginia thinks there'll be a good few there. I called her old number on the off chance when I couldn't get through to Sylvia. Just to confirm my arrival time. Ginny cried when she heard me. Sounded just the same. She was widowed in '55; of course I didn't know. And I didn't know about . . . your mother . . . Well, Ginny was very kind. She wants me to stop by and see her, but I don't think that's such a great idea.'

Virginia Flood was a friend of Sylvia's dating from the 1940s; she made costumes for the local repertory company. Harold had never liked her. She had an over-affectionate white Pomeranian dog with red-rimmed eyes. Eleven-year-old Harold once pushed it away and it bit the back of his leg.

After twenty minutes, Stanley slept. 'Getting old. I'm jetlagged.'

Harold sat and stared. He didn't look genuine. Too fit, too clean, all his clothes too new, with a springy, creaseless,

252

synthetic look. Yet the face, with the skin so tight across the bone, was horribly like his own.

Bastard, you abandoned me. Now you come back and expect me to be nice to you. I hardly remember what you were like. You were always playing the piano, too loud, and the house was full of screaming grownups. I never knew if it was acting or rowing. I suppose they were Mother's friends.

It was awkward, being two men on their own, strangers pretending to be father and son. A woman would have made this easier (Sylvia was gone, Lottie was gone.) And he had to mother his father, this person supposed to be his father. Harold ushered him into the little house, watching him look around, bemused.

'Wow. I mean, almost nothing's changed. It's like a museum, isn't it. I guess she couldn't afford to change things. You know I sent money every year . . . I figured it would be enough.'

'She was OK,' Harold said defensively, trying not to show the last detail surprised him. 'She wasn't poor. She was quite extravagant. This is just the way our houses look.'

The bedroom issue was quickly settled; Stanley would sleep in Sylvia's room. He seemed surprised the question was asked. 'It *was* our bedroom, after all.'

Harold was busy in the kitchen making tea and piling iced biscuits on two plates. As an afterthought he added the Dundee cake, juggling it gingerly on to the tray.

Stanley gazed at it all, looking awkward.

'Say, can you hold it for a moment? The tea would be just great on its own. I'm going to have a little workout.'

Harold watched him through the window. He was standing in the middle of the lawn, visible above a thick frieze of red dahlias. Then he disappeared. Harold knelt on a chair to look.

Christ, he's doing press-ups. He hasn't any feelings. He comes back here after thirty-odd years and all he wants to do is his press-ups. He does them with remarkable efficiency, too, considering he must be nearly seventy. He can't be fitter than I am, surely. Maybe he's trying to show me he is.

I am the child of monsters.

By the time that Stanley returned, lightly gleaming with sweat, the tea was thoroughly stewed. It emerged he ate no refined sugar or starch in any form, including cakes and biscuits.

253

'Used to be crazy about them. Ate cookies all day long. Your mother used to try and stop me . . . I'm pretty careful, diet-wise, now.'

Harold ate too many biscuits, trying not to stare at the lined brown face which was like and unlike his own.

What the hell do we eat tonight? A Seafood Pie was defrosting in the fridge. The picture showed ample pastry. With Mother dead, he might stretch a point. *Prig.*

He forgave him a little when Stanley came down after putting his stuff in the bedroom. His eyes (*my eyes in thirty years' time*) were red. He had clearly been weeping.

'She's got a picture of me in there. Right in the middle of the mantelpiece. It broke me up, Harry.'

That picture. Harold realized the truth. *It wasn't a picture of me at all.* Pity struggled with jealousy. And *why the hell* does he call me Harry?

When Stanley left for the undertaker's, Harold rushed out to do some fresh shopping. The local shop was uninspired; he bought eggs, lettuce, fruit, potatoes. An omelette with boiled potatoes. It sounded dull, but not refined.

Harold was drinking a glass of red wine by the time that Stanley returned from his mission. He looked thinner, and less tanned. Harold offered him a drink.

'I don't drink alcohol, thanks. I used to love a good red . . . but, well, I kicked the habit. Look – if you don't need me to help out, I think I'll just catch some sleep before supper.'

But I need alcohol badly, thought Harold, draining his glass and splashing some more.

At eight, they sat stiffly in upright chairs, at the small, square table. Harold was full of suppressed rage. *He won't drink, he eats like a rabbit – what does that leave us to hide behind?* The light-bulbs were 150-watt giants; Sylvia was short-sighted, and too vain to wear her glasses. On the two of them now, the light was unforgiving. Two pernickety, miserable old men.

'I suppose you think I'm a failure,' Harold said abruptly, putting down his glass.

'How the hell can I think you're a failure? I'm a dry old physicist, boy.'

'But you're a well-known professor. And I'm a layabout non-writing writer.'

'But physics bores me silly. It stops me playing the piano.'

'I remember you and that piano. Mother used to shout at you . . . but you've been an academic all your life.'

'You try becoming a concert pianist at the age of forty-five. I guess I was that old before I really knew how pissed off I was. Up to my eyes in research and admin. I'm a lousy pianist, in any case . . .'

'That's how old I am now. And I'm up to my eyes in nothing.'

Stanley chewed a very small mouthful of lettuce for what seemed like a very long time. Then he swallowed, a lurch of his sharp Adam's apple. 'OK, are you happy? Apart from your mother's death, I mean.'

Harold almost said nothing, and said it all instead. No one had listened to him in months.

'Well, no. I'm – low, at the moment. Pretty low all round, you could say. Look, I've broken up with Lottie. My wife, I mentioned her. Haven't seen her since last Christmas. Or her son Davey . . . he feels like mine. Now Davey says she's got someone else. *Plus*, I've got nowhere to live. And no career. And no clear ambitions. And forty-five is *old*, if you've got nothing to show for it. That's about it,' he ended, wryly. Then, 'I do miss Mother. I can't believe she's . . . gone.'

His father nodded with a neutral face. Maybe he's made of plaster-of-Paris.

'Do you need a loan? You only have to ask.'

'No', said Harold, nettled (but he *did* need a loan).

'Do you still love your wife?'

Pause. 'Yes.'

'Have you tried to get together again?'

'Yes. No. Not enough, no.'

'Will you?'

'Yes!' Harold suddenly meant it.

'Your mother and I tried for three years, after . . . what happened. We still didn't try hard enough. And after the divorce . . . I *thought* about her. Again and again. I would never have remarried. But pride – you have your pride. And the years piled up. They do pile up.'

They sat in a silence which was much less hostile. Harold's father had got some colour back, and grease round his mouth from the omelette. He looked almost human, in fact. Another long swallow. He had more to say.

'Go back to this failure business, a moment. You talk about being a failure. I just wanna know – have you been happy?'

An odd question, after Harold's lament.

'How could I be happy, with my achievements?'

'I mean with what you've done. Have you been happy – *doing* it?'

Harold reflected. It was still an odd question, but it opened a little door in his head.

'Well – yes. If you put it like that. I have been happy. *Not* with the achievements. Maybe a few kids passed their exams who wouldn't have passed them if it weren't for me. I certainly wasn't happy teaching. Or writing textbooks. I gave that up. Since then . . . I have been happy. The days with Lottie. Too happy, maybe. So I did almost nothing.'

'I can tell you, Harry, I've hated my days. And that's what counts in the end. They total up into years, a lifetime. What does achievement mean? There have been hundreds of physicists more brilliant than me. Most of them entirely forgotten. You don't live an achievement. What you live is days.'

'But there *were* good days. You had good days?'

Harold's father's smile was amused and sad.

'Oh yes, I had good days. They mostly ended too long ago. The best days.' He had to stop, and look down. 'Everything seemed so . . . light. The best days were here in this house. First years we were married.'

'I remember . . . a lot of rows. But I remember later.'

'Sure. We screamed and yelled and fought. But as well as that, we had such fun . . . we adored each other.' He looked hard at his son. 'You probably think that's sentimental.'

'No,' said Harold, thinking *yes*.

'It isn't. *That* isn't. It was sentimental – coming back like this, on the strength of a telegram. The telegram Sylvia sent me was as if she was twenty-five again. It got to me, like she always did. I came running back like a puppy-dog.' A pause. With his knife he was scraping agonized circles on his empty plate. 'Only – she wasn't here.'

'Look, have some wine, Dad,' said Harold on impulse,

swallowing the 'Dad'. The brown face cracked open. Either a smile or the beginning of a howl.

'OK, I think this is a special occasion.'

Harold emptied the bottle and went for another.

'What was she like?' It was a silly question, since Harold knew what his mother was like. Except children don't know their parents.

'Well. Impossible, of course. You must know that. But also – like no one else. She was very funny. She laughed like a kid. She thought up crazy ideas, and until you were born we ran off and did them. She – well, she did love me once. You might find that hard to take on board, if you remember the end of it. But . . . she made me feel she loved me more than anyone else has ever done. And – maybe it's not so important, but it is when you're left with just memories . . . She was very, very beautiful. People stared at her in the street.'

'It must have been very difficult, then. Seeing her . . . like that. So much older.'

His father looked at him blankly. 'It was kind of hard to take, sure. Because she was *exactly* the same. Don't you think so? She hadn't aged a bit.'

'No,' said Harold, thinking *Christ, he's deluded*. So love was still blind after thirty-two years.

There was one more question he wanted to ask, now the drink made him feel all things were sayable.

'Look, if you loved her so much. Why did you leave? What happened?'

His father stared at his leathery hands. The silence stretched. Harold's anger returned.

'Well?' he demanded belligerently. 'It wasn't easy, on my own with Mother.'

'It's hard to talk about. Especially to you. I guess . . . you have a right to know.' He was well down his second glass by now. His voice was becoming more English. 'I suppose you'll hate me. But try to understand. I had an affair. With a friend of hers. Oh, what the hell. With Virginia.'

Harold stared at his father, every muscle of his face demanding to know more.

'You want to know the details, so help me. It wasn't love, it was something of nothing. On her side, maybe jealousy of Sylvia. Yet she really did love Sylvia. Me, I can't explain. But

everyone wanted Sylvia. All our friends were Sylvia's friends . . .
she had enormous charm, your mother. I suddenly saw Ginny
wanted me. Sylvia was away on tour. When she came back,
Ginny told her. She couldn't stand the guilt, she said. It seems
your mother slapped her. That astonished me. She never hit
you, once. But after that, she forgave her, completely. And she
never, ever forgave me. We went on for three years after that,
but *everything* had changed. Whatever I did was wrong. In the
end I just gave up.'

He held his hands, bony old hands, up towards the glaring
bulb. The gesture said he was innocent. Yet he said, 'I still feel
guilty. Shabby little story, huh?'

The story ran round and round Harold's head, striking echoes
wherever it touched. So now I know, after all these years.

Do I find my father contemptible?

Yes. I was never unfaithful to Lottie.

Then he thought about and retrenched a little.

After I left her, I wasted no time. And *I* left *her*. Just like my
father. Maybe desertion's in the family.

'I never liked Virginia,' he mused. 'Maybe I guessed. Kids do.
Her dog bit me. Do you remember? A fat, white, horrible dog.'

'Yeah. It was *gross*.' His father smiled. The tension eased
between them.

'You know, I don't think Mother . . . ever had anyone else. I
never remember anyone else . . . '

'That would figure. She was a great – romantic.'

A momentary savage blaze of feeling transformed the old
man's face. Harold dropped his eyes, embarrassed. Yet afterwards he would not forget seeing love crawl out into the naked
light.

'Well, but you never got reconciled. It seems a waste.'

'Perhaps we are now,' said his father, and raised his last half-
inch of wine. 'It's for the best we didn't meet again, maybe.
Maybe we shouldn't have got along. I've *seen* her, at least. I've
met my son.'

☆

As he washed the dishes after midnight, with his father safe
upstairs, Harold remembered those words. He wondered if his
father was asleep. In the bathroom there was a new armoury of
things: toothpicks, floss, disclosing tablets, gum massagers,

Tom's Natural Toothpaste, Natural Mouthwash, cologne. It must take him ages to get ready for bed. Mother would be pleased he's looking after his teeth.

Next day Harold's father left. He was wearing a complete fresh change of clothes, yet he had become familiar. The bathroom shelves cleared by magic.

Glad he was going, Harold asked him to stay. But he had a girlfriend, a 'really special person', and deadlines on the other side of the world, and days, American, utterly strange to Harold, to live through.

All the same. They embraced again, as they had long ago at the airport. This time they held something more than a shadow.

And then Harold is alone in the house with the autumn coming all round him. The Autumn Equinox passes; the last week of September. Each day the colours are brighter, the nights colder, more leaves have fallen. The rope of white stars in a London garden has changed to a rope of silky white seed-heads. Nobody sees it. In Poole, birds peck the rowans bare.

As Harold sorts through Sylvia's things, picking up memories, putting them down, he thinks about fossils, craters, shells, forms of life from which life has gone.

Trying to sleep, he can only dream. Cast up alone on his narrow bed, he falls through the coils of sound of his boyhood. Father and Mother, shouting. The yapping of Ginny's dog. Slowly they grow more distant. The sea faints in a spiral shell.

But the grief wells up, hot and immediate, whenever he starts to think it has gone. Grief for whatever Sylvia missed, but also grief for himself, in the present.

Everything changed. Everything different.

The solar system is sudden and violent.

Mercury is very small, very fast, not the easiest target as it sprints across the sun. Yet it is covered with impact craters.

The largest is the most recent. Caloris Basin is a massive crater eight hundred and fifty miles across.

The explosion shakes the whole planet, breaks open thousands of smaller wounds in the surface through which molten lava streams.

September

Still Mercury sprints on across the sun.
A long darkness, a final brightness.
The first planet that the sun consumes.

October

CHAPTER FORTY

A golden autumn in Northern Europe. Autumns have been growing warmer, they say. On the beaches there is still naked skin, humans hungry for the last of the sun.

At the centre of the solar system the sun burns on as it has done for five billion years, as it will do for another five billion years. Hydrogen flames into helium. Each second, the sun produces more energy than humans have used in the whole of their history. In the blazing body of the sun is over 99 per cent of all the matter in the solar system.

'I suppose this is the last of the really hot sun.'

They say it each year as their small planet turns.

If the sun were the size of a very large orange, Earth would be the size of a very small pip. But the sun is not the size of an orange. The sun powers everything that lives.

Over three and a half billion years ago, the first stirring of life on Earth. For two billion years, the sun pours down on nothing but single-celled blue-green algae. Then sex begins. Evolution moves on. It is autumn in the year of life.

Six million years ago they start coming, multi-celled forms in a dancing chain: the ancestors of sponges, jellyfish, worms, corals, trilobites, ammonites, shellfish, starfish, true fish, spiders and scorpions, ferns, millipedes, mosses, lungfish, conifers, dragonflies, ginkgoes, primitive reptiles with primitive penises, turtles, crocodiles, dinosaurs, more dinosaurs, tree-shrews, duck-billed platypuses, birds, magnolias, water-lilies, moon-rats, bats, sloths, lemurs, whales, elephants, more and more flowers, grass and grazers, dogs and cats, small monkeys, big monkeys, apes and ape-men, and half a million years ago,

261

October

Upright Man, living and dying by the light of the sun.

☆

The window of a Paris *chocolatier*, shaded from the sun by a pure yellow lime-tree. Two months ago it held symbols of summer, exquisitely moulded in dark chocolate, shells and starfish, buckets and spades. Now there are truffles, chocolate mushrooms, *marrons glacés* in beribboned jars.

Lottie walks on into the Luxembourg Gardens, frightening a fat pink pigeon away, a hop and then an undignified scramble. The horse-chestnut leaves have turned golden. Two little boys are on their knees, polishing conkers on the sleeves of their jackets.

Lottie smiles a smile of pure pleasure. One smiles back, and one stares gravely, trying to hide behind his friend. He reminds her a little of Davey.

I'm glad I have children. Well – I have my son. Maybe I should have more children . . .

☆

In Provence, Lottie had longed for André. She came back to Paris and her feelings changed. Paris was cooling down. She enjoyed it . . . on her own.

But sex seemed hotter, and less appropriate. André was still as inventive, as endlessly demanding. Once that quality thrilled her. Now she just thought, his demands are endless.

She didn't want to feel like that. She still thought André was an acquisition. She still enjoyed the respectful way heads turned when they swept into a room together. She was still quite touched by the way he played the (faintly silly) game of protecting her.

Of course, we both know it's nonsense, but it is terribly nice.

His strong hand guided her around street corners, his arm went round her and the traffic stopped by magic as they stepped on to a crossing together. Occasionally she was irritated. However well meant, it could push you off balance. Sometimes, perhaps, she resented the heavy weight of his arm upon her shoulders. He never let her carry the lightest coat or the smallest shopping-bag.

He knew it was nonsense, of course. She *supposed* he knew it was nonsense.

'André, you'll be carrying my handbag next.'

'For you, darling, I even do it.'

André's English had started to strike her as comic. (It was unfair of her, she knew. He was Swiss, he spoke six languages, he couldn't be perfect in all of them.) Even – faintly *ridiculous*. And you mustn't find a lover ridiculous.

One day she found his love-making ridiculous, and then they were really in trouble. It took two to play at erotic games. She wanted to keep him; for a while, she pretended; but her voice rang embarrassingly false in her ears.

Why the hell am I letting him do this? I must be too old to be his Big Bad Girl.

Sometimes she found herself staring at his penis (too often she found herself staring at his penis, just a few inches from her wide open eyes) as if it were some strange animal or vegetable, something she knew well and yet couldn't explain. She felt she spent too much time with it, anyhow. She felt she was wasting herself on it.

She preferred to have dealings with his opposite end, although that was growing less appealing. He had seemed unimpeachably handsome, once, with his satin-smooth golden skin. She used to imagine him, stretched out naked, perfectly matching her coverlet at home.

Now he began to make her think of something carved from butter. Now she knew she would never take him home. She imagined introducing him to Davey; Davey would hate him on sight. Davey would say, 'Mum, honestly. You *cannot* be serious.'

She tried to remember what she'd written in the vaguely tipsy letter she wrote. Davey had never answered. I shouldn't write letters, she thought. I write marvellous letters, but they're evidence.

'I think you will like André a lot.' (She didn't think that, not even at the time.) 'He is not an intellectual like Harold, which as you can imagine is a change for the better. And he knows how to enjoy himself, which gives me a chance to enjoy myself too. After all the trouble I've had with Harold, I don't think you'll object to your mother enjoying herself.' (She knew he would object, even at the time.) 'He's a businessman; nothing wrong with that.' (She knew he would think there was plenty wrong . . .)

Alas, she had signed it, sent it. She'd enclosed a photograph Trudi had taken of the two of them at André's request. They were standing in the morning sunlight on the steps of André's hotel. It wasn't a totally flattering photograph. Trudi had come in too close, so André looked bulbous, out of proportion. Even at the time, she knew he looked heavy. Now she realised he must have looked gross.

One morning she woke up and looked at him, lying on his back with his pink lips open, his little nose foreshortened, smiling slightly, the weight of his cheeks overhanging his ears. Little pink ears which made the rest look enormous. She knew by now why his hair was so shiny; the pillow always showed traces of grease, an oil he furtively applied in the bathroom when he hoped she was far enough away.

Oh dear. I'm afraid he simply *is* gross.

And then he woke up, and the grossness possessed her, swarming all over her, panting and grunting and finally snouting his happy way inside her.

Safe in the bathroom, she bolted the door, which she'd never done before. She scrubbed at her body, grimly.

Maybe it isn't him at all. Maybe I've just been having sex too long. It's nearly twenty years since I started. Maybe I've just had enough.

Actually, it's overrated. Davey isn't missing anything.

André was knocking on the door. She let her legs float out on the water, clear, soft, cooling water, and listened, amused, while he knocked some more.

Davey was also in the water that morning, up to his armpits in the warm strong waves which broke around Boscombe Pier. Mary had gone in deeper and was sending up great fans of white water, swimming easily on her back. Davey was utterly content; he had almost forgotten Sylvia.

When Davey had told Amanda he was going to Poole to see Sylvia, he hadn't mentioned Mary. Nor had he mentioned hitching. The trip seemed a good idea to Amanda; it was nice that he wanted to see his grandma (step-grandma – things did get complicated). She'd loaded him up with asters and dahlias and blackberry jam she had made last year. (*Good – a weekend to herself. I might ·stop the night with Doris again.*)

They presented the flowers to a very imposing lady tramp at the top of their street. She bowed and placed them beside her bags. All day she sat pulling them to pieces, making gold buttons without any petals.

The jam got eaten on the journey. By evening, Mary and Davey were at Christchurch, washing off the stains in the sunset sea. Then they clambered up on Hengistbury Head and huddled together as the winds cut round them. They looked along the coast at the pattern of lights.

'That must be Bournemouth, the longest pier. I think Poole's over there, round the bay. It's not far, where Sylvia lives. I'm sure we can find her somehow.'

He had left her address at home, and failed to find her in the local phone book. (In fact, she was listed under Delaire; but he only thought of her as Harold's mother.) *Seferis, Sefton,* and a column of *Seiferts,* sighing down the page, all strangers to him. Only Mary's name really mattered now. They had entered a different story.

Battered by the cold, hand in hand, they'd found their way down to the beach again. She had brought some blankets, and some biscuits. In Christchurch, he'd bought a bottle of wine, but no corkscrew, and anyway they didn't really want it.

He was not so scared as he thought he would be, because it was Mary, and he knew she liked him (she said she loved him, but he couldn't quite believe it . . . and love wasn't always such a good thing).

Her body, in the shelter, by the promenade lights, was beautiful and touching and quite unfamiliar, much better than he'd hoped for. He had already seen lots of bits of her body, but it was so different when you saw them all together.

She'd done it with her last boyfriend, and the doctor had put her on the pill. 'But I don't like using that, not really,' she whispered, kissing his neck and ear. She was paler than ever in the strange coloured lights. 'Maybe – you know, if we go together, *you* could do something instead. Rubbers are supposed to be quite easy,' she added, kissing him again.

(It was lovely, being his first. He was a beautiful, interesting, amazing boy, not at all like most of the boys at school, and she knew he'd get better at it. She would help him get better at it.)

'Oh, rubbers, of course,' said Davey, with pride, tucking the blanket around them both. Could he go in the chemist and ask for them? He hardly believed it was happening. Her lips smelled faintly of blackberry jam.

How could someone so thin be so soft and warm? How could he suddenly be so happy?

'Before we go to sleep, I'll go outside and make sure there's no one about,' he said. Surely he ought to protect her.

'No, I'll come too.'

They pulled on their trousers and crept out on to the promenade. No one about. The world was their own. A narrow dim beach, an enormous sea. The stars were faint but the stars were there.

'Think how many people have stood there like this.'

'Doesn't matter, does it? There's only us.'

They looked at the lights of faraway Poole; one of those lights might have had a meaning. If so, the nearby illuminations dwarfed it. A Butterfly, a Kingfisher, a crimson Tulip, a pompous Owl with a single blue eye. Boldly outlined in coloured bulbs, the innocent images were stamped on the darkness.

Mary said, 'My favourite's the Bluebird.'

Davey agreed.

Rising, wings spread, brilliantly blue, just a triangle of yellow pointing the beak, it flew for them and for perfect happiness, hung from the stars on the autumn sky.

CHAPTER FORTY-ONE

Harold would soon have cleared everything up. In the house, not in his head. A slow process as the tide receded and he cleared the jetsam away. Grief still came unpredictably.

I did so little. I omitted so much. I never said, just as simply as breathing, I love you, Mum. I really love you. Now he said it, to the empty house, 'I loved you, Mum,' but the tense was wrong.

In some respects it was easier on the days when Virginia came and 'helped' him. She was fatter, more hectically painted than before. She often wept, and talked unstoppably, crowding out the space where Harold might have grieved. She was useful though. Great piles of belongings were carted away in her battered old van. She didn't seem choosy about what she took.

At the cremation he had heard her wrenching sobs in the row behind. Their little party had tea at a hideous, fluorescent-lit hotel, and he couldn't forget the alcohol on her breath or her bright, streaked makeup.

On the final day of her helping, he gave her, on impulse, Sylvia's car. Virginia was ecstatic; she kissed him several times, leaving trails of powder.

'Let's have a drink,' she said.

'Thanks, but I'm going for a walk.'

He waved her down the drive with a hand which also barred her way back. The little mauve insect buzzed off down Tatnam Road at a speed which reminded him briefly of Sylvia.

Eleven o'clock on a golden day. Wrapped in a scarf he would soon discard, he set off with a young, light heart, the *Pocket Guide to Plants* in his jacket. Since he had been tied to the house so much, Harold had developed a compensating passionate interest in the local world outside. He'd thought he 'knew' the coast around Poole. Now he realized he'd just sleepwalked across it.

Today he caught an open-topped bus to Sandbanks, where the ferry would take him across to Shell Bay.

The sky and the trees were all round his head, loud and wild and vivid. On the top deck he was glad of his scarf, swaddling it round his singing ears. Horse-chestnut leaves blew into the bus, some of them already brown and dead but some of them colouring symmetrically, golden borders on living green fingers. A conker fell, loud on the metal. You could almost see into people's bedrooms; a hint of lace, a jug of yellow dahlias. One face smiled at him, caught out. Too bright to stay in bed today.

The harbour suddenly stretched wide below, the foreground gleaming mud at low tide. Beached boats canted to left or right, and a thousand white gulls picked delicately, greedily. The landlocked water smelled faintly of sulphur, but the big ox-eye daisies and straggling yellow ragwort which fringed the bay looked healthy enough.

The ferry, loaded alarmingly with a bus *and* a coach as well as cars, ground across on its mighty chains which as a boy he'd always expected to break. Did ferries *usually* run on chains? It seemed a confession of weakness. Harold discovered how eager he was to live. He almost ran off the ferry.

Shell Bay was as soft and softly curved and white as memory made it, still without shops or shelters, a crescent of sand with a cupping crescent of crested dunes behind it, then miles of heathland. The light was radiant, summer-bright, and each of the thousands of tiny, circular pearl-shells sewn along the edge of the sea had a rainbow sheen.

The sand sparkled; the sea leaped on to it, fell away gracefully, leaped again. He walked round the bay, as near to the water as he could without staining his shoes with salt. As he rounded the point into Studland Bay, he thought *what the hell*, took off shoes and socks and plunged into the surf (*just to the ankle, but didn't I plunge?*) The sand was warm, the sea was warm.

Half way along, he saw flesh. A reddish-blonde man was posed like a statue, talking attentively to a girl who sat with arms folded, peering carefully up at him. She had yellow hair, a pink bikini.

Something odd.

The man was wearing no clothes.

Harold looked away at once.

He remembered something April had said. Nudists came to Studland Bay. They were out here as long as there was sun in the sky. They called people with clothes on 'textiles'. So Harold was a textile. It made him feel slightly less daring and free. He took off his scarf, though a breeze still blew, and rolled up his jeans a little. He tried to look mostly at the glittering surf but sometimes he glanced to his right and caught glimpses of couples and foursomes, often patchily naked – two or three clothed, one or two naked – which made the nakedness slightly more shocking, and slightly comic at the same time.

But from a distance, if both were naked, men and women looked puzzlingly alike.

Why have we spent so much time and trouble making them look so different?

There was one glimpse, painfully idyllic, of a naked family, nested in the dunes. Two little children, one on the man's shoulders, one half-wrapped in its mother's long hair. The nakedness seemed utterly appropriate, then. On the edge of the sea, where life began.

I don't want to be alone. But Harold shook the thought away.

Studland itself was a little scruffy: fencing, beach-huts, a car park. The last drunk wasps wove above the sand, drowsy, hoping for dirt or sugar. Beyond, the cliffs reached round to the end of the bay where two chalk pillars stood against the waves, 'Old Harry' and his 'Wife'. They looked very near, from here. He thought he could walk towards them, but the sand came to an end, and the intervening rocks were treacherously slippy, slicked with green weed. He waved to Old Harry and nearly lost his footing. He couldn't get there today.

Another time, he informed the sea. *Plenty of time*, he informed the sea. It was only October. He could still make good.

And he didn't feel downhearted as he walked back to the ferry across the Heath behind the sand-dunes. They said there were snakes, but he wasn't going to worry. The *Pocket Guide* grew hot in his hands.

There were mauve sea asters like Michaelmas Daisies; bright yellow Autumn Hawkbit; softer yellow, satiny Evening Primroses; blackberry bushes with berries of red and green and black on the same plant. Across the dark nettles a ladybird whirred and settled on his jacket, sharp as a pin of red enamel. He brushed it off; it turned brown again as the wings whirred out from their scarlet case.

He began to feel confused. The banked dark purples of the heather dissolved as he looked into a hundred different shades, from mauve through crimson to dusty pink, touched with brown in places. Bracken grew up through the heather, single yellow feathers waving on the dark. The silver birches had lost enough leaves for the bark to show pale as a baby's skin. The leaves which remained were half-gold, half-green as the little trees shivered against the sky. And everything seemed to swell and burn, trees and flowers and flying things, in a dance so rich and dense and particular, endlessly shifting, growing, surging, that suddenly he felt stunned and dizzy and longed for the simpler sweep of the sea. Everything hummed, everything moved, a pattern which did not let him in.

Was it easier when I saw nothing?

I think I'd better go back to the beginning. I'll take a last look at the sea, and Old Harry.

Cutting back to the beach through the dunes, he recognized ahead of him the first naked man he'd seen that day. His reddish-gold beard and self-consciously healthy posture were unmistakable; his skin was mahogany. As Harold passed close he briefly glimpsed great swathes of red peel. He winced and looked again.

And he noticed something else. Redbeard was displaying himself to a different girl this time. *Green* bikini, *brownish* hair, arms folded protectively across her torso. Not very young, not very pretty, not very interested in what she was offered.

He plunged back down on to the level sand and trotted back to the vast bright sea. Back to beginnings, back to the start. But was there any way to get back – home?

I don't want to be a lonely naked man, strutting the beach for company.

That night Harold lay and tried to sleep while voices called from the edge of the sea. Beaches were places for lovers – had they been there, stifling laughter, just out of sight in the dips of the dunes?

He remembered that naked family, with the child covered by

its mother's hair. Why did it hurt, when he didn't want children?

Because they looked so . . . part of each other.

In the end he put the light on, got out his notebook, groped for words.

Perspective was what he needed. There was more than just his loneliness. More than Sylvia dying on her own. More than this seemingly endless present.

Life had been here on earth, after all, for over three and a half billion years. Here he lay in the middle of the night, hand very white in the pool of light, fingers wriggling like an amoeba, three and a half billion years later. Trying to understand. Trying to fly down vast tracts of time, enormous electrical leaps and circuits.

Sex and Death, he wrote.

It was sexless blue-green algae, going on boringly for two billion years, that built up the oxygen to fuel what followed. Splitting into two identical cells, then in two again, going on and on. If you were sexless, you didn't have to die.

(Just for a moment, he envied them.)

But if you constantly split or budded you couldn't have an individual self at all. The blue-greens were just a kind of endless stream.

Sexual reproduction was utterly different. Two living things produce a third being, in which their genes are mixed. But they don't *turn into* the new being. The original parents remain intact.

Then the new being goes on without them. Life goes on, and leaves the parents behind. They have to wear down and die in the end.

So sex means death, and a kind of selfhood. Sex and death were inextricably linked. He underlined it: *Sex and Death.*

Selfhood and death were linked just as closely. A self means something which has to end. The mother dies, the son goes on.

He thought about his mother. He thought, more keenly, about himself. When he died, would there be anything left?

Human beings have the most sense of self of all. Individual life is so important to us that we don't even want to reproduce any more. Lots of us don't. I don't, particularly. Most humans seem to have almost no interest in the pattern continuing after their death.

It isn't so surprising. We live long childhoods and a long old age, time when we're too young or too old to reproduce, so all we can do is become ourselves. Wishing and thinking and dreaming. No wonder we don't want to lose those selves. No wonder death appals us.

There must be some point to developed selves. There must be some point to me lying here alone in the middle of the night, puzzling and scribbling.

(Was that the point? To puzzle and scribble?)

Suddenly the larger puzzling stopped, and all he felt was small and alone. I don't want to die that way, like Mother. If I could feel part of the earth, just once . . .

Death must be easier for animals like iguanas and boa constrictors, which live more closely. Lying in coils and piles in the Snake House, so no one can see where they begin or end.

Harold had only once known that. Curled with Lottie as they fell asleep, and skin no longer separated them. Waking still tangled together. Nearly every night, even when we'd quarrelled.

With humans, it's not automatic. You have to learn to be close to someone. You have to learn to love someone.

Oh, oh. He missed it so badly.

Suddenly he scrawled out *Sex and Death*.

Love, he wrote.

Was that the point?

I suppose we make such a thing about love because nothing *natural* binds us together, with each other or the rest of the world. I shan't have sons or daughters (shall I?) My father's on the other side of the earth. My mother died on her own. I'm not locked into the pattern. The rhythm is all outside me.

I can't bear always to be outside. I must have someone to . . . fold me in. Someone to cushion the ache. Someone to cushion the intellect. Lottie loved me. And cushioned me . . . I cushioned her, as well.

Does she miss me, though?

Lottie.

Utterly weary, he switched off the light.

The beach came back, as clear as before. Bright skin flickered on the dark of his lid.

Just out of sight, the lovers kissed.

CHAPTER FORTY-TWO

Davey kissed Mary goodbye at the tube so passionately that she pushed him away.

'*Look*, I'm going to see you tomorrow.'

'Thank you – thank you for everything.'

She was pleased, but hid it by sounding sharp. 'Ssshh. Don't tell *everybody*.'

She ran down the escalator, hair flying. Rooted to the spot, he watched her go.

Walking alone down Darlington Road, he wasn't looking forward to going home. There wasn't really a home to go to. Even Amanda was out all the time. He only hoped she was there at the moment; no one had answered the telephone. If she wasn't, he couldn't get in. His sodding keys still hadn't turned up. He had a nagging worry.

And then it sharpened to a razor-edge.

Almost expected that the front door gaped. One stocking was curled on the step, outside. Inside, strange trails of mess – bright cloth, spilled beads, torn wings of paper – were draped down the stairs like a decoration.

Now everything would go wrong.

He went upstairs into Lottie's room. The drawers hung open at odd angles, colour looping out like entrails. A big kiss had been marked with orange lipstick on the mirror. Or else a crude X, crossing Mum out. He felt as if he had been punched in the stomach.

He knew at once who had done it. He knew where he'd lost his keys. It's my fault, then. I let it happen. Fucking bastard. He would go round and kill him.

Instead, he picked up the phone.

A woman, must be the mother, answered. A hostile 'Yer?'

Davey asked to speak to 'Simon'.

' 'Oo's that wants 'im?'

'Davey, tell him.' She sounded frightful.

She yelled like a maniac 'Si-mon! Someone wants yer! Davey wants yer!' He clearly heard Smeggy's voice yell back, 'Well, I ain't *'ere!'* The accent was a little broader than usual, but the voice was just the same.

Davey suddenly shouted into the phone, 'You tell him to come and speak to me or else I'll send the police straight round!'

She said nothing, but went away, and he could hear muffled shouts in the background.

Eventually Smeggy arrived at the phone, falsely matey.

' 'Allo, Davey, me old pal. Whasthis about – '

'Look, you bloody well come round and bring it all back and clear everything up or I'll – '

'Yeah?' It was hard to know if the jeer was a little bit frightened, or totally bold. It sounded more like totally bold.

' – I'll send the police round to sort you out.'

'I don't know what you're on about. Big Mouth. Little Mummy's Boy. Little *rich* boy. Will'oo tell Mummy den?' The voice was full of loathing and envy, things which must have always been there, in secret.

Davey's anger threatened to explode his chest. He crashed the phone down, suddenly.

What do I do, what do I do.

Amanda might come back at any minute. In the next hour or so, for certain, and she'd call the police at once. Millions of policemen everywhere. Policemen sneaking about looking for things.

Somewhere or other, they'd find some dope – he had got less careful with Mum away. Amanda was too naïve to notice. Statements, notebooks, police stations. Anyway, Mum was allergic to police. 'Never trust a man in uniform – they're pompous enough without uniform.'

Suddenly the phone rang, under his hand, making his heart jump horribly.

'Yes?'

'It's your friend *Simon.* Listen, if you make any trouble for me, I'll make sure the police know a thing or two about you. Right? *Right.'*

The phone was dead.

In a way it was ludicrous, Smeggy sounding like a gangster.

He told himself, *that's ludicrous.*

In another way, things were far too serious for him to cope

with on his own. I'll have to ring her, he thought. It isn't fair. She ought to be here. I'd give anything for a proper mother.

After ten minutes' panicky searching, he found the repulsive photo she'd sent, on the back of which she had written Creep's phone number. 'In emergencies, I'm probably at this number now. C/o André Legros. PS He's actually more handsome than this.'

Belatedly, in total frustration, he tore the photo across. He was relieved to see when he looked at the pieces that the tear hadn't touched his mother's body but had severed one of Creep's great fat arms, which she wore on one shoulder like an ornament.

Davey managed to misdial three times. In the end he got a plummy-voiced receptionist who switched effortlessly into bored English. In seconds he was speaking to Monsieur Legros.

Creepy somehow extracted too much information, since Davey wasn't collected enough to stall. Creepy sounded creepily helpful, concerned, outraged, almost – *paternal*.

Nausea made Davey cut him short. 'Look I just want to speak to my mother.' He had wasted almost an hour. She was at the old number, all the time.

He felt transcendent relief when he finally reached his mother. Her throaty, delighted voice, which changed in seconds to a furious roar.

She was coming home at once, this minute. She would *murder* Smeggy with her own hands. He was not on any account to call the police. He must *forcibly restrain* Amanda.

(For a start, she had never been quite sure if the Bonnard was quite legit; Hugo had some strange friends. The kind of police who knew about jewellery might also know about paintings. She didn't say that to Davey. Davey was still quite an innocent child.)

'By the way, he didn't take the Bonnard?'

'Mum, he wouldn't know what a Bonnard *was*.'

When the first roar had subsided, she sounded almost exhilarated. She had toned things down a little. She was coming home *tomorrow*, instead. She would *sort Smeggy out*, not kill him. Davey wasn't to worry. She loved him. She adored him. He was her baby. She would come home.

Lottie put down the phone and blew one more kiss, just to seal the bargain. She looked in the mirror. Her cheeks were flushed, her eyes were bright with determination.

A summons. A mission. I must go and save my son.

The phone rang again. It was André.

'André. Something I must tell you.'

'Darling, I know already. I ring to tell you, I am yours for service. Everything will be put in order by me. You will not worry – '

'What I have to tell you is, I'm leaving in the morning. Probably for g – '

'Of course, we go together, Lottie. At once. We shall talk to the police, the insurers, everything together – '

'André, no.'

His tone became more portentous, like a politician at a funeral.

'Darling, it is in the emergency that you really know the man who is your true, deep lover. And – who will be your husband. Yes, Lottie, I will marry you.'

'This is *not* the time . . . I'm worried about my son! I don't in the slightest – '

'Your son, Lottie, will be like my son. This is the time for the father, I think . . . '

He was unstoppable, possibly drunk, more likely full of cocaine. He informed her what plane they were catching. He told her what time the car would collect her. Before she had caught her breath, he was gone. In a second he rang back again. Did Lottie need him tonight? He had some little ideas which might comfort her, she knew the ones he meant.

'No, André, for God's sake, I . . . look . . . '

But he had presented his enormous kisses, and as she still spluttered, the phone went dead.

Her reflection no longer looked pink and triumphant. She looked – flustered, toppled. This wouldn't do at all. This must be dealt with, once and for all.

She asked Room Service to bring her a vodka with *lots* of ice, and drank it slowly. She sucked the ice. Delicious. It chinked agreeably on her strong teeth. She was soon perfectly cool.

She brushed her hair. She would give this thought. The black dress was not assertive enough. She put on a wide-shouldered scarlet jacket which made her look even larger than usual, painted a bold and scarlet mouth, an unequivocal, no-saying mouth, refrained from the Shalimar she usually wore like an overcoat, rang for a taxi, swept into the night. A sudden attack. He'd be unprepared.

And he was unprepared. Quite unprepared. Perhaps not in quite the way she'd expected.

The receptionist smiled at her as she passed.

'Fait frais, ce soir,' said Lottie.

André never locked his door. It was a splendid door, a panelled black door. She paused for a second just before she got there. Looks like a bloody funeral parlour. *Never again, never again.*

'André,' she called, commandingly, pushed the door open, swept inside.

The scene inside was a brothel. She paused for a moment, stunned. There was André, transfixed, kneeling on the bed, belly bulging over leopard-skin printed shorts. Something probed underneath like a tent-pole. He also wore shiny black boots, knee-length, with little gold bits, *spurs*. They made his pink thighs look exceptionally stout. He also carried, my God, a *whip*, with a black leather plaited handle.

And on the bed (I don't believe this, I *do* believe this) – standing on the bed in front of him, spreadeagled forward so her sharp magenta nails were splayed on the wall – longer and whiter than anyone real – was *Trudi*. Yes, of course.

She turned her tired, sculpted head, saw Lottie, crumpled to her knees, hid her face in her magenta-slashed hands. A split second of complete stillness. Then she had scuttled under the bedspread. From underneath came strangled groans.

And André? He is red, very red, and his torso has slumped over his leopard-skin shorts in thick pink rolls, and the tent-pole has shrunk to nothing, and all of him, voice, legs, red appalled face, is trying to hide inside the shorts, and failing.

'I . . .' A hoarse, tortured sound.

'Poor Trudi,' said Lottie, very distinctly. 'I'm sorry, Trudi.'

She started to laugh as she walked with great dignity along the landing, huge merry gurgles and shouts which left her empty, silent.

CHAPTER FORTY-THREE

When Harold had first arrived, Sylvia's kitchen was so crammed with biscuits and cakes and packets and tins that he thought the food would go on for ever. He ate like a greedy boy as he sorted through what remained of her life. The rustle of starches cheered him up. One day the cupboard was bare and silent. Mother had really gone.

Ted offered to have him at a peppercorn rent. Harold took him up on it; Boscombe would do as a temporary base-camp. Now he decided to do a grand shop in Poole's huge Arndale Centre. The van which was coming for his packing-cases could take his provisions, too.

The day was wild, comfortless, ripping the leaves from the trees. Harold turned up his collar and reminded himself that the radio said the sun 'would break through later'. The air is good for me, he thought, butting across the giant roundabout.

In the Arndale Centre there was no air. It was Saturday; it was very crowded. Harold realized he hated shopping. Everything was outsize, the shops as well as the Economy Packs. A monstrous Littlwoods, a vast Tesco. Did anyone really need such variety? All those shelves just made him feel tired.

Do I want that choice? Do I need that choice?

No. He just wanted to walk to the sea. It was his last day in Poole, after all. Last chance to revisit his childhood.

It was mad to go with all that shopping. I hate my shopping. I want to be free (how on earth did women put up with shopping?). But he didn't dump it all there on the pavement. Don't be silly, it cost good money.

This part of Poole was utterly changed. Surely that road once led to the sea. But a sign said NO ACCESS TO PEDESTRIANS. The traffic roared, triumphant. The sky was grey as metal. Harold turned back through the centre.

That way led to Poole Quay, where he hadn't been for maybe twenty years. The sea could not be far; the quay was beside the harbour. After the vastness of the supermarkets its chief attraction was littleness. Souvenir shops, potteries, pubs, narrow turnings with Victorian views, everything for the strolling tourist. Even on this grey day some strolled, dwarfed by the cranes leaning over like dinosaurs, one woman happily munching haddock without removing her purple gloves.

There was a 'Modern Style' joke shop, very small. Its window seemed to have been bleached by the sun of endless blankly sunny days. Plastic fried eggs with whitening yolks, a hateful – what was it? – drinking-cup shaped like a woman's breast, with a spout at the nipple, *One Dozen Horrible Snake Eggs, Talking Toilet, Magic Spot, Dirty Nose Drop* (Roars of Laughter!!) *'Quality Self-Adhesive Stickers', I LOVE WELSH CORGIS, I LOVE DORSET, I LOVE MY DATSUN . . .*

Disgusting.

Someone had to spend time making these things. Someone had to spend time selling these things. Sometimes he hated the twentieth century.

Gratefully Harold plunged back into the turnings behind the shops. There the nineteenth century remained intact. A little street called Paradise Street led away from the Maritime Museum. The name was almost worn away; the brick underneath it was old and black. Something from Dickens. Lottie would love it. She always wanted him to write like Dickens.

A beautifully restored blue lamp post on which plump dolphins reared and curved. Maybe there were brothels here once for the sailors. Sex must be paradise for sailors. Sex would be paradise for Harold. Maybe he would end up going to a brothel.

But the street was cut off short. *No Through Road,* said the sign at the end. Harold walked back into the twentieth century, where brothels were something only other men did . . . (men without shopping-bags, younger men? Stupid men, unafraid of AIDS.)

You couldn't get to the sea this way. Should he go home instead? He sat and ate a bar of chocolate, watching the big boats swell and fall. His blood sugar rose. The boats were still splendid. On cue, the sun lit up the harbour. That settled it. Optimism broke through. Harold turned to pick up his shopping-bags again. He had leaned them against a wooden structure which was labelled 'The Office of the Berthing Master'. Under the label, he saw a notice.

NOTIFICATION OF INDUSTRIAL POISONING AND
DISEASE
Cases of poisoning by beryllium, cadmium, lead, phos-
phorus, arsenic, mercury, carbon bisulphide, manganese,
or aniline; toxic jaundice due to tetrachloroethane or nitro-
or amido-derivatives of benzene or other poisonous
substance; toxic anaemia; epitheliomatous ulceration, and
chronic ulceration, must be reported on form F41 to the
District Inspector and to the Employment Medical Ad-
viser . . . and entered in the General Register (Sections 82
and 40 and regulations).

Harold stomped away with his eyes on the ground. He'd loved
these docks and ships as a child. Was it an advance, to see
everything black? Human beings were good at some things,
surely.

What, precisely? What was he good at?

Grasping the web of connections. That was what he was
trying to do. Understanding. But he didn't yet. Perceiving. But
his eyes weren't good.

What *are* you good at, Harold?

Carrying shopping-bags.

Leaving people.

Sod, sod. Could he ever improve? His eyes stung, his ears complained. On the long meander of the road round the harbour no
one else was fool enough to be walking, into the autumn wind.

Harold, why are you here?

The wind brought him an answer, the noise of a train running into
Poole station. He remembered the miniature train which used to
run in Poole Park. There was a vast blue lake, with – swans? The
train ran right round the edge of it. Between some willows, his
parents waved, their smiles coming clearer as the train roared
round a bend and six-year-old Harold was there in glory, in the
very front carriage, helping the driver. Mother and Father had
waved so hard their hands nearly came off and flew across the
water.

It could still be there. I could go again.

He started to walk a bit faster, though the weight of the

shopping, by now so familiar it felt like the weight of his own tired body, made him feel older (but he *was not* old: nothing was impossible: love could return).

He followed his instincts. Behind those trees . . .

And there it waited, the little green train. Very much smaller; that was predictable. The icing-sugar colours (every carriage different: pale mauve, pale yellow, pale blue, pale green) were lighter, more playful than he remembered. Harold remembered quite a *serious* train. The driver looked at him rather oddly as he paid his money and clambered aboard.

Harold's upper half poked out of the carriage. He felt very bald, and much too large, and he knew all the mothers would assume he was a maniac, but still he was where he wanted to be, and nothing was going to spoil it.

The train whistled, and was off. He imagined the lake would open up at any second behind the screen of osiers and ashes. With real surprise he saw a pretty little pond, not more than fifty yards long. He just about had time to admire two fluffy grey cygnets and then boys on bikes were racing the train, and could they be winning? – BEWARE OF THE TRAIN, flashed a notice, too late, behind some silver-white poplars, too late, for the bikes had already won and the train was slowing, slowing, it can't be, the train shunted back into the white-staked station.

He sat for a moment bemused.

Flexing his fingers, by now rather sore, round the weary plastic handles of his bags. Lumbering out on to the boring land.

He could go *again*.

He could have another trip.

But he knew there wasn't any point. He no longer fitted the little train. He could ride round and round, but never go back to the lake with the flying hands and swans. Still, he wasn't ashamed of wanting to.

He hated things to be spoiled or lost. The town he grew up in, the woman he loved. Everyone wants things to come again. Poets, novelists, lovesick girls. And boys, of course, he added, hastily. Me, for example.

But it couldn't be that simple. Not for him, anyway. Or him and Lottie. If we get back together, it will never be the same. We've had other people. We've managed without each other. You can't erase that. You might not want to. It might be better; it can't be the same.

(Harold kept going towards the bus stop. By bus, he could still reach the sea before sunset.)

It can't be a circle, but was there a pattern? Perhaps it was one more problem of scale. You longed above all for some sense of a whole. You tried to go back and look for a meaning. You thought the past would make everything plain. But the pattern you ached for might be here all the time, now, in the present, if you weren't so nearsighted. If you just kept going, you might understand.

A straight road might bring you back again, if you followed it far enough, right round the world. And the world would have changed by the time you came back. It wouldn't be a circle, but something more interesting.

Perhaps the road wasn't what was important; some object you glimpsed for a second on the verge, half-hidden in the grass, might have been the point, and you'd suddenly know it long afterwards. A face half-seen in a foreign city, a ripped envelope someone dropped.

Or maybe we're objects left on the verge and other searchers go running past us. Maybe we're meanings for other people. Maybe our personal selves don't matter (*but they hurt; they cry. That matters to me*).

As he reached the bus stop, the light was changing, growing warmer and pinker as the sun began to dip. A cloud of birds flew across the sun, making their escape before the real cold caught them. Was it too late for him to get to the sea? However much he thought, time still *felt* linear.

But he wouldn't be beaten. He paid his fare, and hauled his great baggages of worry upstairs.

The stairs. That was it. He gasped to the top, collapsed on a seat and thought about it.

Time isn't a circle. But nor is it straight. There was hope in a spiral (*well* – the stairs of the bus were only half a spiral, but nothing in life is perfect).

We have to die. That's clear. And the Earth will die, as a separate planet, when the sun becomes a red giant. In five billion years or so (but already, the sun as he gazed through the window was swelling and reddening, *wait for me*). It will swallow the Earth, with Mercury and Venus, and throw them out in a halo of gas, and the gas may condense into stars again . . . but all the time, we'll be losing energy.

In the end, the whole universe will run down. It will expand too far, it will thin to nothing, nothing but endless dark and cold.

But there's another possibility. Astronomers say so, and we can hope . . . At some final point of expansion, the universe will rush together again. Over billions of years, time will run backwards, until all matter shrinks to a singularity. And then the Big Bang will happen again, and everything will emerge again, utterly different but still in motion. And in some sense we shall still be there, Lottie and Davey and Sylvia and I, as energy, completely transformed.

We were stardust once. We could be stars again.

Somehow we shall go on. Not as ourselves, but in everything else.

We shall shine for other living things. Others will look for a meaning in us.

He climbed back down the metal stairs. The bags went lumping against the sides. The vision faded, but he wasn't defeated.

Five o'clock. If he hurried, he would still get a look at the sunset sea. He half-trotted down the zig-zag path.

The wind off the waves was as cold as ice and the sun had reddened, darkened. The remains of the cloud were a conflagration, twists of apricot burning to grey. The promenade was empty.

Below, on the beach, a black dog jumped and howled after a ball someone out of sight bowled again and again across the liquid crimson. The cold down there must be intense; but so was the animal's desperate energy, clear as print on the flaming water, so was the will of the hidden arm which sent the ball up again and again.

Harold stood and stared at the sun. You could only look at it at this time of day when the thicknesses of air made it bearable. You could suddenly see it as something with form, not just a blinding daze of light.

The centre of everything he knew, it sank like a massive spherical stone behind a land-mass which was suddenly simplified, a body of dark, no tat, no mess. The dark was simply a planet, turning, outlined against the starlight; a blaze of crimson, amber, gold.

Sunlight. Starlight. He stared it out.

The sun was nearly touching the rim of the land, then touching, sinking.

Stop, that's wrong.

For it wasn't sinking at all. He had always known it, like everyone else, but now he knew it with his whole body, suddenly felt that the sun hadn't moved but the weight of the Earth was turning away from it, carrying him with it, over and back, carrying everything back into shadow . . . as they rolled over, the cliffs rose dark between the bright sea and the blazing star, fingers of shadow ran out through the waves and then the nearest light had gone out, from the beach at his feet, then the waves just beyond it, and dark spread outwards, swallowing light, though the crests were still silver-pink in the distance, and the light shrank steadily back towards Poole as the earth rolled all of them down into darkness. On the far horizon, the edge of the Earth, just a final sliver of brilliance: gone.

He shook, with a mixture of thrill and terror.

At last I felt it. I understood. Not with my brain, but with my body. I felt where I was in the universe. On a planet, rolling away from a star.

I grasped a tiny part of the pattern.

He shut his eyes for a moment. The after-image was still dazzlingly bright, a ruby blazing inside his eyeball.

But the wicked wind blew. The moment had passed. He was left dizzy, and very cold. He must get indoors.

I want to tell Lottie . . .

Gasping in the wind, he remembered his bags. Oh no, I can't have forgotten them . . . But he'd only wandered a little way away.

They stood on the edge of the promenade, dully abandoned, two bags of litter.

Thank God, he thought, clutching them protectively. I couldn't have borne to do the shopping again.

CHAPTER FORTY-FOUR

On the map it looked so near that Lottie set off on foot without a thought. She hadn't had a walk in ages. It was a cold bright day with a hard red sunset, the sun sinking down into a crack between the buildings like a massive spherical stone.

I want you back. I'm coming to find you . . .

She thought of her heavy gold, amber, rubies piled like treasure trove. She would run her fingers through the cold chains. Her mouth watered; she would snatch it all back.

And then her whole life would somehow come right. *Things would be back as they were before . . .*

Sodium lights flashed on as she walked, starting off crimson, glowing up to orange, traffic-light bright against the clear pale sky: very soon brighter than the last of the sunset.

Perhaps I should have driven. I'll pick up a taxi on the way, probably.

There would be taxis nearer the address. Davey had told her the address, under protest. He'd made her promise not on any account to go near it on her own. He had made it sound, well, *rough*. It couldn't be really rough, however. It was just at the back of King's Cross and Euston. At the back of the Town Hall, in fact. *Camden* wasn't rough.

Still she had flat shoes on, and in her handbag a sweet little gun which was legal in Paris but certainly not in London. The Vanguard took percussion caps or teargas. With pleasure and concentration, she had loaded it before she went out, laying out the caps and the teargas cartridges across the gold satin of the bedspread, inserting them alternately, one by one. As she crossed the five o'clock roar of traffic in Euston Road it occurred to her that she hadn't a clue whether caps or teargas would come out first. But then, she wasn't going to *use* the gun. She didn't *need* it, no. But its weight in her handbag made her feel – *even* more buoyant, more *entirely* invulnerable.

The Town Hall. She consulted her *A to Z*. On the page it

appeared to be minutes away. Not allowing herself to pause for too long, she licked her lips, straightened her hair, squared her shoulders and marched into Judd Street, from which she bore left into smaller streets.

Darker streets.

Rougher streets.

What happened for the next hour or so would never be quite forgotten by Lottie. The city she entered now was a hundred times more alien to her than the boy she was hunting. Having been here once, she was doomed to come again, in broken dreams she would not remember, in sudden disorienting gaps opening up at her feet as she ate a croissant, or bought a print, or gazed at her Bonnard, her beautiful, radiant Bonnard.

It wouldn't last for ever, in its sharpest form. But it left a little shadow, the smallest stain. Something shadowing the silvers and pinks and golds of the skin in the Bonnard bedroom. A tiny puzzlement that somewhere else the light could be so different. A little crack that might finally open and let in more of the darkness than she'd ever allowed to be here before. Say a square inch or so. About a hundredth the size of her Bonnard.

At the time, the unsettling thing about the world behind the Town Hall was that it seemed to go on for ever. Streets began without shops or gardens, without any variation of architecture, stretching unrelieved until the interminable strings of numbers exhausted themselves. Lottie began to feel tired, though she hadn't been walking long. It was time to pick up a taxi. But there wasn't a hint of a taxi. There was nothing but fortresses of flats, with hundreds and hundreds of cells inside. 307, 308 . . .

The first blocks she came to were dingy and grey, asbestos-coloured, not very old. They looked as though they had started off shabby: 1950s or 1960s.

So this is what Davey meant, she thought. Well, it *is* depressing. But at least it's a home for them. I suppose this explains a lot. He must have thought my jewellery would cheer the place up a bit.

And then she imagined putting the diamonds round his scrawny neck and choking him. It didn't work, as a fantasy. The hard stones knocked against his boy's Adam's apple.

Christ, I hope he hasn't sold them already. Silly little bugger, did he think he'd get away with it?

There weren't many people about. Some noisy schoolkids hung around in uniform, not eager to go home. Most of the faces seemed to be black. They looked at her a little curiously. She kept on walking briskly, although she wanted to look at her map.

Why no shops? They must need shops. We'd *die* without the deli on the corner.

And then things got a lot darker, though the sky was progressing at its usual rate. She seemed to walk back in time. All around her were walls of steep dark brick. Blackened brick from another century. It was not quite believable, a set from a film. Like Dickens, but changing the flavour of Dickens, as if Dickens meant to depress everyone when he did those wonderfully squalid descriptions. The windows were tiny eyes, set high, grilled with wood to stop them seeing. Some of the street lamps had not lit up. They couldn't; they were useless stumps.

A dog ran out and barked at her furiously, making her think of Paris and rabies, and shrink against the wall. Then a man came round the corner after the dog, a tall thin man who stared unsmiling, black as his dog but with wild grey hair, and she shrank back very slightly again.

Come on, Lottie, this is ridiculous, you're going to give that little runt what for.

But she waited till the man and the dog had gone before she pulled the *A to Z* out of her handbag and almost tore the page in her hurry, scoring the paper with one sharp finger, missing the square of the map she wanted again and again in the flickering light. The map above her seemed to fade as she stared. There was a plaque above her on the wall which might be a street name. She peered up, but all it said was

EAST END DWELLINGS CORPORATION, 1884

Didn't that make them listed buildings? Lottie was genuinely shocked.

Then it struck her.

These are slums.

This is what slums are.

But the map had no different symbol for slums.

And surely they had made it look small on purpose. They couldn't have drawn it to scale. It's vast. She imagined the centre of the *A to Z* entirely given over to grimy blackness. She was glad they had made it look small. Close up, full-size, it was out of control.

When she finally found where she was on the map, she knew she must penetrate further in. Into that vast brick block with its tiny, sometimes broken windows.

She went through a brightly-lit archway into emptiness. An enormous courtyard. Like a prison exercise yard might be. Above it, the oblong of sky, now blue and glowing, was surprisingly smaller. She longed for it, briefly. The light from the archway fell on the nearer parts of the facing wall. It was like a hallucination, but Lottie never had those.

A mural ran along the bricks, painted in colours which if the sun ever fell in this courtyard might have been brilliant. Painted by an amateur artist, unrecognizable plants and running children with their mouths propped wide. Perhaps they were smiling. Perhaps they were screaming. In the lessening light they began to grow. The other three walls were black. The only illumination came from the stairways which transected the black. Not all of the stairways were illuminated. Raggedly separated stripes of light.

Each stairway had probably started off with a legible notice of the numbers it contained. But innumerable hands had seen to it that such notices were so heavily scrawled with signatures, claims to oral sex, threats of murder, drawings of cocks, that many of the numbers were illegible. Footfalls in this courtyard were impossibly loud. Not all of them were hers. Some must belong to the graffiti artists.

WATCH OUT PIGTITTS ILE KILL YOU (TRUE)

Keeping as close as she could to the walls, away from the exposure of the centre of the courtyard, she finally found the right staircase.

The stairs were stone so you couldn't be quiet, and she heard herself panting as she neared the top. The numbers didn't seem to go in order, or else her thoughts were not in order. You couldn't have a world where you didn't trust numbers. Right at the top, where the stairs guttered out, she read his number on a

pitted door. The final three turned into an eight, and back to
three as she looked. It settled at three. This was it.

The bell didn't work. Lottie beat with her fist.

The woman who came to the door was so big that she was like
a second, inner door. The television blared behind her. Guns
fired great volleys, hooves ran away. She was red and steaming,
presumably from the cooking that Lottie could smell.

Something fried. Lottie loved all food, but this smelled like no
food she knew. Fish with an undertone of pork, or pork with an
overtone of fish. The woman had flat greasy hair, and could
have been any age from thirty-five to sixty. Her eyes were small
and cold, assessing, running over Lottie as if she was a tart.

Christ, she probably thinks I am.

'Mrs McGuire?'

' 'Ooer you? I'm busy.'

In her hand was an empty, open tin. Lottie felt it might be
thrust in her face at any moment, and kept one eye on it
carefully. (Later she remembered the label. It said *Luncheon
Meat*. What was Luncheon Meat?)

'I'm a friend of Smegg – I'm a friend of Simon's.'

She changed it just in time. In the face of that gaze, however,
'friend' seemed wildly suggestive. Lottie tried smiling brightly,
commandingly, proceeding forwards ('Can I come in?') till she
actually touched the enormous flowered bust with her own
relatively insignificant front. The enormity suddenly yielded.
Assert yourself, and things yield before you. The door of flesh
swung wearily backwards.

'Well, 'e's inside. We never see 'im out 'ere.'

Lottie hurried past, and as she turned right down the corridor
she saw the woman staring, stock still, mouth working, and
caught the words, 'Dirty little bugger.'

Music drifted down the corridor. The bulb was forty-watt or
less, and she nearly tripped over a bucket which seemed to hold
dirty nappies. The music got louder in front of a door with a
piece of paper Sellotaped to it.

A crude drawing of a skull and crossbones, yellow chalk on
black paper. The bones were tumescent, the skull leered
horribly.

DO NOT ENTER ON PAIN OF DEATH

Too late to go back. Too late to be scared. *I am not scared. I refuse to be scared.* But just before Lottie jerked the door open, she transferred the little gun, looking smaller than before, from her handbag to her jacket pocket. It felt like a film, not a very good film, a film she desperately wanted to end.

OK, Lottie, show 'em you can do it.

(A sudden *déjà vu:* yesterday in Paris, standing in front of that black, polished door.)

She pushed the door open. What she saw was no less astonishing. At first she thought the room was on fire. Everywhere, smoke curled up in slow feathers, an overpowering smell of wax and incense, but then she saw candles, a bulb glowing red, the red gleaming back from the dressing-table mirror. Music beat through her whole body.

In and out of the glass, dancing to the music, Smeggy, seven-eighths naked, paused in mid-leap, but the energy carried him spinning onwards, slower and slower, his great ruff of red and blue hair shaking and spinning outside him. For a moment, she felt sharp desire. Tiny black pants, white arms and legs as narrow as parts of some underground plant but the narrow white muscles had a sheen in the candlelight, the crazy eyes shone alive and startling from their circles of paint; utterly theatrical, almost fragile with the stones wrapped round his arms and throat, dropping scintillae of rainbow light and then all she felt was blinding anger, *her* light, her rubies, diamonds, sapphires, spinning with this hateful little animal.

'Right!' she shouted at the top of her voice, a voice a sergeant would have envied. 'You cheeky little sod, let's have those diamonds!' and on impulse, while his gape was transforming itself into an insolent smile, she bent into the darkness, found the plug of the record-player, pulled it from the wall; and because as he bent she felt a stab of fear, she closed her hand around the gun in her pocket and was suddenly holding it out towards him, not knowing she'd planned to do any such thing, holding it still and straight towards him.

His smile stopped, died.

'Blimey, Mrs Segall. I mean, *blimey.'*

He started to unwind the stones from his neck. He was shivering a little and couldn't find the catches.

'You'd better switch on the overhead light,' said Lottie, gun perfectly steady.

When he did, there was a sudden stab of pity. His pale, slightly pock-marked body was boyish in the light of the unshaded bulb, reminding her now of Davey.

I bet no one ever pulled a gun on him before, whatever the little sod's done.

But she restrained herself from helping him undo the catches, though she was almost sure that she could have risked it, that some game of wills was definitively won.

She had spotted the coats in the corner of the room, piled like dirty dead animals against the other bed. He must share this room with another kid. The thought of the furs became rather disgusting. The floor was dirty. The walls were dirty. Davey never liked furs anyway. The coats became confused with Smeggy's dirty white skin.

Bare of jewels, he was a kid in his underpants who'd painted himself for a fancy dress party, a kid she had frightened till he stood there and shook. His eyes slid up towards hers again, and one more time he said, 'Blimey, Mrs Segall,' and shook his ragged crimson head.

Ah yes, it was the flowers. In spring, when I bought all those flowers. For one last moment, she wanted to touch him.

She suddenly stuffed the gun back into her jacket, shoved the jewellery into both pockets, swept out, strode into the kitchen, skirted the mountain of Mrs McGuire. Just as she was closing the front door behind her, she turned and shouted above the gunshots and the cowboy music, 'Do you want a fur coat? Your son's got three. Three of mine. I don't want them. Make sure he gives you one.'

The door slammed hard as Mrs McGuire's little mouth dropped open.

('Dirty old scrubber,' she said to the door. 'Patronizing bloody old cunt!' And she heaved down the dim corridor towards Smeggy's room. Time for a sorting-out with this one.)

Lottie was frightened, more frightened than she'd ever been in her life, as she walked back through the courtyard with her jewels in her pockets and her heart thudding, thudding, like her feet on the stone. What if they follow me? What if they catch me? Every face was a mugger's face. She pulled up her coat-collar and kept her head down but her eyes looked everywhere, in every dark corner. It felt several lifetimes later that she waved down a cab on Euston Road. She could hardly pronounce her address. The cab driver looked at her curiously.

She ran up the stairs to her own bright house and rang wildly, instead of looking for her key. When Davey opened the door, she hugged him to death.

In the hall she pulled the jewels from both pockets, laughing like a kid with presents from a party.

But when she sat down she felt utterly weak.

On the dining-room table, the stones didn't look so large or brilliant as she had expected.

Inside, she was a kid who wanted to tell Harold.

Oh, I want him back. It'll soon be his birthday.

Days are getting shorter; mists drift over. Conkers are forgotten in boys' pockets, wrinkling a little out of the light.

Lottie stands in her garden, wishing.

The Stags'-horn Sumach has orange-yellow leaves and purple-red fruit, hard to the touch, long horns pushing up towards the sun. Her spindle tree has heart-shaped seed-cases, pink, split open. The seeds hang down.

If the sun were the size of a very large orange, the moon would be the size of a pinhead. Yet when the moon passes between Earth and sun, the sun goes out, for viewers on Earth. As the moon moves black across the disc of the sun, darkness starts to come. In the final seconds before total eclipse, sunlight pours through the gaps between the mountains on the rugged edge of the moon; a string of diamonds, flaring, dwindling. Then it has all gone out.

It only lasts for two or three minutes. But animals sleep, and humans are frightened.

Actually, something very very small has passed across something immensely bright.

November

CHAPTER FORTY-FIVE

The first frost turn the dahlias grey. A Small White butterfly staggers, crawls.

'We've lost the last warm days, I suppose.'

'Violet, dearest – shall we go away?'

As it gets colder in Northern Europe, humans burn more fossilized sunlight. Sulphur and nitrogen rise in the air.

There are lakes in Sweden which are quite transparent, silent, a frighteningly brilliant blue. They are beautiful, but nothing lives there. Thousands of lakes as clear as acid.

On the other side of the earth, it is warmer, but plenty of trees are crashing down. Mahogany trees and cedars first, then anything that gets in the way. Between thirty and fifty hectares per minute. The tamarins fly, brief as meteors, darting out into too much sunlight.

'A pinch, a punch, the first of the month,' Lottie sang as she pinched and punched her son. One day till Harold's birthday.

'Oh, *Mum*,' he complained, squirming away.

The first blush of uncritical joy at having her back had faded quite quickly. Now he was almost back to normal, but Lottie was much more affectionate, trying to fit in all the hugs he had missed, not to mention the hugs she needed herself as the weather got colder and Harold didn't ring.

The first week she had been back, vast funeral bouquets of red roses had arrived from André every day. He was clearly too afraid to phone. The messages on the little cards, doubly garbled by André and the florist, were farcically importunate. *Most beloved darling woman, I am implore you forgiving me . . .*

She piled them still in their Cellophane in the utility room, which smelled sweet, then rotten. She had lost her temper with Amanda for unwrapping and arranging the first lot. She lost her temper again when Amanda tried to throw them all away. When there were eight dead and dying bunches, she asked Amanda to wrap them carefully in strong brown paper and post them back to André, in Paris.

'*That* ought to stop him,' she said.

Amanda did it, but her face was grim.

It finally stopped Amanda.

☆

She was loyal. She had always been loyal. But she had her limits. Everyone did.

A person has feelings after all. And a person *is* a person.

She explained it to Doris, who agreed with every word, tut-tutting gently, pouring more tea.

All year this had been boiling up inside her. Things weren't right in that house, any more. Nice Mr Segall gone away. Some terrible story Davey had told her about a dead monkey, all Mrs S's doing. Killing a poor little innocent animal. In the utility room, of all places. She tried so hard to keep it nice.

In any case monkeys were dirty creatures. Filthy. Disgusting. Everyone knew that. It made her itch, just thinking about it. Since Mrs Segall had deigned to come home she was always round at the zoo. What if next time she took it into her head to bring home an alligator or a hippo to murder?

Then there was the burglary. She liked things straightforward. A burglar's a burglar, and police is police.

'It probably makes me a Accessory, not telling the police,' she hissed.

Enough was enough. She didn't like nonsense. And beautiful flowers which cost a packet being left to go rotten in *her* utility room was more than enough for a saint. ('And I'm not a saint.' But Doris demurred.) And having to post the whole nasty mess to Paris was putting the lid on it. 'It probably broke the Quarantine Laws. It probably makes me a Smuggler! And so, I'm handing in me notice,' she ended, in a triumphant flourish. 'I'll tell her what she can do with her job! A person is not a stick or stone!'

And so she did, to Lottie's total discomfiture. It was as if the garden had got up and walked, hitched itself over the wall, and vanished.

The letter was phrased like a Home Office circular. Amanda had learned how to hand in her notice from Arthur, while they were married. Arthur was an expert at handing in notice. For Amanda, though, it was a first, and she put a great deal into it.

Dear Mrs Segall
TERMINATION OF EMPLOYMENT
With reference to above topic, I beg to submit . . .

The reason she gave was 'due to matters arising', which covered an awful lot of ground.

The note was left on the hall table, where Lottie always left the Sunday papers for Amanda, who never read the papers, because they depressed her. Lottie read it; she read it again; such language from dumb Amanda. She took it upstairs, and thought about it. She was staggered, but also a little amused.

The ensuing audience with Amanda was not as awkward as she expected. Amanda was impassive and docile as ever, though perhaps, when Lottie asked, smiling with all her famous charm, if she wouldn't miss her just the tiniest bit, there was a certain glint in the eyes that met Lottie's and held them seconds longer than was usual for Amanda.

'An employer's an employer, Mrs Segall.'

Lottie's smile became uneasy. She was more than a trifle hurt. She said Amanda needn't work her notice, and to her surprise Amanda agreed. At Davey's suggestion, Lottie added a leaving present of two thousand pounds.

'But she won't expect it, Davey. I mean – a servant's a servant. She was only doing her job.'

'Bollocks. Amanda loves me. If you don't, I'll take all my savings out.'

He's a very nice boy, thought Lottie. How did I come to have such a nice boy? I really don't think I deserve him.

'Will you miss her terribly, Davey? I mean, I could beg and plead with her to stay.'

'No. Yes. It doesn't matter. I mean, everyone's always walking out of here. And I shan't live here for ever.'

And *that* caught Lottie right under the ribs, though she

guessed he only meant, in some unfocused way, *I'm in love with Mary, so the rest of you don't matter.*

When Amanda had removed the last of her possessions, leaving the basement spotless and bare, Lottie went down and stood on the basement stairs and looked about her.

Yes. The idea of change had a certain charm. Of course we ought to get another housekeeper. But maybe we could muddle through without. If we got someone in to clean. We could eat out more. Or get food brought in . . .

'Harold always needed a bigger study,' she muttered to herself, and the stairwell amplified it.

Davey, in the hall, about to phone Mary, heard what she said and was worried. She's kidding herself, he thought. There's precisely one day to go till his birthday. She's got this fantasy he's going to come home. She's really counting on it. And there isn't any reason to think he'll show up (though Davey had sent a birthday postcard to the address that Sylvia gave for him. It should have arrived today. So he wasn't there, or he wasn't interested.)

Davey had seen the champagne in the fridge, two bottles of vintage Krug. There was also some Beluga caviare, and a cake in a Harrods' box. Worse than all that, the bulky packages delivered yesterday. A *word processor.* It could only be for Harold. Mum was insane. Harold wouldn't even *want* one. Harold was hopeless with mechanical things. Machines turned Harold into a drip. More of a drip *(I miss him, though).*

She pours her money down the drain.

That reminded him of something he had on his mind, and he forgot the phone call, went back upstairs.

The list was typed on bright yellow paper. He had found it that morning, lying on the doormat.

Food and Supplies for Striking Miners
For food parcels:
Tins of: Stew
             Peas

> Carrots
> Corned beef
> Beans . . .
> Packets 'Smash'
> Powdered milk
> Packets of teabags . . .

He started looking carefully through the kitchen cupboards. Amanda believed in storing food for emergencies, so he was pretty sure there would be lots of things spare. This *was* an emergency, after all. The food was to be taken to a collection point in Camden Library. He would take it tomorrow, when Mum was not around.

Lottie called out from the doorway behind him, 'Darling, are you going to be in for a bit? I'm off to the zoo, I'll be back around five.'

She'd startled him, so he sounded cross. 'Not really. I'm just going round to Mary's. Probably shan't be back till late.'

'Well, make sure you switch the answerphone on. And don't, for God's sake, touch the cake in the fridge.'

He didn't turn round that time, just grunted. Lottie went off feeling distinctly neglected.

The zoo had got progressively nicer the fewer people there were to share it with, which wasn't always true of houses, she reflected, smiling brilliantly at the bored gatekeeper. The weather was getting cooler, of course. Not everyone was as hardy as she was.

Lottie had made friends with two of the keepers, one young and blond, one grey and talkative. Men had always liked talking to her. And she'd always been a good listener . . . well, sometimes she talked a lot, it was true, but in this case she'd really concentrated. She had to know everything before Harold came back. Thanks to those sweet men, she already knew a lot. The important things, names and faces.

Even in the months she'd been coming, they'd changed. Possibly she had changed slightly as well; she had been a little blind to the orang-utans, at first. Now her favourite, an adolescent male called Bin-Tang, had disappeared to a Danish zoo. Lottie was surprised at her sense of loss, and the mother and baby who had been with Bin-Tang seemed more lethargic, less extrovert, clinging together as if they were afraid. The other orang-utans didn't seem to care. They cartwheeled and cuddled as usual.

The gorilla group was transformed, though not entirely successfully. The adolescent male, Kumba, who she'd seen holding hands with the female, Salome, had been exchanged for a new massively handsome full-grown silverback male. His name was also Kumba, so at first when she heard the keeper call him she wondered if gorillas had periods of exceptionally rapid growth. And she thought of Harold with painful intensity; what if he had changed entirely? What if that really *was* him in Paris, tanned, with dark glasses and a beautiful schoolgirl?

Salome was clearly besotted at first with the new, hunky Kumba. Sometimes she lay and gazed at him as he sat sternly on his concrete ledge. She patted him gingerly when she dared, even sniffed at his genitals, jumping away if he showed irritation, then lying down a little way off and gazing moon-eyed again. Often she bent in front of him, presenting her square rear, but he chased her briskly away. He wasn't hostile, he was simply detached. He looked as if he was dreaming of jungles.

After a few weeks of this abortive courtship, a new female had suddenly appeared, around Salome's age, but friskier, lacking Salome's wrinkled nose and melancholy smile. Today Lottie was tickled to see that the two females were hugging and patting each other, casting anxious glances at Kumba occasionally, but having rather a good time on their own, chasing and clapping hands, or walking about with their arms round each other, rather like girls at boarding-school.

Maybe I should ring up Claudia. I haven't talked to a friend for months. And sometimes it helps to talk to a woman.

Somone familiar, too. Claudia, at least, was always the same. Lottie knew where she was with Claudia.

But really it was Kumba she wanted, beautiful, remote, showing no interest. Kumba, turned silver, astonishingly changed.

You turned your back and the whole world shifted.

The phone was silent. The evening passed.

CHAPTER FORTY-SIX

I know I shall ring her today – Boscombe, 9 a.m., November 2.

I know he will ring me today – Camden, 9 a.m., November 2.

November 2 in Dorset was the kind of a day a man should be born on. Clear, crisp, cold.

Quite early, Ted Sedley knocked on the door. Harold came in from the balcony where he was drinking coffee.

"Ow old are yer then?' Ted asked without ceremony. 'And 'Appy Birthday, if they're 'appy.'

The old man handed over a postcard.

> H. SEGALL Please forward URGENT please
> Happy Birthday, wherever you are. Mum's back. I went down to see Sylvia but I couldn't find her address. Hope she's all right. Give her my love, tell her we tried. Creep's overcrept himself. RING. Love Davey.

Posted the day before yesterday.

Harold felt a lump in his throat. He suddenly missed Davey so badly. On the very rare occasions that Davey had hugged him, bones and the noisy beat of a heart . . . Harold saw him, felt him with absolute clarity, just for a second, then he was gone.

What did that mean, 'Creep's overcrept himself'?

Either Creep was out on his neck; or else he had crept himself into the house, *our* bedroom, *our* bathroom. 'RING. Love Davey.'

He suddenly remembered Ted's question.

'Er – I'm forty-six.'

' 'At's nothin',' said Ted. ' 'Ow old am *I*? Go on, *guess.*'

He lifted his head and smirked rather horribly, expanding his rib-cage to its fullest extent.

With an effort, Harold concentrated. Ted was probably fabulously old, mythopoeically healthy. That tan like leather cured by centuries of sun. Eighty at least. Probably ninety (how old is Creep? Thirty? *Twenty-five?*)

'Seventy,' he tried, a sycophant.

'*Sixty*,' said Ted, visibly winded.

'I never could guess ages.'

'Well, I'd have given *you* fifty any day,' Ted came back with a left to the chin.

Once Ted had gone Harold counted his tenpenny pieces. He had eleven. Plenty enough to ring London. But the money goes so fast on a weekday morning. Really it was better to wait till later. When he came back from Swanage. This evening.

Relieved, he set off on his birthday outing.

Harold went lightly, like a twenty-year-old, up the little road which wound up from Swanage harbour to the steep green head beyond. To the right he saw a tiny chalk path going up almost vertically to a point that the road would eventually reach.

Was he young enough? He was young enough.

Was he fit enough? He was strong as an ox.

High spirits took him halfway up at a run, three-quarters of the way at a stumbling trot, and he reached the top almost on his knees; but when he had got his breath back, he saw his birthday treat all about him.

The green field rose in a steady arc to the sky which suddenly cut it off. Not a soul in sight, not a sound but the sea and a solitary seagull crying. But that couldn't be the edge of the cliff, up there. There would be signs and barbed-wire fences. Still he went a little gingerly as he got near.

Glancing down he suddenly saw that a webbing of stretch-marks covered the earth, dark weals held together by the roots of the grass, and then it crumbled away to nothing.

The very edge.

A sheer drop, then the blaze of light from the distant sea. He half-closed his eyes against the glare and dropped to his knees and looked over. A fleshy green plant that might be samphire hung on the dreadful cliff, unafraid. Then he lay spreadeagled on the earth's torn side, feeling safer on his stomach, with his heart thumping. The sun was suddenly hot on his neck as the wind dropped for a moment.

In that second, he heard the sea clearly. For a second of stillness, he concentrated. Neither a roar nor a whisper. The sound of millions of pieces of shell and shingle, breaking and swirling, under and over, thousands of millions of grains of sand, turning and stirring against each other. Indifferent to boats or beach-huts. Indifferent to any mess we made. The sound was four thousand million years old. It would outlast whatever we did.

And Harold, however brief and small, was part of that sound as he listened. The grass pricked under his hands. *I'm alive*, he thought. *The earth is alive. Nothing much matters but being alive.*

But the tenpenny pieces pressed in his pocket. His heart beat harder.

Lottie matters.

☆

He rang her from a coinbox in Swanage.

The familiar ringing tone. In the background, a conversation on another line, two women talking chirpily. Harold wished them dead, but didn't give up. Eight rings. Nine rings. The voices got louder. They were laughing at someone, probably him.

On the tenth ring, someone picked up the receiver. Harold shoved in the coin, nearly dropping it, there was a tiny pause in which his tongue turned to sawdust then a man's voice, blurred by the two women's, drawled, 'Hell-o-o--ah?'

Creep. It must be.

Everything seized up. He half-dropped the phone, tried to snatch it up, clashed it on the coinbox, was left with the flex as the phone went crashing horribly earthwards, swore, gave up. Held it away from him, slammed it on the cradle. 'Fuck, fuck, *fuck.*' He was almost weeping.

I'll . . . mangle him. I'll *crush* him. I'll cut out his tongue.

I'll have to ring back. They'll guess it was me.

But the fat woman waiting outside the box swung the door open and asked him anxiously, 'Are you gointer be very long? It's urgent, see. I want to ring my mother. She's very very ill.'

Scrabbling up his money, not meeting her eyes, he left the phone box, defeated.

(The woman rang her boyfriend. She wanted to tell him she wasn't pregnant.)

☆

In London, Hugo, who'd dropped round before lunch and surprised Lottie with some orchids, put down the phone with a bored little yawn. Lottie yelled a query from the bathroom.

'Just a wrong number, darling.'

It sounded as if she yelled, 'Shit,' but maybe she'd just dropped the soap. He'd come round hoping for the dirt on her and André, but Lottie was distinctly unchatty.

She came down in the end wrapped from head to toe in a shaggy coat of white wool. With it, a tiny white velvet hat, under which her yellow hair poured like water. Her jaw was set, but she was still stunning.

'Come on, Hugo, you can take me out to lunch.'

The white made her cheeks look very pink, and the wrinkles were fine, but he noted them. When women were stroppy, a sharp eye helped. The brilliance of her irises made them show more, a regular fan of them across her high cheekbones.

Perhaps it was the age thing that did it with André. Yes, I expect he jilted her.

He quite liked to think of his cousin jilting her. Do her no harm to be jilted a bit.

'Well, come *on*, Hugo, honestly, you've got the most *peculiar* expression!'

☆

Davey, who was longing for her to go out, was delighted to hear the front door close behind them. She'd been utterly foul since suppertime last night when it occurred to her that Harold might not show up.

She'd complained about the toast Davey did for their breakfast, she'd complained about his haircut, she'd complained about his clothes. She'd complained that he 'wasn't company'. She'd complained that he didn't understand her.

He understood her all right. At the moment he didn't like her.

In the kitchen he was very efficient, keeping the yellow list to hand. He was packing it all into a box on the floor. Some of the items he just couldn't find; they had four tins of water-chestnuts, for example, but not one tin of corned beef; they had tinned asparagus, but not tinned peas; the only tinned soup they had was Vichyssoise, and he wasn't quite sure that was right for the miners.

But miners were sensible people. Heated up it was probably like any other soup.

The items he did best with were those headed *'For the kitchen'*. Amanda had a cupboard which groaned with cleaning things. It seemed that she used just the same as the miners,

Scourers
Brillo pads
Washing-up liquid
J cloths . . .

So money didn't change *everything*.

Davey wriggled down to the back of the cupboard to make sure he hadn't missed anything useful. Two brooms toppled down upon his head, then more.

In the kerfuffle, he didn't hear the front door, he didn't hear the feet coming back upstairs, angry feet, his mother's feet, the feet of a mother with very low blood sugar, Lottie who after a small fracas with Hugo had decided to spite him by crying off lunch. Lottie who was spoiling for a bigger fracas.

'What a mess! What on earth do you think you're doing?'

Her voice cut sharply over his shoulder. He jumped, knocked the brooms over again and crawled out of the cupboard backwards with tea-towels on his head.

'Look, Amanda left this kitchen perfectly tidy. I can't get the new girl to come till next week . . . but what on earth is this great box?' Her voice suddenly changed, became utterly repentant, her hand started stroking his hair. 'Oh darling, you've been doing the shopping. You must have worn yourself out, bringing this lot back. Oh, Mum *is* sorry, you're a marvellous boy . . .'

Davey couldn't take it. Time for the truth. He stood up properly, held out the list.

'No, it's not shopping. It's . . . I was going to ask you . . . actually I wasn't. I *wasn't* going to ask you in case you got annoyed. It's a list of things the miners need.'

She looked bewildered, in her beautiful hat. For a moment he felt pity. Then it vanished.

'The miners who are on strike, you know. They put this list through the door . . .'

She was starting to understand. Her cheeks grew darker, her brows came together.

'What? Are you raiding my kitchen? To subsidize some *mob*? Are they making children do their dirty work? Do you realize what you're doing is stealing? You've been picking up tricks from your dirty little friends . . .'

'Shut up, shut up, I'm *not* a child, I'm *not* stealing! It's my kitchen too! You don't know *anything* about the miners . . .'

'I don't want to know anything about the miners! I know quite enough, thank you! I know you're sometimes a silly little boy!'

Lottie wanted to hurt, she was mad with rage.

(Harold hadn't come back. He would never come back.)

'And you! *You!*' Davey was screaming. He had spent too long not screaming at her. 'You don't know anything about yourself! You're . . . a *rotten, selfish, bully*, that's what you are!'

Tears rushed to her eyes in a sudden flood but she sprang for him like an animal, seizing his shoulders and trying to shake him, and now he was dreadfully afraid, staring at her red face distorted with anger, her mouth dragged open in a wordless scream, a bursting red mess under a flap of white velvet . . . terror gave him strength to break away. He darted round the table and on impulse leant across, gripped the sides and half-lifted it against her, staggering slightly but holding her off, and his brain began to clear as he held the weight between them.

He was shouting now, not screaming. 'This is all about Harold, isn't it? Listen to me. It is.' She started to sob. He let her, electric with fear and anger. For the first time in his life, it was him or her. 'Well, I want to tell you something. You don't love Harold at all. You don't even know what Harold's really like. Do you know what Harold is? Harold's a *socialist!* You know, S-O-C-I-A-L- . . .'

'I *know* he's a socialist,' she sobbed, flinging her hat on the table. 'It doesn't *matter* what people are . . .'

' – Harold would *like* the miners. He's probably really *depressed* about the miners. Harold's *on their side*. You don't take Harold seriously. You just want him to be like you. That's probably why he walked out on you. But you haven't changed a bit. You

304

spend all that money on a fucking *word processor*. Harold doesn't *like* machines, Harold even fused the electric kettle. You're *selfish . . . selfish . . . selfish . . .* you think we all want whatever you want . . . I hope he doesn't come back to you! You don't deserve it! You don't! And I'll leave you too! It's what you deserve!'

As he finished, he also started to cry, and the kitchen was silent except for the sound of them weeping and gasping, very far apart. Then he ran past her out of the kitchen. She reached out her hand and tried to pull her son towards her, but Davey was stronger. He brushed her away.

She sat down, elbows on the table, and wept till her eyes were sore. She was abandoned; her life was over. Her coat got in the way, so she took it off, sat down again, sobbed on with quiet determination. If she sobbed long enough she always felt better.

At two o'clock, she made two large cheese sandwiches.

'Davey!' She called upstairs. No answer.

She ate them both with a cup of hot chocolate, and thought about many things.

Perhaps there was a tiny bit in what the child said. She had always believed in bargains with fate; transactions with her God. God hadn't been much in evidence, of late. Perhaps she had been a little bit forgetful. Perhaps she had seemed a little mean about the miners. And Lottie wasn't mean. She had never been mean. She prided herself on being wildly generous.

She rifled through the top layers of his box, and started to feel quite guilty. There wasn't any good stuff there. There was nothing that she herself liked. He had really been quite thoughtful. *Over*-thoughtful, indeed . . .

You could hardly just give people beans and Brillo pads. Sighing, she added some *petits fours*, two tins of hare pâté and a jar of pears in brandy. She cast an eye heavenwards. God seemed to approve, but she knew it wasn't enough.

A little gingerly, she went upstairs.

Her knock on his door was the merest shadow of her usual knock, but her voice was quite calm.

'Davey, come out. Look, you can have your Brillo pads. Where is it to go to? I suppose I'll drive you.'

There was silence, then, 'I don't need you to drive me.'

(He heard her sigh through the thickness of door.)

'I've decided to give something away. For Harold. It's a sacrifice. To get him back.'

'I can't hear you.'

'Then open the door!'

A further silence. He opened the door. Just a crack, but they could see each other.

(Her eyes were swollen, but she looked more normal.)

'I love you, Davey. I really do.'

(She obviously meant it, but he didn't forgive her.)

'You should have *asked* me. I'd have agreed.'

'You wouldn't have agreed.'

'I suppose I wouldn't.'

(He grinned a little, despite himself. She was mostly deluded, but sometimes very honest.)

'I'm going to give some money away.'

'You've got enough of it, haven't you?'

'I don't need you to tell me what I've got.'

'Are you going to give it to the miners?'

'Don't be ridiculous, of course I'm not. *Hordes* of people are giving them money.'

'Well, don't give anything to me. I don't need anything. I don't want anything.'

'I give you things *all the time, endlessly.* But never mind that. I'm not talking about you. I'm going to give the money to someone in need.'

(Pompous, and not at all convincing.)

'I don't believe you. You're just trying to get round me.'

'I'm going out now to give some money away!'

He watched her face going pink and cross. A long narrow line of it hissed through the crack. It was a strange feeling, to have power over her. He wondered whether he liked it or not. He found himself pushing his door closed, firmly, not really knowing he meant to. It was nice to make the crack of pink face disappear.

She kicked the door once.

He bolted it.

Lottie left the house very fast, but with no clear idea where she was going. She had five hundred pounds in her handbag, the kind of amount that she often carried. She knew what she had to do. It would be quite simple, she wasn't afraid. And she knew the one thing she wanted.

Four p.m., November 2.

Still eight hours left when the phone might ring.

Teatime in Boscombe. It had clouded over. Harold wandered aimlessly down the promenade, back from Swanage with nothing to do. He had ten tenpenny pieces in his jacket pocket. It ought to be simple, but he was afraid.

Still eight hours left when I could ring her.

CHAPTER FORTY-SEVEN

Instinct took Lottie towards the park. The obvious place would have been the road off Parkway with the enormous redbrick doss-houses. There were always men on the pavement outside, drunken, tottery men with strange-coloured skins and rasping voices. Perfect for what she wanted, except that there were too many of them. That building ought to be pulled down. It just encouraged them, having doss-houses.

She wanted one on his own. She imagined a man, but it could be a woman. (If it was a woman, she hoped it was a gipsy – she'd always had a soft spot for gipsies.)

She would find him slumped against a wall, or busking weakly with a mouth-organ.

She walked along the road by the railway-cutting. Not so many leaves on the plane trees now. As the leaves disappeared the fruit became clearer, little round balls like ornaments.

She saw him first from thirty yards away as a sack of rubbish leaning with some others against the black wall of the cutting. Then he moved a little. Her heart started beating. *Oh yes. This was hers.*

Her left hand moved to the clasp of the heavy crocodile handbag she held in her right. There were half a dozen fifty-pound notes, and some twenties and tens. It would probably be easier to give him just one, but she had to give it all; that was the point of it.

All of it, Harold. All for you. I do understand you. I can be different.

The other bags must be his possessions. He was sitting on some, the others slumped beside him. His face was very grimy. The eyes which flicked up at her were white by comparison, but actually reddish, smeary. When eyes like that looked at Lottie, she always looked away. It was strange to be looking back, making contact.

His eyes dropped first, and his mouth was moving. Coming level with him, she stopped and stared down.

'Um – hallo,' she said, trying to sound confident. (*Good morning* would have seemed too formal.) 'Do you need some money? I'm sure you do.'

There must be words for this kind of thing.

His eyes flicked up and down and away, he locked his arms around himself and muttered unintelligibly. He was shaking, she supposed with cold. Must be in his – seventies? She hoped he wasn't crazy. Yellow-grey stubbled flesh, rough as an animal's. She inched back minutely, but her voice grew louder.

'*Money. For YOU. I've got some.* See?'

And as he continued to mutter and shake, she took out the notes from her handbag, holding them tightly because of the wind, held them out towards him with her gloved left hand (but was it rude to keep her gloves on?).

Everything happened much too fast.

His eyes grew sharp, his grimy mask crumpled, and with a vague roar he lunged up for the money, a stench of alcohol and filth and two red huge hands were pawing the front of her coat as he missed her hand, tried again, grabbed it, but her body was under independent orders, her tightly-clenched hands couldn't let the notes go, and as the vile smell and the rasping of his breath grew unbearably strong she found she was pushing him, shouting, 'Get *off* me,' and when he didn't yield but hung there half-upright clinging to her coat she suddenly swung at his head with her handbag, losing her grip on the money as she whacked the heavy leather and metal thing into the mess of his face, as hard as she could, *thuck, thack,* so he sagged and yielded, and her handbag made contact again and again while the money escaped her and fluttered to the pavement, and he suddenly sprawled on top of the money, groaning but clutching the slithering notes with terrific willpower, clawing them under him.

Lottie nearly kicked him out of the way. Then she remembered that this was the point. She was trying to give him the money. It wasn't supposed to be like this.

Trembling, legless, with new tears streaming, she walked back home. She would never tell anyone.

She went up to her bedroom and slept for two hours. Davey woke her up, knocking gently.

'Oh, come in, darling.'

Why had she got her coat on? She looked as if she'd been asleep.

'Are you all right? Are you cold, or something?'

'No. I just – fell asleep as I was.'

They were embarrassed with each other, their eyes not meeting.

'I'm sorry if I upset you,' said Davey.

'It doesn't make any difference,' said Lottie.

'You do give me things. I don't think you're mean.'

'I . . . don't let's talk about it.'

'Will you let me take you to *Tarzan*? It's on at the Camden Plaza. I'd like to treat you.'

For once she didn't say, *Don't be ridiculous, of course you won't pay.*

'Is it for children?'

'Nah. The apes are supposed to be terrific.'

She sat up. Her hair was tangled. She looked very strange, and she started to cry as she smiled and said, 'I'd love to.'

'Are you all right? Shall I make some tea?'

'No, let's go out . . . *Oh. Davey.* Sometimes I'm such a fool.'

He looked at her carefully. Not *at all* like his mother. Perhaps he was supposed to contradict. On the whole he thought he wouldn't.

But he walked down the road with his arm around her. She looked very tired, and leant against his shoulder.

That evening, Harold rang their answerphone with steadily diminishing nerves. Once he was sure that no one was there he rang them dashingly again and again. So much less trouble this way.

On a sudden whim, a few pints later, he changed his mind and rang Claudia's number.

The voice that answered was depressed.

'Hallo.'

'Claudia, it's Harold.'

'Hey, *Harold!*' Her voice became a shout of glee. She always had a soft spot for me, thought Harold. 'Long time no see! What's been happening? – I was *devastated* about you and Lottie.'

The news was mostly banal, but they laughed and exclaimed a great deal. Harold sounded almost *extravagantly* friendly. Claudia was rather flattered.

But I think he always had a soft spot for me.

'God, it's good to hear you,' she sighed. She was sitting at her desk, not writing an article, drinking her second gin. 'I've really been quite lonely, just lately. Lottie's been away – haven't seen her. That little runt Justin walked out on me. It's marvellous to hear someone I really like.'

She was almost *extravagantly* friendly. Harold was rather flattered.

By the time the call was ended, various things were settled, though other little ends were unravelling, ready to reweave in Claudia's mind. Harold was going to come and stay with her till he found somewhere of his own in London. She would *adore* the company, she said. It would be nice to have a man around again.

Harold concurred, the warm beer lifting him. Maybe he didn't make his much simpler motive clear. Harold would adore to be back in London, a hundred miles nearer Lottie.

Claudia's delight was a little tempered when she saw all the packing-cases.

'I see, you've brought *all* your things. This isn't a palace, you know.'

'Claudia, I know it looks a lot. But I probably shan't even unpack them.'

That made her anxious to reassure him. 'Oh, it's quite all right, really. As long as you don't mind a bit of a squash.'

She was thinner and looked older than Harold remembered. He'd never spent a lot of time alone with her. He hoped it was going to be all right.

London was darker than he'd expected. Colder too, as he stood on the doorstep. A sense that things were shrinking around him. Harold would miss the sea.

He packed the bulk of his possessions into the smallish bedroom just across from hers. Some wouldn't fit; some stayed in the hall. Just a few boxes, he hoped it wouldn't bother her. She managed to keep smiling, but her jaw was tense.

'Just for a few days,' he said placatingly. 'I'll be off soon.' (But where? and when? . . . He would reconnoitre in Darlington Road. If need be, he would simply burn down the house, murder his rival, kidnap Lottie.)

But first, he started to see that evening, he would have to deal with Claudia. He had offered to take her out to dinner; it seemed the least he could do. She wasn't utterly keen at first on the Indian restaurant he suggested, but inside it was warm and dark and once the candles were lit and the flames danced in their two large whiskies, she shrugged off her shawl to show sharp bare shoulders and smiled a smile which was entirely hopeful.

She held out her glass. 'Cheers,' she said. He suddenly picked up a subtext: *To us.* But his glass was already moving towards hers, the smile was already formed on his face.

You're imagining things, he told himself. And in any case, outside the window was the straight black rain of November. Claudia's eyes brimmed with warmth. He gazed back, laughed, chinked glasses.

That night when they got out of her car outside her house she said, 'I'm freezing,' and pressed close to him, and after a second he slipped his arm around her. He'd done it before in the time he'd known her. But still, he knew there was danger.

'Shall we have another brandy, Harold?' she asked, walking ahead of him down the hall in her perilously high heels. She was slightly unstable, her narrow hips swayed.

The drink was high in his cheeks and his brain but something tapped him sternly on the shoulder, *you'll regret this all your life.* And when she turned in the doorway as if to embrace him he stepped aside smartly, not so very smartly since he slammed his shoulder hard into the doorframe, smiled affectionately at her with his arms firmly crossed, and said, 'That was a wonderful evening. But I think I really ought to hit the sack.'

In bed on her own, Claudia pondered. I should have pressed the point. He's a shy man really . . . All the same, it's always more exciting if you wait.

I ought to have it out with her, thought Harold, just a corridor away, grimacing in the darkness. But what if it's all in my mind.

Hell, hell, hell. I'll ring Lottie tomorrow. Then everything will be sorted out.

By 10 a.m. the die was cast.

Claudia was at her typewriter, Harold was making his breakfast in the kitchen. The phone rang. As he brought Claudia coffee he suddenly heard, 'Oh Lottie, what a shame.'

Slopping coffee, he flailed his free hand towards her. But she frowned a *be quiet* and pulled a face of such intensity her skin was absorbed into a wrinkled mask of rubber which surprisingly fell back into skin in a second. He started pointing vigorously to himself (*give me   my turn   me speak   my wife*) but she shook her head emphatically, and now a distant, tiny voice could be heard or imagined. Harold's gestures grew wilder. Claudia suddenly broke in, 'Look, darling, there's someone at the door, I must fly. I'll ring you soonest and we must have lunch.'

Ping. The phone was down.

'Harold,' said Claudia, 'I hope you're going to be tactful. Lottie is practically my best friend. You know how unstoppable she is in mid-flood. Well, the time went by when I could say you were here without it seeming like . . . well . . . something she ought to have known. Even though it's all over between you. I didn't say a word, so neither must you. Not yet, at any rate. All in good time.'

She smiled a restrainedly erotic smile. And Harold, God forgive him, mimed some smile back though his heart cried a terrible sequence of *Lottie*s.

CHAPTER FORTY-EIGHT

Claudia tells herself, *all in good time.*

But that week slips by, the second in November. The weather grows wilder, crueller, murkier. November slips by in semi-darkness. Harold hasn't seen the sun in days. The little black balls blow wild on the plane trees. All living things shrink into themselves. Harold lies in bed, planning and brooding, and gets a little lazy about doing the housework. In the zoo, the cold apes huddle together, but the time isn't right for the two of them; and Claudia's hope slowly slips away, and the black rain falls perpendicular.

Now it is the last week in November.

This morning Harold doesn't want to get up. He lies there reading *The World of Wonders.*

> In the British Museum there is to be seen a fine stuffed specimen of the little nocturnal, grub-eating, climbing quadruped . . . called 'Aye-Aye' . . . What a strange physiognomy is given to the skull of the little rarity by the enormous, curved, chisel-shaped pair of teeth at the fore part of the upper and under jaws! What can be the meaning of that long, shrivelled finger on each of the hands? . . . Dr Sandwich . . . desired to know whether it should be transmitted to the British Museum dead or alive? To this the superintendent replied, 'It might be more advantageous to science if the animal were killed by chloroform, and properly preserved.' . . . In that state the specimen reached the Museum, where its stuffed skin, its skeleton, its brain, and some other parts in spirits, are evidence of the use made of the opportunity.

Suddenly Harold gets up. It is eleven o'clock.

Claudia was making her third cup of coffee. She watched Harold break an egg straight off the edge of the bowl, so the yolk slid slowly down the draining-board, very yellow and absurd on the shining chrome.

Claudia thought, *he is actually a drip. I am sharing my house with a hopeless drip.*

Seven hours later she came home exhausted, sat down and drank half a bottle of wine with her feet up, staring at the television. Then she yelled an imperious 'HAROLD!' in the direction of his bedroom. He had started calling it his 'study', for God's sake, doubtless to excuse sticking in it all day.

He emerged in a crumpled tracksuit, looking as if he had been asleep. A few strands of hair stood up at right angles, making him look balder. Did he just sleep *all day?*

'Been running?' she asked, sardonically. 'You're going to escort me to a party.'

'Whose party?' he sounded suspicious. There were food stains on his tracksuit jacket.

'Nobody you and Lottie knew, if that's what's bothering you. Hilary Granger – journalist pal of mine.'

'Never heard of her. Super. Marvellous.'

He meant, *all right, since I have to.*

'Then go and clean yourself up.'

'Naturally, Claudia.' Harold smiled, an unshaven but still dazzling smile. He couldn't afford to lose her favour.

'By the way, Harold, have you made any plans?'

'Plans?'

'You know, what you're going to do.'

A terrible blankness. Then inspiration.

'Ah yes. I'm going to work in the British Museum. That's where I'm going to be working, for a bit.'

Her expression suggested that wasn't what she meant.

She softened towards him as they walked into the party and

faces swivelled towards her escort. He was certainly a good-looking man. More than that: a *distinguished*-looking man.

'All the ladies are giving you the eye, did you notice?'

'I'm blind to everyone but you,' he said, playfully *galant*.

Claudia was drunk enough not to pay attention to the tiny pause before delivery. She smiled and was suddenly a hundred times prettier, whispering up into his ear.

Observing them through the cigarette smog from the other side of the room, the editor of a national paper decided it might be worth having a crack at Claudia Cutler. He'd always thought she wasn't keen on it. Now she was positively creaming. Nice legs, non-existent tits.

'Take my word for it, darling. Let's face it, what have women got to choose from? Nearly all successful men are pot-bellied and decrepit . . .'

'Well, I'm bald, but I'm not successful . . .'

'They're bald as well. And hideous to boot. Like Poached-Egg-Eyes over there . . .' (she gestured towards the editor). 'Don't look now, he's staring at us. They all smoke like fish and drink like chimneys . . .'

'Claudia, I think you're tipsy!'

'. . . So y'see, there really isn't any competition, darling!'

By now she was almost shrieking with glee, and a few people looked at them enviously, the thin, ecstatic woman clinging to that tall distinguished-looking man.

I probably need an older man, thought Mary, sulking behind her mother. I like the look of that one.

She'd hardly spoken to Davey all evening, because he'd chickened out of confronting his mother over whether he could have her to stay. Together, in the same room. He said he couldn't ask when his mother was depressed. But she knew he was simply chicken.

'Mum,' she hissed at her mother. 'Who's that with Claudia?'

'Don't know,' said her mother, sorting canapés. By now she had canapés before the eyes. Anchovy and cream cheese, smoked salmon and cucumber. The combinations began to seem random. Oh for the days of crisps and peanuts. 'I gather she's got a new bloke.'

'Well, he's lovely, look.'

'Mmmm,' said Mrs Granger, appreciative. 'You're right.'

She and her husband were getting divorced. That was partly

why she was having the party. Scanning the males who had come so far, there wasn't a lot of point. But if Claudia could get herself one like that . . . She swallowed a fat cheese straw with relish.

The editor with the poached-egg eyes was trying to find out who Claudia's escort was. In the end he discovered Harold was nobody. That rather took the spice away.

Davey was in the next room feeling sick, squashed up too close to the body of the buffet. Lurid pink hams with borders of white, a greasy gape-eyed trout, a hacked joint of beef whose centre shone like a bloody wound. The room was very hot. Two greedy people were gouging out the Stilton together, plainly in competition.

'I'm rather keen on this Star Wars business. Mankind's always thought too small. You've got to think bigger than nuclear weapons.'

'Yes, but how far do we trust the Yanks? If only Britain could get stuck in. We used to have the vision.'

He was in this room to escape the rhythmic beat which made his headache worse. He'd thought that Mary would follow him, but she pointedly did not. The conversations were unbelievable. He tried not to listen, but most people were shouting.

' . . . When it came to the point, he couldn't rise to the occasion.'

'Darling! *Really?* He looks so butch.'

Grownup conversations were shamefully stupid. He vowed he'd never have conversations like these.

'Roberta's having another abortion.'

'I thought she was rather keen on that fellow?'

'She is. But she thinks they'll adopt, later.'

All the same, he quite wished that *someone* would talk to him. Someone, preferably Mary.

'The *on dit* is, Bozo's getting over two hundred grand as an advance on that Jean Seberg story.'

'Is that the woman who was keen on darkies? I thought that had rather been done to death.'

'Reginald – don't be so *frightful.* That girl just behind you is not exactly *Caucasian. Don't* stare! Reggie! *Hon*estly!'

Screams of laughter, male and female.

'I must say I'm boggling about Bozo. Can the old bugger write? I doubt it.'

'You don't suppose he's going to write it himself!' More hoots and squeals. That woman didn't sound human.

Mary's laugh was so different from that. Why doesn't Mary come and talk to me?

'Bournemouth? How peculiar. You don't suppose he's gone queer. One in four, they say, in Bournemouth.'

'One in four? That's less than in London.'

Then someone kissed him smack on the cheek.

'Da-vey!'

It was Claudia. She hailed him like a long-lost lover. He was pleased to see her, and proud to be claimed by someone so very glamorous. But soon he began to feel uncomfortable. She was staring at him as if she wanted to eat him, a hungry gaze that was slightly glazed, and her mouth was exaggerated, pouting and curling like a gadget of shiny plastic.

I don't like parties, he thought. *I'm never going to give parties.* He gazed away helplessly over her shoulder.

And then he saw him from behind. Standing in the doorway, deep in conversation. It must be, it can't be.

'Claudia. Listen.' He interrupted. 'That's *Harold*, isn't it? It must be.'

'Oh yes, that's Harold,' she said, sounding slightly bored but also – *intimate*. 'Yes, that's Harold . . . Shtaying with me.'

And as soon as she had made that slurred pronouncement, her white, sharp face collapsed into worry.

Horrible. Please. It mustn't be. Davey turned away, the food rising in his stomach. To his right a fat man in a three-piece suit was stuffing a folded piece of meat into his mouth. *Harold and Claudia. Claudia and Harold.*

'Christ!' he yelled, with what he hoped was distaste, but all that came out was a child's despair. Their generation were disgusting. And Claudia was flirting with *me.*

Five red fingernails clawed at his shoulder.

'Don't tell your mother.'

'I'll do what I like.'

And he went, without speaking to Harold, without saying goodbye to Mary or her mother.

This is how love ends, he thought. Harold said he loved Mum, but he didn't care at all. Mum said she loved Harold, but she went off with Creep. Mary's already tired of me.

Pretending not to look, Mary saw him leave.

If I can't have him, I'll die.

After this, events began to move very fast, or rather the speed with which they moved became apparent, for all the time they were going very fast, as the Earth spun on its axis at a thousand miles an hour, and moved round the sun at fifty thousand miles an hour, and the sun moved around the Milky Way galaxy at over six hundred thousand miles an hour, and the Milky Way spun upon its centre as it rushed across space towards the Virgo cluster of galaxies at more than a million miles an hour, and the universe itself kept rushing apart, at millions and millions of miles an hour . . . and on our tiny planet, the tiny people chattered, taking every move tremendously seriously. If they couldn't have what they wanted, they'd die.

First, Lottie rang Claudia, the morning after the party. They hadn't spoken for weeks; Lottie had news which had left her shaken.

But Claudia sounded extremely strange; frightened, dim and rather ill.

'Claudia, have you got a hangover?'

'*Frightful*, Lottie. Look I can explain . . .'

'Darling, will you listen for a minute, please? Elspeth Davenport wrote this morning. She enclosed an obituary from the *Telegraph*, months out of date. It's *Sylvia*. Harold's ma, I think you met her once. They gave her three lines . . . She died in September. I can't believe it. Davey's at school. I just had to talk to somebody.'

'What was it like?' said Claudia. 'I didn't see it either.'

There was a pause while Lottie registered things.

'You don't sound surprised. Did you know she was dead?'

Pause the other end. 'Yes.'

'You've – heard from Harold?'

'OK,' said Claudia. Grim and weary. 'I thought Davey would have already told you. Harold's – well, he's staying with me at the moment. It wasn't deliberate, not telling you . . .'

'He's staying with *you? And Davey knew? Is he there now?*'

'He's in the British Museum.'

Silence. The silence was very angry.

'I see. Splendid. I worry myself sick, and all the time my bloody husband is staying with my best friend half a mile away and working in the British Museum. Oh, terrific. Oh, fucking bloody sodding MARVELLOUS!!'

☆

Over a long and sober lunch which neither of them could eat, Claudia and Lottie talked it out.

'Does he still love me?' The hardest question for Lottie to ask. 'At all?' That was even harder.

'He doesn't say so.' Claudia paused. Her voice became a little more weary. 'I think he does though, actually. He doesn't say so in case it makes me jealous.'

'And you. Does he . . . Are you?' The second hardest question.

'No such luck,' said Claudia. 'Look, I did think it was over between you. I thought he *wanted* me. Well, more fool me. And lucky old you. You whistle and they come running, Lottie.'

Lottie smiled a small smile.

'You were always jealous of me, Claudia.'

'I just admitted as much.' *This time I might as well stand up to her.* 'So what? I'm still your friend.'

'Are you?' The voice was mocking, but Lottie's lips shook. 'Do you – *promise, promise* – nothing happened? Do you *promise* you didn't . . .?' She half-hid her mouth.

'I promise. Look, he *didn't want* me.' Those words were never easy to say.

Lottie's hand came away from her mouth in a gesture so sudden that Claudia expected to be struck.

'No, he didn't want you. He *wouldn't have done.* Oh, I hate you, hate you. No, I'm sorry.'

There was silence for a moment. Lottie was crying. She reached out one hand to Claudia, didn't quite touch her, leaning forward into the afternoon sun. Her tears shone on her splendid cheekbones, her hair sprayed out in a white-gold fountain.

Claudia saw her very clearly. Life was different if you looked like that. Lucky, lucky Lottie.

'Claudia, there's one thing you've got to understand. It's different, a husband. It means you're saying, *he's my person, I'm his person.* And everything about them matters to you. In a way, that's what I mind most of all, not knowing that Sylvia was dead. She loved me about as much as rat poison, but she was his mother, she *belonged* to me. Do you see? I should have been there. We should have been there together. I could have helped him. I should have been there.'

Claudia was tired. *Does she need my sympathy? She'll always have most of what she wants.* But she caught dead fatigue in Lottie's face. *Sod it, I'll make an effort.*

'There's one thing you should remember. It's . . . dangerous, as well. Starting to think you own things. You have to be careful with belongings.'

'Hmm. But nobody gives you warning, they'll be gone tomorrow if you take them for granted today. I did use to tell him I loved him . . . *Bastard,*' she added in an undertone. 'How is he, Claudia? Is he *all right?*'

And then, 'I'll be different, if he comes back.'

But she didn't *sound* different, two hours later, when Harold rang at the precise second she walked back through the front door, exhausted.

Harold was in any case half-dead with fear, clutching the phone with shrivelled fingers.

'So you know I've found you out, do you? And you thought you'd better come clean . . . ' she yelled, astonishing herself with her fury.

'What . . .?'

'Don't pretend you don't know I just had lunch with Claudia.'

'I haven't seen her since last night, *evening.* I left for the library at eight this morning. Lottie, please don't be angry. Whatever Claudia told you . . .'

'You mean there are things to tell? Oh *bastard, bastard,* I hope you die . . .'

'Look, I'm ringing from the *British Museum.* We can't have a row in the *British Museum.* We have to meet. We have to . . .'

'*Fuck* the British Museum. You've stayed away a year!'

'Just under a year.'

She slammed the phone down so violently that a little piece of plastic snapped off and fell. She sat down on the stairs. It was very quiet. The slow water ran down under her lids.

Oh why did I do that? I shouldn't have done that.

These days I'm always crying. *I shan't let this happen to me . . .*

Harold stood with his face wretchedly averted inside the shallow egg of Perspex which protected him quite inadequately from the gaze of a uniformed keeper. He felt like a specimen on display. He was clutching the phone like a relay baton. Life was slipping away, it was going down the drain.

I can't give up now. I shan't give up now.

And he dialled again, not speaking until she had answered in case she just slammed the phone down, then explaining himself in a steady flow. 'I don't *like* Claudia. I *never* liked Claudia.' This time she was terse; he could hear she had a cold. She was unforthcoming, and busy. She was going to be in Scotland for a week, making sure the workmen didn't ruin the heating. She agreed to meet him, as if he were a workman. In seven days' time. She thought she was free. All right, she was free.

'My treat,' he said. 'Our local Greek.'

'*The* local Greek,' she corrected him. 'The sixth of December. Eight p.m.'

'Yes. Yes. Yes please, Lottie.'

At least she'll see me. It has to go right.

A week. *A week.* A lifetime to wait.

Or ·004 of his life to date.

Human beings' sense of time is eccentric. They have been here for half a million years, ·0000001 of the age of the planet.

They are bursting to set things right; felling and levelling, heating and drying, governing, defending, planting, transplanting . . .

November in California. A doctor transplants the heart of a baboon into a human baby, sixteen days old.

November in Europe. The papers discover that millions of humans are starving in Africa. How can things be getting worse, not better? Hilary Granger sends a cheque for ten pounds.

Harold has other things to think about.

Outside his window, a few bright leaves. Red in the rain, they give him hope.

Inside the house, he forgets his duties. Claudia's hibiscus dries and wilts.

December

CHAPTER FORTY-NINE

In a year, light travels six thousand thousand thousand thousand miles.

(Hope may come very fast and be extinguished very quickly.)

How immensely far light has travelled since the universe began; thirteen billion years times six million million miles of light moving over the emptiness, streaming between the billions of stars.

A small solar system is utterly lost among such enormous spaces. Light sprints from the sun past Mercury, Venus, to Earth in eight minutes flat. It joins two faces in a hundred-millionth of a second; just too late.

December, California. A human baby with the heart of a baboon dies, a few weeks old. Later a child is found frozen solid in a garden; he will recover.

December, Regent's Park. At four o'clock the sun looks gigantic, a scarlet blaze staying steady as the black trees roll up to cover it. Compared to all this Harold feels very small. How can Lottie ever love him again?

(Love slips away in the beat of a heart.)

A half-dozen seagulls cover the crown of a leafless Weeping Ash, still in the sun when the rest of the tree has slipped into the dark. Their wings and backs are bathed in rose-pink light. One of them flutters up, turns into the sunset. Harold is hopeful, by the icy lake. A second later, the sun has gone out.

He shivers as he remembers its power. Ninety-three million miles away, it moves the Earth, the lovers, love (but if there are ten billion trillion stars, if some of them are a thousand times larger . . .)

Humans could slip into nothingness.

Lovers could lose each other.

Harold sleeps very little, on the eve of the sixth. He rehearses what he will say to her.

In the first rehearsals he has a clear run. Lottie sits and listens uncritically. Near the end he scraps the whole thing and tries it again with her sneering, interrupting, tearing her food like a Giant Condor. Nothing he says can change that face.

It is 3 a.m. Across the corridor, he can hear Claudia coughing. For the past three days he has skulked in the library and then in his bedroom, avoiding her.

There has been a showdown, which left him bruised.

'I think you two had better sort yourselves out.'

'I'm trying to, Claudia. She won't meet me till the sixth.'

'I'm sure she would if you begged her to.'

'Look, I begged her. She put the phone down. She was going to Perth, she refused to change it. I was in the *British Museum*, for God's sake. Have you ever tried begging in the British Museum?'

'I really don't care. It isn't my business. But *you* have been taking advantage of me. That *is* my business. Think about it.'

Harold has made an effort *not* to think about it. He has quite a lot not to think about.

He expected December 6 to crawl, but it started to gallop around lunch-time.

She appeared before him in a hundred forms. Lottie in the sun in the early morning, opening her eyes then closing her eyes, a tiny slit of brightness between short sandy lashes. Lottie shouting with laughter at something in the middle of making love, pummelling his back with her strong fists. Lottie gasping, gasping and closing her eyes, helplessly groaning, convulsed in orgasm. Lottie in the bath with her hair tied up in a yellow ribbon, straight neck, broad shoulders, five crimson toes on the tap, complaining about her 'peasanty' calves as the water ran glittering off their muscles.

Lottie, Lottie. The way she encouraged me. The way she admired me. She didn't have a crush on me like April, but she saw me as bigger and better than I am. Or maybe she saw what I could really be if some lack of confidence didn't prevent me.

And yet, she was terribly selfish; the most selfish woman I've ever known.

How could she have so much patience for me? I suppose she saw me as part of herself. I suppose we were part of each other. Until I tore us apart.

Three o'clock, four o'clock, five o'clock. He combed his hair a great number of times. Half-past six. He needed a drink. He looked at Claudia's whisky. But she might come back at any minute. He would have one near the restaurant.

The Edinburgh Castle. Why not? Into their local, one for luck. What if he met her on the way? It might make it easier if he did.

The wide streets of Camden were reassuringly the same. Tall houses, undrawn curtains revealing lanterns which shone like moons. Underneath them were mysterious intimacies, half-seen humans grouping and regrouping.

How Harold wanted to get back inside. Things would be all right if he followed his feet. Things would be all right, *please*. Nothing could change absolutely.

He followed his feet to the Edinburgh Castle and found it a burnt-out ruin. A hulk of black with sheets of corrugated metal covering the windows. In the garden where they had often sat the only survivors were two sun umbrellas, forlornly bright against the blackened brick wall. No tables, no benches, no familiar sign. A new one was tacked up: FREEHOLD FOR SALE. That was a joke. Who the hell would want it?

Where had the poor ghosts gone?

Feeling very sick he walked round the corner and swigged a warm pint in a pub he didn't know. It was a quarter to eight. He took the long way back, his stomach cramping.

Down the little alley near his old home. The usual two drunks lunged amiably at him (he supposed it was amiable from their blurred voices, but it never felt entirely amiable). How cold they must get, always outside. His heart thudded, out of rhythm with his footsteps.

Just as he got to the Taverna's painted window, he saw her approaching in the opposite direction. She wore a long blonde trenchcoat like a 1940s spy and her hair burned out under the street light, which made her face look blank and pale. In the white, her eyes were unlit coal. She didn't smile, she stopped. Harold's heart stopped too.

Then they both returned to a skin-thin semblance of normal behaviour.

'Hallo.'

'Hallo.'

His hallo was warmer.

They were a foot from each other. She didn't meet his eyes. He wanted to kiss her but his lips were dry. Instead he groped blindly for her hand and wrung it, her hand, her flesh, after all this time. It was colder than his. He couldn't see her properly. He opened the door and pulled her inside. As the warmth came out and held them, she disengaged her hand.

He didn't even kiss me.

Inside the doors reality vanished. For Harold, today had one meaning only. For the Taverna, though, it was a fortnight to Christmas. The walls were hung with rainbow bulbs, red and green tinsel, paper Santa Clauses. Each picture had a few twigs of holly. A tiny tree was weighted down with light.

A familiar waiter rushed up to greet them. 'Ah! Mr and Mrs . . . ' memory failed him. 'Happy Christmas! You see, we decorate today. Ve-ry beautiful. Long time, huh?'

His smile was a sparkling wreath of good will. He shook Harold's hand, patted Lottie's shoulder, and for him (not for Harold) she smiled her smile: her magic, untroubled, enchanting smile, as he took her coat and she shook out her hair (every man in this restaurant is looking at her, thought Harold, suddenly hopeless).

For she would not smile at him. He asked for a bottle of Demestica while they ordered. When the waiter went to get it she said, 'Thank you Harold, I actually prefer to start with a gin.'

'Oh, sorry, sorry, I'll ask him.'

'*I'll* ask him,' she said, and did.

In the candlelight, she was looking marvellous; glossy, well cared-for, maybe slimmer. His eyes never left her face for a moment. *She hasn't been missing me, then.*

Her handsome face was impassive. She gazed at the menu, she gazed at her drink, she examined the other diners.

'Lottie, I'm so pleased to see you.' He was leaning so far forward that the edge of the table dug uncomfortably into his ribs.

'Thank you, Harold.' She kept thanking him. That was not a good sign, with Lottie.

They ordered. He ordered two different starters, a mixed kebab, and a Greek salad. She ordered houmous and an omelette. (Is that what she eats? Christ, I've forgotten.)

Things improved a little with the first two drinks. At least they were talking. But what were they saying?

They asked each other careful, polite questions about non-controversial topics. She asked about Sylvia judicially, distantly, as if she was an aunt or a neighbour. She said how sorry she was, as if the prime minister had died.

He was eating with great concentration now. He no longer dared to gaze at her face. He didn't think it held anything for him. He swallowed everything ravenously down. Mostly unchewed, though she didn't know that.

She observed the speed with which he cleared his plate. He'd kept his appetite, then. It didn't make her better-disposed towards him. She herself had laid her knife and fork aside, and sat looking totally detached from the occasion, yet she drank her wine with uncommon efficiency.

Harold didn't notice that. He was too busy stowing in gobbets of pork and choking them down his gullet.

Each time that she started to say something, his terror hit a new peak. She's going to tell me about her new man. She's going to tell me it's too late for us. He prayed quite simply that he shouldn't have to hear it. He could see it was over. Nobody could miss it. But if she *told* him he would die on the spot. This was all a mistake. He should never have suggested it.

'Aren't you going to finish that omelette?' he asked.

'Are you very hungry, Harold?'

He missed the irony. 'Yes, I'll eat it.' He smiled at no one, grateful, simple, took her plate, slid the yellow glop down.

'How did you like it?' Colder and colder.

'Very pleasant, thank you.' It was greasy and disgusting. 'Now, would you like a sweet?'

'Oh yes! A *sweet!*' she positively trilled. 'That's exactly what I'd like, Harold. I've never felt more like a pudding in my life!'

Harold didn't understand. He scanned the menu obediently.

'I think I fancy a baklava,' he told the waiter, falsely hearty. 'Wonderful baklava you get in here. And we need another bottle of Demestica. How about you, Lottie?'

'Nothing. Nothing.' The waiter went away. 'Look Harold have you . . . have you got . . .'

The sentence died away into less than nothing.

'What? *Please*, finish the question.' For a moment it had sounded as if she actually wanted something from him. His eyes pleaded. He filled up their glasses.

'I was just going to ask . . .' But the baklava arrived, glistening, golden, a sugary enormity. Harold took his spoon and dived straight in. Mouth bulging with syrup and sugar, he mumbled, 'Finish your sentence! Go on, finish your sentence!'

She didn't do it. He had a bad feeling. She downed her glass in a single gulp.

'How do I look?' she asked, not giving him a chance to answer. 'Not nineteen years old, I know, but not bad.'

'You're wonderful . . .'

'Cut it out, Harold, *was it you I saw in Paris?*'

'Aaah . . .'

'Was it or not?'

'Yes, but . . .' He tried to empty his mouth in order to defend himself better. The sticky flakes became enormous, rubbery, refusing to disengage from his palate.

'You saw me all alone, your wife, all alone, and you walked off with some schoolgirl! You care more about feeding your face than talking to your fucking wife! I can see what you are! I've always known! You're just a *pig. PIG! PIG, PIG!!'* Lottie's shout was much louder than he remembered. People were turning to look. Harold started to say, 'But you've got somebody el – '

'Yes I have, pig! I should hope I have!'

She was on her feet, and suddenly she leaned against the table seized the uneaten half of the baklava, and pushed it in his face, so he couldn't breathe; in the moment it hung there, she had swept to the coat rack, every inch a lady, snatched at her coat, pulled the coat rack over with an earth-shattering clatter, tore her coat from under it, and crashed into the night, leaving Harold with Baklava flakes crumbling down his shirt-front.

A room that was silent and appalled.

After a second, a babble of voices.

The waiter was trying to right the coat rack. Harold put his sticky head in his hands and tipped over the bottle of Demestica. It glugged across the tablecloth and dripped on the carpet.

Harold wanted very badly to cry.

'Look, I'm sorry. I'd better páy and go.'

Now the day went into slow motion. The waiter, at first fairly sympathetic, watched Harold's detailed pantomime of looking for his cheque book. In every pocket he put vile sticky hands. In the end he found it, in the place he'd looked first. And then he had to look for his cheque card. After performing the same sequence three times, he knew he did not have it. He had hardly used it, at Claudia's. Life had been cheap, at Claudia's.

When he finally left the restaurant after persuading the no longer cheerful, no longer remotely festive waiter to accept his cheque without a card, he felt that ten years had passed. He was a wife-tormentor, a cheque-defrauder. Everyone in the restaurant knew that.

He had no memory, afterwards, of walking the two miles back to Claudia's.

And Lottie? Who had so nearly managed to ask him, *'Have you got anyone else?'* Who had sat in rigid anger first and rigid misery later, unable to eat or speak or smile because of her fear of what she might hear . . .

Lottie had run up the dim straight street with the night wind turning her tears to ice, nearly falling as her feet clattered up the steps to her cold front door, slipping to her knees. As she rose clumsily, knowing she was drunk, she looked up and swore at those fucking stars, dumb as Harold, hatefully indifferent.

CHAPTER FIFTY

That night Harold slept a terrible dreamless sleep as heavy as death. He didn't wake till twelve; there was nothing to wake up for. And the days that followed were also like death, invariably dark with morning fogs and heavy dark clouds too sluggish to release their rain. The cherry tree outside Claudia's windows had four leaves left, then three. Everything was getting stripped to the bone.

The leafless trees had a certain grim beauty, but Harold was afraid of his life being naked. It wouldn't be beautiful, just very small.

Claudia no longer spoke to him. Fortunately, she was away quite a lot. In the fridge one day there was a piece of paper scrawled in angry capitals: PLEASE REPLACE MILK, BUTTER, CHEESE. THESE THINGS COST MONEY. I AM NOT A COW. But what was the point of shopping? What was the point of eating? He drank black tea, which was bitterly satisfying. He hardly left the bedroom, now.

Where had it gone, that radiant sense of understanding he had had by the sea? A sense that the sky was a limitless window. Looking through at the universe. Knowing where he was. All fantasy, all delusion. Now Harold knew where he was, all right. The world was Harold-sized, opaque and dull, the size of a puny and wretched man.

He kept his door bolted against Claudia's return. Paranoids have enemies. Harold had enemies. The bolt was actually rather slender. What if Claudia attacked him with an axe? There *was* an axe in the kitchen, as it happened, used for chopping firewood. It was oddly cheering, the idea of dying under the blade of Claudia's axe. *Then* Lottie would be sorry . . .

(Or else she would be glad.)

Ten days or so before Christmas. Maybe more, maybe less. Time had lost its meaning. The idea of Christmas left him painfully blank. His second lonely, pointless Christmas. Maybe he'd go back to Mrs Limone's. Lonely, with all those pointless strangers.

He hadn't changed his sheets since he came here. He no longer trimmed his sideburns or the thick hairs which sprouted from his nostrils; his toenails scratched him in the night; he was turning into some mangy wild beast, a shabby thing nobody liked or wanted. Brought here and dumped by some strange mistake. Shrinking back into its own smelly shadows.

I'm nothing on my own, he thought again and again. Together we added up to something. At least what was between us was real. At least we valued each other. Maybe anyone else would say we were worthless. I suppose we were. We just lived our days . . . But however many failures there were in my life, the bond with Lottie was not a failure.

It wasn't a failure until it failed.

Outside the window, gently plopping, the winter rain had started again.

Did the tamarin matter so very much? What she did was stupid, horrible. But that's the kind of creature we are. And it's the kind of thing we do. I never thought Lottie was an angel, not even when I first met her. So why did it suddenly matter so much? I can never remember feeling so angry.

As if it was done to hurt *me*. As if it was me that was dying.

When she woke up the morning after the scene, Lottie felt a thrill of adrenalin. *That* put a stop to him. That must have finally demolished him.

She tried to tell it as a triumph at breakfast, but Davey was unresponsive. He looked at her gravely, with Carl's grey eyes, except they were damnably moral. The young of today had no sense of humour.

'I thought you quite wanted him back.'

'Well, you were wrong. All right, *I* was wrong. If you could have seen him sitting there stuffing, you would have attacked him too.'

'Look, Mum, I'm not like you. I'm not into attacking people. Violence isn't my scene.'

'Are you my son or aren't you?' She was angry too quickly, painfully uncertain.

'That's a stupid question. I don't *belong* to you. I'm a person, aren't I?'

He remembered Amanda. He had seen her yesterday, chaotically but proudly ensconced with Doris. 'At last I can ask you into a *home*. A home's a home.' – Yes, he thought. And a person's a person, Amanda.

☆

Lottie's adrenalin high fell flat.

In the next few days she learned at last what people meant when they said they were depressed. *Unhappy*, she'd known; *furious*, she'd known; now she got to know *depressed*, in depth. Numbness, boredom, a corroding sense of shame. Shame was novel, too.

The days were just light before they grew dark again. She didn't go out, except to the zoo. She didn't put makeup on. She mooched in a dressing-gown, his big, blue dressing-gown, no longer his after a few dry-cleans. The last of Harold had been cleaned away.

Christmas was coming, but for the first time in her life she didn't bother to shop. Who was there left to shop for? Davey was always out with that girl. Davey had been less than grateful for the videos she gave him for his birthday last month. Lottie wanted to spend money to cheer herself up – she had always spent money to cheer herself up – but the idea of Fortnums or Harrods repelled her. Watching from her bedroom window as some of the neighbours' cars disgorged whole food chains of bags and boxes, she started to see how strange it was. Christmas just meant buying things. She was relieved and disturbed that she couldn't take part.

But so much of her seemed to be changing. That is what it means then, being depressed. Losing yourself. Almost nothing was left.

☆

Changes in the Human Frame
The body (says Lord Brougham) is constantly undergoing change in all its parts; probably no person at the age of twenty has one single particle in any part of his body which he had at ten, and still less does any portion of the body he was born with, continue to exist in or with him.

All that he before had has entered into new combinations,
forming parts of other men, or of animals, or of vegetable,
or of mineral substance, exactly as the body he now has
will be resolved into new combinations after his death . . .

Harold got up to prove he still could. What he read seemed dull,
irrelevant. He glanced in the mirror to check on who he was.
Then he went to the kitchen to get breakfast. It was nearly 6
p.m.

He felt horribly guilty about not having shopped, and terrified
Claudia would come back and catch him. Her note still lay in the
empty fridge. Could he face dry cornflakes? No.

The vegetable basket held a shrivelled carrot, and an orange
which looked relatively brilliant and fresh. Hearing a threatening
noise outside, he snatched them up and scampered back along
the corridor, dived into bed in the far corner of the room and
pulled the bedclothes up to his chest.

He started to eat the carrot in a panic. Just as he did so, his
door jerked open – damn, damn, forgot to bolt it – and light
poured in from the hall outside. Claudia stood outlined against
the brightness. He shrank even further into his nest.

'*Harold!*' she called. 'Have you gone crazy? I glimpse you
through the kitchen window looking like a tramp. You frightened
me for a moment. And now you hide in a corner like some
demented animal. I've really had enough of all this. Remember,
I'm not responsible for you. I'm not your mother and I'm not
your keeper.'

He listened without feeling any need to reply. When she
came no closer, his fear subsided. It all seemed to happen a long
way away. He munched more carrot while she talked at him. He
was glad that her face was in darkness. He hoped she would
soon go away.

'Have you *any* idea what you look like?'

Slam.

Good.

Now I'll eat the orange.

Of all Lottie's habits, only the zoo remained. Perhaps it was too
recent to count as a habit. Never mind, she was grateful for it.

She could still raise a smile for the orang-utans. No one could fail to smile at those.

If only she could have an orang-utan. Then she would be happy, she was sure. Their endless cuddling, nipping and kissing at each other with curled lips, tickling, hugging.

I'm sure they would do it to *me*.

I shouldn't be happy. It would only die. It would only die, like the tamarin.

So even the zoo could make her depressed. She would die of gloom before the year was out.

One day, she saw a notice. She read it, then read it again, so fast that she didn't really take it in.

ADOPT AN ANIMAL AT LONDON ZOO . . .

Members of the public could adopt an animal. Several animals. You just paid some money. Lottie could hardly believe it. Something she wanted. Something she could still get with money.

She assumed that *adopting* must mean you could take it home with you sometimes to play with. Perhaps with a keeper, out on loan. Or perhaps it would mean special visiting rights, popping in to see it sometimes late at night with specialized animal snacks.

The man she spoke to explained rather coolly that it was just a question of paying for their food.

'In the case of the Golden Lion Tamarins, though, it's really worth doing. Less than a hundred of them left in the wild . . . the forests where they live are being cut down. They'd die out if it weren't for the efforts of zoos. Have you changed your mind, madam?'

Madam had not. The man's eyes opened as she took out a fat wad of notes. She adopted four on the spot.

It was a shame that she couldn't take them home. But she would know they were there, even if she couldn't have them. The terrible gloom began to lift just a little.

She hoped God had noticed she was doing something useful. She might be helping to keep something alive.

One of them became her special favourite. She knew his face; luxuriously golden, with round frightened eyes which she thought had become a little *less* frightened.

When she was actually there, she felt better, pressing her face up as close as she could to the bright swift things in their silent cage.

But when she had to leave them behind the thick glass, she felt as lonely as ever.

She began to be afraid they would go away and leave her, after Davey showed her a news story.

> *Rare Zoo-Bred Monkeys Returned To Wild*
> Hoping to set a precedent, researchers from the National Zoo in Washington have returned fourteen captive-bred Golden Lion Tamarins to their native forest home outside Rio de Janeiro. It was the first time that an attempt had been made to return this small monkey species, *Leontopithecus rosalia rosalia*, to its native habitat.
>
> After the tamarins were raised in the National Zoo and before they were released into the wild, they were trained in a Brazilian acclimation centre to hunt for fruit and insects, to avoid poisonous foods and to avoid jumping on dead branches, situations which they did not face in captivity. After their release, they were carefully monitored. Two disappeared and a third was killed by a venomous snake bite. The other eleven survived.
>
> The Golden Lion Tamarin, numbering fewer than a hundred in the wild, all of them in Brazil, is one of the rarest and most beautiful primates. It has been highly prized by collectors for its brilliant coat and mane. It is now threatened in the wild by deforestation. There are more than 400 of them in zoos.

'What's the point of putting them back again if the forests are being cut down?'

'That TV programme said lots of people were trying to save the rain-forest.'

She knew she ought to feel pleased about it. She ought to feel glad they were free. She could *almost* manage it; she thought very hard. Eleven golden bodies leaped through the greenness. No more glass. No more keepers. She saw it for a second. Then she just felt lonely. The flying bodies vanished in the distance.

She was glad they weren't dead. She was glad they were free. She was even glad that filthy tramp had taken her money, though she couldn't help wishing she had kicked him first. She was trying to change. She had changed quite a lot.

But did it have to mean she lost *everything?*

Couldn't she keep *anything* of her own?

CHAPTER FIFTY-ONE

And then the rain turned to snow. In the middle of the night, the world turned white. What was black and inchoate became brilliant, precise. It was done in hours, without fuss.

Harold, who lately had slept till noon, woke around ten. Something was different. A radiance behind the curtains. Sunlight?

What day was it? He counted through. The twentieth, the *twenty-first. Yes.* The Winter Solstice.

He pushed off the bedclothes, parted the curtains. Yes. Two cloud-white leaves on Claudia's tree.

It had snowed on the Winter Solstice. It felt like a personal present to him. Until something changed, *he* couldn't change. Now the snow had cleared away the mess. He would – clean this place up. He would go for a walk. He would . . . go to the zoo, of course.

First he took a bath, scrubbing himself fiercely. The water turned grey and his skin was very white. Pure as the snow, he went to make breakfast, only to remember there *was* no breakfast.

In the kitchen was a Christmas card from Claudia. It *looked* like a Christmas card, from the outside. HAROLD, the envelope said, mildly.

Within was a rather small card, a robin perched on some very sharp tinsel. The greeting inside was scored out by two toboggan tracks of ink.

> HAROLD, SORRY BUT MUST MAKE THIS PLAIN.
> CLEAR OUT BEFORE I RETURN FROM NEW YORK JAN
> 1 *LATEST.* ANY RENT YOU THINK SUITABLE WELCOME.
> CHEER UP. WHILE THERE'S LIFE . . . Yr friend
> CLAUDIA.

It could have been worse, he thought. It probably should have been worse. I suppose I've been a bit vague. Everyone said he was vague. It probably just meant selfish.

Resolution: BE LESS SELFISH.

I'm only forty-six. There's time to change.

He started working doggedly to clean things up. His bedroom was carpeted with fluff, old socks, chocolate wrappings, bus tickets, orange peel, orange pips, unplaceable file cards, scattered sheets of paper. There was more for his file than he realized. He brushed on his knees, penitentially.

But the light had also changed.

The clouds had come back, softly and certainly, silting together, growing heavier now with the colours of a bruise which announced more snow.

Unbelievably, it was already two o'clock. He ought to get a bite before he went to the zoo. By that time, it would be rather late . . .

Get on with it, Harold. Get out of here. Go to the zoo while you've still got time.

He found his gloves quite quickly, but he wasted time looking for Lottie's bright scarf. Found it. Looked for *The World of Wonders*.

Half-past two, and he was ready to go.

He'd forgotten the Christmas shoppers. They streamed like a steady column of ants clutching parcels of food down Kentish Town High Street, and the snow was turning to slush or black oily liquid under their feet. Their faces were grey in the leaden light as they tried not to slip, eyes on the pavement, but their grasp on their parcels was content. The traffic was solid, an army convoy, two armies passing and forgetting to fight. The day had the feel of a mighty emergency, a national happening which left him out.

Most national happenings would leave him out. Harold felt marginal, frivolous, light, but enabled by that to trot on the edge of things, watching the serious cortèges with their boxes, trollies, tethered children, a light man slithering and smiling down the kerb, though what had he got to smile about?

It doesn't matter. I'm smiling anyway.

He nearly fell flat on his back as he began to skirt the park. Here fewer ants had trodden. They had dented the snow, then the cold had bitten back and turned their tracks to shiny black ice. There wouldn't be many at the zoo today.

I'm smiling because of the orang-utans, he realized. *Pongo pygmaeus.* I'm longing to see them again.

Their friendly, elastic, affectionate bodies, tangled together, gazing at each other. How lovely to wear no clothes. How lovely *never* to wear clothes. But the world was cold and dark and hostile. Human beings would *die* without clothes.

☆

The gatekeeper had his black greatcoat on and an unofficial-looking purple scarf. His face was purplish, too.

'Not much of a day,' said Harold.

'There's a lot like that,' said the gatekeeper. He smelled pleasantly of whisky and ginger. 'You know you only got an hour or so, sir.'

'You can see a lot in an hour.'

You could see a lot in a year. You could live a lot in a year. A year ago we were still together. It didn't seem possible.

Why am I back here again, less than a mile from the place where we first started?

The orang-utans whirled like comedians, glad to have someone come and see them. They stared at him mildly until they got bored, thick matted hair pressed flat against the glass, stuck with pieces of straw. Then they went off and played with some empty boxes.

Maybe the year has taken me nowhere. I think I've changed, but maybe I haven't. I've picked up bits and pieces of things. Bits of straw, empty boxes. I understood *something* about the planet. I had a vision. I still think it's true. But I'm not my vision, I am just one man. Maybe my range is incredibly limited.

In the end there's only one thing I want.

CHAPTER FIFTY-TWO

Lottie opened her eyes very late indeed. No Amanda, now, to wake her up.

Wasn't that . . . ? Yes, it was snow-light. The child in her still responded. But the adult said grimly, *Things to do. I've got things to do, today.*

I ought to get *something* in, for Davey. Lottie wasn't used to thinking like that. Basics for Christmas, dammit. Turkey? Chickens? Is he vegetarian at Christmas too? I suppose he is. He's such a little spoilsport.

Still Lottie herself was (*purely temporarily*) not so keen on meat as before. She didn't understand why. Something to do with the baby orang-utan whose tiny mottled body showed so clearly through his dark hair. His round pot belly as he dashed about was around the size of a plucked white chicken. He was so *alive*, crawling over his mother. His curious, unfolding limbs were so tender.

Of course, that was it. Go to the zoo.

Go to the zoo, said the voice in her head. *It's not too late. Get on with it, Lottie.*

But shouldn't I do some shopping? she wondered, feeling guilty as she pulled on her Armani tracksuit and her boots, worn once, from Dido and Aeneas.

You've done enough shopping, in your life. No one will starve – not in this household. Follow your instincts. Go to the zoo.

The light was fading as she got outside, and the snow had begun again, light as salt. The boots weren't as comfortable as she thought. In the first few blocks she passed at least three people who reminded her stupidly, painfully of Harold. I've had enough of that, she informed them, silent.

The zoo seemed a very long way away. She'd only have half an hour there before it closed. She had got halfway when a sharp gust of wind dumped an armful of snow from a tree down her neck. The first blow shocked her, but the slow icy trickle down her spine was infinitely worse.

Right, that does it. I'm not an Aunt Sally, she informed the heavens. I'm going home.

But as she stood there on a straight stretch of white, snow filtering all round her, she suddenly realized how small she was, cold and wet and quite alone.

It isn't a home. There's no one else in it. You'd better keep going, said the voice, firmly. *Pity you had to get so wet. You deserved it though. Remember the baklava?*

The gatekeeper looked drunk, and leered as he said, 'There's only twenty minutes. Are you sure it's worthwhile?'

'No,' she said, frostily. 'I'm going, though.'

She tried to walk away from him very upright, but the leather pressed horribly against her toe. I never did like that fucking shop. I'm never going to go near it again.

The fat old mother was apparently asleep but the baby orangutan was playing with a box. Seeing Lottie, he ran like a drunk to the glass, and pressed both his hands against it. It's almost as if he recognized me.

While she was with him, the pain decreased.

Where to now? It was hard to decide. The grey sky fell in a thousand pieces. Single grey figures were already making towards the exit, indistinguishable.

She was near the Snake House. She'd go and see that. *Dry and warm.* Snakes and lizards. The choice somehow felt important, though nothing was really important. Everything was coming to an end, an end in dull anonymous cold . . .

But the exhibits inside the deserted hall could not have been less anonymous. The leathery old turtles were fiercely different as they heaved their way through an unimaginable life. The great boa slowly and silently uncoiled, surging up smoothly against the warm glass. Three cobras slept in parallel meanders, three bizarre heads laid down together.

Humbled and cheered, with her last ten minutes she went to visit the tamarins. That was the point of it all. She wanted to smile at her own special one.

Ladies and gentlemen, the zoo will be closing in ten minutes. Ten minutes.

She ran under the tunnel with its mock cave paintings and her boots began to stab again, more painfully than ever. Running out of time. So much had been wasted. The cavemen left their paintings, I'll just be dust. But the pain nearly tripped her, and cut off thought.

As she hobbled on, now looking straight ahead, she glimpsed in passing one last mock-Harold, a thin tired man in a multi-coloured scarf. In the dim light of the tunnel he was so very like that for a moment her crippled steps almost stopped, but she was too exhausted by her own obsession. So little time, and she wanted to be done with it, she wanted to see the tamarins and leave.

PAVILION FOR SMALL MAMMALS

At least inside she could rest her feet. But how would she get home?

Ladies and gentlemen, the zoo . . . the 74 bus to Camden Town . . .

She shuffled, panting, through the warm corridors. She heard feet somewhere. Must be a keeper. They mustn't turn me out, not before I've seen him. She tried to limp more quietly, but the pain prevented her. Lottie was no longer in control of her movements.

Ladies and gentlemen . . . ladies and gentlemen . . . time to go home . . . time to go home . . .

The man was standing staring at the tamarins, hand shading his eyes from reflections. Inside he saw the tamarin staring back with its bright myopic gaze, quivering, hopeful.

The hand concealed the man's face from her.

It was Harold's hand.

It was Harold's face.

'Harold.'

He jumped.

'Lottie.'

A moment's pause, then they flung themselves together with the desperate force of two worlds colliding, hands clutching and clawing at hair, coats, necks. Harold dropped his book; Lottie scooped it up again.

'I love you.'

'I love you.'

'Don't let go.'

'Don't let go.'
They don't let go. They cling there, helplessly.
'Do you mean it?'
'Do you? Oh, *darling, darling.'*
Ladies and gentlemen, please proceed . . .
As soon as they started, she remembered the pain, and
realized that she could not proceed.

That was why the gatekeeper, anxious to get off home and
finish his bottle of whisky, saw a fantasy monster loom through
the snow, shrieking and laughing like two human beings, a
double-headed, eight-foot giant.

As it reached the shelter of the gates, it split into two human
beings. *They've* had a few, he thought.

It was that sexy blonde who always came on her own. Used to
wear that fur. I gave her one of my looks. After that there had
been no trouble. She slid off the back of a man whose face was
familiar, though the keeper had never seen them together. He
looked a bit fragile for that kind of thing. They were *both* a bit old
for that kind of thing.

She had no shoes on. It took all sorts. He watched judicially as
the man took off his gloves and pulled them over her feet. Two
black boots stuck out of the man's coat pockets. Bloody hell. He
must be a very fast worker.

'This is my wife!' yelled Harold suddenly, mostly at the
gatekeeper, partly at the world, bending double and gasping as
she mounted him.

'This is my husband,' panted Lottie.

Oh yers, thought the gatekeeper, and he smiled a thin smile,
and one finger rubbed the side of his grog-blossomed nose. The
funny thing was that both their faces were streaming with tears,
although they were laughing.

'Enjoy yourselves,' he murmured, only half out of envy, and
louder, in good heart, 'Goodnight. Happy Christmas.'

And now it was his turn to get ready to go home.

It was queer dos, being in charge of a zoo. You never knew
what might happen. And he *was* in charge, because if you were
sensible you set a lot of store by the way things ended. And he
locked the gate carefully, so nothing could go wrong.

Not that anything *could* go wrong. But sometimes, in winter, when night came early and he hadn't had a chance for his usual nip, he would see all the animals come tumbling through the shadows, shambling orang-utans, long arms linked, scarlet ibises flying like a banner, chimpanzees sprinting and nipping each other, lumbering rhinoceros you wouldn't care to tangle with, ostriches, feet flying, leading the stampede . . . they would pass his sentry-box in seconds, and make in a wave for Primrose Hill.

EPILOGUE

Davey's mouth dropped helplessly open as he came downstairs at the sound of the row and saw from above Lottie and Harold fall into the hall in what looked like a fight with Lottie on top and collapse in a heap on the bottom three stairs. A split second explained it. They were hugging, kissing. Now they were kissing *again*.

'Well,' he said with an enormous grin, picking his way past them. 'What have we here?'

'Oh, *Davey*,' Lottie tried to clutch his ankle, and missed. 'It's Harold.'

'Yes, Mum, I can see that.'

'I'm back,' said Harold, a wild-eyed Harold with his strands of black hair pulled utterly haywire. 'For good.'

'Yes,' said Lottie, 'he is,' and he saw that his mother had *gloves* on her feet.

'Are you two drunk? Not that it matters,' and Davey, who needed to express his feelings, ran his hand over the top of Harold's head. 'Hallo,' he said, surprised how bare it was.

'He sounds like our parent, doesn't he?' said Lottie. 'Lovely Davey. I think he missed you, Harold.'

'Missed *you*, and all,' said Davey. 'Look, I've got to go out. I only came back for a minute. I'm going to a play with Mary. Will you be all right, if I leave you together? Or will it be all off again, when I come back?'

When he got back, they had long ago disappeared, leaving a note on the kitchen table.

> We love you, Davey. See you in the morning. Failing that, in the afternoon. Both of us XXXXXX P.S. *We apologise.*

And so they should, he reflected.

☆

345

Upstairs they are talking, talking. She tells him a bit about André; such a boring man, such a hopeless lover. She tells him things about the zoo; rhinoceros piss backwards. He tells her about Violet and Pamela; he tells her about his sunset. He shows her the *World of Wonders*, and reads her a bit, which she adores:

Snow in the Ball-Room
– The following anecdote is told by Professor Dove, of Berlin, in illustration of the production of snow by change of temperature. On an extremely cold but starlight night, a large company had assembled in a ballroom in Sweden, which in the course of the evening became so warm that some of the ladies fainted. An officer tried to open the window, but found it was frozen to the sill. He then broke a pane of glass, and the rush of cold air from without produced a fall of snow in the room. Its atmosphere was charged with vapour, which, becoming suddenly condensed and frozen, fell in the form of snow upon the astonished dancers.

'I love it, darling. You're a fascinating man.'

Now they are talking nonsense, staring at each other, taking off their clothes, as intent as if they had never seen each other's bodies before.

Lottie suddenly says, *'Harold'* so urgently he wonders if his balls have turned orange.

'I chucked that bloody thing away in Paris. Never wanted to see it again, after André . . . oh no, I don't *believe* this. *You* haven't got anything, have you?'

'No. I've been living like a monk.'

'What are we going to do?'

They stare at each other's nakedness, nonplussed.

Then Harold says, 'Look . . . would it be so awful if . . . it *happened* to happen. If we did have a child . . .'

'Do you mean you'd like one?'

'No, of course not. I don't think so. Not unless *you* . . .'

'I'm much too old to start all that again. Oh, but Harold, I do love you. I want you. Yes. Oh . . .'

'If it happens. If it's meant to . . .'

'But do you *want* one? Could you bear to be a father?'

'Yes. I'm dying for you. Yes. Yes.'

He's a wonderful, wonderful man, thought Lottie, sighing with pleasure as they slipped together. Everything was like dancing. The snow would fall but they would be warm. Lottie knew they would dance all night.

In fact, by twelve they were deep asleep.

Lottie was dreaming of dove feathers, falling like snow on her naked shoulders, light as snow but as warm as skin, covering the two of them over and over so nothing could ever come between them. Light as snow, they could float together . . .

That night there fell a deeper snow, an erasing snow, a cleansing snow. It muffled the noise of cars and doors and let them sleep till late. It blurred the lines between discrete objects, smoothed the plaited forms together.

They woke to each other in the cinematic light. As they kissed, each one thought the other looked older, and did not love them any the less.

And they lay and talked of what they wanted.

'I'll love you for ever,' said Harold. 'If you want me to, I mean. I'm going to write my book. I shan't be . . . useless. I've decided that writing isn't useless.'

'You know I want you,' said Lottie, kissing his eyes, his nose. She sat upright to sound more certain. 'Of course you're not useless. You never were. You're brilliant, and creative. You'll write your book. It will explain . . . *everything*. *Big* things, as well as small things. But are you sure you want me?' She was pulling, twisting her thick yellow hair. 'I mean, I'm the one who's useless. I always have been useless. Quite pretty, darling, and bags of energy, and . . . definitely *generous* . . . and I have my talents. I could have done *so much* . . .' (Harold nodded, pre-emptively) '. . . but not a bit useful. Well, neither of us is if useful means things like polio vaccine, or social workers, or miners . . . you know what I mean, don't you?'

He did. He stared up at her, smiling like an idiot.

'I am going to try to be more informed,' Lottie continued, more earnestly. 'I've learned a lot while you were away. Not just about art, either. I've decided the world's very interesting . . . But I don't expect I'll improve with age. I shall get louder. And more embarrassing – '

'You never embarrassed me, ever – '

'*Liar!* How about me standing by the window with no clothes on? You growled at me nearly every morning! Well, I'm sure I'll get worse. I expect I'll be a drunk. I'll probably end up a Bag Lady – '

' – the only one with bags from Harrods – '

'Harold, are you sure you know what you're in for?'

She gazed at the wall as she asked him, sitting very straight with two pillows behind her, but when she had finished she turned towards him, her dazzling eyes for once uncertain, her bright hair knotted and wreathed like a nest.

Harold stared back. She saw his nostrils had tensed as they did when he was brought to a pitch of nerves or emotion. Before he spoke, his face cried *love*.

'I shall follow you about and stop you falling in the fire,' he said, in a voice which trembled. She dived towards him and buried her face against his neck so her tears fell down her cheek and his neck and his tears, having further to go, ran down from his cheek to her temple, and the tears which confused them one with another still made things seem simpler.

'It might be the other way around,' she gasped, trying to sound controlled. 'I might have to look after *you*, Harold.'

'Yes,' he said, 'but you let me say it. Thank you, darling, for letting me say it.'

'No one ever said anything better.'

'I love you, I love you,' Harold moaned. 'I'll always love you. I know what that means.'

'Oh, let's have a happy ending,' she cried, sniffing grossly against his shoulder.

They will grow old, and they will be ill, but they will not often be unhappy.

They will quarrel, massively, briefly.

Harold will be appalled by her and laugh at her and sometimes ignore her. Harold will fuss, and be crotchety. But he will also adore her. Lottie will be cross and bossy with Harold and sometimes take him for granted again, but not for more than a month or so.

Love will surprise them, in the middle of the night.

She will love him to death, she will love him till they die, will wake up for a second in the early hours to find him aged seventy, eighty, beside her, and still be grateful, and kiss his shoulder.

Happiness is a lottery. Harold and Lottie may have won.

Points of light as rare as stars seem to give form to the universe. It isn't so, of course. There are stars and there is emptiness. But round the stars the planets spin, small and random as pollen grains. In millions of years, life takes, and grows. This happened. This will happen. The infinitely rare still happens.

'We're lucky,' Harold gabbled tenderly, kissing her damp hair.

'We nearly weren't,' Lottie replied.

Beat of his heart, their heart, their skin.

He will not let me fall.

She will not let me fall.

'What shall we do this afternoon?'

'Let's go to the Planetarium.'

They got up and dressed, and she kept him waiting, and he exclaimed at the price of the seats. He wasn't paying, but he still exclaimed. They are not transfigured; they are only human.

In the long view, though, they become the stars.

They sit in the seats tipped back like a bed, holding hands in the darkness. The stars, projected by a thousand-eyed machines, move softly above them on the map of night. The recorded voice seems to wish them well. Great constellations wheel overhead. The moon swells full and then sinks again. White in the distance, crescent Venus.

They listen to the end of the story.

The earth will go on circling the sun for another five thousand million years. Then the sun will slowly expand and redden, the earth will be drawn, with Venus and Mercury, into a new red giant star, and the star will pulsate and shoot most of its contents out across the emptiness. They will hang on the dark, the ghost of the sun, a red-blue ring of gas and dust. (*It looks like Smeggy's hair*, thinks Lottie, *it looks like Smeggy, dancing*.) In billions of years, the gas may condense and grow hot again and form new stars; around some stars there will be worlds; and on

349

some worlds there will be life. The stars will go on rushing apart, until gravity saves them at the last, when they have grown infinitely distant . . . then they will rush together again. When everything has shrunk to a single point, the point can explode into a new beginning.

They sit, the tiniest living points, light as dust beneath the dome, spread on the long curve back to stardust. Holding each other, they pale into the future.

Passing as stardust through the long years of light, for nothing is lost but everything goes onward, the snow in the ballroom and the puzzled dancers, tamarins flying like golden comets, Venus, seen from a proper distance, rising white soon after the sun; Violet and Pamela, Mary and Davey; the weeping stranger on New Year's morning; Sylvia, laughing as she tears her telegram, *Yes, my darling, yes;* April Green and the cruel party-goers; those who were lucky and those who suffered; climbers, one with their bright horizon; sleepy butterflies, florist's roses, shells which broke to make the sound of the sea, all streaming on across the emptiness till the cosmos beats, beats like a heart

emptiness, then the heart beats

the heart beats

the heart beats

light runs faster than love or writing across the enormous absences